Peter Lovesey was born in Middlesex and studied at Hampton Grammar School and Reading University, where he met his wife Jax. He won a competition with his first crime fiction novel, *Wobble to Death*, and has never looked back, with his numerous books winning and being shortlisted for nearly all the prizes in the international crime writing world. He was Chairman of the Crime Writers' Association and has been presented with Lifetime Achievement awards both in the UK and the US.

'Peter Lovesey has an **extraordinary talent** for picking up the conventions of the classic English detective novel and delivering them with an **entirely contemporary twist**'
Val McDermid

'The plotting is **devilish**, the writing a **pleasure**'
Donna Leon

'Sheer **entertainment**'
The Times

'It looks deceptively easy, but this is an author who **excels at his craft** and keeps coming up with books that **entertain and puzzle**'
Sunday Telegraph

'Peter Diamond may be my **favourite** fictional police detective – perky, dogged and **very clever**'
Scotsman

'Peter Lovesey is **undeniably** one of the best practitioners of the genre'
Financial Times

Also by Peter Lovesey

Sergeant Cribb series
WOBBLE TO DEATH
THE DETECTIVE WORE SILK DRAWERS
ABRACADAVER
MAD HATTER'S HOLIDAY
INVITATION TO A DYNAMITE PARTY
A CASE OF SPIRITS
SWING, SWING TOGETHER
WAXWORK

Albert Edward, Prince of Wales series
BERTIE AND THE TINMAN
BERTIE AND THE SEVEN BODIES
BERTIE AND THE CRIME OF PASSION

Peter Diamond series
THE LAST DETECTIVE
DIAMOND SOLITAIRE
THE SUMMONS
BLOODHOUNDS
UPON A DARK NIGHT
THE VAULT
DIAMOND DUST
THE HOUSE SITTER
THE SECRET HANGMAN
SKELETON HILL
STAGESTRUCK
COP TO CORPSE

Hen Mallin series
THE CIRCLE
THE HEADHUNTERS

Other fiction
GOLDENGIRL (AS PETER LEAR)
SPIDER GIRL (AS PETER LEAR)
THE FALSE INSPECTOR DEW
KEYSTONE
ROUGH CIDER
ON THE EDGE
THE SECRET OF SPANDAU (AS PETER LEAR)
THE REAPER

Short stories
BUTCHERS AND OTHER STORIES OF CRIME
THE CRIME OF MISS OYSTER BROWN AND OTHER STORIES
DO NOT EXCEED THE STATED DOSE
THE SEDGEMOOR STRANGLER AND OTHER STORIES OF CRIME

Peter
LOVESEY
THE TOOTH TATTOO

SPHERE

First published in Great Britain in 2013 by Sphere
This paperback edition published in 2014 by Sphere

A CIP catalogue record for this book
is available from the British Library.

ISBN 978-0-7515-5060-3

Typeset in ITC New Baskerville by Palimpsest Book Production Limited,
Falkirk, Stirlingshire
Printed and bound in Great Britain by Clays Ltd, St Ives plc

Papers used by Sphere are from well-managed forests
and other responsible sources.

MIX
Paper from
responsible sources
FSC® C104740

Sphere
An imprint of
Little, Brown Book Group
100 Victoria Embankment
London EC4Y 0DY

An Hachette UK Company
www.hachette.co.uk

www.littlebrown.co.uk

THE TOOTH TATTOO

1

SOUTH BANK, LONDON, 2005

Eleven thirty at night, sweaty in his evening suit and shattered after a heavy night playing Rachmaninov, Mel Farran plodded out of the artists' exit on the south side of the Royal Festival Hall. Good thing his legs didn't need telling the way to Waterloo station and the tube. He'd done it a thousand times. Rachmaninov was said to be the ultimate romantic – miserable old git. The six-foot scowl, as Stravinsky called him, had been a pianist through and through. He worked the string section like galley slaves to show off the joanna man, and Mel Farran was a viola player, so thank you, Sergei.

The moon was up, spreading the shadow of Hungerford Bridge across the paved square called Beacon Market Place.

He was forced to stop. A young woman was blocking his path, one of those situations where each takes a sideways step the same way. It happened twice and they were still face to face.

She said, 'Do you mind?'

Mel took it as a statement of annoyance. He was annoyed, too, wanting to move on, but what's to be gained from complaining?

Then she surprised him by saying, 'Please.'

How dense am I, he thought, not realising she always

1

intended to stop me. Something glossy and flimsy was being waved under his nose. The concert programme. She was holding a pen in the other hand.

Mel forced himself out of his stupor. She wants my autograph, for God's sake. She can't have confused me with the pianist, else why does she think I'm carrying an instrument case?

Quick impression: she was the typical music student, bright-eyed, intense, dark hair in a bunch tied with red velvet. It wasn't that long since Mel had gone through college himself, passionate about all things musical. He'd queued through the night for the proms, cut back on cigarettes to buy the latest Nigel Kennedy, busked in Covent Garden to pay for a trip to Bayreuth. But he'd never understood the point of collecting autographs, still less the autographs of mere orchestra members.

She pleaded with her eyes. Almond eyes. Nothing remarkable in that. Every college has a large quota of students from the Far East.

He succumbed. 'Are you sure it's me you want?'

'Absolutely.'

'I'm only one of the orchestra.'

'Principal viola. You were wonderful.'

'Get away.'

'Truly.'

Well.

Maybe I was, he told himself, and his self-esteem got a lift. I'm good at what I do and some people appreciate my playing, even when ninety-nine per cent are there to hear the pianist. This well-informed young lady knows who I am, so I'd better sign and be on my way.

He tucked the fiddle under his arm to free his hands. 'Where are you from?'

'Tokyo. Have you been there?'

He shook his head. 'One day, maybe. Just my signature?'

'Whatever you want to write.'

That was a facer. At the end of a long concert he couldn't think of two words together. 'May I make it personal and put your name?'

Instead of the gasp of pleasure he was expecting, she curled her lip.

He was thrown. Had he said something wrong?

She gave a laugh – a throaty, mocking laugh, meant to hurt – and took a step back. 'You don't know who I am, dumbo.'

At the same time Mel felt a sharp, strong tug from behind. He flexed his arm. Too late. His viola had been snatched.

He swung round in time to see a young guy on a bike in baseball cap, T-shirt and jeans pedalling away across the square. He was riding one-handed with Mel's instrument case in his free hand. It was a set-up. He must have sneaked up behind while Mel – shit-for-brains – was being soft-soaped by the girl. He'd been mugged.

Life was unthinkable without that viola. It wasn't a Strad. It was not particularly valuable, not even old in instrument-making terms, but it was Mel's voice, his art, his constant companion, his living. You'd need to be a professional musician to understand how he felt.

Hell, he decided, I won't allow this.

He was no athlete, but he started running. Later he realised he should have chased the girl, who was clearly the accomplice. She would have been easier to catch than a bloke on a bike. Instead, all of Mel's focus was on his viola and the thief himself, fast escaping along the side of the Festival Hall.

The concert audience had long since dispersed. At that time of night people were keen to get away. The great palaces of culture along the South Bank are locked, impenetrable,

3

but all around – for those who know – are places of refuge, arches, stairwells and underpasses. The whole area becomes a haven for dossers and derelicts.

Mel doubted that the thief was a down-and-out. For one thing, he'd grabbed the fiddle, not his wallet. For another, he was working with the girl, who looked and sounded Royal College of Music. And he was on an expensive-looking bike.

Spurred by a degree of anger he didn't know he possessed, Mel kept up the chase. The thief was faster, but one thing was in Mel's favour: they'd turned left towards the Thames and he couldn't cycle across.

No use shouting. There wasn't anyone else in sight. Taking increasingly shallow gasps, Mel sprinted the length of the building as well as he could, resolved to get the thief in sight again. He turned the corner by the main entrance, already in darkness.

The guy was there, up ahead.

Mel's legs were heavier with each stride and a band of pain was tightening across his chest. He was slowing, for all his strength of will. The buildings were a blur when he started. Now he could see them clearly.

But the thief would have a problem. The riverside walkway was at a higher level and a set of about a dozen steps formed a barrier ahead of him. He'd need to dismount. It wouldn't be easy carrying both bike and viola up there.

Mel urged himself into another spurt.

He was running in the space between the front of the Festival Hall and the side of the Queen Elizabeth Hall. No one was around to help. It's me and him, Mel thought. If I keep going I may catch up before he gets up those steps.

The guy's head turned, checking, Mel guessed, whether he was still in pursuit.

Then he surprised Mel by veering to the right just before the steps, straight towards the QEH. What was he doing?

Mel had been assuming the high wall was solid concrete like the rest of the building.

He appeared to cycle straight through and vanish.

Disbelieving, in despair, at the limit of his strength, Mel staggered along the remaining stretch and discovered how it had been done. There was a hidden ramp just before the steps, obviously meant for wheelchair access. The thief must have skimmed up there without breaking sweat.

Suddenly he was back in view on the walkway, pedalling across Mel's line of vision as if to mock him. But he stopped just to the right of the gated entrance to the Festival Pier, still astride the bike, with his feet on the ground.

He was up against the railing by the water's edge. He swung the viola case back to get momentum. Jesus Christ, Mel thought, he's about to throw it over.

'No!' he yelled. 'For God's sake, no.'

He was powerless to stop it. The thief couldn't hear him this far off.

There was a freeze-frame moment as if he was having second thoughts. Then Mel's precious fiddle was hurled over the edge.

Water is the worst enemy. No stringed instrument will survive immersion. The canvas case wasn't waterproof. It would fill with filthy water. Whether it floated or got dragged down was immaterial.

To Mel, what had just happened was akin to murder. Anyone who has listened to music, who has heard a violin or a viola sing, must know it has life. It's a unique individual with the power to speak directly to the soul, to calm, heal, inspire, uplift the spirit in ways beyond man's capability. Mel would defy anyone not to respond to the purity of legato bowing, the eloquence of the flowing tone. Each instrument has its own voice.

He'd stopped running. His muscles were refusing to function, his brain spinning between disbelief and panic.

5

Why? What malice drives anyone to such an act?

'Bastard!'

Already the cyclist was moving off left. And now Mel saw he'd get clean away, under the bridge and past the London Eye. All day there is a queue outside the huge observation wheel. But the place closed at nine thirty. Nobody would be there to stop him at this hour.

In reality his attention wasn't on the thief any longer. He could go. Mel wasn't thinking about justice or revenge. He wanted the impossible: to put the last five minutes into reverse and undo what had happened. Real life isn't like that.

He'd got the shakes now. The shock was consuming him.

He knew he should mount the steps and look over the edge. It was too late to leap over and recover the poor, damaged thing. The only reason for jumping would be suicide. He was almost of a mind to do it.

He forced himself upwards, stiff-legged, still shaking, right up to the railing, and peered over. It was too far down and too dark to spot anything floating there. All the filth of the river spreads to the banks like scum in a sink. The black water caught some ripples of reflected light from the ornate globe lamp-stand and that was all.

Out in the middle there were lights. A small vessel was chugging past the pier towards Waterloo Bridge. A police launch? No such luck. It was more like a powerboat moving sedately because of the conditions. Too far out to hail.

He heard water slurping against the embankment wall below him. The boat's backwash had reached there. He stared down and saw nothing.

Hours later, in his flat, he drank coffee and replayed the scene in his mind. He'd recalled it already for the police, given them such descriptions as he could – the Japanese girl

6

with the red scrunch, the guy on the bike, and his poor, benighted instrument. The constable taking the statement hadn't understood his desolation. He hadn't even promised to pursue the thieves. 'Look at it from our point of view,' he'd said. 'Where would we start? I don't suppose they'll try it with anyone else.'

Obviously they had conspired to rob Mel and it wasn't an opportunist crime. There had been planning behind it. But what was the reason? Surely not malice alone? They don't know Mel, so why should they hate him? There was no profit in it. A good, much valued instrument was destroyed and his livelihood put at risk. They couldn't know if he had other violas.

Senseless.

Or was it? His memory retrieved an image, the powerboat he'd noticed out in the middle of the river. Could it have come close enough for someone aboard to catch the viola as it was slung over the railing? This would provide a cruel logic to what had happened, a well organised plan to rob him.

Now that the finality of his loss had come home to him, he was discovering dark places in his psyche that he didn't know existed. He believed he could kill those two if he met them again.

Would he recognise the girl? He thought so. The light hadn't been good, but he'd seen her up close. He could remember the eyes wide in appeal when they'd first met, catching the light of the streetlamps, yet shot with scorn when she was sure he'd been suckered. He had a clear, raw memory of how her mouth had opened to mock him and most of all he could hear the cruel glissando of her laughter. Was he right in thinking she had been a music student? If so, the mugging was even harder to understand.

Of her partner in crime he could recall only the clothes. He hadn't once seen his face.

Did it matter any more? Did he want to hunt them down? He could search the common rooms of all the music colleges in London and maybe find them, but he wouldn't get his viola back.

Anger didn't begin to describe his state of mind.

2

VIENNA, 2012

'How much longer does it last?' Paloma Kean asked Peter Diamond.

'Aren't you enjoying it?'

'I'm trying not to breathe.'

Diamond felt in his pocket and produced a tube of peppermints. 'The man who thinks of everything.'

'Thanks, but an oxygen mask would be better.'

There are days when the Vienna sewer tour is more odorous than others. Wise tourists take note of the humidity before booking. Diamond and Paloma, on their weekend city break, had no choice, Saturday afternoon or nothing. It happened that this Saturday in July was warm, with a thunderstorm threatening. Even Diamond had noticed that the smell was not Chanel No. 5.

'After this, you'll appreciate the Ferris wheel,' he told her.

She was silent. She'd brought this on herself when reminding him that his favourite film, *The Third Man*, was set in Vienna. At the time, she'd congratulated herself for thinking of it. Otherwise they wouldn't have been here.

The adventure had begun back in April with a scratch card she had found on the floor of his car. Diamond hadn't bothered to check it. He'd said they were giving them away at the petrol station.

She'd revealed three matching symbols and told him he was a winner.

'Everyone is.'

She had insisted on phoning the number on the back of the card.

Deeply sceptical, Diamond had told her, 'That's how they make their money.'

But it had turned out that he really had won a weekend break for two in a city of his choice: Paris, Amsterdam or Vienna. True to form, he'd dismissed Europe's historic capitals with a dogmatic, 'I don't do abroad.'

'Come on,' Paloma had said. 'Lighten up, Peter. This could be so romantic.'

'I'm too busy at work.' Work for Diamond was heading the CID section at Bath police station. There were always matters to be investigated.

Then Paloma had remembered *The Third Man* and whistled the Harry Lime Theme.

'What did you say those cities were?' he'd said, looking up.

And here they were trudging through a reeking sewer with a bunch of elderly tourists carrying flashlights. At intervals everyone stopped to be shown a clip of the film projected on to the brick wall opposite. Paloma could see Diamond's lips move silently in sync with the soundtrack. '*It's the main sewer. Runs right into the blue Danube.*' So obviously was he relishing the experience that it would have been churlish to complain.

The day had started agreeably enough in the Café Mozart, another of the film locations. The coffee and *Sachertorte* were expensive, even for a couple used to Bath prices, but Diamond had basked in the ambience and said the experience was worth every Euro, and talked about Graham Greene being a regular there in 1947 when he was researching the story. From there they'd moved on to a side street off the Naschmarkt and he'd stressed how fortunate they were to be here on a Saturday, the only day of the week the Third Man Museum opened. Displayed along with countless stills and posters was the actual zither Anton Karas had used to play the haunting theme. You could select from four hundred cover versions of the tune. Paloma had left the place with a headache that Diamond said was surely something to do with the weather. A short walk had brought them to Esperantopark and the brick-built spiral staircase down to the oldest part of Vienna's sewer system. Proceedings underground had begun with a film explaining how the cholera epidemic of 1830 had made a better sanitation system necessary. Then, after warnings to watch their footing, the guide had led them into the glistening brick-lined drains.

Atmospheric? Paloma couldn't argue with that. She just wished every film clip wasn't punctuated with another head-numbing burst of the zither music.

'Are you enjoying this?' she asked Diamond in the faint hope that he'd had enough.

'Brilliant.'

There was no opting out. This was not the best place to get lost if she tried returning to the stairs.

'How's your head now?' Diamond asked.

'About the same.'

'I think I should warn you that at the end of the tour a man dressed as Harry Lime steps out and fires a gun at us.'

'I can't wait.'

That evening at the Prater they rode the Riesenrad, the giant Ferris wheel that had featured in the film. The worst of the clouds had rolled away to the south and Paloma's headache had departed with them. She was actually enjoying the ride

11

in the rickety old cabin. They were definitely cabins and not pods or capsules. Each was a little room like a railway compartment with a curved roof and windows. They shared theirs with an elderly man in a brown Tyrolean hat with a feather trim who was at the far end surveying the view with a benign smile. Below, ribbons of light stretched to infinity. The wheel itself periodically flashed silver and gold.

'I don't really mind hearing it again,' she told Diamond with a smile.

'What's that?'

'The Harry Lime speech about Switzerland, five hundred years of brotherly love, democracy and peace producing the cuckoo clock.'

'I was going to spare you that. It wasn't in the original script, you know.'

'You tell me that each time.'

'Orson Welles—'

'That, too.'

He placed a hand over hers. 'You've shown the patience of a saint all day.'

'If I'm honest, I haven't been feeling that way,' she said. 'But I can see how much it means to you, reliving the film.'

'The old black and white movies have got it for me.'

'I know. Giant shadows, sudden shafts of light.'

He took a deep, appreciative breath. 'Like the night scene when Lime appears in the doorway.'

'With a blast of zither music just in case anyone in the cinema isn't paying attention.'

'Er, yes. Well, it is called the Harry Lime Theme.'

'And you grew up with it.'

He baulked at that. 'The film was released before I was born. Orson Welles was old enough to have been my grandfather.'

'Sorry.'

'But that scene gets to me every time.'

'Strange.'

He frowned. 'Why do you say that?'

'Harry Lime was the villain, selling adulterated penicillin. You're supposed to be on the opposite side. You should identify with the Joseph Cotten character.'

'But Welles had all the charisma. The film is clever, playing with your loyalties.'

She tried to see it from his point of view. 'I suppose as a policeman you have to get inside the minds of bad people.'

'Sometimes – but you aren't supposed to admire them. Each time I see it, I really want him to stay at liberty. And today we walked in his footsteps.'

'With great care, watching where we trod,' Paloma said.

There was a movement at the far end of the cabin. The elderly man turned from the window and raised his hat. He may even have clicked his heels. 'Excuse me. I heard what you said. You were talking about the sewers, am I right?'

'You are,' Paloma said. 'We did the tour this afternoon.'

'It wasn't Orson Welles.'

There was an awkward silence.

'Believe me, it was,' Diamond told him. 'I've seen that film more times than I care to count.'

'Mr Welles took one look and refused to work in such a place,' the old man said.

Diamond was speechless, shaking his head.

'Most of the scenes featuring him were filmed with a double, or in Shepperton studio in England.' The old man seemed to know what he was talking about.

Paloma laughed. 'Do you mean we traipsed through all those dreadful-smelling tunnels for no reason at all?'

'I wouldn't say that,' the old man said. 'They did hours of filming down there, but little, if any, with Orson Welles.'

'Why not?'

'He was being difficult at the time, playing – what is the expression? – hard to get. He had an agreement with Mr Korda, the producer, to star in three films, but nothing much had come of it and he was annoyed. This was only a cameo role. He is on screen for less than ten minutes of the entire film. I believe he was taken down to the sewer once to see a place where water cascaded from one of the ducts. Harry Lime was supposed to run underneath and get drips running down his face. Welles absolutely refused.'

'You seem to know a lot about it.'

'I'm a Viennese. It's part of our city history.'

'So they built a studio mock-up of the sewer?' Paloma said, and she seemed to be leading him on.

'That is my understanding.'

Determined not to have his day spoilt, Diamond rubbed his hands and said with conviction, 'Well, at least Orson Welles did what we're doing now – rode the Ferris wheel.'

The old man turned and looked out of the window again. 'Have you heard of back projection? Look carefully next time you watch the film.'

Back in their hotel room, Paloma saw how deflated Diamond was and said, 'We've only got his word for it.'

'He seemed to know what he was talking about. I did read once that they shot parts of the film at Shepperton.'

'Bits, I expect. It was the way they worked. It's still a classic.'

'You're right about that.'

'Silly old man. I bet he rides the damn Ferris wheel for hours on end lying in wait for fans like us.'

'Do you think so?'

'Destroying people's illusions – that's his game. Don't let him ruin our day, Peter. We did the tour. We visited the right places. You'll spot them next time you see the film.'

He was grateful for her words. Paloma was a terrific

14

support. She knew how his pleasure in the day had been undermined. And the weekend hadn't offered much for her to enjoy. He'd been planning to fit in a visit to another of the film locations – the cemetery – next morning and now he changed his mind. 'I'm going to suggest we do something different tomorrow. Our flight home isn't until the evening. Let's make it your day. How would you like to spend it?'

She took off her shoes and flopped back on the bed, hands clasped behind her head. 'That's a lovely suggestion. Let me give it serious thought.'

'There's some wine left. I'll pour you a drink while you decide.'

'Now you're talking.'

But when he returned from the bathroom with the two glasses, Paloma's eyes were closed and she was breathing evenly. It had been an exhausting day.

Over coffee next morning in a small shop near the hotel with a display of irresistible fruit tarts, they debated how to spend their last hours in Vienna. 'Knowing you,' she said, 'and I don't mean to sound offensive, you may not be too thrilled about this. So many great musicians lived and composed their masterpieces here. Could we find Beethoven's house?'

'Why not?' he said, doing his best to sound enthusiastic. 'Where is it?'

They opened their map and asked the waitress, but she didn't seem to understand.

'We need a phrasebook,' Diamond muttered.

From behind them a voice said, 'If it's Beethoven's house you want, you have about forty to choose from in Vienna. He was constantly on the move.'

'Excuse me?' Diamond turned in his chair, peeved that somebody had been eavesdropping.

The speaker wasn't the old man from the Ferris wheel,

but he could have been his brother. He had the same gnomish look and a voice like a scraper stripping wallpaper. Probably a Tyrolean hat was tucked under the table on one of the other chairs.

'There are two of any note,' the man went on. 'The first is the Beethoven Memorial House, but you are too late for that. It is closed this month. The other is the Pasqualati House where he composed his fourth, fifth and sixth symphonies and the opera *Fidelio*.'

'That'll do us,' Diamond said. 'Is it open?'

'I believe so.'

'Where exactly is it?'

'Before you dash off, I think I should inform you that Beethoven didn't actually live there.'

'I thought you said he did.'

'The rooms open to visitors are furnished to look as if Beethoven was the tenant, but in reality his home was in the adjacent flat – which is privately owned and not open to the public.'

It was like being told Orson Welles hadn't run through the sewers.

'I give up,' Diamond said. 'Where do we go to see something authentic in this city?'

'Some of the exhibits are authentic. The salt and pepper pots unquestionably belonged to Beethoven.'

'Big deal,' Diamond murmured to Paloma.

'You asked where it is,' the old man said. 'You'll find it west of Freyung. This is an old part of the city. You go up a cobbled lane called Schreyvogelgasse to the Mölker Bastei and the Pasqualati House is there. I'll show you.'

'Is it worth it?' Diamond asked Paloma, but she had already passed their map across.

'Here.' A bony finger pinned down the map. 'At the western margin of the Innere Stadt.'

'Some way off, then,' Diamond said. 'Maybe we should choose another composer's house.'

'This is Schreyvogelgasse. As you pass along, you may wish to glance at number eight. The doorway is famous. It's where Harry Lime first appears in that film, *The Third Man*.'

Diamond's eyes widened.

'It looks as if we'll be going there after all,' Paloma said.

In the taxi, Diamond said, 'I'm beginning to understand. They post little old men all over the city to bring innocent tourists down to earth with a bump.'

'He was trying to be helpful.'

'So was the guy on the Ferris wheel. There are some things I'd rather not be helped with.'

'That's rich – from a professional detective.'

'A secret romantic.'

Her eyebrows popped up.

In the cobbled street she told him to stand in the doorway of number eight for a photo.

'I can't. It's so cheesy.'

'But you want to.'

He didn't need any more persuading. He took up the pose, even giving his straw hat a rakish tilt.

The Beethoven house pleased Paloma. There was a good atmosphere and enough genuine relics to make the old man's criticisms unimportant. 'To think *Fidelio* was created here,' she said.

'Next door.'

'It doesn't seem to matter any more. Are you impressed? I'm sure I can feel his presence.'

'It's not my strongest suit, classical music,' he admitted.

'What is, apart from the Harry Lime Theme?'

'Queen's greatest hits, I suppose.'

'I can see I'll have to work on you.'

'You can try. It's still your day. How shall we spend our last couple of hours here?'

'Let's take a look at the Danube. Is it really blue? We haven't seen it by daylight.'

The nearest bridge wasn't far from their hotel. They packed, cleared their room, left the cases in a storeroom and strolled down Schwedenplatz.

'You're not going to believe this,' Diamond said, studying the map. 'It isn't actually the Danube.'

'Get away.'

'It's the Danube canal. The river is way off to the north-east.'

'Second best as usual, then.'

Blue the water was, under a clear sky. They walked to the centre of the bridge and watched the shipping gliding underneath. A breeze ruffled Paloma's hair.

'This has been a treat,' she said, linking her arm with his.

'All of it?'

'Every minute, now I look back. We got you out of the CID room for a whole weekend. Go on, admit it, you needed the break.'

'It's done me good,' he said.

'And all because of that scratch card. Next time we shouldn't rely on a piece of luck. I'll try persuading you to look at a travel brochure.'

'Don't push it.'

With more time in hand they bought ice creams and took a walk along the embankment.

'Look, someone's dropped some flowers,' Paloma said as they approached a point where some steps led down to a mooring. A bunch of pinkish-white flowers wrapped in paper was lying on the pavement. When they got closer, they saw more flowers pressed into the lattice mouldings in the wall. Most were dead carnations. 'It must have fallen out.' She stooped to lodge the fresh flowers back into a space in the stonework. They were star-shaped with long, yellow-tipped stamens. 'The scent is powerful. Must be some type of lily. The place has been made into a little shrine. Do you think someone drowned here?'

'Hard to say,' he said, wanting to lighten the mood. 'Where are the little old men of Vienna when we need one?'

'There's a card with one of these dead bunches, some kind of message. But it isn't in German. I think it's Japanese.'

3

ACTON, WEST LONDON, 2012

Temptation arrives in many forms. For Mel, it was cued by the opening notes of Beethoven's Fifth, the ringtone on his phone.

'Yes?'

'Mr Farran, the viola player?' A male voice, educated, middle-aged and as imperious as Sir Thomas Beecham's in rehearsal.

'That's me.'

'Do you have a moment?'

'Depends. Are you selling something?'

'Certainly not. This is a serious call.'

A rap over the knuckles. Mel should have cut the call immediately and saved himself from the wrecking ball that was swinging his way.

'Who are you?' he asked.

'That's immaterial at this juncture. Call me Ivan, if you wish. I have a proposal massively to your advantage.'

'You *are* trying to sell something.'

'Pay attention, please. This is about your professional career.'

'As a musician?'

'Naturally.'

'A gig?'

A pause. Ivan was plainly unhappy with the expression and considering whether to hang up. 'More than that, much more – if you're prepared to cooperate. But this is too important to discuss over the phone. Are you free tomorrow evening?'

'Free for what?'

'For a drink and a chance to discuss the opportunity. I'll send a car at seven thirty.'

'You know where I live?'

'This isn't spur of the moment, Mr Farran. I've heard you play, or I wouldn't be bothering.'

Let's admit it – flattery is a sure-fire persuader. 'Where are we having this drink?'

'At my club. There's a dress code, by the way. Lounge suit and tie. You do possess a suit?'

Irritated by the patronising tone, sceptical, yet intrigued, Mel switched off and pocketed the phone. In truth, he was in no position to turn down the invitation. A life in classical music is precarious. His income from orchestral work and teaching was barely a living wage. Yet he was good at what he did. He'd been gifted with perfect pitch and a mother hooked on Mozart. Handed a miniature violin at an age when other kids were learning to tie their shoelaces, he'd mastered the basics within days. He was taught by an elderly Polish maestro and within a year on his advice switched to a miniature viola. Really. They do exist. Violists, the maestro told him, were always in demand, whereas there was a glut of violinists. The old man had been right – to a degree. Mel had never gone for long without ensemble work. He'd survived. However, there wasn't much prospect of advancement. Solo opportunities with the viola were rare. If he'd excelled at the violin – as everyone suggested he could have done – the repertoire is huge and he could have toughed it out with the army of East Asian players who came along at that time. No use complaining now. He could play both instruments to a good level, but it was the viola he was known for. He'd trained at the Royal College and filled in with some of the great orchestras of Europe. Violists are an endangered species. If he'd known just how endangered he wouldn't have listened to Ivan. But he was an innocent. At twenty-nine, he needed an opportunity and this promised to be it.

Single, hetero, not bad looking, he was originally from Beaconsfield and currently living in a poky first-floor flat in Acton, West London. Fingis Street had never seen the like of the gleaming black limo that drew up outside at seven thirty. Good thing he didn't keep it waiting or the local youths would have unscrewed the Mercedes logo in seconds and scraped a coin along the bodywork to see if it was real.

He was wearing an almost new pinstripe suit from Oxfam. You can bet the original owner had died, but you can't get fussed about stuff like that when you're skint and need to look respectable. All of his work clothes, evening suits, dress shirts and bow ties, black and white, also came from charity shops. Bargains, every one.

'Where exactly are we going?' he asked the driver.

'Clubland, sir. St James's.'

'Which club?'

'I was told it's confidential.'

'Well, I'm being driven there, so I'm going to find out.'

'And I have my orders, sir.'

Mel didn't press him. If Ivan wanted to make a cloak-and-dagger occasion out of the meeting, let it be, he told himself to calm his nerves. He hoped this wouldn't turn out to be a huge let-down.

For all the man-about-town bluster, Mel couldn't say he was familiar with the St James's area of London. He'd never set foot in a gentlemen's club, and when they drew up outside a set of white steps to a shiny black door with brass fittings, he forgot to look for the name.

The doorman had his instructions and waved Mel through when he said who he was. Carpeted entrance hall, grand staircase and oil paintings in gold frames. Mel couldn't say who painted them, except it wasn't Andy Warhol or Francis Bacon. A short, bald man appeared from behind a potted fern and extended his hand. The grip was firm, as if they were old chums.

'So glad you came. There's an anteroom we can have to ourselves. Have you eaten?'

'Yes,' Mel lied, not wanting to be treated to a meal before he knew what this was about.

'In that case, cognac should go down well. Agreed?'

A beer would have been more to Mel's liking, but he didn't have the neck to ask for one. A club servant was sent for the cognac.

Bound copies of *Punch* lined the anteroom. Laughs all round.

'I still don't know your surname,' Mel said when they were seated in leather armchairs either side of a marble fireplace big enough to park a car in.

'Better you don't unless and until we come to an agreement,' his host said. 'You will have guessed I, too, am a musician. Violin. You've heard me play.'

'Have I?'

'Possibly in the concert hall and certainly on disc.'

What do you say to that? If the guy was a soloist, Mel didn't recognise him. He could think of dozens he'd heard in the last eight years.

'In a well-known string quartet,' he added.

'Ah. Am I supposed to guess which?'

'No.'

Be mysterious, Mel thought. See if I care. The cognac

23

arrived in a cut-glass decanter and was poured into balloon glasses. Ivan waited for the flunkey to leave the room.

'There could be a vacancy in the quartet,' Ivan said.

'Could be?'

'Is.'

'For a violist? And you have me in mind?'

'In mind is a good way of putting it.'

Mel waited, but nothing else followed. 'Is this an offer?'

'Not yet. The others will have a say.'

'Are they coming here to join us?'

'No.'

'Who are they?'

'That's not for me to say.'

All this stonewalling was hard to take. Ivan had issued the invitation. He should have been selling the deal. Instead he was swirling the brandy in the glass as if he was reading tea-leaves.

At last, he said, 'It's not straightforward.'

'That's getting obvious,' Mel said.

'The others don't know I've approached you. I believe I can persuade them. We play as a unit, but we're all individuals, which is our strength. A quartet of yes-men would never make fine music. Playing in a quartet is all about dialogue, distinct voices that respond to each other, but not passively. There's question and answer in musical terms, sharp debate, argument even. It isn't all resolution and harmony.'

Mel felt like saying he wasn't a total beginner. He'd played in quartets. 'You said they don't know about me. What if they don't approve?'

'I would expect to persuade them – if I'm persuaded myself.'

'You said on the phone you've heard me play.'

'But can you commit?'

'Commit what – murder?' A cheap remark. Something had to be said to lighten the mood.

24

Ivan didn't smile. 'Commit to a trial period of, say, a year? It would mean total loyalty to the quartet, rehearsals, business meetings, performances, recordings and touring.'

'I'd need to know more.'

'In particular?'

'Who am I replacing?'

'That I can't say.'

'Has he retired – or have you given him the elbow?'

'Neither.'

'Died?'

Silence.

'He's still playing? You're plotting to dump him and he doesn't know?'

A shake of the head. 'We're professionals, Mr Farran. We have our disagreements, but we're not like that.'

'Speaking of the professional part, how much would I expect to earn? I need to live.'

'Enough for that, and more. We divide all the income equally and that includes our manager. As a new member, you'd take home precisely the same as the rest of us. Not as much as a bank executive earns, but better than you're used to getting.'

'How much approximately?'

'Just under six figures in a good year.'

Yoiks. This was the first thing Mel had heard that he liked. 'At some point soon, you'll have to come clean about who you are, the name of the quartet. If you're earning that money, you must be famous.'

'The fame is immaterial. You're single, yes?'

'I am.'

'So touring shouldn't be a problem?'

'I guess not.'

'We don't live in each other's pockets. There's no sharing of rooms, no forced mingling. All we would insist on is that

25

you are there for rehearsals and concerts. If we take on a residency, as we may, that can involve some teaching. Are you comfortable with that?'

'I've done some. I'd still want to meet the others before deciding.'

'Naturally – and they will insist on meeting you.'

'So will it be arranged?'

Ivan hesitated. 'Possibly. In the fullness of time.'

The 'fullness of time' was presumably how long it would take to dump the current violist, Mel mused, wondering what the unfortunate musician had done wrong. Difficult to feel comfortable about this set-up, but he was willing to stretch a point for a hundred grand a year.

Nothing more of substance was said and he left soon after. It was clearly a 'don't call us' situation.

Three weeks went by before he was contacted again. He was on the sundeck of a riverboat on the Thames playing in a string trio for someone's wedding. This kind of gig was a steady source of income and he didn't think of it as slumming, as some musicians did. The repertoire was undemanding, but the pieces were popular for a reason. Most were from the shows and it was no hardship to play Gershwin and Bernstein along with others who had written damn good tunes and never aspired to the concert hall. In a mid-session break for drinks Mel was cradling a tankard and leaning on the rail watching ducks and moorhens taking refuge in the reeds along the river bank when a nudge from behind almost sloshed the beer out of his glass.

'Careful, chuck. You don't want to wet your Strad.'

He turned and found himself staring into a cleavage threatening to give him vertigo. He'd noticed this large wedding guest in a lyre-shaped fascinator hat and a wispy, low-cut yellow dress whooping it up with several of the men. The hearty shove in his back had come from her and here she was telling him to be careful.

This lady's had a few, he told himself. People do at weddings. Keep in the spirit of the occasion. 'If this is a Strad,' he said, 'I'm putting it up for sale. What's your best offer?'

'My body,' she said, 'and there's plenty of that, but on closer inspection it looks like a Chinese imitation. The viola, I mean, not me. I withdraw the offer. You're Mel Farran, right?'

Caught by surprise, he said, 'I am.'

She drew back a fraction, allowing him to get a wider focus on her physique. She was exceptionally large in all areas. Under the rake of the hat, blonde curls in profusion surrounded a face that was both pretty and pudgy. 'I came specially to see you. I'm the cellist in the quartet you could be joining.'

He took a moment to absorb this. 'Really? Which quartet is that?'

She wagged her finger. 'I may look decks-awash, buster, but you won't catch me as easily as that. I'm more sober than you think and that's restricted information.'

'Are you allowed to tell me who you are?'

'I've told everyone else, so I might as well tell you. I'm Cat – known for obvious reasons as Cat with Kitties. Rhyming slang.'

Difficult to follow that. Mel summoned a faint grin.

Cat continued blithely, 'You look the part, anyway, and apparently you can play a bit. Have you ever tried the cello?'

'I know enough not to stick it under my chin.'

'Don't get modest with me. I bet you can play, and I could play yours if you'll pardon the expression. At a pinch I can stand in for anyone.'

'Useful.'

'In the quartet we back each other up.'

'Does that mean you get someone else to carry your cello?'

She laughed and everything wobbled. 'Now you're talking, kiddo. If that's a genuine offer, you could have just sealed your place in the famous foursome. Mind if I handle your instrument?'

She had the knack of giving an innuendo to everything, and she had already picked up his viola.

Mel handed the bow across. Cat gripped the fiddle in a way that showed she was no beginner, tucked the chin-rest into her flesh and played a few bars of Elgar's 'Salut d'Amour', inescapable at events like this.

'Would I get by?'

'You know you would.'

With a sure touch, she segued to the opening solo chords of the Telemann Viola Concerto. Much more demanding.

'You don't need me in your quartet,' Mel said.

'I'm a smart gal, but there's a problem. I haven't yet learned how to play my cello whilst holding the viola.' In yet another smooth change of styles she knocked out some bars from one of the numbers the trio had performed, 'Those Were The Days', and did it with gusto. 'Tell you what. Why don't you get yourself another drink and I'll sit in for you? The others won't mind.'

They didn't. She delighted everyone, including Mel's colleagues in the trio, not merely coping with the music, but giving it some welly.

Mel looked on in awe from behind a cluster of guests bobbing to the beat. He was amazed that this boisterous woman belonged to the same quartet as the po-faced Ivan. How on earth did the pair of them relate to each other? Ivan had said something about the members all being individuals, but these two came from different planets.

28

Perhaps the playful Cat was needed as a counter-balance to Ivan's navel-gazing. Mel was in no doubt which of the two he'd rather have for company. What could the others be like? As yet he couldn't picture a rehearsal. String quartets were sometimes known as the 'music of friends'. His own experiences of ensemble playing told him this could be a long way from the truth, but there was an understanding that discussions must take place and agreement reached on fine points as well as the major issues of interpretation.

He still had no clue as to which quartet they were. He knew of many and had played in some. This wasn't to say he was an expert. String quartets were legion, a surprising number top notch, plenty whose best hope was to get through a concert without people leaving, a humble majority who confined themselves to weddings like this and a few who were just abysmal. The high-flyers literally jetted around the world delighting audiences in distant places, so it was understandable that he'd not heard Cat in concert. He was sure he'd have noticed her.

They'd reached the end of a rendering of 'Moon River' that she'd embellished with trills the trio hadn't heard before, all in waltz time, and now she waved the bow for Mel to take over. 'Melly, my dear, I haven't had my second slice of wedding cake. I'm through playing.'

She was given a round of applause and blew kisses to the audience. While changing places with Mel she said with a wink, 'See more of you soon, eh?'

'So I may be in with a chance?'

'Don't push it, ducky. We only met an hour ago.'

'I meant the quartet.'

'Oh, that. Better wait and see. Is this your best instrument?'

'I do have another I keep for concert work.'

'That's a relief. This one isn't fit to use as a doorstop. Promise me you won't show it to any of the others.'

He wasn't going to miss an opening like that. 'I only show mine to girls, really lucky girls.'

'Well, it didn't get my juices going, honey. Keep it hidden.'

'Does anyone else need to vet me?'

'You bet.' She blew a kiss. 'Thanks for today. Wild.'

He didn't see her again that afternoon. At the end of the river trip, when they were packing up, one of the ushers asked him who the woman in yellow had been.

'That was Cat,' Mel said.

'Your girlfriend?'

'D'you mind? We only met today.'

'The reason I asked,' the usher said, 'is that no one seems to know who invited her. The bride's people thought she was one of the groom's family and the groom thought she was on the bride's side. We decided in the end she must have come with you.'

4

BATH, 2012

'It was a suicide,' Diamond told Paloma. 'Want to hear more, or would you rather not know?'

Back in Bath, on an overcast evening with soft rain in the air, they were taking one of their walks along the industrial stretch of the river west of the city, crammed on the south side with warehouses and factories, a far cry from the elegant part of Vienna they'd stayed in, but there was a compensation: they were only five minutes, he judged, from the Dolphin in Lower Weston. Walking wasn't a pleasurable activity for Diamond unless there was a pint and a pie when it finished.

'Every suicide is a tragedy,' Paloma said.

'Of course.'

'It's been on my mind ever since I saw all those flowers people had left. I want to know the details – and yet in a way I don't.'

'Best forget it, then.'

On the opposite side of the river an InterCity train bound for Bristol enforced a timely pause, long enough for Paloma to come to a decision.

'I'm sorry. I know I shan't stop thinking about it. You'd better tell me what you found out.'

'Then we leave it and move on?'

'Agreed.'

'Okay,' he said. 'I asked Ingeborg. She's a whizz at winkling out information. Even so, it took her a while on the internet. Four years ago the body of a tourist was found in the Danube canal close to those steps. A Japanese woman in her twenties.'

Paloma's sympathy now had more to latch on to. 'A tourist? Poor soul. Was she travelling alone?'

'Apparently.'

'I wonder what drove her to do such a thing. Did they identify her?'

'Months later, through her DNA. She'd been in the water too long to be recognised.'

'How do they do that?'

'DNA is unique to each individual, as you know. They take a sample from the remains and once they know of a missing person they can compare the profiles.'

'What with?'

'Traces found in the home – hair follicles, skin cells, blood, saliva. A comb or a toothbrush will often have DNA attached.'

'I suppose the family reported her missing.'

'Not immediately. She'd been away some time. Her travel arrangements were open-ended.'

Paloma took a sharp, pitying breath. 'So easy to get depressed when you're alone in a strange city.'

'She must have known what to expect.'

'Yes, but things can easily go wrong. You find you're running through your cash, or you lose your credit cards, or you just get ill and there's no one with you to share your troubles and laugh them off. The world can seem a hostile place.'

'It would take more than that to make me jump into a canal.'

She didn't take the remark as lightly as he intended. 'We're not all men of steel.'

'Just trying to keep a sense of proportion.'

'Not always so simple. You said she was Japanese. They think differently about suicide. It's rooted in their culture.'

'What – harry-karry?'

'Hara-kiri, actually. No, that's part of the samurai tradition and too gory to go into. I'm talking about the mass of the people, and the way they think. I'm trying to think of the name of the most famous Japanese dramatist. Anyway, he specialised in plays about lovers who commit suicide, and he was writing over three hundred years ago.'

Paloma's knowledge of international drama had to be respected. She had her own company advising on historical costume for theatre, film and television.

Diamond said, 'I heard somewhere that the Japanese are in the premier league for suicide. If you fail in your job, topping yourself is the honourable thing to do. Politicians, bankers, business managers. It wouldn't happen here. You write a book about your failings and make another fortune.'

His efforts to raise a smile weren't working.

'Did this poor girl leave a note?'

'No.'

'Then how do they know she killed herself?'

'They found something with the body that was almost the same as a suicide note. What are those little carved ivory things people collect? They have some sort of practical function.'

'Netsuke?'

'Right.'

'They go with traditional Japanese costume, fixed to the sash of a kimono so that personal items can be suspended from them.'

'Well, this one was found inside her T-shirt. She may have been holding it to her chest when she jumped. Two embracing figures in snow up to their waists.'

'Chubei and Umegawa.'

His high opinion of Paloma's expertise went up several more notches. 'You know their names?'

'They're well known, almost universal characters. And now I've remembered the name of the playwright: Chikamatsu. He used them in one of his plays. It ends with the lovers going out into the snow to die.'

'You're way ahead of me. The point of this is that the police took the netsuke to be a suicide emblem.'

'Symbolically, it does make sense,' she said. 'I've seen the story represented in woodcuts, paintings and netsuke. This poor woman may have been in love.'

'Not just missing her credit cards, then?'

She finally produced a smile, more in charity than humour. 'Probably not. Had she met someone?'

'Couldn't tell you. I don't suppose the Vienna police could, either.'

'Aren't you interested in why she died?'

'The "how" matters more than the "why". If it happened here and it became obvious she'd killed herself, with no possibility of anyone else being involved, we wouldn't go into all the possible reasons. The inquest will do that. It's not up to the police to find out her state of mind.'

'Peter, you probably don't mean it, but that sounds so uncaring.'

Smarting from that, he justified his statement. 'We're not social workers or psychologists. We'd be wrong to try.'

'But you'd try if she'd been murdered. That's where your argument breaks down.'

He shrugged. 'I didn't think we were arguing. Besides, it's not my case. The Vienna police dealt with it.'

'And decided it was suicide because of nothing more substantial than the netsuke? Didn't they go into it any more deeply than that? Someone could have stuffed the netsuke into her clothes and pushed her in.'

'Murder, you mean?'

'Or manslaughter, horseplay that went wrong.'

'Unlikely.'

'Why?'

'If they used the netsuke to delude the police the killing would be premeditated. But it wouldn't be a very reliable way of going about it. You couldn't guarantee the police would find the thing. It was not much bigger than a walnut.'

'So you agree with the official line – it was suicide?'

'I've no doubt they looked at all the evidence.'

'And this was how long ago? Four years? People still care enough to leave flowers.'

'It's a modern custom.'

'And a nice one. Her family must be devastated. For this to have happened thousands of miles from home – that's heartbreaking.'

He couldn't prevent Paloma identifying strongly with the people involved. He'd hoped she would be satisfied knowing the main facts. She'd spoken of the temporary shrine of flowers several times since returning from Vienna.

He tried one more time to draw a line under the incident. 'Nothing we can do about it. Bad things are happening every day in this world. It's no good letting them get to you.'

She rounded on him with more passion than he expected. 'That's bloody typical of a policeman, if I may say so. Cut yourself off from reality. Develop the hide of a rhinoceros. This was a tragic suicide, a young life sacrificed and probably for love, if the netsuke means anything.'

'Paloma, we didn't know her. I haven't even told you her name.'

'It's the offhand way you said it: "Nothing we can do" – as if she's just a statistic. I know there's nothing we can do. It's up to the Austrian police. But I can't forget we were there and I picked up the flowers. Someone obviously cares about her enough to place a bunch of lilies there four years after the event, even if you want to turn your back.'

He ignored the last remark. 'Japanese friends, I should think, or local people with more sympathy than most of us, like you.'

'There you go again, analysing, looking for explanations. I'm saying it's a personal tragedy. It's real.'

No question: the very thing he'd wanted to avoid was happening. Paloma was reliving the incident and more upset than ever. Worse, it was becoming an issue between them.

She continued, 'We spent most of our time in Vienna tracking that bloody film as if the events actually happened. It was only a story, but you seemed more affected by it than the real human tragedy we stumbled over. I tell you, that scene has been on my mind a lot since we got back.'

'That much is obvious,' he said. 'You don't have to keep telling me. That's why I asked Ingeborg to find out more. Maybe I shouldn't have done.'

She turned her head, as if talking to the river. 'It's better knowing, even if we can't do anything about it.'

They walked as far as Weston footbridge before Diamond spoke again, trying to make peace.

'You had a basinful of *The Third Man*. Selfish of me. I should have given you more choice in what we did.'

'I'm not complaining about that. What I find hard to stomach is that you can get emotionally involved in a film, yet cut off from a real death.'

'My job. Simple as that.'

'Being detached, you mean?'

'Any professional will tell you the same – doctor, paramedic, fireman.'

'Yet you're a softie underneath. I've seen you in tears at the end of the film when the woman walks straight past Joseph Cotten and into the distance.'

'You weren't supposed to notice. I'm just the same in *Casablanca*. She was Anna, by the way.'

'Who was?'

'The woman in the film, played by Alida Valli.'

'For pity's sake, Peter, I despair of you. Yet you won't name the Japanese suicide victim.'

'If it mattered, I would.'

At Twerton, the river divides to accommodate a weir. They followed the towpath along the Western Cut as far as the small humpback bridge that takes its name from the Dolphin.

'This is almost three hundred years old, did you know?' Diamond said with a too-obvious shift in the conversation.

'It can't be.'

'Most of it is. One side was bombed in the Bath Blitz and had to be rebuilt. The pub copped it, too. It's said to be equally old.'

'How do you know this?'

'I live just down the road, don't I? This is one of my locals.'

'One of them. I like that.'

It was too damp to sit in the garden, so they found a table in one of the eating areas inside. He brought a pint for himself and a glass of Chablis for Paloma from the bar.

She was still tetchy with him, as if more needed to be said. He wittered on for a while, explaining that the Dolphin hadn't got its name from a small whale that had strayed up the Avon, but an old word for a mooring post.

Only when their meal arrived did Paloma say, 'When I called you a softie just now, it wasn't meant as an insult. I don't think it's bad if you shed a few tears over a film. It shows you have emotions that are bottled up mostly. You keep them hidden in your working life and I understand why. What I can't work out is why you don't relax enough to let your feelings show when you're off work, such as now.'

'What do you expect? I'm a bloke.'

'There you go again, putting up the shutters.'

At a loss, he stared across the room. He could think of nothing to say. He'd never been comfortable talking about what he thought of as personal. Even with his beloved wife Steph he'd rarely opened up and after her sudden and violent death he'd confided in nobody, preferring to endure the unimaginable grief in isolation. The wound would never heal and he was certain that no one, however well-meaning, could assist. He'd put the shutters up – as Paloma had expressed it – for a reason. He couldn't predict how he would react if she were to probe his hidden emotions. Paloma was a valued friend and an occasional lover. Up to now she'd been willing to conduct their relationship on those terms. Unless he was mistaken she seemed this evening to be demanding a change in him that he didn't think he could make.

When it became obvious Diamond wasn't going to speak, Paloma said, 'I know what you're thinking. Let me remind you that we've both got painful areas in our lives – totally different, but hard to bear. My ex-husband, my son. I'll never come to terms with what happened, just as I wouldn't expect you to get over your personal tragedy. We're scarred for life, both of us. But we still *have* a life. Surely it helps to share joys and sadnesses?'

'I prefer to keep my sadnesses to myself,' he said.

She looked surprised. 'But a trouble shared is a trouble halved – or so they say.'

'Claptrap.'

She didn't speak for a moment, but her face drained of colour. 'I beg your pardon.'

'What you just said – it's only a saying and it's rubbish. I'm not discussing my private life with anyone.'

She caught her breath. 'I thought I was a part of your private life.'

'It doesn't mean you're on the inside with a licence to go where you want.'

'You don't know how hurtful you're being.'

'I'll shut up, then.'

He finished the pie and chips in silence. Although rows with work colleagues were his stock-in-trade, this was his first serious difference with Paloma and he knew he was handling it badly. He offered to get another drink.

She was tight-lipped.

'Shall we go, then?' he suggested.

Still silent, she got up from the table and walked to the door. The barman shouted, 'Cheers, folks. Have a great evening.' Neither Diamond nor Paloma answered.

Out on the towpath, something definitely needed to be said. In ordinary circumstances they would head towards his house and she would spend the night with him. But it wasn't as if they were married. These intimacies were occasional and by arrangement – a subtle, consensual understanding.

He said, 'Perhaps it's a sign that we've moved on, having a few strong words with each other.' He meant to say they'd grown closer and could speak their differences without the relationship breaking down.

That wasn't how Paloma took it. 'Moved on? Are you saying you want to end it?' She stopped walking and swung round to face him. 'Are you?'

'Paloma, it's not me making an issue out of nothing.'

'So I'm to blame, am I?'

'I didn't say that.'

'Not in as many words, but that's obviously what you meant. It may sound like nothing to you but I'm not used to being told my opinions are claptrap, especially when I was reaching out to you, doing my best to understand you.'

'I don't want to be understood – not like that, anyway.'

Her face reddened and her eyes filled with tears. 'In that

case you don't need me around. Find some other woman to shag, someone who doesn't give a damn about you. You and I are through.'

She turned and stepped briskly away without looking back.

5

Two weeks passed and Mel heard nothing more from the 'Famous Foursome', Cat's term for the mysterious string quartet. Thinking they may have decided he wasn't the right choice for violist, he made up his mind not to lose any sleep over it. Sure, the money was tempting, but he didn't care for their methods, acting like Cold War spies, obtaining his address, whisking him off for a secret meeting in a London club, refusing to say who they were and gatecrashing a private wedding party for a second look at him. Out of curiosity he'd Googled string quartets. Would a reputable, high-earning ensemble group be able to exist in the twenty-first century without its own website with pictures of the performers? Even if Ivan was a shadowy figure, the rumbustious Cat was not. He'd found more ensembles online than he had ever dreamed existed, plenty with female cellists and their pictures, too, but none looked like her. If he'd been able to supply a name for the quartet he might have had more success. After numerous tries he decided his time would be better spent practising.

He was starting to think the whole thing could be an elaborate hoax. Classical music wasn't without its jokers, however solemn its reputation. Generally they struck in rehearsal sessions when fooling about was excusable. Most of it was at the level of sabotaging piano stools, music stands and sometimes even the instruments. On occasions the trickery was more sophisticated, involving players being sent wrong instructions. He'd heard of an unfortunate first violin led to believe everyone would be wearing a red bow-tie for a concert of Russian music. Then there was the percussionist tricked into moving his entire set of instruments into the royal box at the Albert Hall for a performance of the '1812 Overture'.

The more he thought about this leg-pull theory, the more plausible it became, but where it was leading? Presumably some kind of humiliation was in store. He'd be notified he was picked for the quartet, turn up somewhere for a rehearsal, open a door and be greeted by all his jeering mates. Was that the sting? It didn't seem enough after such a build-up. Better think again.

There had to be a bigger pay-off.

With a sinking heart he recalled the *Candid Camera* show that had run for so many years taking advantage of unsuspecting members of the public. Surely that had disappeared from TV screens, along with its imitators? They'd spared no expense in staging elaborate cons. What if some crap TV company had decided to dust off the formula and serve it up again?

His comeuppance as mass entertainment? He didn't want that.

Either way, he was obviously the fall guy. Why? He hadn't been getting above himself, had he? He was an even-tempered, unassuming bloke, or so he liked to think. He didn't go out of his way to annoy people.

Maybe he did, and was not aware of it.

Or he was a born sucker. He still recalled with pain the night he'd been robbed of his viola outside the Festival Hall.

If this was a con, he knew musicians were involved. Ivan could have been an actor, but Cat was not. She was a damn good cellist. Someone in the business must have persuaded her to join in the fun.

Next question: who, of all the players he knew, was devious enough to have picked on him? Actually, plenty. In his situation, filling in often for violists in ensemble groups and orchestras, there were hundreds who knew him by name. Generally there's some banter when you return to a bunch of people you've met before. A few might want to take it further.

His thoughts veered in another, darker direction. This could be a revenge thing. He'd once had sex with a flautist called Destiny who played for the Royal Opera, a haughty-looking lady with hidden lusts. She'd approached him first, literally put her arm around him and led him below stage at Covent Garden where they'd had a vigorous session on the single-ended sofa normally used for the dying Violetta in *La Traviata*. This didn't inhibit Destiny in the least. Mel was left with soreness amidships and multiple scratches to arms and back. He'd vowed not to repeat the experience, but Destiny had other ideas. For the rest of Mel's stint with the Opera orchestra she made sure everyone knew he'd scored with her and she was up for more. Months afterwards he was still getting phone calls and texts suggesting another session. Everyone in the music world seemed to know. He got weary of being asked when he was planning another date with Destiny.

Could she have hatched this plot? On reflection, probably not: she believed in the direct approach.

But once he'd started on this tack, he thought of other affairs with musicians. Playing in an orchestra tends to encourage close relationships. Sitting for hours in rehearsal with attractive, creative people, you find yourself becoming fascinated by physical details, how her hair is fastened to leave the nape of her neck exposed, or how she crosses her legs at the ankles. The discipline of the music means that in moments between playing, a glance, a smile, a raised eyebrow can convey more than it would outside. With a love of music in common and the shared experience of making it as near to the ideal as possible, responding to the conductor, to the harmonics, you already have everything in place for some flirting when the formalities end.

That was how Mel had scored a number of times. Some romances lasted longer than others, but all had come to an end, almost always with unhappiness on one side or the other. It was not impossible that some of the hurt had lingered. He tried to imagine which former girlfriends were capable of engineering a plot like this, designed to raise his expectations and then humiliate him, and he just couldn't see it. What was happening to him called for a degree of organisation, of bringing in people to help, that didn't square with any of the women he'd slept with.

Currently he was going out with Dolores, the redheaded fount of all knowledge from his local record shop. She didn't play (or wouldn't admit to it), but knew more than he did about all the great artists and ensembles. And while she had a quirky sense of humour that made her approachable, she was most unlikely to be behind what was currently happening to him.

Tonight they were drinking the house Merlot at the Coach and Horses on Kew Green and she looked at him over her rimless specs and said, 'Something bugging you?'

'Why?'

'You're miles away.'

He decided to tell all.

Dolores listened with increasing interest.

'The thing is,' Mel summed up, 'I hate uncertainty. These people could be taking me for a ride, getting my hopes up about a well-paid job in a high-class quartet. If it's a hoax,

I need to know. But it's just possible it's on the level and I can't afford to let a good opportunity pass by.'

'How long is it since you met the cellist lady?'

'Couple of weeks.'

'Didn't she give any clue what happens next?'

'She was upbeat. Said something about seeing more of me soon.'

'Suggestive.'

'Just about everything she said was, but she can get away with it. She's big, wall-to-wall. Have you heard of anyone like that?'

'Playing cello in a string quartet? I can't say I have.'

'But you know all the top ensemble groups.'

'On CD, yes. I haven't watched them all perform. Sometimes they're pictured on the cover, but not always. You said her name is Cat. Would that be short for Catherine?'

'She didn't say. Katrina? Kathleen? It may be a nickname.'

'I'm trying to think of cellists,' Dolores said.

He sipped the wine and waited.

She took a different tack. 'You've met two of them. Logic suggests that the third will want to vet you soon.'

He nodded. 'They've got me on a piece of string.'

'Not necessarily. I expect they're as nervous as you are. It's a massive decision. Get someone who isn't compatible and he could destroy the group in a very short time. Did they say what happened to their violist?'

'That's another mystery. I asked Ivan straight out if he died or is being given the push. He more or less told me to back off. He's a hard man, is Ivan. There's some East European in his manner as well as his name – if that is his name.'

'Yet he was the first to approach you, and he told you he'd heard you play, so he must be on your side.'

'You're talking as if this is going to happen.'

'I think it will,' she said.

'But you can't identify the quartet. They've got to be famous if they're earning the money Ivan spoke about.'

'I'm not infallible, Mel. Yes, I may have heard them. I may even recognise their playing, but that doesn't mean I'd know them if they walked in here this minute and bought us a drink.'

'And do the personnel change much?'

'In some groups, yes. Others stay together forever. The same four guys played in the Amadeus for forty years and the Guarneri weren't far behind. Their cellist retired, but the others carried on. Four people coming together to play music can't predict what life will throw at them. Someone gets ill or dies and the others have to decide whether to call it a day or look for a replacement.'

'And is it blindingly obvious when someone new comes in?'

'To me? I can usually hear the difference in a recording of the same piece. To the players I'm sure there are major adjustments.'

'And some resentment, no doubt,' he said, confiding yet another worry that had been gnawing away at his confidence. 'I don't particularly relish being the new boy. Comparisons are going to be made. I wouldn't wish to ape the playing of the previous incumbent just to make the process easy for the others. I doubt if it's possible, anyway.'

'They'll understand,' Dolores said. 'Everything I've heard about string quartets and the way they work suggests that there's debate going on all the time in rehearsal. And sometimes in performance. I don't need to tell you this. You've played in ensembles.'

'Filling in isn't the same as taking over from someone who has left,' Mel said. 'The two people I've met are formidable characters in their different ways. They're not going to give me an easy ride.'

'Would you want one?'

'An easy ride?' He smiled. 'Of course not.'

Then his phone beeped.

'D'you mind if I take this?'

'Feel free.'

'Mr Farran?' Mel tensed. The voice was Ivan's, the same Beechamesque tone as if he was speaking to an audience. 'We spoke before, about the quartet.'

'Yes.'

'We'd like to arrange an opportunity for you to play with us.'

'In concert?'

'No, in more of a soirée situation, a private house, with the three of us and possibly our manager.'

'Where is this?'

'We will send a car, as before. Would next Sunday afternoon suit you?'

'I suppose.' His brain was racing. He almost forgot to ask the basic question: 'What are we playing?'

'Are you familiar with Beethoven's Opus 131?'

He took a deep breath. The Quartet in C sharp minor is one of the most challenging in the repertoire, a forty-minute masterpiece. He'd have five days to prepare. 'I wouldn't say familiar. I've played it.'

'That's all right, then,' Ivan said. 'Be sure to bring your best instrument. We need to hear the sound.'

'Is this an audition, then?'

'Don't think of it as such. Treat it as an afternoon of making music. The car will pick you up at two. Do you eat smoked salmon?'

'When I get the chance, yes.'

'We'll have some for tea. Oh, and there's no need to dress

47

up this time. Come in your weekend attire, whatever that may be.' This was Ivan at his most human. Apparently deciding he'd gone overboard, he abruptly ended the call.

'I'm about to find out if this is genuine,' Mel told Dolores. 'Sunday afternoon, Beethoven Opus 131. In at the deep end.'

'You'll be fine,' she said. 'Think of it as—'

'An afternoon of making music?'

'Exactly.'

6

An afternoon of making music?
Some chance.

Mel wasn't treating this lightly. He was about to be put to the test. Each waking hour must be devoted to preparing the piece, learning the seven movements passage by passage in readiness to respond to the other instruments, letting the viola speak, sing, inspire, transform, in harmony with the rest. And of course the difficulty was not being able to predict how the others would interpret their parts. The preparation you can do in isolation is limited.

For encouragement he kept telling himself that this wouldn't be a memory test like a solo performance. Quartet-playing is almost always from the sheet. They'd have the score in front of them with the composer's markings.

Opus 131 is said to have been Beethoven's favourite of all his string quartets. It is also said to be the ultimate in difficulty, in places almost beyond comprehension. Enough to make a nervous player take up drumming.

Yet more than once Mel had filled in for a quartet when the violist had become ill between final rehearsal and concert. He'd gone in cold and performed well enough to get through. Nobody had thrown anything.

Surely these people would make allowance.

Or would they? Ivan was the sort who expected perfection, gritting his teeth at anything less. Cat would treat any false note as hilarious. Hard to say which would be less mortifying. The great unknown was the mysterious third member, the second violin, who hadn't shown any interest yet. Mel tried to put all three out of his mind and steep himself in the work, but he knew in his heart that the personalities in a quartet are fundamental to its performance.

By Saturday he was up with the piece, as well prepared as anyone could expect to be. Sunday morning he went through it twice without fluffing a note. He drank a large black espresso, packed the instrument in its case and started looking out of the window for the black Mercedes.

But it never arrived.

Instead, around ten past two, a red convertible with the roof down rattled the Fingis Street window frames. The driver – not the man he'd met before – got out, gave the house a long look and decided against all appearance to the contrary it must be correct.

Mel saved him the trouble of ringing the doorbell. 'It's me you're picking up, I think. Mel Farran.'

'Good man. Set to go, then?' There was none of the deference of the previous chauffeur. This guy looked and behaved as if he owned the Aston Martin. 'I'm Doug, of Douglas Christmas Management.'

Pause for thought. 'You manage the quartet?'

'Try to – on their more agreeable days. Hop in. We're running late.'

'I need my instrument.'

The driver flashed his whitened teeth. 'Of course.' He took a key from his pocket, pointed it at the car and the boot lid opened.

'Thanks,' Mel said, 'but I'd rather keep it by me.'

'You fiddle players are all the same. Treat them like newborn babies.'

They left Fingis Street behind, roaring through West

London, the sound exaggerated by the roof being down. Mel kept the case containing his baby between his knees, deciding this gave more protection in case of a collision. Conversation would have been difficult anyway, and was rendered impossible by rock music at high volume. Doug wasn't a Radio Three man.

Somewhere west of Acton they joined the North Circular and stayed with it as far as Friern Barnet, at which point Mel gave up trying to track the route. Soon they were travelling into an area lush with greenery and golf courses. A right turn, a private road, an electronic gate and they moved up a red-tiled drive and stopped outside a residence like the backdrop to a Gainsborough portrait. Mel shed all doubts about the quartet earning six-figure salaries.

'Whose place is this?' he asked when the engine was switched off.

'Mine, actually. The talent, as I call them, will tell you I'm an extortionist, but that's their little game. In my position you have to have a reasonable lifestyle or people don't believe you're good at what you do.'

'Is this where we're playing?' All week he'd pictured four upright chairs in someone's living room with the other furniture pushed to the walls.

'That's the plan.'

'Are the others inside?'

'And getting stroppy by now.' Doug marched to the front door, opened it and shouted, 'We made it, musos.'

Mel followed, his knuckles turning white around the handle of his viola case.

The Georgian front of the house was no preparation for the interior, an open-plan conversion, a monument to the possibilities of the rolled steel joist, with several stone pillars where solid walls once stood. The spaces were defined in a conventional way, dining area, kitchen, office, library and a

51

couple of lounges. At the far end three people waited, already seated with stands in front of them in what was evidently the music space. A fourth chair had been put out for the newcomer. Mel spotted Cat first, not unlike Britannia on an old penny coin, her cello leaning against her thigh. She raised her bow.

'Glad you made it, kiddo.'

Ivan was opposite her, checking his watch. His weekend casuals were a three-piece suit and striped tie.

'My fault we're a trifle late,' Doug said. 'Couldn't find the street and ended up on the Hammersmith Flyover.'

Mel was looking at the one musician he hadn't already met, a guy more his own age, with brown hair to his shoulders and dressed in a black shirt and red corduroy trousers, but unwilling, it seemed, to make eye contact.

Doug made the introduction.

'Good to meet you,' Mel said to Anthony and could have saved his breath. The second violin showed no intention of shaking hands or offering any kind of greeting.

Now Doug took a step back. 'I'm going to make myself scarce, people. I'm an unrewarding audience, as you know. Take the hot seat, Mel. They're on pins to know if you'll fit in.'

Thanks for that boost to my confidence, Mel thought.

Cat called out as Doug was leaving, 'Keep your thieving hands off the sandwiches, boyo. I've counted them.'

Heart pumping faster at the ordeal to come, Mel removed his viola and bow from the case and joined the quartet.

'You did tell him on the phone it's Beethoven's Opus 133?' Cat said to Ivan.

Mel's jaw dropped. 'I heard 131.'

'Joke,' she said. 'You'll get used to me, sunshine. We may be tough nuts, but we're not asking you to tangle with the *Grosse Fuge,* not before the first break.'

52

'Can we be serious?' Ivan said. 'Mr Farran is our guest for the afternoon. Let's treat him with respect.'

'No need for that,' Mel was quick to tell them. 'I'd rather be informal.'

'Me, too,' Cat said. 'What do you have in mind?'

'I meant—'

'Relax, my pet. You're one of us.'

Ivan gave her a sharp glance. 'Don't be premature. Nothing is decided.' To Mel, he said with a twitch of the lips that was the nearest he would get to cordiality, 'Ready?'

'Of course.'

'We won't treat this as a rehearsal, because it isn't. We'll play the whole quartet as we would if you were our regular violist. No one is expecting a miracle. You'll be adjusting to our tempo and voicing just as we will respond to yours. When infelicities occur—'

'Don't you love that?' Cat broke in. '"When infelicities occur." He means when someone plays a bum note.'

'We'll make allowance,' Ivan said. 'After all, we're human.'

'Some of us,' Cat murmured. She was doing her best to take the stress out of the situation, even if Ivan didn't care for it.

As for Anthony, he remained expressionless, as if he'd heard all this before.

'Shall we tune the instruments?' Ivan said. 'And by the way, because of the length of the piece and the room temperature it's to be expected that they'll go out of tune before the end. No matter.'

'We'll wing it, bossy boots,' Cat said. 'We always do.'

Ivan lifted the violin to his chin and played a note that acted on Mel's nerves like a thousand volts.

Get a grip, he told himself. You prepared for this all week.

He raised his viola, waited for a lead from the cello, tried the note several times, gave a small twist to the fine tuner, was satisfied, nodded, took a deep breath and waited.

Anthony had come to life and looked a different man tuning his violin. Cat drew her bow several times more across the cello strings and winked. They tried a few chords in the C sharp minor key.

Then it got serious.

The opening movement of Opus 131 is majestic, yet with a sense of foreboding. Beethoven's first mark says 'Adagio ma non troppo e molto espressivo' and presents an immediate test for the first violin. Ivan sounded the first dramatic bars expressing the anguish that mirrored Mel's state of mind. And as Anthony took up the fugal theme on a single up-bow it was apparent how seamlessly the two blended. This was playing of rare quality. The second violin might be a social misfit, but he was a fine musician.

Poised for his entrance in bar nine, Mel knew it had to be spot on. The score called for him to join the playing of the others at precisely the same bow speed. There was no hiding.

His timing was right. He conquered his nerves, launched into the piece and played the crescendo in bar eleven in the knowledge that he needed to top the two violins with the complete fugue subject, a theme that is heard in various guises throughout. A lift of Ivan's right eyebrow signalled satisfaction. Under way and making music as requested.

Now was the moment for the fourth voice, Cat's cello, and she supplied a strong, sonorous note in no danger of being drowned by the others. With all four instruments in play, the harmonics came under scrutiny and to Mel's ear blended well. Even while straining to concentrate he felt lifted by the company he was in. They were spectacularly good. Ivan was a skilful leader, setting the tempo, making way when necessary, yet filling in the harmony with precisely the right strength when required.

Towards the middle of the first movement the violins speak to each other with the last six notes of the fugue motif and then viola and cello take up the dialogue in one of the loveliest passages in the entire quartet repertoire. An immense test, and Mel was equal to it, removing everything from his mind except the purity of the sound. His eyes didn't meet Cat's, yet he felt an emotional affinity with her that only musicians could appreciate.

It was a seminal moment. Performing with such gifted artists was uplifting, however mismatched they were as personalities. I want to be part of this, he thought. I want it more than I ever suspected.

So as movement succeeded movement, he felt buoyed up by the quality of the playing, growing in belief, inspired to new heights. In the jarring transition from the breakneck speed of the scherzo to the poignant adagio of the sixth movement, the viola takes centre stage. All those hours of practice gave him the confidence to play this heart-rending passage from memory, his bowing prolonging the intensity at slow tempo without sacrificing the sense of motion.

The fireworks of Beethoven's seventh and final movement have a huge impact after this. Four instruments in unison from the jolt of the first note on a downward stroke into a rapid pounding rhythm played right at the frog of the bow will startle any audience. With no one else present, not even Douglas, there were only the four musicians to thrill to the vitality of the music, the culmination of all that had gone before. Spells of ferocious playing were separated by those gorgeous lyrical oases. Excited, energised, the quartet performed the finale relentlessly until its sudden, challenging stop.

No one spoke.

After a piece of such range and power, mere words seem crass.

Some seconds passed before Ivan tapped his stand several times with the bow, a gesture of satisfaction. Cat nodded her agreement. Anthony had slumped again, a puppet with slack strings.

At a loss as to how to behave with these people he'd joined intimately through the music but hardly at all as companions, Mel propped the viola in the angle of his lap and waited. He'd raised his level of playing beyond anything he'd achieved before. He was emotionally drained.

Finally, Cat spoke. 'Don't know about you dudes, but that was good enough for me.' She turned to Anthony. 'What do you say?'

'I'm easy.'

'We know that, honey, but what about the playing?'

'I said – I'm easy.'

Cat turned to Ivan. 'We can take that as affirmative – I think. What's your opinion?'

'Of what?'

'Of the combo.'

'I wish you wouldn't use that expression.'

'Here we go again,' she said. 'Forty minutes of bliss with Beethoven and it doesn't take ten seconds to start another spat.'

'It's unseemly.'

'Give me strength. What do you want us to be known as – the Ivan Bogdanov Players?'

'Now you're being offensive.'

'It would be, stuck with a name like yours.' She raised a hand. 'All right, that was out of order. Sometimes you drive me to it. Back to my question: do we have a future together? I think we do, and Anthony is easy – which coming from him is as good as a twenty-one-gun salute. Are you up for it?'

Ivan sniffed. 'Allowing that Mr Farran was my suggestion in the first place, I give my consent, but with reservations.'

'What's your problem?' Cat said.

Mel was increasingly uncomfortable. 'Should I go outside while you discuss this?'

'For the love of Mike, no,' Cat said. 'We're talking about reviving the quartet and everyone deserves a say.'

'Then we'd better bring in Douglas,' Ivan said.

'He can go bark at the moon. He'll take his twenty per cent whatever we decide. And if we're down to a trio he'll want twenty-five. What's eating you, Ivan?'

'I'm going to propose we agree to a trial period of, say, three months. If, for some reason, it doesn't work as well as we hope, we can review it then.'

'Why? When you and I started there was no trial period or the rest of us would have kicked you out for sure.'

'You don't mean that.'

'I mean the first bit – no trial period. I like equality. If Mel is joining us, he won't want second-class status.'

'Perhaps we should ask him.'

And that was how Mel found himself in the hot seat. He cleared his throat and said, 'If you're serious about inviting me in, I'd like to know more about you.'

This silenced them for a beat or two.

Cat said, 'Such as?'

'What's the name of your quartet?'

Even more hesitation.

Ivan said, 'One matter we must discuss at an early stage is whether to adopt a new name.'

Mel gained in confidence. 'What's wrong with the old one?'

'We had a quartet, a successful one, but it no longer exists.'

'What happened?'

'Our violist left.'

No one added to the bald statement. Mel could hear them breathing.

'Over a disagreement?'

'Not that I'm aware of.'

Finally Cat said, 'You don't have to be so mysterious, Ivan. Harry went missing in Budapest four years ago when we were playing there. Nobody has seen him since. He's a missing person. We've been marking time ever since in the hope he'll walk in one day. It hasn't happened so we faced reality and started looking for a replacement.'

Mel turned to Ivan. 'And you want to buy more time in case he does turn up?'

Ivan reddened.

'He won't,' Cat said. 'We would have heard by now. Something final must have happened.'

'Was he acting strangely?'

'We're all strange, ducky, as you must have worked out for yourself by now. If you want my opinion, Harry was the closest to normal.'

'Was there a disagreement?'

'Disagreements are the stock-in-trade of string quartets. We're strong-minded people, even Anthony, as you'll discover. But there was nothing more than the usual to and fro over the score of whichever piece we were playing. We all bring something to the party and it makes for a more exciting performance.'

'Then you haven't played together for how long?'

'A couple of years, give or take. We tried, but for one reason and another – most of them crap viola players – it hasn't worked out, so we've had to do our own thing – teaching and orchestral work and stuff we wouldn't want anyone else to know.'

Ivan said, 'We haven't made it public that the quartet stopped appearing. We've been fading away.'

'Faded,' Cat said.

'I'd still like to know the name.'

'The Staccati.'

Mel's skin prickled. The Staccati had been an international name. He owned some of their recordings. The only reason he'd overlooked them when he'd racked his brain for likely quartets was that nothing had been heard of them recently. Their great period was five or six years back. They'd been in demand at all the great music festivals across the world. 'I know about you, of course, but never had the pleasure of hearing you in concert.'

'We do most of our playing abroad,' Ivan said. 'You're able to travel, are you?'

'I enjoy it.'

'You won't when it seems never-ending, one hotel after the next.'

'The best deal is a residency,' Cat said. 'A few paid months in one place. Time to chill out, go shopping, get your hair done and find the hottest clubs in town. Heaven.'

'We give a fixed number of concerts and do some teaching,' Ivan said. 'It isn't all about self-indulgence.'

'Listen to him talking,' Cat said. 'Who was always in the park playing chess with the old men?'

Mel said, 'How soon would you want me to make a decision?'

'Yesterday isn't soon enough,' Cat said. 'We need to be concert-ready when Doug swings into action and gets us some gigs. Let's talk about repertoire. Any obvious blind spots?'

'I wish I knew more contemporary music.'

'Put it there, buddy. We stop at Schoenberg.'

'I haven't specialised in quartet music. I had to work hard at this.'

'You think we were playing off the cuff? I haven't watched TV all week. You can play. You should have heard some of the others.'

'Your standard is very high.'

'Bollocks.' She pointed her bow at Ivan. 'What do you say, Rasputin? Do we give it a whirl with Mel on full membership?'

A sigh. 'Very well.'

'Anthony?'

Anthony managed a nod.

'He's easy,' Cat said. 'Why don't we call in Doug and start on the salmon sandwiches?'

The deal was sealed. A verbal agreement would do, Doug said. And, just as Ivan had promised, Mel would earn one-fifth of the profits. The only undertaking he had to give was that the quartet's engagements had priority over everything short of acute appendicitis.

'And what if the original violist turns up?'

'I wouldn't worry about Harry,' Doug said in his nonchalant way. 'He's history. Nice man, wonderful musician, but out of the picture now.'

Years of working in an insecure profession had toughened Mel. 'Sorry. If I'm going to give up all my freelance work I need more of a guarantee.'

'I'll speak to the talent.'

'They said full membership. Can I take that as permanent?'

'If they already agreed, yes.'

'Then it has your approval?'

'Let's shake on it.' His grip reinforced the pact.

Mel still felt he had a right to know more. 'Has Harry ever gone missing before this?'

'Missing? No. They all go their own ways in free time on tour. They don't live in each other's pockets. The embassy kept asking us where he was supposed to have gone that evening and nobody knew. Ghastly time. We had to bring in a local musician to play the viola part in the last three concerts and he wasn't terribly good. I was forced to cancel the rest of the tour. Endless wrangling with the Hungarians over breach of contract and compensation claims. Made my life hell. If Harry had turned up at that point I'd cheerfully have shot him. Have another sandwich.'

'So will you make it clear to the others that I'm the permanent replacement?'

'Absolutely.'

Mel raised another concern. 'Won't it be difficult getting engagements after so long?'

A shake of the head. 'The name still has plenty of currency.'

'They want to change the name.'

Doug almost dropped the plate. 'Who does?'

Some inner censor stopped Mel from naming anyone. 'You'd better ask them. Personally, I'd be proud to join the Staccati.'

But Doug wasn't there to hear the last words. He was striding across the room to speak to Ivan.

The clash of wills was won by Doug. They would continue to be known as the Staccati Quartet. Once again, Cat waded in with a wisecrack: 'Staccato is all about sharp, disconnected notes and no four people are more disconnected than we are.' The dynamics of the group were becoming clearer. Ivan was not so dominant as he had first appeared. Cat could undermine him with her streetwise humour. Anthony allowed the others to make all the running, but might yet pounce. For the time being, Doug was the decision-maker.

'How soon will you be up to concert pitch?'

'We need to prepare,' Ivan said with all the earnestness of Noah before the rains came. 'Weeks, maybe months.'

'Why don't you fix up some gigs and tell us?' Cat said to Doug. 'Give some focus to the preparation.'

'I have a few ideas already,' Doug said, and any half-decent manager would have said as much. 'I was thinking of letting you in gently. There are various festivals coming up in this country – Cheltenham, Cambridge, York. Their programmes will already be arranged, but I can't see any of them turning down a chance to slot in the Staccati at short notice.'

Ivan was shaking his head. 'Too soon.'

'Tucson, Arizona? That's an awful long way for a single performance,' Cat said. 'Doug, I think you've got it. Better still, how about trying for a residency? Would you care for that, Anthony?'

Anthony said, 'Cool.'

'That's two of us, then. Mel, are you on board?'

'If there's half a chance, yes.'

'Three.' She turned to Ivan. 'We'd get paid to rehearse in a practice room. Isn't that better than weeks and months squatting in Doug's house?'

He still looked doubtful. 'I suppose if it could be arranged . . .'

'Sponsors, endowments. There's money out there. That's why we employ the best manager in the business.'

Doug almost purred. 'No promises. I'll do my best.'

With that settled, and the sandwiches all but gone, Ivan suggested they should rehearse another quartet while Doug went off to make phone calls.

Another quartet? Mel's heart sank and it must have been obvious.

'No sweat, kiddo,' Cat told him. 'When we rehearse, we take the thing apart, bar by bar, as if we never played it before. We're all learning together.'

'I didn't bring any other music.'

'You see that printer over there on Doug's computer desk? It's also a photocopier.'

*   *   *

Not long after, they were back with their instruments. They worked on a Schubert quartet familiar to most chamber musicians. Cat's reassuring words on a first rehearsal were borne out. The playing was in fragments, every phrase open to analysis. Strong views were voiced, but the arguing was of a different order from the debates on how the group was managed. These were points of interpretation and nuance, each player speaking with the authority of the score. Anthony found his voice and made clear that the term 'second violin' is misleading. He was not subordinate to Ivan or anyone else. And Mel, for his part, made sure that the viola was given its due.

Quite when Doug returned wasn't clear. By then the concentration was pretty intense. He must have been standing nearby for some minutes waiting for a break. He wasn't fussed. He was like the cat with the cream.

'Sorry to interrupt. Breaking news, as they say. You asked for a residency and I may have got one, a university with a substantial endowment for a series of master classes and concerts. They are willing to engage us for six months when the new term starts.'

'Who are?' Ivan said.

'Bath Spa University.'

'Bath.' Ivan spoke the word as if it were Lubianka Prison.

Cat overrode him. 'Not a bad place to spend half a year. Is there enough for us to live on?'

'Approved lodgings, all meals found and twenty grand each plus concert fees.'

'I could survive on that. When do they need to know?'

'I said I'd give them an answer today. It's a fantastic deal. To sugar the pill I said you'd also make a recording in aid of university funds.'

Cat looked at the others. 'Any objections?'

Anthony said, 'How many concerts?'

'You're going to like this,' Doug said. 'What they suggest is a series of soirées, fortnightly musical evenings in private houses, chamber music as it was originally performed. The audiences will be limited to the size of the venue and in most cases this will mean twenty-five to thirty at most. There are some beautiful houses around Bath. I can picture you by candlelight in gracious rooms of the sort the composers themselves must have known.'

'By Jesus, you're a wicked salesman,' Cat said.

'That's what you pay me for.'

'I'm in. How about the rest of you?'

Ivan was straight to where the shoe pinched. 'Fortnightly, I think I heard you say. With a new programme each time? That's a tall order.'

'What I'm suggesting is no more than one string quartet per evening, followed by a champagne interval and then some solo pieces. How does that seem?'

'I could endure that,' Cat said.

'If you like, you can repeat the programmes,' Doug said. 'Your audiences will be different each time, I expect.'

'Presumably they pay for the privilege?' Ivan said.

'The sale of tickets and all profits are handled by the university. They intend to put it towards the sponsorship – which I may say is very generous.'

'So we perform for nothing?'

'It's all part of the deal, Ivan, as I've tried to explain. Personally, I'd be thrilled to play in such surroundings if I had your talent.'

'You think Ivan plays the fiddle well?' Cat said. 'His main instrument is the cash register. He's a virtuoso.' She turned to Mel. 'Are you up for it, new boy?'

Mel was still in a spin from being admitted to the quartet. Right now, he would have agreed to anything.

Doug asked for a show of hands.

Nobody objected. Ivan seemed to have changed his mind about Bath.

'I'll confirm, then,' Doug said. 'That was a good sound, by the way. What's the piece?'

'That's our manager talking,' Cat said, 'and he doesn't know what we were playing.'

'Schubert,' Ivan said. 'Quartet Number 14 in D minor, better known as "Death and the Maiden".'

7

Ingeborg Smith said, 'Something is up with him.'

The rest of the CID room must have heard, yet nobody else spoke. The central heating was set too high for a mild October afternoon. Lethargy was the prevailing mood.

'He's been out of sorts all week. Longer really.' No one could be in any doubt who she meant. Ingeborg was the Diamond-watcher on the squad.

And on a day like today no one except Ingeborg cared much.

She tried a third time. 'I don't think he's had a civil word for any of us.'

DI John Leaman finally responded with, 'Tell us something new.' Which was rich coming from the misery-guts of CID.

From across the room, Paul Gilbert, the youngest on the team, said, 'It's the trend, isn't it? All those Scandinavian detectives, so depressed you wonder if they'll hold out until the last chapter.'

'What the hell are you talking about?' Leaman said.

'Don't you read?'

'Read what?'

'Some of them get on TV as well.'

'I don't have time for that stuff. I look at science-based series like *CSI* and *Bones*.'

'Be fair, you guys,' Ingeborg said. 'The boss treats us right and he can be amusing when he's on form. You have to tune in to his sense of humour, that's all.'

'My tuning must have gone to pot, then.'

'Bosses come a lot worse than him.'

Gilbert was quick to take her up on this. 'Why do you say that, Inge? Do you know something we don't?'

'I'm wondering if *he* knows something we don't.'

Leaman swung round in his chair. 'Hang about – do you think Diamond's on the way out?'

This possibility galvanised everyone. Keith Halliwell, the most senior man present, said, 'Get away. He's said nothing to me.'

'Whatever is bugging him, he's internalising it,' Ingeborg said. 'With all the government cuts he could be looking at early retirement.'

'Voluntary, you mean?'

'He wouldn't walk,' Halliwell said. 'Not the guv'nor.'

'But he'd take it badly if they forced him out.'

Mental pictures of Diamond being dragged from the building.

'There is another possibility,' Gilbert said.

'Give it to us, then.'

'It could be some of us for the chop. He's been told and he doesn't want to break the news to us.'

Rumours of redundancies had been circulating for months and now something close to panic ensued.

'They can't do that,' Leaman said. 'We're overstretched already.'

'Overstretched when there's a major enquiry,' Halliwell said, 'but that isn't every week of the year. We could be vulnerable.'

'All the public services are taking cuts,' Gilbert said. 'We can't expect to escape.'

Leaman said, 'And it's always last in, first out. So don't look so pleased with yourself, young man.'

By now every head was buzzing with thoughts of unemployment. Some twenty minutes later, Halliwell stood up. 'I'm going to ask him.'

Diamond was at his desk with his chin propped on both hands like a medieval gargoyle, but chunkier. He'd discarded his jacket and loosened his tie. 'What is it now?'

'Nothing special, guv. I was wondering . . . do you fancy a cuppa?'

'A cold drink would suit me better. They never get the heating right in this place.'

'Want to slip out for ten minutes?'

'While you mind the shop?'

'Actually I was thinking you might want company.'

'Something on your mind, is there? All right. John can hold the fort. It's not as if we're snowed under. Be better if we were.'

In the Royal Hotel just down the street, Halliwell brought the drinks to the table where Diamond had resumed his chin-in-hands posture.

'Did you want crisps or anything?'

'No. What's your problem?'

'Not mine specially, guv. There were some murmurings in the office about lay-offs.'

'Why? Do they know something?'

'They're thinking maybe you do, and you don't want to tell us.'

Diamond grinned faintly. 'Have I ever shied away from passing on bad news?'

'So we're safe?'

'I wouldn't bet on it, but I haven't heard yet, and if I do I'll fight tooth and nail to keep the squad together, even the layabouts.'

'That's all right, then.'

'What put this into their heads?'

'Nothing really.' Now that the team's concerns were put at rest Halliwell was ready to talk about the weather, or television, or the quality of the beer.

But Diamond wasn't. 'Murmurings, you said. Who was murmuring?'

'No one in particular.'

'Leaman, I bet.'

'To be fair, he isn't the only one, but I didn't come here to tell tales. They study your moods and they reckon you've been under a cloud these last weeks.'

'Study my moods sounds like Ingeborg.'

'So the general opinion is that there has to be something you're hiding from us, such as redundancies.'

'Bullshit.' Diamond rolled his eyes. 'For as long as I can remember, Keith, the politicians have banged on about getting more coppers on the streets. Even now, with all the cuts, they're saying it. How will it be done? By cutting down on the backroom staff. Backroom is the dirty word. That's you and me if we're stuck in the office all day. We need to get out more.'

'Like this?'

He couldn't raise another smile. 'Front-line is the buzzword. If you're front-line you're in no danger of the chop.'

'There hasn't been much serious crime lately.'

'Too true. A major incident would solve everything, keep us in work, get us away from our desks and stop stupid rumours flying around.'

'What do we do – tell the criminal class to step up productivity?'

'Not a bad idea.'

They brooded on this until Halliwell said, 'You do seem more depressed than usual. Is anything wrong?'

'With the CID room? Where shall I start? A DI who likes nothing better than spreading alarm and dissension. A recently promoted sergeant who watches my every move. A DCI who believes all that garbage enough to dump it on me.'

'You once said you wanted to be told if anyone was unhappy.'

Diamond shrugged. 'Fair enough, Keith. I'd forgotten.'

'When I asked if there's anything wrong, I meant in your life.'

The big man glanced away, across the room. 'If there was, I wouldn't tell you.'

'Your health is okay, I hope?'

'Now you're sounding like the idiot doctor who does the annual medical. Of course I'm okay. I don't make a point of taking my blood pressure or weighing myself, but I'm as fit as you or anyone else. Shall we end this pointless conversation and go back to work in case some of them think I've decided to end it all and jump off Pulteney Bridge?'

He'd had enough of this probing. Well intentioned it may have been, but he wouldn't be telling Halliwell or anyone else about the break-up with Paloma. Months had gone by since that walk along the towpath. Yes, he was unhappy, bloody miserable, and now CID had picked up on it, but he wouldn't be calling Paloma to try and make up. He had his pride and she had hers.

Two days passed before the team was gifted the suspicious death they needed. A couple walking the towpath near Lower Weston – much as Diamond and Paloma had done – spotted a floating object that at a closer look turned out to have arms and legs. They called the emergency number and a patrol car and an ambulance went to the scene.

Normally a dead body is left where it is found so that the

police can inspect the scene. This one was moving with the current and there was no telling when or where it had entered the water. A boat was used to retrieve it near Weston Lock and it was stretchered to a waiting van and taken to the Royal United Hospital mortuary.

The first duty of the police was to identify the dead woman, but this was difficult. She was way past the point when anyone would recognise her. A body in water will sink to the bottom and only rises to the surface when decomposition begins and gases form within the stomach and lungs. The time this takes depends on the water temperature. In icy conditions, months. In the Avon in a typical English summer, not much less.

In this case the decomposition was plain to see. Significant areas of the skin and tissue had peeled away.

The deceased was short, at just under five feet, and slight in build. Her hair was natural black, and cut sheer at the back. She had a full set of teeth, with some whitened fillings. The white T-shirt and black jeans she was wearing gave no clue as to her identity. Nothing was in the pockets. She wore no jewellery.

The missing persons register was consulted. Nobody from the local area matched the description, such as it was.

An early decision was taken by the coroner to order an autopsy. It was carried out by one of the hospital's team of clinical pathologists. The police, who provided continuity of evidence, were in attendance. Sometimes new information is discovered at this stage. Not this time.

Identity: unknown.

Cause of death: uncertain.

The pathologist – a man who didn't like wasting time – was unwilling to speculate how this young woman had died. The obvious assumption would have been that she had drowned – difficult to prove in any case and impossible in

71

this one. Drowning is one of the most problematic of all causes of death to diagnose. For one thing, the immersion in water, possibly for a considerable time, rots the body and vitiates the evidence. If the internal organs have deteriorated, as they do in quite a short time, they won't provide confirmation that the victim was struggling to breathe.

In this case, the classic signs, the plumes of froth at the mouth and nostrils, must have dispersed long ago and any internal froth at the trachea and bronchi would have vanished. There were no obvious external marks of injury apart from minor lacerations probably caused by the body being moved with the current and striking submerged rocks and objects. Anyway, the state of putrefaction would have masked anything less than severe wounding. All the pathologist would say was that from the general deterioration she must have been immersed for a minimum of two weeks and probably longer.

He added that a diagnosis of drowning is invariably a best-guess situation and this would be a very inferior guess that he wasn't willing to hazard.

He estimated her age at between twenty and thirty.

As for identification, her own family would not have recognised her. Under water the body assumes a face-down position, with the face, arms and legs dragging along the bottom.

It was only after the post-mortem, when the clothes were being put in a bag for storage, that a medical student assisting the pathologist happened to draw his attention to a faded label on the white cotton knickers.

'Sir, have you noticed this?'

He had not, whatever it was, and he was not overjoyed to be told. 'Noticed what?'

'I believe this writing is Japanese.'

'Why? Can you read it?'

The student reddened. 'No, but I spent some of my gap year in Tokyo. I can tell the difference from Chinese.'

'So?'

'So if her knickers were made in Japan, isn't there a chance she was Japanese?'

'Unless, like you, she travelled to Japan in her gap year. Or unless Japanese knickers happen to be on sale at Marks and Spencer. Or Tesco. I'm a histopathologist. My expertise doesn't stretch to ladies' underwear.'

'It was just something I noticed.'

'Full marks.' Said with no gratitude.

'Isn't there a way of telling?'

The pathologist gave a long-suffering look to the police witnesses, pulled up his face mask and asked the mortuary attendant to return the body to the table. 'You thought we were through, ladies and gentlemen, and so did I. From the state of her, I wouldn't know if she's Japanese or from up the road, but there is a way of finding out a person's racial origin from the teeth. There's a difference between people of Caucasian origin and the Mongoloid group of Asia and it's known as the shovel tooth – a concavity at the back of the upper incisors.' He leaned over the skull and opened the jaws. 'We don't routinely go into this kind of detail. Can we get a better light on this?' First, he ran his little finger along the back of the teeth. Then he used a dental mirror.

An uncomfortable silence followed.

'Hey ho,' the pathologist said without a glimmer of pleasure, 'this may be significant. These appear to be shovel teeth.'

The student had the sense not to shout, 'Told you so.'

The pathologist said, 'I'd better get one of my colleagues from odontology to confirm this. Sorry, folks, but if you want to follow this autopsy all the way through to the land of the rising sun I must invite you to return next week.'

* * *

The following Monday, the remains were brought out again for the dental expert. She was expected to confirm the pathologist's finding, but before starting she announced that she was not confident she could help. 'I know what you're talking about. Shovel teeth are typical of East Asians, but there are all sorts of exceptions and I wouldn't say it's reliable. Native Americans have them and I've seen many examples in Europeans.'

'So you can't tell us if she's Japanese?'

'Frankly, the knickers may be a better guide, but as I'm here, I might as well take a look. Oh dear, she *is* in a sorry state.'

The examination was painstaking, using a magnifier with a halogen light. The odontologist said at one point, 'Plenty of dental work and of excellent quality.'

She straightened up and turned to the student. 'Was it you who noticed the label?'

'Yes, ma'am.'

'And you thought she might be Japanese? Well, you could be right. Have you heard of tooth tattoos?'

A frown said the student had not.

'They're the big thing in Japan, like nail art, but for teeth, and she seems to have the residue of one. Didn't anyone spot this?'

Silence from the onlookers and a stony gaze from the pathologist.

'They're not really tattoos at all,' the dental expert explained. 'They're attached. If you fancy yourself with a mouthful of bling you get them applied with a special glue using an LED light to fix them. They can be removed quite easily and there isn't much left of this one, but take a look with my magnifier and tell me what you see.'

The student leaned over and looked through the lens at where the jaw was held apart. The tiny black symbol on one of the upper incisors was chipped in a couple of places, but clearly an embellishment. 'I do see it. Is it a Japanese character? No, I don't think it is.'

'Agreed.'

'It's a music note, isn't it? Looks to me like a quaver.'

'I never even got to first grade, but I'm willing to take your word for it.' The odontologist stood back. 'This all proves nothing, but if you're wanting to find out who she is, I would check for a missing Japanese woman with a possible interest in music.'

'Not my job,' the pathologist said.

At the request of the coroner, the job was passed to the police, but not yet to Diamond's CID team. The Missing Persons Register was checked again. No obvious leads were found. The supposed Japanese connection yielded nothing. Of seventeen young women reported missing in Bath and Bristol since the start of the year, none were from Japan. Fourteen had already been eliminated from the enquiry because of their height and hair colour. The tooth tattoo was thought to be an unlikely decoration for the remaining three.

CID were brought in after a couple of days.

'Any suggestion she was attacked?' Diamond asked the uniformed inspector who had handed over the paperwork.

'Impossible to say, but she did end up in the river Avon.'

'No marks of violence?'

'The body was too far gone to tell.'

'Could be an accident, then, or suicide. Was she fully dressed?'

'The shoes were missing.'

'They could easily have come off in the water.' He glanced through the post-mortem report. 'I've heard of tattoos in weird parts of the anatomy, but a tooth?'

'It's the best clue we've got, apart from the Japanese knickers.'

'Ah – the Japanese knickers.' Diamond rolled his eyes.

'We managed to confirm that the manufacturer doesn't export them. Mind, someone from Britain could have travelled there and bought a few pairs.'

'Someone from Britain or anywhere else on the globe.'

'True. But the tooth tattooing is a Japanese thing. It's popular there.'

'And I'm supposed to work with that?'

'Plus the music connection.'

'One note.'

'What do you expect – the Japanese National Anthem?'

Diamond raised his finger. 'I do the jokes here.'

Back in the CID room, he told the team, 'This is gainful employment, so we're not knocking it. In fact, we're going to make a big production of it. I want a display board with photos of the deceased and all the evidence, a map of the river and anything else you can think of. That's your job, John.'

Leaman beamed. Incident rooms were his speciality.

'Ingeborg, you get a front-line job, checking the two universities and all the private language colleges to see if any Japanese students have stopped attending in the past three months. Sometimes these things don't get reported. And Paul . . .'

'Yes, guv?'

'You're on hotels. Examine the registers for yourself. Don't just ask the reception people. Japanese names are pretty easy to spot. Get the details of all of them who stayed here and when they checked out.'

'Isn't some of that confidential?'

'What do you mean?'

'Data protection.'

'Don't talk to me about data protection. You're in CID, doing a job, trying to trace a missing person.'

John Leaman said, 'Strictly speaking, she isn't missing. We know where she is.'

Diamond didn't appreciate the logic. 'She's missing from somewhere, clever clogs, has to be. It's our job to find out where, college, hotel, tour group. That's how we'll find her name.'

'Precisely,' Leaman said. 'It's the name that's missing, not the person.'

'Any more lip from you, John, and you'll find yourself on knicker duty.' He addressed the team in general. 'Anyone here clued up on music?'

'Depends what sort,' Halliwell said.

'We don't know what sort. We have one musical note.'

'Personally, I like the Big Band sound.'

'Big Band. What's that – Glenn Miller? Duke Ellington? You're just the man to conduct this big band. I need an office manager. It's backroom, I know, but how could we manage without you?'

Halliwell gave the grin of a man who'd spoken once too often.

'Ingeborg?' Diamond said.

'You already gave me a job, guv.'

'Yes, but what's your taste in music?'

'I'm into roots.'

'What on earth . . .?'

'Folk, Celtic, blues, country and western.'

Paul Gilbert added, 'When it's not rock, jazz or classical, it must be roots. Me, I go for modern rock.'

'This isn't getting us anywhere,' Diamond said. 'I had a weekend in Vienna and visited Beethoven's house, but I wouldn't call myself an expert.'

'We have a wide spectrum, then,' Leaman said. 'I enjoy decent music of all kinds, but for preference I'm a Savoyard.'

'I thought that was a variety of sausage.'

'Gilbert and Sullivan,' Leaman said, not appreciating the laughs.

'The thing is, why did she choose to get a musical note glued to her tooth? Is she a performer? If so, we'd probably have heard. When a musician goes missing, people notice. It gets in the news.'

'She doesn't have to be a musician,' Halliwell said. 'She could be a music lover, just like any of us. I'm not sure if the tooth tattoo is going to help us much more now we know she's almost certainly Japanese.'

Ingeborg had been doing some lateral thinking. 'Guv, is it just a coincidence that you asked me some weeks back to get some background on that Japanese tourist who was found in the canal in Vienna?'

'Must be,' he said to cut her off, wanting to confine the discussion to what was happening in Bath. 'Better get started on this, boys and girls. Until something bigger comes along, it's the best way to defend our jobs. All the apparatus of an incident room. Computer back-up. Whiteboard. Photos. Action files. Big wheel – that's me. Let's get this show on the road.'

After that, no one had any other option than to look busy. Paul Gilbert remarked to Ingeborg as they headed for the door, 'Looks like the boss is coming out of his Swedish detective phase.'

'We can hope,' she said. 'I wouldn't put money on it yet.'

8

'One more time. She won't be back for ages.' Tippi Carlyle, in her bed facing Mel, ruffled his hair and smoothed her hand across his cheek and jaw. 'She's at Weightwatchers until seven and she always goes for a McDonald's after.'

'It's her house and you're her daughter.'

'The apple of her eye.'

'Okay, which makes it worse if she comes home early and finds me in bed with the apple of her eye.'

She wriggled and her nipples skimmed his chest. 'You can't deny you're up for it.'

'I don't want to upset her and nor do you.'

'Come on, big boy. Have another bite of the apple.'

'And get asked to leave? I like it here.'

She pressed closer. 'This is what you like.'

'I think we should each have a shower – separately – and be in our own rooms when she gets back.'

'You're scared of her.'

'I respect her. She's my landlady.'

'Get real, Mel. She must have guessed about us in – how long? – nearly two months? My mum's not daft. It's not as if I'm under age.'

'Agreed, but she hasn't seen us at it. Let's show respect and leave her guessing.'

'You're terrified she'll kick you out. You prefer her cooked breakfasts to sex with me.'

'Tippi, I want both to continue.'

'Honest? Prove it, then.'

'Not right now.' He kissed her forehead, eased away, rolled over, emerged from under the quilt and started gathering his clothes.

Tippi watched him. 'Tosser.'

'Tomorrow.'

'You must be joking.'

He padded back to his room, closed the door and took that shower. It doesn't get better than this, he thought. A regular income, nice lodgings, a friendly landlady with a dreamboat daughter who can't get enough, and any amount of music. I've hit the jackpot here in Bath.

Two months into the residency, the quartet remained an eccentric bunch, but by mutual consent they stayed apart from each other except when rehearsing and performing. The accommodations office at the university had first offered them a large Victorian house on Lansdown Road to share, and Ivan had behaved as if he was being sent to Siberia. 'That's out of the question, wholly unsuitable,' he'd said. 'Can't you give us separate lodgings?' The others had felt the same way – nothing is more calculated to disturb than overhearing a fellow artist at practice – and said so in unison. Four addresses spread across the city were found. The quartet would need to meet only when music-making. And Douglas, having set up the residency, scarpered back to London.

Part of Mel's contract was giving solo classes for third-year BA music students and postgraduates. The standard was high, the teaching a joy. Little different in method, though, from the lessons he had given at Fingis Road. He had five talented violists not far short of professional standard. In addition, three mornings each week the quartet drove out to the Newton Park campus and attended the Michael Tippett Centre, the university's pride and joy, one of the best locations in the country for ensemble playing. Rehearsals were private at this stage. Later they would allow some undergraduates in.

The first of the 'soirées' Doug had negotiated as part of the deal had been held in a beautifully panelled room at Dyrham Park, high in the Cotswolds north of the city. In consideration for Mel the ensemble played the Beethoven Quartet in C sharp minor he'd learned for his audition and they delivered its subtle mood changes and breathtaking extravagance with finesse. The audience of thirty or so, including a number of final-year students, received it with shouts of appreciation out of keeping with the surroundings. They seemed to feel mere clapping was not enough.

Everyone agreed that these musical evenings were a good thing. In later concerts, they moved on to Haydn and Mozart. Tickets were hugely in demand. Ivan was annoyed to hear that one had been sold on eBay for £250. 'Doug is hopeless. He should have cut us in on the deal. I could have bought my own Strad with the money we're losing over this.'

'Misery-guts,' Cat said. 'This is the best time we've had since Harry left. Don't knock it.'

At the Michael Tippett Centre, Ivan and Cat gave regular master classes in front of audiences, an ordeal Mel was spared on the grounds that he was still bedding in (as Cat expressed it with a wink); and Anthony because of his poor communication skills ('and he's no fool,' Cat said).

Mrs Carlyle came home just before nine and knocked on Mel's door with an offer of tea and biscuits. 'You can't spend all evening on your own,' she said. 'Come and watch telly in the lounge with Tippi and me. You'll have to excuse her bathrobe. That girl is always showering.'

When Mel entered, Tippi was on the sofa with her legs curled under her. She didn't look away from the TV screen.

'I lost five pounds today,' Mrs Carlyle said to Mel.

'Too bad. Where was that?'

'Pounds in weight, silly. I'm not saying where from, but I hope you notice. How was your day?'

'Fine.'

'Giving lessons as usual?'

'Mainly.'

'When's the next concert with the others?'

'The seventh of November.'

'Do you think Tippi and I would enjoy it? We're not highbrow, but we know a good tune when we hear one.'

'Hard to say. Some people obviously enjoy it.'

'Strauss waltzes?'

'Actually, no.'

'Shame. They really get me humming. I dare say you could wangle some tickets. How would you like to see Mel perform, Tippi?'

Tippi may have thought of a rude answer. She didn't give one.

Mel filled the gap. 'Quartet music asks a tad more of the audience than spotting a good tune. There's usually a theme or message that the composer develops in subtle ways. You need to listen – rather than just hearing – and the rewards are there.'

'Not so obvious as Strauss, then?'

'I wasn't going to say so, but yes.'

'I expect at a pinch you can play "The Blue Danube".'

'I can, and I have. I've been a jobbing musician for years, playing all sorts, fitting in where I can. And when I couldn't get work, I did busking down the tube, "The Blue Danube" included.'

'Outside the Pump Room is a good pitch.'

'Thanks. I hope it won't come to that.'

'Or inside. There's a trio playing while everyone scoffs

their cream tea. If one of them gets ill, you could help out. Something on the side. We all enjoy something on the side.' She glanced at Tippi, whose eyes didn't move from the TV screen.

Mel said, 'I doubt if the university would approve.'

'It's not slumming, playing in the Pump Room. They have to be good because they get requests. I was told someone asked them to play the "1812 Overture" and they said they'd love to but unfortunately they didn't have the cannon.'

He grinned. 'I like it.'

'A cannon in the Pump Room – that's a laugh. Have you ever played the "1812", Mel?'

'A few times, but not alone. You need an orchestra for that.'

'And a big gun?'

'Ideally, more than one, but it doesn't often happen. There's a story of the Liverpool Philharmonic playing with two cannon mounted at the back of the orchestra. When they fired the first blank the orchestra was deafened and one lady violist fled the stage. Everyone was coated in specks of cordite and the management had to pay the laundry bills.'

'Glory be. What fun.'

'Nothing so dramatic happens in our concerts.'

'I expect you have a few laughs, even so.'

'At rehearsal sometimes. Our cellist has a sense of humour. She's fun to be with.'

Mrs Carlyle's eyebrows pricked up. 'She? Did you hear that, Tippi? You'd better listen up. There's a lady in Mel's quartet.'

Tippi didn't even blink.

Her mother hadn't finished. 'Perhaps all three of the others are ladies. I hadn't thought of that. Who's a lucky boy, then?' She put a hand to her mouth and shook with amusement.

'Cat is the only woman,' Mel said.

'It's the other way round, is it? She's the lucky one, with three fellows to choose from. Cat, did you say? Cat with the cream, I should think.'

'Nothing of that sort goes on. We're professionals.'

'Says you.'

He knew she was making mischief, so he grinned, reached for a biscuit and said nothing.

'More tea?' Mrs Carlyle said. 'Your cup's empty. Tippi can top you up.'

For that remark, she got a glare from her daughter.

'Thanks. I've had all I want,' Mel said, and the words slipped out before he could stop them. 'Busy day coming up. I must read through a score for our next rehearsal, a Mozart I haven't played before.'

'A score sounds like hard work to me,' Mrs Carlyle said. 'You'll be wanting the usual breakfast, then?'

'Please.' He got up and wished them a joint goodnight.

'She's in a world of her own,' Mrs Carlyle said. 'I don't know what she does by day to make her so unsociable of an evening. Sleep soundly, Mel. You look tired yourself.'

Musically, he'd moved to a new level since coming to Bath. The musicianship of the others challenged and energised him. He was getting a crash course in the quartet repertoire – already preparing Brahms, Dvořák, Schubert, Bartók. The learning process was exacting, but so filled with achievement that he didn't begrudge a minute of all the time studying scores. Regularly he would feel he knew a piece and then discover in rehearsal how much more it contained.

Intimate, intense and exhilarating, the fortnightly candle-lit concerts made demands on all the players, yet brought coherence to their programme of work. After the Beethoven at Dyrham Park it had come as some relief to Mel to learn some of the more romantic pieces in the repertoire, or quartets with exciting cello parts like Haydn's Opus 20, No. 6 where the viola was more in a supporting role. His musical education was on a sharply rising curve, but it was all immensely satisfying. These were some of the most rewarding evenings of his life.

It was extraordinary how the other members of the quartet were transformed in the white heat of playing. Ivan – old sobersides – inhabited the soul of the composer and became spirited, playful, ecstatic even. Cat stopped being amusing and brought soulfulness from her cello capable of moving anyone to tears. The biggest change was in Anthony, who came alive in the rehearsal sessions, argued with passion for his interpretation and was usually right. Any quartet is only as good as its members and the fusion of their playing. This one was reaching heights rarely scaled.

They knew it, of course.

During a break from rehearsal one morning, Mel said to Ivan, 'This is more dynamic than anything I've experienced musically before, the way we all contribute ideas.'

'It's how we've always worked.'

'So creative.'

'Nothing is static in ensemble work. We learn from each other constantly.'

'I'm learning in spades.'

'It isn't one-way. We're responding to you.'

Mel blinked. 'Really?'

'I don't say things I don't mean. So you feel you are benefiting from the experience?'

'Enormously, even though I still hardly know you.'

'Me personally?'

'The group. Anthony puzzles me the most. A sort of Jekyll and Hyde.' He stopped, embarrassed at what he'd said. 'No, that's out of order. Do you know what I mean?'

'Bipolar?'

'I wouldn't want to give it a label.'

'Good – because we don't think he's bipolar. That's about highs and lows, isn't it? Manic-depressive stuff. He's not particularly depressed.'

'There's a personality change when we start rehearsing.'

'The music is paramount to Anthony. It dwarfs everything else. The rest of his life bores him. He can't be bothered with it. Playing in the quartet is his only reality.'

'Isn't that dangerous?'

'There are times when we have to remind him over the most mundane things like getting his hair cut or renewing his passport. He needs someone in his life to chivvy him along. But he's not capable of entering into a relationship, so I don't think he'll find anyone.'

'Not capable? He must have emotional needs.'

'Outside music?' Ivan shook his head. 'I'm not aware of any. The emotion is all channelled into his playing. If his body tells him he requires food, he'll eat. He doesn't read or go to the cinema. When he wants sex, he'll pay for it. All those things are functional, unconnected with intellectual pleasure which comes to him only when he picks up his violin.'

Having said he wasn't giving a label to Anthony's behaviour, Mel passed no comment. Privately he thought this sounded like some form of autism.

'It must have been tough for him when Harry quit.'

'Indescribably tough. We worried over him. He was close to suicide. Douglas got him some work with the Hallé which probably saved his life.'

When the session resumed, Mel watched Anthony's eyes light up. Disturbing, really, to see how addictive music can be. They played a few bars of Schubert's *Rosamunde* and Anthony halted the playing himself. 'It's become sentimental,' he said. 'We're losing the truth of the piece. Can we try this section again from the beginning?'

'Not until we agree what is wrong,' Ivan said.

'The tempo. We've never played it this way. Like treacle running off a spoon.'

'Must be my fault,' Mel said. 'I'm making the difference.'

'I'm not blaming anyone,' Anthony said. 'We can rectify this. Didn't you notice, Cat?'

'Sweetie, I was miles away, trying to remember if I sent my dad a birthday card.'

Anthony swung round to face her, all aggression. 'How can you do that when we're playing?'

'All too easily. Haven't you ever driven a car and thought I've come this far and I can't remember any of the traffic lights I passed and the turns I made and if I was watching my speed? One part of my brain is doing these things but I'm in another place. The worst is when it happens in a concert. I can see my bow moving and it isn't my hand that's guiding it, can't be, but Jesus, it is. Shit a brick, I'm in Carnegie Hall, playing Beethoven. If it hasn't happened to you, my chick, be grateful.'

Mel knew exactly what she'd described. He'd experienced the same nightmare more than once, although not with this group.

Anthony was lost for words.

Ivan said, 'Let's reconsider. Anthony may have a point. If I take it with more energy, like so . . .' He played the first bars again. 'What do you think?'

'Still sexless,' Anthony said.

Cat's mouth lifted at the edges, but she said nothing.

'Show us, then,' Ivan said, irritated.

'Your part?' Anthony tucked the violin under his chin and played, and he was right. The section needed a stronger pulse. 'Shall we take it in segments?'

87

Ivan scowled. 'That won't be necessary.'

They went from the start and the improvement was obvious. Nobody said, 'I told you so.' Rehearsals were like this, with music the only winner.

After the session ended, Ivan said, 'At some stage soon we must decide which piece to record.'

'Who's talking about recording?' Cat said. 'We're still finding our way as a quartet.'

'If you remember, it's part of the deal. A recording for their funds. With downloads and sales of the disc it helps to pay for our residency,' he said and added in a casual tone while fitting his violin into its case, 'I'd like to offer the *Grosse Fuge.*'

'That's insane,' Cat said. 'We've only been together six weeks and he wants us to play the most difficult piece in the repertoire. Even with Harry on board, that was always a killer.'

'We made a passable recording,' Ivan said.

'I'm up for it,' Anthony said.

'We all know about you. What about Mel?' Cat said. 'Are you familiar with it? All those fortissimos?'

'I've heard it played and studied the score.'

'With the best will in the world, that isn't the same as cutting a disc, sunshine.'

Ivan said, 'I have confidence in Mel. If we start work immediately, we can be ready in a matter of weeks.'

Cat said, 'We could make life a lot easier for ourselves with a more familiar piece like "Death and the Maiden".'

'We can record that as well,' Ivan said. 'We'll need to offer a programme.' He finished fastening the case. 'What's your opinion, Mel?'

Ivan's unqualified support had been unexpected. Mel felt as if he ought to be worthy of it. 'How soon do we have to commit?'

'They want it by the end of term.'

'*They* want it?' Cat said. 'How about the players? You just said we must start immediately and for once I couldn't agree more – but only if every one of us opts to go for it.'

Anthony raised his hand.

'He's more than willing,' Ivan said, 'and the second violin part is unbelievably demanding on the fingers. You sound reluctant, Cat.'

'For Mel's sake. What Beethoven asks the violist to do isn't shelling peas, you know. The lad's risen admirably to the challenge, but he's not a regular quartet player.'

'We can increase the rehearsal sessions.'

'Slave-driver.'

'I wouldn't suggest it if I thought we'd fail.'

'We've come a long way already.' She sighed and shook her head. 'If Mel is willing, then so am I.'

The three original members looked at Mel.

'Let's give it a go,' he said, trying to sound cool.

He shared a taxi with Cat and her cello. There wasn't room for the others.

'I hope you know what you let yourself in for, new boy.'

'I have some idea. I must get a copy of the recording you three made with Harry.'

'It's not bad.'

He tried obliquely to get more on Harry's disappearance. 'He must have been with you some years.'

'Harry? From the beginning. We're not careless. We don't keep losing violists like beads off a string.'

'Did he have family?'

'None he ever mentioned. It's hard on partners, this wandering existence. Like the rest of us, he was self-reliant. Well, I'm saying that and it's not entirely true. Anthony needs mothering, but he's a special case. Sometimes I feel like smothering him. Harry was all man.'

'In what sense?'

She smiled. 'He took his chances when they came.'

'How do you mean?'

'Groupies. We're not much different to pop groups when it comes to fans. In our peak years we had a huge following. Invitations of all sorts flooded in, from billionaires wanting us to play on their Strads to schoolgirls asking us to autograph their bras. Asking the guys, that is. Even they got bored with it after a time.'

'And you think Harry took advantage?'

'Of schoolgirls? No, he wasn't that way inclined. What he got up to was grown-up stuff and he didn't like me asking about it.'

'Was he gay?'

'Harry? No, don't get me wrong. I've seen how pleased he was when women came on to him. The first commandment of quartet life is that you don't pry into each other's goings-on, but laws are meant to be broken and I'm curious by nature, and it sounds like you are, too.'

'He interests me for obvious reasons,' Mel said. 'I've stepped into his shoes.'

'All I can tell you is that he covered his tracks. When we needed to get hold of him at short notice – as you do at times because of a change in arrangements – it was the devil's own job trying to reach him. He was never at his lodgings. But you couldn't fault him for reliability. He turned up at the hall in good time for concerts and rehearsals. Looked a little jaded on occasions, but I guess we all do from time to time.'

'So when he disappeared, it came as a shock?'

'Panic stations. We had to cancel that night's concert with the audience already in their seats. I was all for improvising with some solo numbers, but the others couldn't cope. Ivan was a dead loss. He's no use at all when things go belly up.

And Anthony is an ensemble player first and last. Doesn't do solos. I could easily have given them "The Swan" and there are hundreds of pieces for the fiddle that Ivan could have picked from, but no, he insisted we cancelled the show. Good thing Douglas was with us. He found a local stand-in for the remaining concerts and we got through somehow, but it wasn't pretty.'

'And you never heard any more from Harry?'

'Nothing. None of us knew where he went in his time off. The embassy found that hard to believe, but it's the way we are. So the local police didn't know where to start looking.'

'Do you think he's dead?'

'I hate to think it, because he was a lovely guy, but what else could have happened? If he'd gone on a bender that night he'd surely have got in touch when he got his head together. He needed the quartet. It was his living.'

'He could have had an accident and lost his memory.'

'Some kind of freak event? We can only hope, but as every day passes . . . You see, being the female in the group, I'm locked in, heart and soul. You guys belong to me, even bossy old Ivan, bless his little cotton socks.'

He was about to say something about the maternal instinct and stopped himself in time. She didn't mean that at all. Behind all the brazen chat was a woman getting emotional – if not sexual – fulfilment from being so close to three men. 'We're lucky to have you.'

She smiled. 'You'd better believe it.'

9

You couldn't have mistaken it for anything else but an incident room. Desks, computers, phones. Graphic photos of the corpse, with a close-up of the tooth tattoo. A large-scale map of the Avon. Lines of enquiry listed on the whiteboard. Plenty of noise and movement from the CID regulars and civilian staff. Presiding over it all, Peter Diamond, much more his old imposing self.

'I've asked for a second autopsy,' he announced to the few members of the team who weren't out of the building on active enquiries.

'Can you do that?' Halliwell asked. 'Isn't it the coroner's call?'

'The coroner isn't God. He's a public servant, same as you and me. I'm not satisfied, and I told him. The medic who did the first one wasn't a forensic pathologist at all. He was a hospital man, a histopathologist. What's that when it's at home?'

'Not sure.'

'Neither am I, not at all sure. He writes a two-sheet report and comes to no conclusion except that the woman had been dead for some time. I could have told him that.'

'He found the tooth tattoo.'

'No, he didn't. He asked some dental expert to look at the teeth and she spotted it. No wonder I don't have any confidence.'

John Leaman looked up from his computer screen. 'Histopathology: the branch of medicine concerned with changes in tissues caused by disease.'

'There you go. It's not disease we're bothered about, it's crime. No use to us at all. I want a proper forensic man like Bert Sealy. Sarcastic swine, but at least he does the job and misses nothing. You don't get short-changed by Sealy.'

'What did the coroner say?'

'He'll look into it. He will.'

'Does the ACC know you spoke to him?'

'She's away on some course, isn't she? Can't reach her. If I could, she'd be the first to know.'

Halliwell grinned.

Energised, Diamond stalked the CID room delegating duties to anyone unlucky enough to catch his eye.

'Haven't we heard back from Paul Gilbert? He's taking his time round the hotels. What's he doing – testing the beds? You.'

'Me, sir?' some hapless DC said.

'Give Gilbert a call and tell him we need a progress report.'

'Very good.'

'It had better be. And why is Ingeborg so silent? She should have got some names out of the colleges by this time.'

Towards the end of the morning, he used the marker pen to list the hotels Gilbert had visited. 'This is taking too long,' he said. 'We need more manpower. I'll ask for back-up from uniform. The plods are as capable as we are of checking names.'

Ingeborg looked in at lunchtime. 'It isn't easy, guv. Some of the private colleges are hopeless at keeping records. They can tell you who joined and when, but there's no check on day-to-day attendance. As one college secretary said to me, it's the students' loss if they don't put in the hours.'

'And if one goes missing altogether?'

93

'Could be weeks or months before the system picks it up. Most have personal tutors, but the tutors aren't overly concerned if the students don't appear. There's often a valid reason, they say, like a change of course or a transfer to another college, and they aren't always notified.'

'Sounds like the perfect set-up for absenteeism. It wasn't like that when I went through police college.'

Ingeborg was briefly lost for words, struggling, no doubt, with the thought of Diamond as a police cadet. 'I was told the attendance record for Japanese students is above average.'

He nodded. 'They're a law-abiding race. The Japanese police spend most of their time helping people find their way.'

'Nice work if you can get it,' Halliwell said.

'Foreign students come here on visas,' Diamond said. 'There must be a record.'

John Leaman, the resident know-it-all, said, 'That would be with the UK Border Agency.'

'They decide who gets in, right?'

'Through a points system. All students from abroad need a valid visa letter to say they've been accepted by an approved college. That gets them thirty points. Then they must prove they've got several thousand pounds in the bank for twenty-eight days. That gives them the remaining ten points they need.'

'And you and I know there are loopholes. The money can easily be borrowed.'

'Right. And the letters have been forged on occasions, but not by the Japanese. Like you said, it would be highly unusual to find them fiddling the system. If our young woman was a student, it's more than likely she came officially and her name is known.'

'Along with several thousand others.'

'I'm not sure of the numbers,' Leaman said.

'Let's assume she's on the books. Can the Border Agency tell us if she's dropped out?'

'They'd rely on the colleges informing them.'

Diamond sighed. He'd found the flaw. 'Which they don't.'

Ingeborg said, 'To be fair, guv, some of them do.'

'Why would anyone drop out? Anyone from Japan, brought up to do the right thing, work hard and get results?'

'Can't keep up with their studies. Loss of face.'

He glanced across at the photos of the victim on the display board. 'Can't argue with that.'

No one smiled.

'If the Border Agency doesn't have a grip on this, we're dependent on the colleges,' Diamond said.

'This is the problem I'm finding,' Ingeborg said. 'The colleges are a law unto themselves.'

'Or no law at all?'

'Not much of one, anyway.'

'Haven't they given you any names?'

'Three are being followed up as we speak. It's a matter of contacting the staff concerned and that takes time because the lecturers aren't all in college at one time.'

'Speak to the students. They'll tell you if one of their mates has gone missing.'

Diamond had put his finger on it, as usual. Students would surely cooperate, especially if it was made clear that a body had been discovered. Going through official channels wasn't the only option.

'Thanks, guv. I'll give it a go.'

By the end of the day all the checking had come to nothing. Everyone had been accounted for, even the three Ingeborg had mentioned. She had tried questioning groups of Japanese students. They were keen to help when they heard what she said and there was a useful grapevine of information between different colleges. They had answered the few queries that had come up.

'It's looking more and more as if she was a tourist,' Halliwell said.

'So what did Paul Gilbert find?'

Silence.

'He must be still out there.'

The hotels had been easier to check than the colleges. Registers existed and were reliable. It was just a matter of getting round to them all. The extra help from uniformed officers had lightened the load. There remained a number of bed and breakfast houses that would wait for the morning.

'A day visitor?' Halliwell said.

'In a coach party? They count them back in, don't they?'

'I was thinking she may have been travelling alone – by train, say, from London. Plenty do.'

'There's no way of finding out.'

'Unless her people back in Japan report that she hasn't returned. Have we asked the embassy?'

'One of the first calls I made – and wouldn't you know it, there's a chain of command. It's always the way with bureaucracy. They have to check ten times over before they tell you what day of the week it is.'

'It's in their interest to cooperate.'

'I'm not saying anyone is being obstructive. The people I spoke to were ultra-polite. They'll check with their government and the police and we'll get a response by Christmas.'

'We haven't much to help them apart from describing the clothes.'

'We emailed the dental record and the all-important tooth tattoo.'

'DNA?'

'DNA as well.'

'Did we send a photo?' Halliwell said.

Diamond tilted his head towards the shots of the corpse. 'That? You wouldn't identify anyone from that.'

From across the room John Leaman had overheard what was said. 'Just a thought, guv.'

'What's that?'

'Something we may be able to do. There are experts who can reconstruct a face from a skull.'

'A decomposing skull?'

'They put it through a CT scanner and get the digital data to produce a computer image, one you can rotate and look at from all angles. From that, they make an exact model in styrene foam with a computer-controlled milling machine—'

'You're losing me,' Diamond said.

'A replica of the actual skull. Then they use wax or clay to add the muscles and tissue.'

'Hold on. How do they know how much wax to add on?'

'I'm not sure. Generally you've got an artist – a sculptor – working closely with a forensic anthropologist.'

'Not the best of combinations.'

'It's not infallible, I grant you.'

'And slow, I wouldn't mind betting.'

'But there is a quicker method.'

'What's that?'

'When it's all done on the computer, using a high-resolution 3D image of the skull. They have a large stock of facial features that they manipulate into place until something fits.'

Diamond gave him a squint. 'Is that more reliable than the wax?'

A pause. 'I couldn't say. I'm not an expert.'

'Sounds like trial and error. Where did you pick up these pearls of wisdom?'

'From one of those *CSI* shows on TV.'

'Say no more.'

Halliwell came to Leaman's defence. 'Some computer-generated images would look good on the display board.'

Swayed by the suggestion, Diamond tapped the point of his chin. 'D'you think so?'

'Doesn't matter what I think. The ACC would like it.'

'Georgina?' A fleeting smile. He knew exactly what Halliwell was getting at. The Assistant Chief Constable, Georgina Dallymore, had him down as a technophobe. 'On second thoughts, maybe it's worth a try.'

'The computer graphics option?' Leaman said.

'Definitely.' Even Georgina would think a wax head was over the top.

'Why don't you find out some more?' Halliwell said to Leaman.

That evening Diamond walked the towpath alone. He'd heard nothing from Paloma since the bust-up at the Dolphin and his pride wouldn't allow him to call her. She'd dumped him, so it was up to her to get in touch if she still had any regard for him. Actually the speed of her departure had caught him unprepared. A few unguarded words from him and she was off.

You and I are through.

He'd gone over it repeatedly. Maybe she had a point, he had decided as the days went on. He'd treated her as if she was staff. What was the word he'd used when she'd told him a trouble shared was a trouble halved? Claptrap. Not a nice thing to say in the circumstances, and she didn't know she'd touched a raw nerve. He didn't want to share his troubles with anyone.

Yet he knew the seed of the misunderstanding had been sown earlier, in Vienna, when they had come across the little shrine by the canal. It was clear from what she'd said that he shouldn't have distanced himself from the death of the woman. He'd treated the tragedy professionally, as a policeman, sidestepping the sympathy Paloma had obviously felt. Someone had come to a tragic end and he'd not shown the concern expected of him. Paloma had wanted to learn more about the victim while his instinct was to move on and be grateful it was someone else's case.

His bigger misjudgement had been to follow up on the Vienna incident, asking Ingeborg to find out the facts. If he'd been consistent, he would have let well alone. Stupidly, he'd wanted Paloma to be pleased he'd gone to this extra trouble – even allowing that he'd only delegated the duty. He hadn't thought ahead, hadn't sensed that by raising the subject again he was giving her a rerun of the same scene: his professional way of dealing with the fact of death against her heartfelt sympathy.

The outrage she'd kept in check in Vienna had reared up. A moment of turmoil neither of them could have prepared for.

Would she come round?

Women could be every bit as obstinate as men.

Without much to console him, he stopped to watch the steady flow of the river. Recent heavy rain had quickened the current and pieces of driftwood were being carried quite swiftly. Any one of them could have resembled the body when it was first noticed, demonstrating the impossibility of finding exactly where it had entered the water. It must have been submerged somewhere upriver for a considerable time before the internal gases made it buoyant and mobile.

He'd ruled out a search of the river banks.

But there were finites he hadn't taken into account until

now. The Avon wasn't free-flowing from source to sea. He should have remembered it had man-made barriers. Only a few hundred metres upstream from here was Pulteney weir, where he'd often seen floating objects trapped by the curved wall. And not far downstream was Weston lock.

The obvious conclusion was that the body had entered the water somewhere below the weir. It had been recovered some way short of the lock, not much over a mile away.

He revised his plan of action. Both river banks along this stretch needed to be searched, a real fingertip search for possible items belonging to the deceased. Her shoes may well have been lost while in the water, but what about her bag, phone, watch or an item of jewellery? Find some object belonging to her and you would almost certainly know where she'd got into the river. Then the sub-aqua team could go to work.

He'd have a search squad make a start in the morning.

With that decided, he resumed his walk and almost immediately his pulse quickened. Ahead on the towpath, approaching from the Saltford direction, was a familiar figure. He recognised the way she walked, her height and the cut of her hair. Coincidence, or had she chosen to walk the towpath knowing he often came here at this time in the evening?

He'd spotted her, so she must have seen him. She continued her approach at the same deliberate rate.

What now? he asked himself. Do I say I behaved abysmally and ask her to forgive and forget? The fact that she's chosen to come this way at this time of day must surely mean she's in a forgiving frame of mind. She's missing me as much as I'm missing her.

Best offer her a drink, but not – for an obvious reason – in the Dolphin, and not the Old Crown, his local, where some of the regulars still remembered Steph. He was still dithering between pubs when he became conscious of a movement by his feet. A small dog, a dachshund, had trotted past and then returned, as if checking if it knew Diamond. It had a confident look, head cocked to the right, although who was the owner of this silky charmer wasn't clear. Having decided, apparently, that Diamond was a disappointment, it turned and scampered off – straight towards the woman he had taken to be Paloma.

Odd.

So far as he was aware, Paloma didn't possess a dog.

He watched the dachshund run the short distance, stop, turn and apparently come to heel – and the woman stooped to fasten the lead to its collar. Now he saw with crushing certainty that she wasn't who he'd supposed. She had the same style of walking, but she was undeniably someone else. He'd superimposed his image of Paloma on to this stranger, a younger woman with lighter-coloured hair.

How pathetic was that? He was as churned up inside as a smitten teenager.

He about-turned and retraced his steps. The world wasn't a romantic novel. Chance meetings don't happen when you need them. If he wanted an improvement in his wretched situation he'd better do something active towards it.

Like what?

Picking up a phone? Ringing her doorbell?

No chance, he told himself.

The search of the river banks got under way in the morning, twelve officers in overalls and boots progressing methodically along both sides below Pulteney weir. As one constable cynically remarked, it was a cheap way for the council to get its rubbish collected. Everything from cigarette stubs to beer cans was painstakingly picked up, and its position noted.

The first stretch as far as North Parade Bridge was

deceptively easy. Then the footpath along the west bank came to an end and the footing became perilous. One side of a river is generally easier than another to move along, so they switched duties when possible and everyone was given a share of wrestling with brambles and scrambling along the muddy, uncultivated side. The quality of the finds didn't do much to improve morale. They were the boring throwaway items you would expect and mostly coated in 'grime or slime', as one of the searchers put it.

Diamond put in a mid-morning appearance at Ferry Lane, alongside the cricket ground, and watched the unfortunates making slow progress through the undergrowth. He didn't have much sympathy, especially when he learned that nothing of interest had been found. He'd endured worse in his days as a rookie sifting the contents of a London council tip for bits of a dismembered corpse.

While he was there someone picked up a clay pipe and said it might interest the local historians. The sergeant in charge said it was probably at least a century old and could have been smoked by one of the bargees who once navigated the canal.

'It's a river, not a canal,' Diamond said.

'A waterway,' the sergeant said.

'So what?'

'So it was used by the barges that used the Kennet and Avon canal. To all intents and purposes it's part of the canal. The man-made bit feeds in at Dolemeads. They came down from Reading and linked up with the river for the last stretch to the docks at Bristol.'

The man was right. Never having taken much interest in the canal system, Diamond hadn't given any thought to the river as a waterway. In his mind there was a clear distinction between a river and a canal. A canal was a man-made thing, like the one he'd walked beside in Vienna.

And now that the Danube canal popped into his mind, he thought fleetingly about the woman murdered there.

One dead Japanese woman in a canal in Vienna and another here in the Kennet and Avon.

Coincidence?

Sensible thinking suggested nothing more. It wouldn't be wise or profitable to start constructing theories of an international killer.

'Keep up the good work,' he told the sergeant, 'but tell them I'm not really interested in clay pipes.'

Back in Manvers Street, he found John Leaman practically turning cartwheels in excitement. 'It's all under way, guv.'

'What is?'

'The facial reconstruction. I found a really helpful technician at the Royal United who arranges the CT scans and he knew exactly what I wanted. In fact, he's really chuffed to be helping us.'

'Probably watches *CSI* on the telly.'

Leaman took this as encouragement. 'He does. So he's already done the scan and emailed it to Philadelphia.'

'Whatever for?'

'I found Professor Hackenschmidt through the internet. He's a world expert in plastic surgery and uses computer imaging all the time. We're hoping he can use his skills to recreate her face. We could have a result in a matter of hours.'

'Let me get this straight,' Diamond said. 'The skull was put through the scanner in Bath and the pictures sent to Philadelphia?'

Leaman's face betrayed some nervousness, as if he knew he'd overstepped the mark. Budgetary considerations were always a worry. 'Correct.'

'Did you ask for any to be sent here?'

'Well, no. We wouldn't know what to do with them.'

'Oh yes we would,' Diamond said. 'You missed the point, John. We'd stick them on our board and look as if we're going places with this investigation. Get on to your friend at the RUH and tell him this is our baby and we need a copy of everything.'

In other respects the progress was less spectacular. All the listed hotels and boarding houses had been checked and there was not a single report of a missing Japanese woman.

'If some of you can't look busier than this,' Diamond said, 'I'll tell the search party on the river bank that reinforcements are on the way.'

After he'd gone into his office and slammed the door, there was a spell of silence. Then Paul Gilbert said, 'Who's that Swedish detective Kenneth Branagh plays on TV?'

Better news came through after lunch. The coroner had reviewed the autopsy report and decided on a second post-mortem to be conducted by a Home Office approved forensic pathologist at 8 a.m. next day. Diamond was invited to attend. He thanked the coroner and said he would do his level best to be there. If, however, something came up, his deputy would attend. After switching off the phone, he called across the room, 'Keith.'

Halliwell looked up. 'Guv?'

'Are you a big breakfast man, bacon, eggs, the full English, as they say?'

'When I can get it.'

'Have a light one tomorrow. Early start for you.'

Autopsies and Peter Diamond didn't mix.

Later in the afternoon came a call from the search squad. They'd found an iPod on the Green Park stretch of river bank between the Churchill Bridge and Midland Bridge. It looked as if it had been there some time.

Diamond said he would come at once. He asked Ingeborg to join him.

Green Park is a wedge-shaped space on the north side of the river, a piece of land that somehow escaped the builders of centuries past and enjoys some seclusion simply because it borders on the river and is a good distance from the main shops and tourist attractions.

'I lose track,' Diamond said to Ingeborg as they drove along Green Park Road. 'What's an iPod?'

'You really don't know?' she said in disbelief.

'I don't have the patience to keep up.'

'There are iPods and then there are iPods,' she said.

'Now you're poking fun. It's some kind of audio device, right?'

'Or much more. There are touch-screen versions, video versions. Technology moves on.'

'I can use a mobile phone.'

'After much prodding.'

'Am I missing something, not owning an iPod?'

'Depends,' Ingeborg said. 'They can be good if you work out at the gym or go for a jog.'

He looked out of the window instead.

The sergeant from the search team was waiting for them beside a section of the river bank below the towpath now cordoned off with crime scene tape. Alder trees and bushes would have provided a useful screen for anyone up to no good.

'Where is it?' Diamond asked.

A transparent evidence bag was handed over. The object inside was small and square and so coated in mud you couldn't tell what colour it was. A lead with two earpieces was coiled in one corner.

'Good spotting on someone's part,' Diamond said. 'This would have been easy to miss.'

'There's no certainty it belonged to the dead woman,' the sergeant said. 'On the other hand, people aren't in the habit of slinging things like this away.'

'One of the earpieces is broken,' Ingeborg said. 'It looks as if it's been crushed, stepped on, or something.'

'We noticed.'

'The iPod itself looks all right. You might chuck out the earphones, but not that.'

'I agree.'

'The damage could have been done in a struggle.'

Diamond took a closer look. 'Are there any signs of violence where it was picked up?'

'Hard to tell, sir,' the sergeant said. 'Take a look if you like. We've marked an approach path. I made sure my lads didn't trample all over the scene.'

Diamond could take a hint. His big feet wouldn't aid the investigation. 'We'll get the crime scene professionals out here and have it mapped and photographed. Where are your people now?'

'The other side of Midland Bridge continuing the search.'

Diamond turned to Ingeborg. 'What do you think? Any way we can link the iPod with the victim?'

'The best chance is to find some hair at the scene or match some fibres with her clothes.'

'Put a call through to the men in blue overalls, then. I'll get a sense of where we are and how she might have got here.' He told the sergeant that the search could stop at Windsor Bridge. The body must have entered the water way before there.

If, as he was tempted to suspect, the Japanese woman had been murdered, this little triangle of parkland was as good a spot as any to dump the body in the river. Quiet, well away from houses, with plenty of trees and scrub screening the view, the site had much to commend itself to a killer. You could get a vehicle right to the end of the road known as Green Park, no great distance from the river bank.

And no one would hear the screams.

10

Georgina Dallymore, the Assistant Chief Constable, had spent the past week attending a Home Office course. Rumour had it that the top bananas were being instructed on how to maximise resources – government-speak for cuts. So a collective shudder should have gone through CID when she reappeared. In fact, the team were so busy that Georgina was scarcely noticed.

'What's going on here?' she asked Peter Diamond. 'I wasn't told we had a major incident.'

'You've been away, ma'am.'

'I wasn't away from my BlackBerry, if you know what that is. I expect to be kept informed. What's it about?'

'A body found in the river. We're treating it as suspicious.'

She eyed the display board. 'It looks like a full-blown murder investigation. Is all this justified?'

'It is when there's an international dimension.'

She twitched in alarm. 'In what way?'

'The victim – the deceased, I should say – is almost certainly from Japan.'

'A tourist?'

'Possibly. We're working closely with the Border Agency and the Japanese embassy.'

'Do you know who it is?'

He shook his head. 'Female, below average height, twenty to thirty, with a tooth tattoo as the only distinguishing feature.'

'What on earth . . . ?'

Diamond explained. After the dig about the BlackBerry he wasn't missing a chance to let the boss know he was street-smart.

Georgina peered at the close-up. 'It looks like a music note.'

'A quaver, actually.'

'I didn't know you read music, Peter.'

'I have hidden depths, ma'am.'

'I've known that for a long time, but music is something else. So is this the only clue?'

'An iPod has been found on the river bank in Green Park.'

'Hers?'

'We can't say yet. I'm having the scene examined for evidence of violence.'

'Was she attacked, then?'

'Unfortunately she was in the water too long to tell.'

She paused as if to play the statement over. 'I hate to say it, but this has all the hallmarks of an unsolved case.'

He wasn't being goaded into submission. 'You're entitled to your opinion, ma'am.'

'What makes you think this isn't an accidental drowning?'

'In all my time here, I can't recall any accidents below Pulteney weir, where she was found. You don't find swimmers or canoeists there.'

'She could have climbed over the railing,' Georgina said.
'Why?'

'Suicide, obviously.'

'But the iPod was found on the river bank further down.'

'So you're working on the basis that she was murdered and dumped in the river? A pretty big assumption from one lost iPod.'

'We'll know more when the crime scene investigators

report.' He decided this wasn't the best time to tell her he'd asked for a second autopsy.

'You *may* know more. Have you checked with missing persons?'

'The first thing we did. Since then we've enquired at all the colleges and hotels.'

'No names yet?'

'So far, no.'

'You've hit the buffers, then. Better scale everything down and get the room back to normal.'

'I haven't told you about Professor Hackenschmidt.'

She blinked rapidly. 'Who's he?'

'The world expert on facial reconstruction using computer imaging. He and his team in Philadelphia are already at work.'

'Did you say Philadelphia?' Georgina was tight-lipped now.

'He works from CT scans.' Another bit of technological jargon coming to his aid.

'Is this coming out of your budget?'

Diamond's way of dealing with awkward questions was to ask one himself. 'I expect you're up with computer imaging, ma'am?'

'I've heard of it, but I didn't expect you of all people to give any credence to it. How much will this cost?'

'I'm told the professor is only too pleased to be involved.'

'Small wonder, if we're paying. I hope you asked for an estimate.'

'One of my team is dealing with it.'

'Who's that?'

'John Leaman.'

'Good. He's no fool.' Having said this, even Georgina seemed to realise Diamond could take offence. 'This is just the kind of outsourcing we've been discussing on the Home

Office course. These are tough economic times. We can't employ experts for this and that and go way over budget. We need to make better use of our own resources.'

Diamond wasn't backing down. 'I wouldn't trust this lot to reconstruct a face. We'd end up with something out of *Frankenstein*.'

'Be serious, Peter.'

'I am. You asked if we've hit the buffers and I'm telling you we haven't. It's all in train, if you'll excuse the pun. Can't be stopped now. As soon as the professor sends us a likeness we'll forward copies to Japan and get them on TV and in the papers. Speeds up the whole enquiry. Once the woman is identified we'll get to the truth of it, I promise you. Maximise our resources.' The last words tripped off his tongue so glibly that Georgina was caught off guard. She drew a long, fatalistic breath and returned upstairs to consider her options. Dismantling the incident room might not be the best way forward.

Mid-morning, significant news came in from Keith Halliwell at the mortuary. The second autopsy had been conducted by Dr Bertram Sealy, as Diamond had hoped.

'And what did he find?'

'He asked me to tell you he was sorry to have missed you, guv.'

'Typical bloody Sealy.'

'But he did find something the first man missed. There's a bone called the hyoid in the throat, above the Adam's apple, quite small and delicate and shaped like a horseshoe and not attached to any other bones. He removed it and pointed out that it was damaged, fractured at one end.'

'Meaning that violence has been done to the neck?'

'It's the only sign of violence he could find, because of the bad condition of the flesh.'

111

Diamond whistled. 'Fracturing of the hyoid bone is a common sign of manual strangulation. This could be it.'

'I think it must be. He says it's highly unlikely this was caused accidentally when the body was being recovered from the river, or while it was submerged. To break a young person's hyoid bone you have to exert real pressure on the neck.'

'Is this going into Sealy's report?'

'I asked him. He's a pain. He kept me dangling for about ten minutes while he went through all the other symptoms of strangling: bruising, facial congestion, bleeding into the neck muscles. None of this showed because so much of the flesh had gone rotten in the water. Finally I got it from him. Cause of death: asphyxia by compression of the neck. His words.'

'That's all we need, Keith. We're in business.'

'I thought we were already.'

'Nothing can stop us now, not Georgina, the coroner, Portishead. Tell Bert Sealy he's my hero.'

There are times in police work when nothing goes right. Most days seemed like that to Diamond. Just occasionally there's a break in the clouds and you have to make the most of such moments. Within twenty minutes of the call from Halliwell he heard from the search team at Green Park. Fibres had been found on a bramble bush on the river bank, and there were twin lines in the mud suggesting somebody had been dragged down the slope to the water.

'Heel marks?' Diamond said on the phone to the supervisor of the crime scene team. These days crime scene investigations were farmed out to private firms; outsourcing, as Georgina would put it.

'Very likely.'

'If she was wearing shoes, they may be in the water. I'll arrange for the sub-aqua team to take a look. Is it deep there?'

'Don't know. I haven't been for a swim.'

Now Diamond remembered the voice of a man he'd tangled with before, a smart-arse with a liking for sarcasm. 'You're Duckett, aren't you?'

'Who else did you expect? We're a small business, not the Co-op.'

'Surely you can tell at a glance if the river's deep.'

'It shelves steeply.'

'And did you find any shoeprints near these marks?'

'Far too many. We'll need to check what every one of your search team was wearing.'

'You'll be telling me we corrupted your scene.'

'A line of policemen tramping through? Give me a break. And presumably you had a look yourself?'

'Only by the access path.'

'Was there one? It's like a football field here.'

'The fibres,' Diamond said. 'What are they like?'

'Like fibres.'

'Wool, cotton, man-made?'

'We won't know until we get them under a microscope.'

'And I suppose the iPod has gone to the lab as well?'

'Where else?'

After the call had ended, Ingeborg said, 'I heard you asking about the iPod, guv. I wonder if it's still in working order. They're well constructed. It would be good to know what music she liked.'

'How will that help?'

'It kind of brings her alive.'

He gave her a baffled look.

Ingeborg added, 'Well, it tells us more about her. Any new information must be welcome.'

'Give them a call at the lab if you like. I don't fancy discussing music with the guy at the scene.'

* * *

113

Early in the afternoon when America was starting up, John Leaman took a call from Philadelphia. He discussed it with Ingeborg. 'I've just been speaking to one of the professor's team. He wants to know about the dead woman's hair.'

'What about it?'

'The style, I suppose. It doesn't show up in the CT scan, but they'd like to know what we observed. When they send us an image they want the look to be as lifelike as possible.'

'Did you tell him she was in the water for weeks? It doesn't do much for a girl's hair.'

'Can we say anything about the cut?'

'Okay. It's thick, dark hair with a fringe and cut sheer at the back. You can tell him that.'

'I'd be happier if you did.'

She began to laugh 'Aren't you comfortable discussing hairstyles with another guy? I'll speak to them if you like.'

Keith Halliwell was back from the autopsy looking pleased with himself.

Diamond soon altered that. 'Now we know it's murder, we must pull out all the stops. That's a musical expression, in case you weren't aware of it. Try the embassy again for names. They promised to get back to us.'

'Be good if we could send them the computer picture. What's the latest from Philadelphia?'

'Inge was talking to them about hair. They must be close to sending an image.'

'They know she's Japanese, do they? Japanese in our opinion, anyway.'

'They can tell from the shape of the skull, can't they?'

'I was told it isn't obvious.'

Halliwell did his best to reassure. 'I expect they'll give her the almond-shaped eyes.'

'Christ, I hope so.' Diamond had a fleeting vision of a

Betty Boop cartoon. 'You're making me worried. I'm less confident now than I was.'

'About the whole case?'

'The picture they're sending.' Diamond vibrated his lips. 'And the whole case, if I'm honest.'

'But the case is keeping everyone busy. Georgina was gobsmacked.'

He raised a smile. 'Yes, that was a nice moment.'

A knock on the door interrupted them. It was Ingeborg. 'Guv, I'm sorry to butt in, but you ought to hear this. The people at forensics found that the iPod was working okay and I asked them to play it for us. Hold on a mo and I'll put it through to your hands-free.' She touched the amplifying phone on his desk and music filled the room – music of an unexpected kind. She stood with arms folded.

Glances were exchanged. This was the first time Beethoven had been heard in Diamond's office, an event about as likely as finding the *Judgement of Paris* on his wall.

'Bit highbrow for me,' he said. 'I was expecting something Japanese. What is it?'

Halliwell shook his head.

'John Leaman says it's a string quartet,' Ingeborg said. 'At times it sounds like a full orchestra, but four instruments can make a big sound.'

'This is on the iPod?' he said.

'This and a whole lot more. Whoever she was, she was into classical music.'

The heavy notes from the cello were starting to rattle the framed photo of his late wife Steph. 'Turn it down, will you? I can't think with that row going on.'

She did so. 'The point is that it ties in neatly with the tooth tattoo.'

'Any kind of music would have tied in with that,' he said. 'The Stones, the Beatles.'

'Duke Ellington,' Halliwell said.

Ingeborg smiled. She had to admit that they were right. 'And now we know she had better taste than any of us.'

The computer image from Philadelphia appeared on Leaman's screen towards the end of the afternoon. Everyone got up for a look. Leaman rotated the face through several angles. This was definitely a young woman of Eastern appearance, with high cheekbones, a small cupid-bow mouth and widely spaced eyes topped by well-defined eyebrows. She had the fringe and fine head of hair Ingeborg had described.

'How do they know she wore lipstick?' one of the civilian computer operators said.

'They don't. It's a balance of probabilities,' Leaman said. 'Most Japanese women I've seen use make-up.'

'Wouldn't it be more useful to show her without any?'

'I don't see why. We're issuing this to help people recognise her.'

'The eyebrows are a bit thick.'

'They have to give her some, don't they? We told them she had a good growth of hair.'

Halliwell said, 'It seems to me a lot of this is guesswork.'

Leaman wasn't having that. 'Only the superficial stuff. The bone structure is entirely real.'

'But the fleshy bits can't be. How do we know her nose looked like that?'

'They choose from a bank of features. She's what's known as a Mongoloid type and that means small, flat noses. The Japanese were ahead of most other countries in making a data bank of soft tissues.'

'One thing we can all agree on,' Diamond said. 'This is easier on the eye than the photos taken at the autopsy. Back to work, people. I want a copy emailed to the Japanese embassy now and we'll go public with a press release tomorrow morning.' After the first buzz of interest was over, he said to Halliwell, 'What do you think, Keith? Will it help?'

'To me, it looks like everyone's idea of a Japanese woman. There's not much character you can pick out.'

'It's a proper face. Remember the photofit pictures we used to work with? Compared to this, they were like kids' drawings.'

'But is it reliable?'

'We'll find out. If it isn't, it could do more harm than good.'

He gave his attention to the press release. The tooth tattoo would be featured and so would the clothes the dead woman had been wearing. Until a definite connection was made with Green Park he couldn't mention the iPod and the interest in classical music. He seemed to have spent the best years of his career waiting for forensics to go through their painstaking procedures.

But there was a big plus. The printouts of the computerised face from several angles made a pleasing difference to the display board. He thought about sending copies upstairs to Georgina, but in the end decided to let well alone. With any luck the ACC would be dealing with her backlog of paperwork after a week's absence.

That evening he got home to a string of messages on the answerphone. Normally he wouldn't have bothered to play them before supper. Most would be junk calls. He was tired of being told by some fruity voice sounding as if doing him a huge favour, 'This is a free message.' But after all this time he still had hopes of a call from Paloma.

Nothing.

He opened a pouch for the cat and a beer for himself. Put two large potatoes in the microwave. 'What shall I have with it this time, Raffles? Beans, egg or cheese, or all three?'

Paloma had been encouraging him to cut down on the calories and take more exercise. There was a reward system. To earn a pie, he'd had to take a two-mile walk, and she'd come along to make sure. Lately, he'd let himself go again. His ideal had been to look like Orson Welles in *The Third Man*, but he was in danger of ending up like the Welles of the sherry commercials. Did it matter? In his present mood, not a lot.

Baked beans, scrambled egg and grated Cheddar joined the potatoes on his plate. One of those obsessive Swedish detectives was on the TV. He reached for his DVD of *Casablanca*.

More sensational news greeted him at the office next morning. The forensic lab had got through with an early finding. A hair Duckett's team had picked up at the Green Park river bank site matched the DNA of the drowned woman. All doubt was removed that this was where she had entered the water.

A turning point.

'We can forget about suicide or accident now, guv,' Ingeborg said. 'The heel marks prove she was dragged there and dropped in. You were so right to get us up and running.'

Keith Halliwell said, 'What are we suggesting here – that she was killed before she entered the water and this was the murderer's way of disposing of the body?'

'That's obvious, isn't it?' Ingeborg said.

'Then wouldn't the body have floated, rather than sinking? A person who drowns takes water into their lungs. That's why they go down. A corpse still has some air inside.'

John Leaman joined in with one of his erudite contributions. 'It's not as straightforward as that. Other factors come into it. For one thing, it depends how the body enters the water. Face down, any air in the lungs and airways is trapped and will take time to disperse. But if it gets submerged on its back, the weight of the head bears down and there's more chance of water entering the nose and mouth. And anyway, after a corpse has been several hours in the water the airways get filled passively and it will sink. Fresh water is less buoyant than the sea, so the process is quicker in a river.'

Diamond said, 'Where do you learn this stuff?'

'Don't you believe me?'

'Let's deal with what we know for certain. The body was rotting, so it must have been underwater for weeks. We now have a crime scene. With any luck, forensics will give us more information. But we know enough already to get headlines with the press release.'

'Are we going to use the computer image?' Halliwell asked.

'You sound doubtful.'

'I'm not convinced by the science.'

Leaman said at once, 'It's based on a scan.'

'Did you say scam?'

Diamond said, 'Silence in the ranks. The answer, Keith, is yes, I'm going to issue it to the media. A picture is worth a thousand words.'

'And if the picture is nothing like her?'

'There must be some resemblance.'

'May be.'

Ingeborg said, 'People don't expect a computer image to be perfect. There's news value in the fact that we're using this method. And when we finally do get a photo of the victim they'll want to compare it. So we get more publicity, a second bite at the cherry.'

'So speaks our ex-journo,' Diamond said.

Halliwell shrugged and was silent.

The Avon & Somerset sub-aqua team was sent to Green Park.

'Wouldn't it be wonderful if they found her handbag?' Ingeborg said.

'You're joking,' Halliwell said. 'If the killer takes the trouble to dump the body in the river, he's not going to dump her bag in the same place.'

'I was trying to be positive. You're getting as grouchy as the boss. Is it catching?'

Diamond's 11 a.m. press conference was well attended. The Manvers Street media relations manager, John Wigfull, presided. He and Diamond – old adversaries from way back – sat in front of a large projected image of the computerised face. Diamond read his prepared statement and invited questions. It all went well until someone asked about the music on the victim's iPod.

'Classical music, you said, superintendent. The murdered woman liked listening to string quartets, is that right?'

'You'll find a note of it in the release we handed out.'

'Would that be Haydn or Mozart?'

He hesitated. These smart-arse reporters were always trying to put the boot in. 'Beethoven, actually.'

'So you've listened to it. Are you a Beethoven expert, Mr Diamond?'

'I wouldn't claim that, but I'm not a complete duffer.'

'So was it the Amadeus?'

'Trying to catch me with a trick question?' he said. 'That's Mozart.' He didn't add that he'd seen the film.

'The Amadeus Quartet. I thought every music-loving policeman would have heard of them.'

CID press conferences aren't renowned for laughs, so when they come they are appreciated.

Diamond still wasn't sure if he was being tricked. 'I was *stringing* you along,' he said, and got a satisfying groan for the pun. 'And that's a good *note* on which to finish.'

*   *   *

He asked Paul Gilbert to drive him back to Green Park. Already the cameramen were there in force, lined up behind the tape getting shots of the underwater team in their scuba suits. From now on the press would be tracking every development.

Duckett, arms folded, watched him arrive. Neither needed to treat the other with much deference, and neither did. But to their credit Duckett's firm of crime scene investigators had been prompt this time in reporting the significance of the hair found at the scene.

'Any more discoveries?' Diamond asked after dipping under the 'do not pass' tape.

'Haven't they put you out to grass yet?' Duckett said.

'I was going to ask the same question, but come to think of it you look more at home up to your knees in mud.'

'It may look like mud to you, my friend, but it could be the piece of evidence that gets you off the hook.'

'So what else have you found, apart from the hair and the fibres?'

'We won't know until we get it cleaned up.'

'Have you worked out what happened?'

'You want it on a plate, don't you?' Duckett said. 'What do you do all day in that police station – watch the racing on TV? It's a pig of a scene, this one.'

'Always is.'

'Too many coppers have tramped through in their big boots. It's a wonder we found the hair.'

'Where was it?'

'Caught on a bramble, quite low down. If you really want to know what happened, I reckon she was dead or out to the world before she got here. There's no evidence of a struggle except dragging her to the bank and heaving her in. Have you seen the heel marks?'

Diamond nodded. 'If she was dead already, would she have floated?'

'Not for long in the current. You see what it's like. She'd have got waterlogged.'

'And after she sank, wouldn't the flow of the river continue to move her along the bottom?'

'In this case it didn't. My opinion is that the body lodged against something deep down. You want to speak to your frogmen. All kinds of stuff gets tipped into the river over time. We're only a few hundred yards from Sainsbury's here. Nothing pleases the yobbos more than heaving trolleys in.'

'It's true the body didn't travel very far,' Diamond said. 'It was spotted at Lower Weston, three or four hundred yards away. But it had been submerged some weeks from the state of it.'

'It will have inflated, as they do, and the pressure finally lifted it clear. The absence of the corpse at the scene is a real pain for me. We're reduced to looking for traces. It's not good for my back.'

'Any traces of the killer?'

'You're an optimist. What do you expect – another hair? We'll examine everything we've got under the microscope and let you know, but I wouldn't hold your breath. Ninety per cent of it is going to be rubbish blown across the park.'

'When do you reckon to finish?'

'In a couple of hours if people stop asking damn-fool questions.'

Diamond left him to it. To Paul Gilbert, he said, 'You wouldn't think we're his paymasters, would you, cocky bastard? He's not going to get work from anyone else.'

'He seems to know what he's talking about,' Gilbert said.

'He could say it in a more civil way. Now, I'd like your opinion. Come with me.' They left the crime scene and moved some distance from the press people. 'It's a park, right? You can't drive straight through it.'

'You might with a four-by-four.'

'The tyre tracks would be a giveaway. I haven't seen any. And you wouldn't get any kind of four-wheeled vehicle along the towpath. If you wanted to drop a body into the Avon, how would you get it here?'

'Carry it, I suppose.'

'Where from?'

'Your transport.'

He tried picturing someone burdened with a corpse, stumbling the hundred yards or more from where the road ended. 'You'd need to be strong.'

'She was quite small, guv.'

'True. But it would easier with some kind of barrow.'

'A supermarket trolley?'

'Maybe, if there was one handy. And this would be done by night, I imagine. Anyway, the killer got her to the bank and dragged her down the last bit, leaving the heels trailing.'

'You'd need to, just to make sure of your footing,' Gilbert said. 'It can't be easy pitching a body into the river.'

'But still a good method of disposal. People are going to assume she fell in, or jumped. It's unlikely any of the killer's DNA will be recovered, even if some was transferred. And he's buying time. Worth the extra effort, wouldn't you say?'

They checked with the sub-aqua team before leaving. Nothing of interest had yet been found. Visibility was a problem and so was the force of the current. A few days of rain had brought extra water off the hills and may well have contributed to the freeing of the corpse from whatever had trapped it. Several days of searching beckoned and the team didn't hold out much hope of more discoveries.

'We got a few unfriendly looks, I thought,' Diamond said as Gilbert drove them back along Green Park Road. 'They volunteer for this work. It gets them out of the office. What do they expect? Diving for pennies in the hot baths?'

His mood improved in the incident room. The excitement was obvious.

'What's happened?'

'We've got a name. That's what's happened, guv,' Ingeborg said.

'Already? Someone recognised the computer image?'

'No,' said Halliwell. 'That's just confusing everyone. The embassy delivered.'

11

'Have you ever done the towpath walk, Mel?' Mrs Carlyle asked while cooking his breakfast.

'The what?' He was never in the mood for small talk at this time of day and certainly not with his prying landlady.

'The towpath, by the river. You can go for miles. When I was younger, it was the romantic thing to do – if you had someone with you, of course. Mind you, the scenery loses its charm as you go on. Too many factories.'

'I expect so.'

'These eggs are ready now. I'll pop them on the plate with the bacon and tomato. You did say no to fried bread? It's a pity Tippi isn't down yet or I could have cooked hers at the same time. She used to be an early riser. Ever since you arrived she's taken to lying in bed of a morning.'

He didn't want to talk about Tippi's sleep pattern, especially with her mother. He leaned back and allowed Mrs Carlyle to put the plate in front of him.

She didn't go away. 'I think she doesn't want you to see her before she gets her face on.'

He shrugged. 'Thanks for this.'

And still she hovered over him. 'The reason I mentioned the towpath is because of something in the paper this morning. A poor young girl was pulled out of the river a few days ago and they seem to think she was murdered. They're appealing for witnesses who saw anything suspicious down at Green Park in the past eight weeks. She was Japanese.'

'Yes?' Spoken in a monotone, to emphasise his lack of interest.

'They know she was put in the river at Green Park because they found her iPod. And this is the part that will interest you. All the music on it was classical, like you play.'

'Classical can mean all sorts.'

'String quartets?'

Now his interest did quicken a little. 'Is that what it says she had on her iPod?'

'You can read it if you like.'

'It's not so remarkable,' he said. 'A lot of people like listening to chamber music. Could I have my coffee topped up?'

'Need your caffeine, do you? Bad night?' She shuffled towards the kitchen area. 'Or heavy day coming up?

'They're all heavy. I'm learning a difficult piece.'

She returned far too quickly for Mel's liking with the cafetière and the *Daily Mail*. 'You might like to see it. Bath gets in the papers quite often, but unpleasant things like this are rare, thank the Lord.'

'Thanks,' he said, back to his denial of any interest, 'only I don't think I have the time right now.'

'Have a quick look at the picture anyway,' she said. 'One of those artists' impressions, I suppose you'd call it. You wouldn't want to see a dead person's face at breakfast time. I was thinking she could easily have been in the audience for one of your recitals.'

'If she was, I wouldn't have noticed,' Mel said. 'I have to give all my attention to the music.'

She was lingering again, her hand on the back of his chair. 'Or you could have seen her after, hanging about to get your autograph. I've heard that you're famous, you and the Stark Arty Quartet.'

'Staccati. The others may be well known, but I'm not. I'm a late arrival, filling in for someone who dropped out. Nobody wants my autograph.'

'Don't put yourself down, Mel. Plenty of young ladies are dewy-eyed about you when you're playing, I'll be bound.'

The face on the front of the paper lacked any personality. He turned it over and pretended to take an interest in the football. Mrs Carlyle finally moved away. It crossed his mind that in future he might make a show of listening to his own iPod at breakfast. Would she take the hint? He couldn't depend on it.

The quartet was supposed to be rehearsing Schubert's 'Death and the Maiden' at the Michael Tippett Centre, but Cat had phoned to say she had a bad headache and wouldn't be coming in.

Ivan was unforgiving. 'Women and headaches. That can mean anything. If I get a headache I take a painkiller. It's about loyalty to the rest of us. What are we supposed to do – practise our scales?'

Mel said, 'She must be in a bad way to miss a session. Shouldn't we give her the benefit of the doubt?'

Anthony spoke up. 'We can practise without her.'

Ivan shook his head. 'This of all pieces requires the cello at the centre of things. It's the way it's arranged, with the rest of us responding to her variations. We'll be all at sea.'

'We can do the first variation. That's mine essentially.'

'A few bars and then what?' Ivan said. 'She becomes the soloist in the next. We can't work through it piecemeal, picking the sections that suit us.'

'Why not?' Anthony said in his uncompromising way.

'Because it will do more harm than good.'

'I can't think why.'

'We lose the flow, the unity, the tempo, that's why. It's not just a waste of our time, it's an insult to the composer. What do you say, Mel?'

After that, it was hard to know what to say. 'I see the difficulty—'

'In that case, I'm not staying,' Anthony said. He slammed his violin into its case and was off like the bishop who woke up in a brothel.

Ivan sighed and said to Mel, 'I was about to suggest we looked for an alternative piece, something with less cello. He wouldn't have agreed. He can't deal with changes of plan.'

'Pity. We needed him. There isn't much two of us can do.'

'He's a fine player – brilliant, in fact – but as a personality he can be impossible. Well, you just saw. I ought to be used to his ways by now. Cat handles him better than I do. And so did Harry when he was with us.'

'Did you know about this side of him when the quartet formed?'

'Not really. We were so impressed by his musicianship that we overlooked the signs of oddity in his personal dealings with us. You expect eccentricity among musicians and we forgave the occasional outburst.'

'Cat was telling me he doesn't have much of a life outside his music.'

'None at all that I'm aware of – which makes it so much more of a crisis each time anything upsets the arrangements. Shall we go for a coffee?'

In the months so far in Bath, Mel had not spent time alone with Ivan, apart from sharing taxis. He still felt in awe of him. Being told what to wear for that first meeting at the club in St James's had set the tone. A chat over coffee might be a chance to get to know the real Ivan.

Mel made an immediate try to get personal. 'This is my third this morning. All that caffeine. It starts off in my lodgings. Mrs Carlyle, my landlady, wants to talk in the mornings and I don't. I get through more of this than I should.'

'Are you comfortable where you are?'

'No complaints on that score. How's your place?'

Ivan looked into his cup, taking a moment to decide whether he wanted to open up. 'Adequate. I wouldn't put it higher than that. They say they don't mind me practising, but when I do, they turn up the volume on the television. I can hear it in my room with the door closed.'

'A couple, are they?'

'Civil partners, I think, is the term.'

'Same sex?'

'Gay men, yes. I don't mind that. They keep the house in immaculate order. But they like to economise on the heating so the water is barely warm. I don't enjoy getting up in the morning.'

'I thought you'd be used to cold winters.'

'Outside, yes, but we were always warm inside. Old-fashioned brick-built Russian stoves are very efficient.'

'Where were you brought up – Moscow?'

'Odessa.'

'So you're Ukrainian now.'

'Always was,' Ivan said with a defiant tilt of the head.

'Not a bad place to be a string player.'

'The only place. Isaac Stern, the Oistrakhs, Nathan Milstein.'

'What a line-up.'

'There are more I could name. It's a world-wide phenomenon. Do you know the story about Stern when President Kennedy made him responsible for intercultural exchanges with the Soviet Union? Someone said it must be a difficult job. He said, "On the contrary, it's a piece of cake.

They send us their violinists from Odessa and we send them our violinists from Odessa."'

An amusing story from Ivan? This was better than Mel could have wished for. 'You started early, no doubt?'

'Didn't we all?'

Mel nodded. He couldn't think of a top violinist who hadn't begun as a child.

Without any more prompting, Ivan launched into his story. 'I was giving recitals at ten years old. My parents were elderly and wanted to see me established as a musician, good enough to make my own way in the world when they passed on, so I mastered the basics early in life. I was accepted by the State Conservatory at fifteen, and there I learned about intonation and phrasing and so on. At seventeen I was playing in the Odessa Philharmonic. A year later I got an audition for the Moscow Chamber Orchestra and was accepted.'

'Leaving your birthplace?'

'I'd already decided to escape from the Soviet system. It was all the things you hear, oppressive, rigid, without a heart. The music we were playing spoke of joy, freedom, spirit, and didn't square with the life we were living. So I had this unstoppable urge to leave. To defect, I would need to get a trip abroad. Odessa was classed as a regional city by the State, which meant no orchestra from there was allowed to travel. You had to play in Moscow or Leningrad, as St Petersburg was known, if you wanted to visit the West.'

'How old were you when you got out?'

'Barely twenty, but old enough to know what I was doing. This was in the mid-eighties. I was friendly with some of the top chess players. I play a good game, up to tournament standard. At that time chess players were defecting regularly and some of them told me how to go about it. The main thing was to get invited to the West as part of a larger unit.'

'Like the ballet stars who came over with the Kirov company?'

130

'I suppose, yes.' He didn't seem to like the comparison. 'Anyway, I would be well placed with the Moscow Chamber Orchestra.'

'I can understand that. They have a terrific reputation.'

Ivan shrugged. 'More important to me, they often toured abroad. Six months after joining, I travelled with them to Frankfurt, gave the slip to our minders, got in a taxi and paid him over the odds to drive me to another town and stay silent. I asked for political asylum and never saw my parents again. This was 1987. They were dead before the wall came down.'

'That was hard.'

'Life was hard – then and for the next few years. I wasn't a name. I couldn't survive by playing my fiddle, but I had no other trade, so I worked as a hospital porter and mortuary attendant. These hands have performed tasks you wouldn't want to know about.'

'Better than working as a brickie. You wouldn't want to damage your fingers.'

'I would have earned more as a builder or a docker, it's true. You're right. I had to think of my hands.'

'And obviously you got back to playing?'

'I was always playing. Music is therapy. It nurtured my soul.' An extraordinary stillness came over Ivan.

Mel understood why.

'I kept my fiddle through the hard times and didn't change it until I was offered the use of a Strad – practising as often as I could, and I also took on some teaching and ensemble work. If you have a talent and you don't neglect it, the opportunities come. I filled in with various ensembles across western Europe and eventually got to England and found an opening with the Bournemouth Symphony. A happy choice.'

'Have you been back to Odessa?'

'Once, with the quartet. I found it much changed, but the music is still of the highest quality. Do you know it?'

Mel shook his head.

'From now on, you'll travel a lot.'

'I still find it hard to believe you took me on.'

'It wasn't a snap decision. We heard a number of others.'

'Will Douglas be looking for more engagements for us?'

'Undoubtedly. He wanted to see if we got along together, if the chemistry was right.'

'It wasn't this morning.'

'Don't worry. We've come through worse. We can all be prima donnas on our day. It's when we're on tour and compelled to travel with each other and not speaking that things get difficult. But I suspect all quartets are like that. It's not as if we've promised to love, honour and obey. We happen to be stuck with each other like four prisoners in a cell.'

Mel grinned. 'I hadn't thought of it like that.'

'Now you know why I didn't want us sharing a house.'

'I guess respect is what we should aim for.'

'Exactly.'

Becoming more confident, Mel asked, 'You chose me for my musicianship alone, is that right? You didn't ask about my temperament.'

'Or if you're an axe murderer?' Ivan said without a flicker of amusement. 'No, we judged you on your playing, first and last, and we expect the same consideration from you.'

'You've got it.'

He added a sly postscript. 'Of course it will be inconvenient if you're picked up by the police.'

'You'll bail me out?'

This prompted a rare smile. 'If we're not in custody ourselves. You have no idea what we're capable of.'

Not a topic to explore, Mel thought. Ivan had mellowed

in the last few minutes, but there were limits. 'Will Anthony come round, or does he want some kind of apology?'

'It will be as if nothing happened. An apology is needed and it should come from him, but he won't give one. We'll begin again when Cat is restored to her boisterous best. I hope *your* health is reliable.'

'Usually.'

'I haven't missed a rehearsal or a concert since the quartet was formed, so I feel I have a right to expect high standards of others.'

'What's your secret – vitamin pills?' Mel asked, keen to lighten the mood again.

'A balanced life. I still play chess, these days more on the internet than with a real person across the board, more's the pity. Do you play?'

'You wouldn't find me much of a challenge.'

'Plenty of musicians enjoy the game,' Ivan said. 'I expect you have a life outside music. I'm sure you do.'

Now that the focus switched to Mel, he became ill at ease himself. 'Nothing to speak of.'

'Women,' Ivan threw in. 'I've seen you eyeing up the students in short skirts. Have you dated any of them?'

With his chess-playing skill, Ivan had definitely taken the initiative. Mel felt as defensive as when Mrs Carlyle was making barbed hints about what went on with her nubile daughter. 'I can't afford the time. I need hours of practice to keep up with you and the others.'

'Hasn't it occurred to you that we're all practising like fury and not telling each other?'

Mel wasn't sure if this was a heavy-handed attempt at humour. 'That would be a comfort.'

But Ivan was serious as usual. 'You may get the idea that because we played the repertoire many times before, we don't need the preparation you do, but you'd be wrong. I practise several hours each evening, however loudly my landlord turns up the volume. For me, the ideal time would be early in the morning, but they'd treat that as an act of war and I can see their point of view. Anthony does nothing else but practise, as we know, and I'm pretty certain Cat will be bowing her cello at this minute, even in the throes of a headache.'

'Thanks. I'll remember I'm not alone when I put in some hours tonight.'

Ivan became the abbot again. 'Don't get distracted by women.'

Mel felt himself blush, as much in annoyance as embarrassment. 'You're reading too much into a few glances at girls.'

'Some of whom come to one-to-one tutorials.'

'You're out of order now. I can honestly say there's nothing going on with any of my students.'

'Keep it that way, then.' Ivan hesitated, realising, possibly, that he needed to justify interfering. 'We don't know for sure if women were Harry's undoing, but they could have been.'

'In Budapest?'

'Budapest, New York, Tokyo. He was always getting out of contact with the rest of us.'

'But you've often said you respect each other's space.'

'Too much, in the case of Harry. He disappeared into a space none of us were aware of.'

'From all I've heard about Harry, he comes across as a likeable guy.'

'He was – or is, I suppose I'd better say. We valued his company as well as his playing.'

But not the playing away, Mel thought. 'As his replacement, I often find myself wondering what he was like. I don't even know his age. I may be wrong, but I get the impression he was one of my generation.'

'A few years your senior.'

'What was his musical background?'

'He started as a violinist, as most viola players do. Went to the Guildhall School of Music and found he preferred the darker tones of the viola. He was with the Birmingham Symphony Orchestra for a short time before joining a talented quartet based in Dublin. There were personality clashes, I believe. The Irish are an excitable nation. They broke up at about the time Cat and I were looking for an experienced violist.'

'Lucky you,' Mel said.

'It wasn't luck.'

'Nice timing, then.'

'As a musician, you should know that timing is ordered and I always make sure it is.'

'Like when you defected?'

'A perfect example. I planned my escape. You don't leave anything to luck when your freedom depends on it. And when it came to forming the Staccati, we were very deliberate.'

'It wouldn't surprise me if you triggered the break-up of the Irish quartet just to get Harry on board.'

Ivan lifted an eyebrow and said nothing. Mel had spoken in jest, but now he was in two minds. This man with his deep-set, unblinking gaze was starting to come across as willing to stop at nothing to get what he wanted from music.

Soon after, Ivan said he needed some time alone. He was giving a master class in the afternoon.

Mel had no students to teach for the rest of the day, so he phoned for a taxi. He rather hoped Tippi would be at the house. After all that pious stuff from Ivan about not letting women distract him he felt like a damn good screw.

He was in the glass-walled foyer looking out for his cab when a small private car came up the drive. A young blonde

135

woman he didn't recognise got out and came inside. She was about ten years older than most students and didn't look as if she was arriving for a lunchtime concert.

She spoke first. 'Are you on the staff, by any chance?'

'Sort of,' Mel said. 'Can I help?'

'I'm police,' she said. 'Ingeborg Smith, Detective Sergeant.'

12

The dead woman was Mari Hitomi, a twenty-year-old from Yokohama. Her father, Kenji, the owner of a sushi bar on Lavender Hill, Clapham, had informed the embassy three days ago that she was missing, having believed for some weeks she was with friends. She should have come back to London at the weekend prior to catching a return flight to Japan. Mr Hitomi's account of her movements and the tooth tattoo and the interest in classical music had made the identification convincing and a DNA test had confirmed it.

Peter Diamond took Paul Gilbert with him to South London, or, rather, ordered young Gilbert to drive him. Not much was said until they were a few minutes from Clapham. A potential problem was nagging at the big man's confidence. 'Do you eat Japanese food?' he finally asked.

'Why, guv? Do you think we'll be offered some?'

'They're polite people. It's an eating place, a good one, going by the reports.'

'Sushi's okay. I like it.'

'All of it?'

'I can't say I've tried everything.'

'The raw fish?'

'That's all right.'

'Good.' Diamond relaxed. 'If it's offered, I'll pass mine to you when he isn't looking. Between you and me, I prefer my fish cooked in batter.'

'With chips?'

'What else is there?'

With that off his mind, Diamond concentrated on the job. Interviewing a bereaved parent wasn't easy, but at least he didn't have to break the news. The embassy had already done that.

The sushi bar was near enough to Clapham Junction to have a thriving trade from commuters. Every seat was taken at the rotating counter and waitresses in red suits with black bow ties were steadily adding new offerings. Diamond's troubling prospect of questioning Mr Hitomi over a plate of rice-coated suspicious objects was quickly dispelled.

'We get the hell outta here,' the slight, silver-haired father of the victim suggested after they had introduced themselves and dipped their heads in response to his courteous bow. 'Better joint across street.'

The better joint was a dimly lit coffee shop without many customers. They carried their mugs upstairs and found a table that was reasonably private. 'Touch base here, no problem,' Mr Hitomi said. His English sounded as if it was learned mainly from American movies, but the tough talk came in a subdued, husky tone that seemed to show he was still suffering from shock. He was wearing a black tie with a grey pinstripe suit.

'Is your wife here in Clapham?' Diamond asked, wanting to begin as painlessly as possible.

'Yokohama,' Hitomi said. 'Divorce, 2001.'

More of a conversation stopper. It required some sort of respectful response, but 'Ah, so,' wouldn't do. Dive in at the deep end, then. 'And your daughter . . . ?'

'Mari.'

'Was she living at home?'

'Yokohama, also.'

'So Mari was visiting you?'

'Two days only. Then to West Country, to hang out with Japanese school buddies. Exeter University.'

'Exeter? But she was found in Bath.'

He nodded. 'Last week I call Exeter, speak to Japanese friends. Mari no show. No call, no text, no letter.'

'Did she say anything to you about visiting Bath?'

'She say zilch.'

'She wanted to be independent?'

'You bet. Independent.'

'We believe she died four to six weeks ago – a long time for you not to have heard from her. Was she in touch with you at all after leaving here?'

Hitomi raised the palm of his right hand in a sort of salute. 'You said it, chum, independent.'

Diamond wished he hadn't said it. Putting words into the mouths of witnesses wasn't good interviewing technique. 'Weren't you worried?'

'Eyeballs out running restaurant. Mari knew the score.'

'She could have texted. You both have phones, I'm sure.'

He gave a sad smile. 'Much to see, many joints to visit. Texting old man no big deal.'

'Joints to visit? Did she say which?'

Hitomi lifted his palm again, on the point of using that word a third time.

Diamond spoke first. 'She was a music lover, I understand?'

'Check.'

'I mean serious music.'

'From her mother, graduate of famous Kunitachi Music College, Tokyo. Shit-hot violin player.'

'Mari played the violin?'

'Don't get me wrong, man. Mizuki, her mother. But Mari crazy for this music. Boy bands, bluegrass, hip-hop, no chance. Beethoven, Mozart, put it there.'

'I expect you heard there was classical music on the iPod that was found? String quartets.'

'Quartets, sure. Beethoven, Schubert, Haydn since she was a kid this high. Mizuki and me say you dig it, you go for it, babe. Western classical music ginormous in Japan. You seen her phone?'

'We didn't find her mobile, unfortunately.'

'Too bad you miss picture on front.'

Gilbert said to Diamond, 'He means the screen saver.'

'String quartet.'

'She had a quartet as her screen saver? What kind of phone did she have? Do you know which make?'

Hitomi shook his head.

'What was she carrying when she left you? Her clothes – were they in some kind of case or bag?'

'Backpack. Black canvas. Many badges.'

'She had badges attached to it? Places she'd visited?'

He nodded. 'And key-rings.' He made a space between his forefinger and thumb. 'Small violin, clarinet.'

'I understand. In pewter, probably. These were hanging from the backpack, right?'

'You got it.'

'We haven't found the bag. Did she leave anything at your home before going on her travels?'

'Some clothes for laundry. Your guys already took these off.'

'For the DNA testing. Do you have any idea why she would have gone to Bath instead of Exeter?'

This time Hitomi got the word in before Diamond could head it off. 'Independent.'

'She didn't mention friends in Bath, anybody she wanted to visit?'

He shook his head.

'Why Bath?' Diamond said. 'Any clues?'

'Famous place, well known in Japan.'

'She went there as a tourist, then?'

'Tourist, could be.'

'I'd like to ask you about Mari as a person. It may be difficult, even painful, to answer. These are things we need to know. Did she have a boyfriend?'

He rolled his eyes. 'In Yokohama, three, maybe four.'

'And in England?'

'Who knows?'

'If she met someone, was she the sort of girl who made friends easily? Do you understand me?'

'Shack up with guys?'

Diamond hadn't gone as far as that, but now it had been mentioned the answer would be good to get. He raised his eyebrows and waited.

'This is not something Japanese girl speak about to her old man,' Hitomi said, and closed the door on that.

'But did she trust men?' Diamond asked, back to his line of enquiry. 'In a strange city, meeting a man for the first time, would she be on her guard?'

'Her guard? Who the hell you talking about?'

'It's an expression – "on her guard" – meaning careful.'

'You've lost me, buster.'

'Would she let a strange man buy her a drink?'

Hitomi pondered the matter. His hand tightened around his mug of coffee. Clearly he was under strain, trying to be frank and remain dignified. 'I guess is possible.'

'Get into his car? I'm trying to understand what happened. Her iPod was found on the river bank in a quiet place away from the city centre.'

'You telling me all this so I figure it must be so. Nobody told me how she died.'

'Because we aren't a hundred per cent certain,' Diamond said. 'All we know for sure is that she was in the river still

141

in her clothes. She may have been killed before this. We can't tell how, or why.'

'I'm reading you now.' Hitomi sighed and looked down, no doubt picturing the scene. He took another deep breath before going on. 'Mari is modern young woman, hot chick, twenty years old, straight out of college, degree in higher mathematics. As foreign visitor, in Bath for first time, no buddies, she feels lonesome. Some guy gets friendly, comes on to Mari. This I don't like one bit, but I understand.'

'Me, too,' Diamond said with a glance at Paul Gilbert, 'and all too easily. The unfortunate part is that the guy in question was a murdering bastard and she trusted him.'

'Come again,' the father said. 'Murdering bastard?'

'I was speaking to my colleague.'

Hitomi lowered his head. 'What kind of jerk am I, not keeping tabs on my own daughter?'

Now Gilbert spoke up. 'Mr Hitomi, do you by any chance have a picture of Mari?'

'Picture? You bet.' At once, an iPhone was produced. With a couple of touches on the display, Hitomi found not one photo, but a series that he let the phone show as a sequence. He passed it to Gilbert. 'Right here in London town.'

'This visit? That's brilliant.' Diamond was reminded that all the Japanese he'd ever seen were compulsive takers of photographs. He practically snatched the phone from Gilbert. 'Can you show me from the start?'

Hitomi leaned across and touched the screen again.

The shots were sharp and natural, a touching record of a happy young woman in the last hours she had spent with her father, starting with her emerging from the arrivals gate at Heathrow pushing a trolley containing the backpack decorated with badges. Then beside a silver car – presumably Hitomi's – and in the passenger seat. The next was at a front door that must have been his; and indoors at a table, teacup in hand. Several more showed her in the sushi bar, one with her father at her side. There were some street scenes on Lavender Hill, Mari with arms outstretched, revelling in being in this new setting. The sequence ended at a mainline station that had to be Paddington. She was wearing the backpack and turning to wave as she walked towards a train, still smiling – a poignant final picture that moistened even Peter Diamond's eyes.

'These are just what we need. Can we get copies?'

Gilbert said, 'We can send them to Manvers Street right now if Mr Hitomi agrees.'

'Did you hear that?' Diamond asked Hitomi. 'These pictures are precious to you, I'm sure, but they'll help us catch her killer. The only likeness we have isn't much of a likeness at all. Show it to him, Paul.'

Gilbert used his own phone to bring up the computer image and turn it through several angles. For all the work that had been done, it didn't bear much resemblance apart from the hairstyle. Comparison with the genuine images they had just examined was a harsh test. The only test more harsh was showing it to her own father.

'My Mari? You got to be joking,' he said, shaking his head.

'You see why your photos are so vital?' Diamond said. 'It's okay to use them, I hope?'

'Be my guest,' Hitomi said.

'In that case, we'll email them to Bath.'

'Sure. Go ahead.'

For all Diamond's battles with modern technology, he couldn't deny that it had simplified parts of his job – as long as someone else was there to press the right keys. Paul Gilbert made sure the complete set of digital images was sent to Bath. A text from Ingeborg with the one word *Magic* confirmed the transfer.

Hitomi's account of his daughter had been priceless

information. Up to now he was the only person in Britain known for certain to have seen her. Other witnesses might yet see the photos and come forward, but there was no guarantee that they would.

For all the clichéd tough talk, Diamond could sense the pain this father was suffering, and warmed to him for bearing up so bravely. No question about it: Hitomi had loved his daughter and felt guilty for failing to keep tabs on her.

'I need to be clear about this. Did she know anyone in Britain apart from yourself and the Exeter friends?'

He shook his head.

'Had she visited you before?'

'Here in Britain? No.'

'So we have to assume she was killed by someone she met here on this trip, or a total stranger. Difficult.'

'But with her picture you find witness, no problem, yes?' Hitomi said.

'We can hope. It won't be easy. But you've given us a chance we didn't have before.'

For the drive back, Diamond bought pasties from a shop further up Lavender Hill, confiding to Paul Gilbert that the smell was so appetising he had to get some, even though he knew there wouldn't be enough meat for his liking. 'I get caught each time. Sniff the cooking and can't pass the shop entrance. And then I regret it later.' He picked up a six-pack of beer for himself and some bottled water for Gilbert, explaining that they couldn't risk being breathalysed.

Not far along the M4, he opened the last tin and said, 'I feel a lot of sympathy for Mr Hitomi. He was bearing it well, but suffering inside.'

'I expect his ex-wife is having a bad time, too,' Gilbert said. 'Must be worse, being so far away.'

'Tough. Very tough. But Hitomi wasn't just grieving. He felt responsible, guilty even.'

'He wasn't to know what was going to happen.'

'He'll always believe he should have stayed in touch, texting or phoning.'

'She was over twenty, guv. She wasn't a kid. And he was busy with his job. That sushi bar was really humming. It must take most of his time ordering supplies and checking on the kitchen and his waiting staff, taking reservations, being nice to his customers. All these things make a difference in the catering business.'

'But when the job takes you over completely and your nearest and dearest get pushed to the margins, you have to watch out. That's what I'm saying. A lesson for us all.'

Paul Gilbert drove on in silence as if doubtful what to say next.

He needn't have worried. Diamond was deep in thoughts of his own, about Paloma and the conversation on the towpath concerning his bottled-up emotions. Her plea – 'I thought I was a part of your private life' – still pained him. And so did the bust-up that had followed.

13

In the incident room next morning, the whiteboard display was strikingly improved by Kenji Hitomi's photographs of his daughter when alive. Everyone felt the investigation had moved on. The computer-generated images had been removed. Mari the victim didn't much resemble the woman painstakingly assembled in Philadelphia.

'Did they charge us yet?' Halliwell asked John Leaman. 'I don't think we should pay up.'

'Too late. It was fifty per cent up front and the rest on receipt. Already went through the bank.'

'Demand a refund.'

'They had a clause to rule it out.'

'You signed an agreement? They'll have lawyers waiting to pounce.'

'Exactly.'

'So how much of our budget was wasted on this?'

'Don't ask. I haven't even told the guv'nor yet.'

'It's Georgina we need to worry about. She's looking for any excuse to downsize us.'

Diamond himself appeared soon after and called for silence. 'We're going public with these pictures of the victim. Someone in the city must have spotted her. She was here in Bath at least one day – the day she was killed.'

'Not necessarily, guv,' Leaman said in the irritating sing-song he used when he knew he was right.

'What do you mean?'

'She could have been murdered in Exeter and brought here by the killer and disposed of in the river.'

'She never reached Exeter.'

'We don't know that for certain. Her so-called friends told her father she didn't reach there, but one of them could have killed her and driven to Bath with the body. We ought to check the Exeter end.'

Diamond backtracked fast. 'You've got a point. Christ, what's the matter with me, not spotting that? The Exeter lot definitely have to be questioned. There could be some falling-out we haven't heard about.' He looked right and left for help, like a floundering swimmer. 'Paul, did we get their names from Mr Hitomi?'

'He didn't actually name them, guv.'

'Get through to him now. No, better text him. We need the correct spelling.'

'Will do,' Gilbert took out his iPhone.

'Want me to call Exeter CID?' Halliwell asked.

'What – ask them to do the job? We'll handle this ourselves. Even if these friends are innocent as newborn babes it's possible they can tell us stuff about Mari her father doesn't know.'

Leaman couldn't resist rubbing in his small triumph over Diamond. 'Equally she could have been killed in some other place and brought here: Bristol, Swindon, Devizes—'

'All right. We get the drift.'

'Shouldn't we put out a countrywide alert?'

'That'll happen willy-nilly. The press are sure to go national on these pictures. They're quality photos and they tell a story. If she was seen in any place from here to John o'Groats we'll get to hear of it.'

'Better expect some mistaken sightings, then.'

'That's inevitable. I still favour Bath as the location – there was local knowledge at work – but we'll keep an open mind.'

'Why would she have come to Bath?'

'Why do thousands of tourists come every year? You're forgetting this city is known all over the world. Her father said he reckoned she came as a tourist.'

And now, with Diamond shown up once as fallible, Keith Halliwell pitched in. 'He could be wrong. She could have come for some other reason.'

'Such as?'

'Something she didn't want to tell her father about.'

'Go on.'

'Looking up an ex-boyfriend.'

'Japanese?'

'British, American, Japanese – who knows? Someone she knew in Yokohama who is now working or studying in Bath. Mari has set her heart on reviving the relationship. But it turns out he's living with someone else, may have a child as well. Mari is hurt and angry when she finds out.'

'Straight out of *Madame Butterfly*,' Leaman murmured, annoyed that someone had stolen his thunder.

Halliwell wasn't being put off. 'She threatens to tell the new partner about his past. They have a row, it gets violent and he kills her.'

'Quite a theory,' Diamond said.

'You did ask.'

'I'm grateful. And there could be some simple and obvious reason for coming to Bath that nobody has mentioned.'

'What's that?'

An interruption from Paul Gilbert saved him. 'Guv, Mr Hitomi will be texting the names in the next few minutes.'

'Excellent. While we wait we can decide which of his pictures to release to the press.'

This didn't take long. They chose three: a close-up of Mari in Hitomi's house, a street picture with arms outstretched

148

and the shot of her wearing the backpack looking over her shoulder at the camera.

The names of her friends came through soon afterwards: Taki Kihara and Mikio Nambu. Both were ex-pupils of Yokohama High School studying physics at Exeter University.

'Exeter.' Diamond turned to Ingeborg. 'How long would it take you to drive there – a couple of hours?'

'Probably less. Depends who's sitting beside me.'

Smiles all round. Diamond's dislike of high speeds was well known. Even he managed a twisted grin.

'Tee it up with the physics department. We'll go this afternoon.' He continued doggedly with the briefing. 'One thing Mr Hitomi confirmed is that Mari was into classical music in a big way. We already knew there was Beethoven on the iPod. It now turns out that her mother in Yokohama is a violinist who studied to a high level at some music college in Tokyo.'

'Kunitachi,' Paul Gilbert said.

'Someone give him a Kleenex.'

'The Kunitachi College of Music. I made a note of it.'

Leaman took this as the cue to air more of his musical expertise. 'Suzuki trained.'

The only Suzuki Diamond had heard of was a motorbike and he wasn't being lured into admitting that. 'We'll take your word for it. The point is that Mari's mother taught her to love music and she was keen enough to have miniature musical instruments fixed to her backpack. I'm thinking it's possible she was here in Bath for some concert.'

'But we don't know when, so how can we tell?' Halliwell said.

'You want it on a plate. It's a possibility, that's all.'

'The music festival is always at the end of May,' Leaman said, 'but there are concerts of one sort or another all year round.'

'Ingeborg checked all the local music colleges for a

missing Japanese student and came up with nothing,' Halliwell said.

'Get with it,' Diamond said with an opportunity to score. 'We're not looking for a missing student now. Mari wasn't living here. That wouldn't stop her looking up some Japanese friend in a music college. The music may be a huge red herring, but it keeps swimming into view.'

Diamond and Ingeborg got on the road after an early lunch. The Exeter University physics department had set up a meeting with Mari's two Japanese friends at 3.30 p.m.

'It's a learning experience, this,' he said after they were on the M5 and he'd asked Ingeborg to stay in the slow lane. He believed conversation made the journey go just as quickly as belting along at dangerous speeds. 'Classical music and now physics. Quite a mental leap.'

'Einstein managed it,' Ingeborg said. 'He was a keen violinist.'

'You're starting to sound like John Leaman now.'

'In what way?'

'Trotting out facts. I'm not complaining. John's a useful guy on the team. He was right, saying we must investigate these Exeter friends. I don't know why I didn't think of it. Am I losing my grip?'

'You don't miss much, guv.'

'I'm not sleeping all that well.'

'Any reason?'

'Bit of a crisis in my personal life.' He stared at the back of his hand as if it didn't belong to him. 'You might as well know. I split up with Paloma.'

'Really?' She hesitated before saying with sympathy, 'That's tough.'

'My fault. I came out with one stupid remark too many. Any woman who takes me on is asking for trouble.'

'Would you like to make it up with her?'

'Don't know. We're proud people, both. She gave me an earful.'

'Pity if it's only words that came between you.'

'There's more – my attitude. I can't stop being the hard-nosed cop. She thinks I should lighten up when I'm off duty. I try. Obviously not enough.'

'It goes with the job,' Ingeborg said. 'We're never entirely off duty. We see something wrong and can't ignore it.'

'What started this? You mentioning Einstein, making me feel inferior.'

Ingeborg laughed. 'I'm no Einstein myself. I failed physics and I can't read music.'

'Too bad. I was hoping you'd be discussing relativity with these undergraduates.'

'And in Japanese?'

'They must be reasonably fluent in English or they couldn't study here.'

'How do you want to deal with them – as a pair or singly?'

'Definitely one by one. Joint interviews don't work. There's always one loudmouth who dominates and it's sod's law that the quiet one has all the information.'

'And we're treating them as suspects?'

'We must. John Leaman could be right. They may have murdered her in Exeter and dumped the body in Bath as a blind.'

'They're supposed to be her friends.'

'They'd need a motive, yes, like some bad blood we've yet to find out about.'

Even in the slow lane, they reached Exeter ahead of schedule. The university complex north-west of the city was easy to locate. Finding a place to leave the car was more of a

151

problem. 'There was a time when most students couldn't afford a motor,' Diamond said.

'It's now,' Ingeborg said. 'They just run up a bigger debt.'

At the physics department they were told that the professor was off the campus all day, so they were given his office to use as an interview room.

'Chair of physics at Exeter will look good on my CV,' Diamond said as he tried the seat. 'Who's first up?'

'It seems to be decided,' the department secretary said. 'We asked them both to be here at the time you stated. Miss Kihara is waiting outside, but the man is late.'

'The *man?*'

'Mr Nambu.'

'Funny. I assumed they were both female, being friends of Mari. Not obvious from the names.'

'Unless you're Japanese,' Ingeborg said.

'Ask Miss Kihara to step in, will you?'

The student was small and nervous, with powerful glasses that magnified her eyes into a permanent startled look. Being interviewed in the professor's office must have been daunting. She might have been more relaxed in the place Diamond had originally planned to use: the union bar.

'May we call you Taki?'

'Please do.' At once it was clear there would be no problem over the language.

'You knew Mari Hitomi, I believe, and you'll have heard the sad news of her death.'

'It's incredible. A horrible shock.'

'We spoke to her father and he understood she was planning to visit Exeter to see you and Mr Nambu.'

'That's right. She called me after she arrived in London.'

'Did she fix the visit?'

'She didn't put a date on it. She was going to text us nearer the time. I said she was welcome to stay a few days if she wanted. She could sleep at my place. So we left it flexible.'

'And you didn't receive the text?'

'I wasn't worried. It was a casual arrangement and when weeks went by I thought she must have made other plans. The next thing I heard was when her father phoned. He seemed to believe she'd been coming straight to Exeter. He was very upset when I told him she wasn't with us.'

'It seems she planned a visit to Bath without telling him. Do you know if she had friends there?'

'Nobody I heard of. If they were friends from Yokohama, I'd know. We all keep in touch. There are three in Sheffield, two in Bangor, one in Cambridge.'

'Do you visit any of them yourself?'

She shook her head. 'It's too far on a bike. That's my transport.'

'You don't drive?'

'No.'

If this was true – and it was an instant response, spoken without sign of evasion – one crucial question was settled. She hadn't driven to Bath with a body in the back. 'You've known Mari a long time?'

'We went through school together in Yokohama.'

'What was she like?'

'Very good company. She was open and truthful. Laughed a lot. I was looking forward to seeing her again.'

'We need to get a picture of her as a personality, likes and dislikes, that kind of thing.'

'There was the music, of course,' Taki said. 'She was passionate about that. Serious music. She didn't have time for modern pop.'

'When you say passionate . . .?'

'I mean it. She'd travel to concerts in other cities. Her bedroom was full of posters of famous musicians, just like

153

some girls go crazy over rock stars. She had a really top-class sound system and hundreds of CDs. This was before downloading came in. Music was her main thing when we were going through school.'

'Did she play an instrument?'

'I never heard that she did. Her mother was a professional violinist and maybe that put Mari off, thinking she could never live up to that standard. She could read music, I know that. She'd buy the score and follow it.'

'She studied maths, her father told me.'

'Sure, in Yokohama University. There's some kind of link between music and maths, isn't there?'

'Do you know if she had boyfriends?'

'I expect so. I haven't seen her for some time.'

'At school, I mean.'

'We all went out with boys. Mari was no exception.'

'Was Mikio a particular friend?'

'Of Mari's?' She blushed a little. 'You mean Mikio at this university? They were seeing each other at one time. You'd better ask him.'

'Are you and he . . .?' Diamond asked, picking up on the blush.

'Absolutely not.' Her voice shook a little. 'Just because we went through school together it doesn't mean a thing. We happen to be studying in the same department in the same university, that's all.'

The charged quality in her response alerted Diamond. 'Is something the matter between you?'

'This has nothing to do with Mari.'

'But . . . ?'

'We don't get on now.'

'Is that why he wasn't sitting outside when we arrived? To avoid you?'

'It could be.'

154

'Have you spoken to him at all about Mari's death?'

'We don't speak.'

'But after her father phoned and was so distressed, didn't you ask Mikio if he'd heard from her?'

'No.' She was increasingly tight-lipped. And this interview had started so well.

'It's as serious as that, the rift between you? What's behind it, Taki?'

She dipped her head.

Diamond, at a loss, glanced to his left for assistance.

Ingeborg said to Taki in little more than a whisper, 'We need to know. It may seem personal to you, Taki, but we don't ask questions without a good reason.'

Without looking up, she said, 'My trouble with him has nothing to do with Mari.'

'You don't know,' Ingeborg said. 'It could be important. Did he try it on with you?'

After another long pause, Taki lifted her head and faced them, her eyes red-lidded and tearful. 'At the end of summer term, he got me drunk. He wasn't dating me, or anything. We were with other students in a pub in the town and everyone was drinking. He kept filling my glass with cider. When I got up to go I was unsteady. I've never been drunk before. I couldn't stand up properly. Everyone except me seemed to think it was funny. Mikio said he'd take me back to my lodgings. He had to hold me up. I remember him at the house helping me upstairs. After that, it's a blank.'

'Do you think he took advantage?'

'I woke up at some time in the night feeling ill. I was alone in my bed and my head was hurting. I managed to get to the bathroom and threw up. Then I realised I was naked.' She twisted her fingers in an agitated way. 'I have no memory of undressing.'

'He stripped you,' Ingeborg said, making it more of a

155

statement than a question. She was always alert to abuse of any sort.

'What else can I think?'

'Were you bruised? Sore? Do you think he raped you?'

'If he did, it wasn't obvious. I was too drunk to know. It's so humiliating. I can't believe I encouraged him, but even that is possible. You'd think I would have some memory of it, only I don't.'

'He could have added something to your drink.'

'I've thought about that. I simply don't know.'

'It happens. If it was just drink, you'd probably have some recollection. Is there any talk of guys here using the date-rape drug?'

'I haven't heard it mentioned.'

'As you say, you could be mistaken,' Ingeborg said, appearing to sense that her outrage was adding to Taki's distress. 'Maybe you undressed yourself. Where were your clothes?'

'On a chair.'

'That doesn't sound like a man intent on rape.'

Taki made a small movement with her shoulders that suggested she'd like to be persuaded, but wasn't. 'I didn't see him again until the new term started. I was too embarrassed to speak to him. In fact, we haven't spoken since. What makes it worse is that some of the others who were with us in the pub still treat it as a joke.'

'How does he react when they tease you?'

'He doesn't say anything.'

'Does he have a reputation for sleeping around?'

'No. I've heard nothing like that.'

Diamond joined in again. 'Back in Japan, before you came here, what did the girls think of him?'

'Nothing special. He was just another guy.'

'Did you ever go out with him?'

'I don't think he was interested in me.'

'But you said he was interested in Mari.'

'I said they dated a few times. I doubt if it ever got serious.'

'When she spoke to you on the phone about coming to Exeter, did she speak about seeing Mikio as well?'

She gave a nod. 'It was kind of awkward. She asked if I saw him and I said yes because I do in lectures and she said it would be good for the three of us to meet and would I like to tell him she was coming. I didn't want to tell her what happened with Mikio, so I said a better idea was to wait until she arrived and maybe we could fix something then.'

'What did she say to that?'

'She misunderstood me. I must have sounded really cool about her plan, because she jumped to the idea I was dating him and didn't want her to come between us. I insisted that wasn't the case, but I don't know if she believed me.'

'So how did you leave the arrangement?'

'Like I said, we kept it loose. She was going to let me know by text when she was coming.'

'Is it possible she called Mikio herself?'

'I don't know.' Taki frowned. Then her eyes became huge behind the glasses as if an appalling scenario was surfacing in her brain. 'I guess it's possible.'

'Did she have his mobile number?'

'We all had contact numbers.'

'We'll ask him,' Diamond said. 'If you didn't tell him Mari was coming, how else would he have known?'

She still looked deeply troubled. 'What I said to you just now – about what happened to me last term – doesn't have to go any further, does it? I'm not accusing him.'

Ingeborg said, 'That's not up for investigation, and even if it was, proving anything happened would be impossible so long after.'

'You won't mention it when you interview him?'

Diamond had let the exchange between the two women run on for long enough. Sympathy could only go so far. 'Mari was murdered. Nothing is off limits.'

Ingeborg softened the statement by adding, 'If it comes up, we'll be as discreet as possible.'

After Taki had left the room, Diamond said, 'What did I tell you about the quiet ones?'

'How do we know she's the quiet one?' Ingeborg said.

'We'll get his story presently. Did you believe her?'

'Why shouldn't I?'

'She was quick to tell us she doesn't drive and doesn't speak to the guy. We came here to find out if they combined to murder Mari. Everything this one said absolved her from any part in a possible crime. She told us in effect that if Mikio killed Mari and drove her to Bath, he acted alone.'

Ingeborg's eyes narrowed. 'Are you saying she made all this up?'

'I'm saying she's well and truly stitched up her old school buddy Mikio. Could be true, though. If he's a date-rape specialist it's not impossible he drugged Mari and things didn't go to plan. Some of these drugs like ketamine are potentially lethal. He could have given her too much and had a body to dispose of.'

'Manslaughter. I hadn't thought of that.'

'The question is, had Taki?'

The department secretary arrived with tea and biscuits. Switching quickly to his amiable self, Diamond told her he could get used to the academic life. Nobody ever brought tea and biscuits to his office in CID.

'Perhaps you don't treat them right,' the secretary said with a smile.

'I'm like a favourite uncle to them all,' he said, 'but it makes no difference.'

'Try getting tough, then.'

'Now there's an idea.'

Ingeborg was open-mouthed.

'Mr Nambu is here now,' the secretary said.

'We'll see him.'

By student standards, Mikio Nambu was improbably well groomed, in a navy polo shirt and white jeans. He looked as if he couldn't kill a fly, but so did many of the notorious rapists and killers in criminal history, Diamond reflected. As an investigator, you had to accept that wrongdoers aren't necessarily uglier or larger or less presentable than the rest of humanity. Juries were always disarmed by the ordinariness of the people put up before them.

'Sit down, Mr Nambu. Sorry to take you from your studies. This shouldn't be long. We'll call you Mikio if you don't mind. Is that the way you say it?'

'Mickey will do.'

'We won't get too chummy.' He introduced himself and Ingeborg by rank and surname. 'Do you know why we're here?'

'It's about Mari Hitomi.' His English was at least the equal of Taki's.

'A friend from Yokohama, is that right?'

'She was, yes. I saw the TV news. It's difficult to believe.'

'Always is for the nearest and dearest. Would you call yourself one of Mari's nearest and dearest?'

He shifted in the chair. 'I don't know about that.'

'I'm trying to get a sense of your relationship. You must have dated her. Did you ever sleep with her?'

'We were schoolkids.'

'Is that a no?'

'A definite no.' He leaned back in the chair and said, 'I hope you're not trying to connect me with her murder.'

'You're a witness – or I think you are. She arrived in

159

London and stayed for a short time with her father, who thought she was coming directly here to catch up with old friends from Yokohama – you and Taki Kihara. Did you hear from her?'

He paused. 'There was a text to say she was coming and would get in touch when she knew the date.'

'Is it still on your phone, this text?'

'Deleted. I don't keep everything.'

'When did you receive it?'

'At least two months ago, possibly longer.' He was hesitating before each response, as if expecting a trap.

'And I suppose there's no way of telling if it was sent from London or Bath?'

'It's a mobile phone.'

'Right. So did you see her after the text arrived?'

'She didn't get here.'

'Let's not take anything for granted, Mikio. You don't know if she got here. You're telling me you didn't see her here, is that more accurate?'

'I suppose. I thought she was killed in Bath.'

'Her body was found there. It isn't certain she was killed there, unless you know something we don't.'

He blinked rapidly. 'I don't know what you mean.'

'Do you drive?'

'Yes.'

'Got a car, have you?'

'A Nissan Micra.'

Diamond exchanged a glance with Ingeborg. 'It crossed my mind that you could have arranged to meet her in Bath, in which case you could tell us what she was doing there.'

Mikio shook his head. 'I've never been to Bath.'

'Or some place near by?'

The words came rapidly now. 'I didn't see her. I didn't speak to her on the phone. I received one text and that's all.'

'She could have come to Exeter as she promised,' Diamond said.

'If she did, I didn't see her.'

'Okay, don't panic, Mikio. Where do you keep your car?'

If anything was likely to panic him, it was more interest in his car. He swallowed hard. 'On the street outside my lodgings.'

'Is it there now?'

'Now? It's here on the campus.'

'So would you show it to us?'

They didn't have far to go. The physics department had its own parking area behind one of the labs. Mikio's Nissan Micra, a small, blue hatchback, stood only a few spaces from where Ingeborg had parked.

'I haven't washed it lately,' he said.

'It's all right,' Diamond told him. 'We're not thinking of buying it.'

They walked around the mud-spattered car. The back seat was covered with textbooks and file covers.

'There isn't much room for books where I live,' Mikio said.

'Open up, please.'

A sharp odour was apparent as soon as he unlocked the front door.

'What's that – disinfectant?'

'There was a smell I was trying to get rid of. Maybe I should have used something else.'

'What sort of smell?'

'Vomit.'

'Here in the front?'

'That's where it was.'

An insight into student life. Diamond glanced around the interior, which hadn't been cleaned for a considerable time. Forensics would have a field day here if they were ever asked to check it. 'Is the back open?'

161

Mikio took them around to the rear door. More books, up to a hundred probably, filled the boot space. Diamond sniffed and got the smell of books. Nothing else. This end of the car hadn't been disinfected.

'You can close it. We're done.'

Back in the office, Diamond resumed in a disarming way. 'Tell us what Mari was like when you were going out with her in Yokohama.'

Mikio frowned, still wary of being trapped. 'I already told you we were just schoolkids. Nothing happened.'

'You're on about sex, are you?' Diamond said. 'I'm interested more in her personality, but if you want to tell us what you got up to – or didn't – go ahead.'

A sharp breath. 'No. It's okay. There's nothing to say. Personality. What do you want to know? She was popular, good at her studies, especially maths. She lived with her mother in an apartment in one of the best buildings in Yokohama. It was big, well furnished.'

'You've seen inside, then?'

'Only the hallway and living room.'

'I believe her bedroom was quite a sight, filled with posters,' Diamond said.

More nervous blinking. 'I wouldn't know about that.'

'When you took her out, where did you go?'

'The movies, a couple of times. She didn't like clubs. They had the wrong sort of music. She was into serious stuff.'

'So we are finding out. Did you go to any concerts with her?'

'No, she liked to go alone. She spent all her pocket money travelling around to catch her favourite players. She had all the gigs on her iPad calendar and if I wanted a date I had to fit around them.'

'So did you take her drinking?'

'We were under age. Couldn't afford it, anyway.'

162

'Was she better off than you?'

'Definitely. She got an allowance from her dad as well as her mother. But she spent most of it on the music.'

'Tough for you, being second best,' Diamond said. 'How do you make any headway with a girl like that? What did she drink – Coke?'

Mikio reddened. Plainly he saw where this was heading. 'Lemonade actually.'

'Lemonade doesn't have much of a kick.'

'It was her choice.'

'I expect she was drinking stronger stuff these days.'

He was quick to say, 'I wouldn't know. I didn't see her.'

'If she still drinks lemonade, there are ways of pepping it up, aren't there?' Diamond said. 'You know all about getting girls in the mood. Ecstasy, GHB, or whatever the latest is.'

Mikio snapped, his voice rising. 'Look, that's out of order.'

'I wasn't talking about your schooldays. We've moved on. It's a different world here. The girls drink as much as they want of whatever they want and sometimes things get added as well.'

Pushed to the limit, Mikio launched into a defence of his actions. 'Taki's been talking to you about me. If she told you I drugged her at the end of last term, it's a lie. I didn't add anything to her drink. I don't do drugs myself and I wouldn't dream of giving them to girls.'

'What happened, then?' Ingeborg said, fixing him with an uncompromising stare.

'Do you really need to know?'

She didn't answer and neither did Diamond.

'Okay.' Mikio gripped the chair arms. 'There was this end of term booze-up in a pub. We thought it was a laugh when she was getting giggly and I filled her glass to encourage her, but I didn't know she was legless. When it was obvious she couldn't stand properly I felt bloody mean and ashamed. The least I could do was see her home safely, so I drove her back to her place. It wasn't what you're thinking. She threw up in my car. I got her to the house and helped her upstairs. If she told you I did anything else, I didn't. She had vomit down her front. Would you fancy anyone in that state? I opened the door and guided her in and she sat on the edge of her bed and pulled off the smelly top and started unfixing her bra. I decided I'd done my duty and ought to leave fast, so I did. We haven't spoken since.'

The words had come so rapidly and with such strong recollection Diamond found them convincing. None of it sounded rehearsed. 'Did you put disinfectant in the car to take down the smell?'

Mikio needed a few seconds to get over his statement. 'I've given it several goes. Air freshener isn't enough.'

Diamond was ready to move on, whatever Ingeborg had decided. 'What happened between you two isn't my concern unless it touches on the death of Mari. Let's get back to when you were dating her in Yokohama. How did it end? Did you have a row?'

The young man's eyes rolled upwards. 'How did it end? It didn't really. There was never much to it. We stopped seeing each other, but we stayed friends, or she wouldn't have asked to see me on this visit. I couldn't compete with the musicians she idolised, and that's all there is to it.'

'Did she name any of them?'

'I don't remember any names. It was groups mostly, like any pop band, only classical. And you might say she was like any groupie, dead nuts about them.'

'Is that what you really mean?' Ingeborg asked, her feminism challenged yet again. 'A groupie? That's something more than idolising them. It means she was willing to sleep with them.'

'Sorry. I shouldn't have used the word,' he said, on the retreat. 'It's unfair now she's dead. I don't know what was in her mind. The music thing was all a bit obsessive, but that's a stage teenagers go through, isn't it?'

'Who were the groups she liked?'

'They didn't mean much to me.'

'The Staccati?'

He shrugged. 'Don't know.'

'Where did that come from?' Diamond asked Ingeborg.

'Tell you later,' she said. 'But I think we should speak to Taki again before we leave.'

They let Mikio return to his studies. He was out of that office as if a fuse had been lit.

'What did you make of him?' Diamond asked Ingeborg. 'Is this a Japanese crime?'

'If it is, we need to know a lot more about the motive,' she said. 'I was all ready to pin it on him after listening to Taki and how he treated her, but I thought he came across as honest. Jumpy, but truthful.'

Diamond murmured in agreement. 'And the smell of disinfectant in the car definitely came from the floor in front of the passenger seat, which backs his story. When he first opened the door I thought maybe he'd had a corpse in there and tried to clean up, but you wouldn't stick a corpse beside you in the front. The boot area was free of the smell.'

'And he needn't have shown us the car,' Ingeborg said. 'He could have said it was at the other end of the campus.'

Diamond surprised Ingeborg by suggesting she alone should do the follow-up interview with Taki. 'She'll respond better to you. In kindness you should tell her Mikio's version of what happened the night she got drunk. If she's alone with you and more relaxed she may recall something of real importance.'

* * *

On the drive back to Bath, he said, 'Well?'

'Well what, guv?'

'Well, you're looking pleased with yourself. How did it go?'

'It was rather sweet. She wept a few tears, but they were tears of relief. She's given herself a hard time these last few months imagining what happened. I think they'll be back on speaking terms soon.'

'And did you get any more from her?'

Ingeborg smiled. 'I did. I asked about the musicians Mari was keen on. We'd talked earlier about the posters in her room, but we didn't get down to names.'

'We asked Mikio and he couldn't remember any.'

'Taki did. She said there was one string quartet that stood out and it was called the Staccati.'

'The name you brought up earlier?'

'Yes – because they're based in Bath.'

'Really?' He turned to look at her, eyes gleaming. 'How do you know about that?'

She played casual. 'Who's been doing the rounds of all the music colleges? I heard the name and remembered it, and what's more I've met one of the players.'

14

The four were united again for the next rehearsal at the Michael Tippett Centre. As if to compensate for the day before, they had a spat-free session, rounding off with an hour's bar-by-bar dissection of the *Grosse Fuge* and then a run-through.

'The best yet,' Ivan said, resting his instrument on its case. 'We can all improve our intonation, but that will come. Some of your playing was exquisite, Mel.'

'Thanks.'

'Some of it?' Cat said, laughing. 'Good in parts like the curate's egg?'

'I didn't mean that,' Ivan said.

'He can take a joke.' She turned to Mel. 'I liked your sound, too, sunshine, and Anthony won't say a word, but he was quietly purring at those last arpeggios.'

'Do we have a date for this recording?' Mel asked, to steer the attention away from himself.

'That's up to us,' Ivan said. 'We're not ready yet.'

'The recording studio has its own terrors,' Cat said. 'Personally, I prefer performing in front of an audience.'

'Don't we all?' Ivan said. 'I always find I can bring out something extra.'

'Is that one of your Ukrainian customs, bringing out something extra?' Cat said. 'Do that in public here, comrade, and you'll get arrested.'

Ivan clicked his tongue. 'Isn't it possible to say anything serious in present company?'

Anthony stood up and packed his violin away, indifferent to the banter as usual.

Cat said to him, 'Your turn to share a taxi with me and my cello, right? I'll phone for one now. Want me to order a second one, guys?'

Ivan said he was staying on to teach a student, but Mel said he was ready to leave.

When they reached the foyer only a few minutes later, a cab was already outside.

'Can't be ours,' Cat said. 'It's too quick.'

'I'll check,' Mel said.

The driver lowered his window and when Mel asked who he was waiting for, he said, 'Mr Farran.'

'That's me,' Mel said, surprised. 'Is the other cab on its way?'

'I wouldn't know, mate. I was asked to pick up Mr Farran, the viola player.'

'Fair enough.' He gestured through the window to the others that he'd got lucky.

It all happened so fast that the taxi was zooming along the road to Bath before he realised he hadn't given his address. He must have used this driver before, he decided. Often at the end of a rehearsal he felt so wrung out that he wouldn't have recognised his own father in the driver's seat. They were heading in the right direction, so he relaxed and thought about his plans for the rest of the day. He'd need to fit in more practice. In spite of the praise from the others, he knew Ivan was right. His intonation – accuracy of pitch – could be improved. With such latitude possible in their creation of sound, string players had a huge advantage over anyone else in an orchestra, yet there were phrases, say in a long legato line with open strings, when the pitch should be suppressed. He'd noted a couple of passages in the Beethoven when he needed to adapt better to the violins. Ivan would certainly speak up if there wasn't an adjustment next time they practised.

The taxi forked left at Park Lane, heading directly north past Royal Victoria Park – an odd decision considering Mel's lodgings were in Forester Road, north-east of the city. Cab drivers were a law unto themselves, so Mel didn't question the route. Maybe the man knew about some obstruction along the way. Or maybe he was putting another half-mile on the clock. If so, it didn't worry Mel, as all the fares went on the quartet's account and were settled by their agent, Doug.

But when they slowed to a crawl for no obvious reason he tapped on the glass. 'Hey, this isn't where I live.'

'All right, mate. It's under control. I'm picking up another fare.'

'What?'

'Just ahead. Your lucky day, by the look of her.'

A woman was waiting opposite the entrance to the Botanic Garden, hand raised for the taxi to stop. People sometimes shared when cabs were in short supply at the station, but this woman was behaving as if she was hailing an empty one. Mel was on the point of objecting before he saw what a dream she was. She could have stepped off the style pages of a weekend magazine. Blonde, in a short white leather skirt and black top, she was smiling as if she knew exactly who Mel was, even though he was sure he'd never met her. She wasn't in any way forgettable.

Mel was a ladies' man. Any lingering thoughts of protest went out of the cab door when it opened and a tidal wave of cleavage almost engulfed him.

'I'm Olga and you must be Mel.'

Distracted, he almost forgot to move his viola case from the seat beside him. 'How do you know my name?'

'Relax. It's all good news if you're up for it.'

'Up for what?'

She laughed. 'Wait and see. It seems a bit cloak and dagger, but from now it's champagne all the way.'

The taxi was already speeding along Weston Road. Mel had abandoned all thoughts of objecting to the extra passenger.

'Heavy practice this morning?' Olga asked. This close, her perfume was overpowering.

'I'm used to it.'

'But you're new to the quartet.'

'Newish. You seem to know a lot.'

'Only the essentials.'

'Where are we going?'

'The Royal Crescent Hotel.'

The taxi took the turn to Marlborough Buildings and was soon rattling over the cobbles in front of Bath's best-known thirty houses, a five-hundred-foot semi-elliptical terrace faced with Ionic columns. The crescent's position, high above the park with views across lawns and trees to the city, was intrinsic to its glory. Three months into his stay in Bath, Mel hadn't been here before. He was awed.

The famous hotel occupied the space for two houses at the centre, fitting unobtrusively into the architecture. From a distance the only way you could tell it wasn't private dwellings was a pair of ornamental trees in tubs either side of the entrance.

A doorman in dark blue livery stepped forward and opened the cab.

Mel was in such a state that he almost forgot to reach for his viola, an unthinkable oversight ever since he'd been mugged that time in London. He snatched it up and stepped out.

In the front hall, it became obvious Olga knew where to

go when she crossed the chequered floor to the staircase. Mel followed his new companion up the stairs as if her undulating bottom had hypnotic powers. Powers of some sort, for sure. Whatever she planned next he was unlikely to object.

The doors along the first-floor corridor had the names of well-known former residents of Bath. Olga stopped outside the John Wood suite.

'We have the use of this for the afternoon.'

Which beat working on the Beethoven, he decided.

She opened the door.

The suite was spacious and honey-coloured, with a padded sofa and armchairs at the centre and walnut furniture. The windows facing the front were elegantly pelmeted and draped in a gold fabric. To the left, discreetly recessed behind a white wooden balustrade, was a kingsize bed.

At full stretch on it was a man.

Mel came to an abrupt halt. A threesome wasn't in his thoughts, and certainly not a threesome in this combination.

Olga said, 'Mel, this is Mr Hamada. He doesn't speak much English so I'll need to translate.'

'That won't be necessary,' Mel said. 'You've got the wrong idea about me. I'm leaving.' He turned towards the door.

'No, please be reasonable.' She put her hand on his arm.

Something sharp but unintelligible was said from across the room. Mel glanced back.

Mr Hamada had sat up and removed himself from the bed. He was fully dressed in an expensive-looking suit. He stepped over the little balustrade, bowed solemnly and spoke some words in his own language.

Mel reached for the door handle.

Olga said, 'Wait.'

There was such unexpected force in her voice that he froze.

171

She went on with more moderation, 'Mr Hamada apologises for all the inconvenience, the secretive way you were brought here. As a passionate lover of music he has been looking forward to meeting you.'

Mel hadn't supposed this was about music, even though he was holding his viola in its case. After some hesitation he clasped the hand that was offered. Hamada had a strong grip. He was a short man, made shorter because he was in his socks. Mel guessed he was around thirty-five.

'He has a musical matter to discuss with you,' Olga went on, 'but join us first in a drink.'

The bottle was waiting on ice in a silver cooler. The strong grip made short work of the cork. A flute of champagne was placed in Mel's right hand.

'You don't have to hold on to your viola. You're with friends here,' Olga said.

'I won't be staying long.'

Hamada said something to Olga and she said, 'He's asking if he might see your instrument.'

'No chance.'

'He is very knowledgeable about them.'

'Then it won't interest him. It's nothing special.'

'But it plays well, obviously.'

'I'm comfortable with it.'

'Please allow him to see it. He's not fooling. He's a true connoisseur.'

'I don't care what he is. I was brought here under false pretences.'

'Believe me, Mel,' she said. 'It's very much in your interest to cooperate. This could be your lucky day.'

'That's what the taxi driver said before you got in. If this is luck, it's not what I expected.'

She smiled. 'You expected to be here alone with me? That was a little game and I'm sorry. Mr Hamada is my employer.

He has a wife and children. He came to Bath and reserved the suite specially to meet you.'

'I can't think why.'

'Please indulge him. I'll hold your glass.' She must have noted the subtle softening of his protest.

Mel sighed. 'He won't think anything of this.' He unfastened his case, removed the viola and handed it to Hamada, who gripped it by the neck and ran his hand lightly across the soundboard. Then he held it horizontally and examined the rib and the purfling along the edges. He studied the dark wood of the underside before speaking again to Olga.

'He says it's of English manufacture, early twentieth century.'

'He's right about that.'

Mel then heard Hamada say, 'William Hill.'

'Spot on,' Mel said in surprise. 'You do know your stuff.'

Saying you possessed a Hill viola could be embarrassing even among musicians if they weren't specialists in stringed instruments. The name didn't have the cachet of the great Italian instrument makers. Yet William E. Hill of Bond Street produced violins and violas of exceptional quality for fifty years as well as restoring a number of Stradivari instruments.

Nodding his approval, Hamada handed the viola back and spoke more words in Japanese.

'He's asking if you would be so good as to play something,' Olga said.

'I don't think so.'

'Please don't refuse. Just a few bars, to give him the measure of the instrument.'

With reluctance, Mel took the bow from his case, tuned the strings, and played the opening bars of Bach's Chaconne from the Suite in D minor, but a fifth lower, in G minor.

173

Just a snatch of the entire piece was sufficient to demonstrate the timbre of his viola.

Hamada nodded in approval and spoke again. Mel was getting the impression that this little man had a better understanding of English than he was letting on. The translation process kept him at a distance.

'He compliments you on the sound of the instrument and the choice of piece,' Olga said. 'He says he doesn't associate Bach with the viola.'

'It was written for solo violin,' Mel said, 'and transposed by Lionel Tertis, the English master.'

Hamada nodded at the name and spoke some more.

'He says Tertis, more than anyone in the world, raised the status of the viola. He played on an eighteenth-century instrument of exceptional quality.' She turned to Hamada to confirm the name.

'Montagnana.'

A distinguished, but lesser-known maker. Mel couldn't any longer deny that the man was knowledgeable. 'I wish I'd heard Tertis play. He lived to a great age, but he was before my time.'

Olga was translating for them both with apparent ease. She'd lured Mel here, but he still found her attractive. His playing of the Bach had been aimed more at her than her employer.

'Mr Hamada says when Tertis because of infirmity could no longer play to the standard he set for himself, he presented his precious viola to his pupil, Bernard Shore.'

'I didn't know that. How generous.'

This time Hamada didn't wait for a translation of Mel's response. He crossed the room to the wardrobe, opened the door and took a bulky object from the top shelf – an instrument case. He brought this to the middle of the room, placed it on the sofa and unzipped it. The case was modern, but the instrument inside was not. It was of viola length, at least the size of his own, but of lighter, thinly varnished wood, almost apricot in colour, obviously antique.

'So is he a player?' Mel asked Olga.

'A collector. What do you think?'

'It looks special.'

Hamada lifted out the viola and handed it to Mel.

The weight was lighter than his own fiddle.

Olga said, 'He is inviting you to play the Bach piece again, using his instrument.'

Not unreasonable, Mel thought. If you own a fiddle, you want to hear it. Aside from that, he was curious to try it himself. He liked the feel. Now that it was in his hands he could tell it was a fraction longer than his own, but about the same weight. He ran his fingertips along the board. Using his own bow, he began the tuning process. Then he started playing another excerpt from the Chaconne.

The projecting power was a revelation, the depth and fullness of tone a joy. He knew at once that this was an experience to be savoured, so he continued moving through the daunting multiple stops of Bach's composition for longer than he intended.

Hamada's serious look had been supplanted by open-mouthed admiration. And when Mel finally lifted the bow away, Hamada clapped and said, 'Bravo.'

His pulses racing from the experience, Mel did his best to appear calm. 'Who is the maker?'

Olga asked the question, listened to the response, turned to Mel and didn't give an answer. Instead she said, 'If you would be so kind, he would love to hear you play some more. We both would.'

No hardship. Mel launched into Kreisler's arrangement of a Tartini fugue written for piano and viola, yet possible to perform as a solo. He gave them the complete piece.

'Now may I know the history of this instrument?' he asked after finishing.

For the second time, Olga put the question to Hamada.

Mel listened keenly to the answer and wondered if he could believe his ears, or had confused the sounds.

Olga translated for him and confirmed the name of the maker. 'It's an Amati, from 1625.'

'Christ Almighty – I thought it was special.'

Four generations of the Amati family of Cremona were making stringed instruments from at least 1560. Nicolò Amati was said to have taught the craft to Antonio Stradivari and Andrea Guarneri. Amati violas were particularly prized because of their rarity compared with violins. Mel had heard of a 1613 Amati selling at auction for half a million pounds.

With reverence he replaced the instrument in its case. 'That was an experience I wouldn't have missed.'

Olga's eyes shone with amusement. 'Twenty minutes ago you were ready to walk out of here.'

'I had no idea what was coming. Any musician worthy of the name would kill to play a fiddle of that quality.'

'I hope not. We don't want bloodshed.'

'Mr Hamada must be a very rich man as well as a connoisseur.'

'He's both.'

'May I ask what his business is?'

'Shipping, mainly, but he has other companies as well. Your glass is empty.'

'My head is spinning and it isn't the champagne.'

Hamada took this as the cue to refill Mel's glass. He started speaking to Olga and it lasted some time.

She turned to Mel. 'He admires your playing. He says a great instrument needs to be played by a top musician. He arranged for you to come here because he wanted to hear

176

the Amati played by an expert. Now he is certain you must have it.'

'*Have it?*'

'On permanent loan.'

Mel felt the hairs straighten on his skin. 'That's incredible.' He knew millionaire patrons occasionally presented precious instruments to musicians. This was how rising artists came to play some of the finest fiddles in existence. He'd never imagined such an opportunity would come his way.

'How does Mr Hamada know about me?'

'He knew you joined the Staccati Quartet. They are respected throughout the world. They wouldn't play with an inferior artist. The instrument is insured, of course, and so well known to connoisseurs that it could not be stolen and sold on for anything like its true value, but he will expect you to take great care of it.'

'I'm still coming to terms with this,' Mel said. 'He's suggesting I take it away today?'

'This was always his intention. Stringed instruments are not meant to be kept in glass cases. If they are not played regularly they can deteriorate.'

'Believe me, this will be played every day if it's in my care,' Mel said.

A smile as thin as a stray horsehair briefly settled on Hamada's lips.

'Of course he reserves the right to reclaim it at any time,' Olga said, and she was speaking without any obvious prompting from her employer. 'But his view is that an instrument of such quality should be played, and by a leading player.'

'What am I supposed to do – sign an agreement?'

She shook her head. 'Mr Hamada's view is that even if you broke an agreement and failed to return the Amati, nothing you possess could compensate him. He is not

177

interested in financial compensation. This must be a pact of honour. On your side, to value the instrument and play it to its capacity. On his side, to make it available to you free of charge, to treasure and maintain in good condition.'

'That will be my privilege and pleasure.'

'And one more thing must be observed,' she said, still without obvious reference to Hamada. 'The loan is confidential. He doesn't like it known that he collects instruments or makes them available to top musicians. That's why this meeting was arranged in secrecy.'

Mel immediately foresaw a problem. 'Look, the other members of my quartet are sure to notice when I turn up with a new instrument and they'll see at once that it's very special.'

'You can admit that you have it on loan. I dare say you would find if you asked that theirs are not their own. But you are not to tell anyone that Mr Hamada is the owner. He would take that as a breach of faith.'

'Understood. May I take it to rehearsals – or is it just to be used in the concert hall?'

'I'll ask him.' After more consultation she said, 'He says play on this viola and no other. Put in as many hours as you can. It can take several weeks to adjust to a new instrument.'

'I know that from experience.'

'And in addition the rehearsal process must require you to use the same instrument so that the other players can blend with your sound. Does that make sense musically?'

'Perfect sense. I wanted to get the ground rules clear, so to speak. How will I stay in touch with you? Is there a contact number? Do you have a card, or something?'

'Mr Hamada will know where the quartet performs and practises. From time to time you may see him in the audience. Should it ever become necessary, we'll contact you.'

'Is there any time limit on this arrangement?'

'None – for as long as you and he stay alive.'

'We look to be about the same age.'

'Stay fit, then.' She gave him a long, level look. 'I believe he will.'

Mel faced Hamada again and gave a bow that would not have disgraced a Japanese ambassador. It was the best he could think of to demonstrate his thanks.

The same taxi was waiting in front of the hotel with the door open when Mel emerged carrying the two violas. In his state of unimaginable euphoria he climbed in. He continued to grip the handles, even when seated. He wouldn't dare believe he possessed an Amati until he got the little darling home, took it from its case and played something.

The taxi started over the cobbles.

'I haven't told you where we're going,' he said to the driver.

'It's all right, mate. They know where you live.'

Just for a second it was if a cloud passed across the sun, but he didn't let it trouble him.

15

'The Staccati String Quartet.'

The team stared at their boss as if he'd forgotten to dress. Peter Diamond as a classical music buff was hard to swallow.

'Come on. We already know the murdered woman, Mari Hitomi, was wild about music, and we're not talking reggae and rap. This is the serious stuff that goes on in concert halls. Ever heard of the *Nuns' Chorus*, DC Gilbert?'

'Sorry, guv.'

'This will be an education for some of you.'

John Leaman said, 'The *Nuns' Chorus* as a string quartet will be an education for us all.'

Diamond ignored the sarcasm. 'One of Mari's close friends called her a classical music groupie. I didn't know such things existed, but apparently they do – young girls as devoted to nerdy guys in white tie and tails as most kids are to their pop idols. Mari had posters of this string quartet in her bedroom in Yokohama. And for the past two months the Staccati have been resident in Bath.'

'Teaching and performing at the university,' Ingeborg added.

'I'm surprised you're all looking so open-mouthed,' Diamond said. 'They're world famous. This is the breakthrough, the reason the victim came here. Sergeant Smith will now give us her take on the quartet.'

Ingeborg unfurled a poster and pinned it to the board. 'The Staccati have been performing all over the world for at least fifteen years and this could easily be one of the posters Mari had in her room. To be accurate, only three of these people are currently in the quartet. They changed their viola player recently. We'll get a picture of the new guy soon.'

'Are we treating professional musicians as murder suspects?' John Leaman asked.

'Because they can read music it doesn't make them saints,' Keith Halliwell said. The tension between these two never entirely went away.

'Hold on,' Diamond said. 'All we can say for sure is that the string quartet looks like being the reason Mari came to Bath. She was a fan, so she must have known they were based here. Who killed her and why is another question.'

As if she hadn't been interrupted, Ingeborg said, 'I met the new viola player while I was doorstepping the colleges of music. He's a Brit, thirtyish, friendly enough. We didn't talk long, but he showed me where the quartet do their rehearsals out at Newton Park – the Michael Tippett Centre, on the Bath Spa University campus.'

'Michael who?' Halliwell said.

'Only one of the greatest British composers of the twentieth century,' Leaman said to the rest of the room.

'He lived in Corsham and was a strong supporter of university music,' Ingeborg said. 'But I was telling you about the quartet. They teach a series of master classes and in return for a six-month residency give regular concerts.'

'How regular?' Diamond said.

'Every two weeks.'

'Not bad if you can get it,' Gilbert said.

'It's not a cushy number,' Ingeborg said. 'There are hours and hours of rehearsing. They've got a reputation to keep up.'

'Who are they?'

She tapped the poster. 'The bald guy on the left is the first violinist, Ivan Bogdanov, a Ukrainian and one of the founder members. Lived in the West since he was a young man. Learned his music in the old Soviet Union and played with the Moscow Chamber Orchestra until he decided to defect.'

'And the others?'

'The second violin is Anthony Metcalf, from South Africa originally. There isn't a lot on the internet about him, except he joined about seven years ago and fitted seamlessly into the quartet. A very gifted violinist apparently. Their website suggests he's the quiet one. The guy to the right of him is Harry Cornell, the one they replaced, so we can forget him.'

'When did he quit?' Halliwell asked.

'About four years ago, I gather,' Ingeborg said. 'He was their viola player. They tried a number of replacements, but none of them cut the mustard until Mel Farran came along this summer.'

'The large woman with the cello?'

'Cat Kinsella, said to be among the best in the world and with several recordings of cello concertos to her credit, but prefers ensemble playing to the life of a soloist. She's the other original member of the quartet along with Bogdanov.'

'Those are the players, then,' Diamond summed up, wanting to move on. 'A mix of talented people who make very good music. They've got a strong fan base, which is where Mari Hitomi comes in.'

'You said they give concerts,' Halliwell said. 'Are we assuming Mari came to Bath to attend one of them?'

'Good question,' Ingeborg said. 'These soirées, as they call them, are supposed to be for the university community. They're held in big houses like Dyrham and Corsham Court, and the tickets are distributed among the staff, with some music students included as well. They're not open to the public.'

'So if Mari wanted to hear the quartet . . .?'

'She'd have to wait for the Bath Festival, when they're due to perform.'

'Next May,' Leaman said, eager to confirm his status as the only true music expert.

'How else would she get to meet them?'

'Depends,' Ingeborg said. 'A groupie – if that's what she really was – would find a way. If you were nuts on one of them you'd break any rules to get up close. Stalking them, or posing as one of the music students. Nothing would stop you.'

'Ever go through a phase like that?' Leaman asked Ingeborg.

She gave him a glare that could have pinned him to the display board. 'That's got sod all to do with it.'

'Just trying to understand the female psyche. You sounded as if you were speaking from experience.'

'My only ambition at her age was to get into CID. Shows how misguided I was.'

'And who was your idol? The guv'nor?'

'John, get back in the knife box,' Diamond said. 'We're doing a job here. We know Mari left London on September twentieth. We believe she took the train to Bath instead of Exeter. There may have been sightings of her. With her picture in the paper we ought to find out soon if she was here long, if she stayed anywhere. But we also need to know what the Staccati people were doing, where they lodge, how they spend their time off, the company they keep and so on.'

'Whether one of their concerts coincided with Mari's time here,' Ingeborg said.

'You think she gatecrashed a concert?'

'Tricky. They're not listed on the website, being private.

But if she found out they were performing she could have gone to the venue and waited outside.'

Keith Halliwell said, 'A random killing. Someone sees this young woman hanging around on a dark night.'

'A sex attack?' Gilbert said.

'Who can say?' Ingeborg said. 'The pathologist couldn't tell us. She ended up strangled and dumped in the river, that's all we know for certain.'

'All options are open,' Diamond said. 'Meanwhile, we work with what we know. She was a fan of the Staccati, but was it one of them in particular that she idolised?'

'Not the old Ukrainian guy,' Halliwell said.

'Why not?' Diamond said with a touch of injured pride. 'There's such a thing as a father figure.'

'Sorry I spoke.'

'And if any of you are thinking not the big cello lady, let's remember girl on girl is not out of the question. Okay, to be realistic, the second violinist looks the part.'

'Eye candy,' Ingeborg said.

'Ike who?' Leaman said.

She ignored that. 'And you're right, guv. My mind was wandering. Anthony Metcalf is the good-looking one. Isn't that what you're saying?'

'The pin-up boy.'

'Don't forget the guy who isn't on the poster,' Leaman said. 'The viola player, Mel Farran.'

'He's new,' Halliwell said. 'Mari wouldn't have known about him.'

Ingeborg was quick to correct him. 'Not all that new. These things get written up in music magazines and on the internet. She may well have heard of him and seen his picture. He's nice-looking too.'

'Before anyone makes anything of that, here's the game plan,' Diamond said. 'What we've heard from Ingeborg is useful, but basic. Most of it comes from the Staccati website. It's their publicity material. By the end of the day I want the inside story from the people themselves.'

'As soon as that?' Leaman said.

'This afternoon.'

'There's more to discover, that's for sure,' Ingeborg said.

'You're all in on this. Get them talking about themselves. They'll be used to that, so make sure it's not just the standard spiel. Interrupt, question, challenge, get to the truth of how this quartet functions.'

'I thought we were focusing on Mari,' Leaman said.

'You won't get many answers out of her,' Halliwell said, and got a few smiles.

'John's got a point,' Diamond said. 'We'll ask if they had any dealings with Mari before she arrived here and if she approached them in the hours leading up to her death. But that could be a short interview. This is our chance to get to know these people. Be alert to everything they tell you, suspicious incidents, strange goings-on. What they've experienced could be the key to this investigation.'

'So how do we handle this?' Ingeborg asked.

'It's our team taking on their team,' Diamond said. 'Keith, you can tackle Ivan Bogdanov. John, yours is Anthony Metcalf. Ingeborg has already met Farran, so she can deal with him.'

'Does that leave me with the cellist woman?' Paul Gilbert asked.

Diamond was kind enough not to say so, but you only had to look at the poster to see that the youngest member of the squad would be eaten alive by Cat Kinsella. 'I'll take her on myself. You can do some research on the mysterious violist who quit.'

'There's also a manager,' Ingeborg said. 'He seems to work from an office in London.'

'We'll catch up with him later. What's his name?'

'Douglas Christmas.'

Diamond couldn't let that pass. 'I may have sat on his knee. A hoodie with a big white beard? Forget it. You lot are way behind me.'

Ingeborg had checked with the university music department and found that the Staccati would be in rehearsal at the Michael Tippett Centre the same afternoon.

'Perfect,' Diamond said.

'They may not welcome it,' she said. 'They've got one of their soirées tomorrow night. This could be their last rehearsal.'

'They can do overtime. We have to.'

'Musicians can be temperamental.'

'So can I. Haven't you noticed?' He gave the matter more thought. 'Let them know we're coming and it shouldn't take long. A concert tomorrow night, you said? Where are they playing?'

'Corsham Court.'

'I'm thinking I should hear this lot.'

Ingeborg didn't comment. She had an inkling of what he would say next.

As if he'd just thought of it, he said, 'Care to come with me?'

'Well . . . ' she started to say.

'Good, I'll need someone to stop me from clapping at the wrong point. I'd prefer you to John Leaman if you can make it.'

'John knows far more about classical music.'

'But you're better company. Have you got a little black dress? This sounds like a smart occasion.'

Ingeborg didn't pursue the matter of the little black dress. She thought she had another escape route. 'I heard these concerts are hard to get into. There's a long waiting list.'

'Don't worry. I'll get Georgina to pull some strings. She moves in high circles.'

'Perhaps she'd like to partner you.'

'Get outta here.'

The team descended on the Michael Tippett Centre early the same afternoon. They commandeered four practice rooms for interviews before any of the musicians showed up. As a result they were able to separate the quartet as they arrived. A united front might have been difficult to deal with.

Anthony Metcalf was the first. A glaze came over his eyes and he allowed himself to be escorted into a side room by Leaman. As a result, Ingeborg was able to inform Mel Farran when he showed up that interviewing was already under way.

She'd met Mel on her previous visit here. Knowing who she was, he should have been calm, if not relaxed. So it came as a surprise when he appeared startled and on the verge of panic, clutching his viola case to his chest as if Ingeborg was about to snatch it away.

'It's okay,' she said. 'You're not in any kind of trouble. We're looking for help with an ongoing enquiry.'

Still twitchy, he allowed himself to be shown into the woodwind room.

Ivan Bogdanov was difficult in another way. 'It's out of the question,' he told Halliwell. 'We have a performance tomorrow and we need to practise.'

'The sooner we get through, the more time you'll have,' Halliwell said.

'And if I refuse?'

'I arrest you and do it at the police station, ask to see your work permit and proof of identity, take your fingerprints and DNA.'

This put a swift end to Ivan's protest.

Diamond was left to meet Cat Kinsella when she appeared, short of breath, grasping her cello. 'Sorry, young man,' she told him as he brandished his ID. 'No autographs now. I'm late for rehearsal.'

He told her what he was there for. Shaking her head, she allowed him to escort her to the remaining practice room. Once she had rested her cello case against the wall and perched herself precariously on a stool behind a drum kit, Diamond drew up another stool and showed her a picture of Mari.

'Ever seen this young woman before?'

She shook her head.

'She's a major fan. We think she came to Bath specially to see you.'

'Not me, detective. One of the guys, possibly, but not me. I don't have female fans, nor male, now I think about it. I'm past all that.'

'The passions are on their side. You'd only find out if they threw themselves at you.'

She chuckled at that. 'Get real. I'm a cellist. I don't strut about the stage in skimpy underwear and sequins.'

'But you won't deny there are classical music groupies out there who follow the quartets?'

'There may be a few crazies. Is that really what she was? She looks normal enough in the picture.'

'She could have had a crush on one of you.'

'You'd better find out from the men.'

'We're doing that right now. Have you ever performed in Yokohama?'

'Never.'

'Anywhere else in Japan?'

'Tokyo a few times.' Her face softened as she thought back. 'There's a place called Katsushika Symphony Hills. I remember it because of the Kat bit. Huge. Two halls, one seating over a thousand and the other three hundred. In my innocence I thought they'd booked the small hall for us. I was wrong. Every seat was taken in the thousand-seater including one in the front row occupied by an urn containing the ashes of a man who'd booked to see us but died a few days before.'

'That said a lot.'

'Actually, no. Not a damn word.'

He smiled. 'So if Mari had come to see you, she'd have had to travel to Tokyo. That's not a vast distance from Yokohama.'

'I'll take your word for that. Geography passed me by when I was in school. Let me tell you something about quartet playing. You have the score on a stand in front of you with a little light over it. If you look up and you can see anything at all above the light, it's rows of identical heads looking faintly like the beads on an abacus. You don't recognise people.'

'Thanks for explaining,' Diamond said, genuinely pleased she was speaking more freely than she had at the start. 'Let's talk about the quartet. You were one of the founders, right?'

'With Ivan, yes. Back in the last century, that was, when I was young and easy, as the poet said. To be truthful, I wasn't easy, I was bloody difficult. Always have been. I'm surprised Ivan ever asked me to join, but the time was right and I jumped at the chance.'

'You were a soloist before?'

'Going right back, I was one of those child monsters, an infant prodigy. We're Liverpool Irish, the Kinsellas, and my dad played the fiddle around the pubs. My mum was red-hot on the squeezebox. They got me started early and pushed me hard. Recorder, flute, piano, violin. I can knock out a tune on almost anything. Don't ask me why, but I was drawn to the cello. There are all kinds of Freudian theories I draw the line at discussing in polite company, or police company, come to that. I started to play when I was nine and must have looked ridiculous wrestling with it. You need to be an athlete. It's easy for a cellist to get musclebound. But I adored it – the sound, the sweet, rich voice was all that I wanted. So at a young age I got through the drudgery of mastering the thing and won a scholarship to music school in Manchester. You must have heard of Chetham's.'

Diamond tried to look as if he had.

Cat was into her story anyway. 'They worked wonders with me and put me in for Young Musician of the Year. Didn't win, but made the final and got noticed. I must tell you – and you won't believe this – in those days I was thin enough to slot into a toaster. Long, blonde hair that I wore in a pigtail. Anyway I learned the repertoire and at fourteen had the cheek to play the Dvořák with a youth orchestra and overnight I was touted as the next Jacqueline du Pré. They wanted me to loosen my hair and record the Elgar looking all frail and angelic. That's what she made her debut with and is mainly remembered for, but of course she could play anything. She was the real deal. Did you see the movie?'

'Somehow it passed me by,' Diamond said.

'Far better to watch some footage of Jackie herself. There's a lovely video of her with Barbirolli. And to think that they wanted me to ape her just to get famous. Catriona Kinsella, aged fourteen and a half, dug her heels in and said she wanted to be herself. Sucks to the Elgar and sucks to wearing a long white dress. It was a teenage rebellion in a music context. Everyone, my parents, the school, the marketing people, bore down on me and said I was flushing a brilliant career down the toilet. The battle went on for almost a year. I started eating, seriously stuffing myself with chocolate, fried foods, pastry, the lot. In a matter of weeks it started showing and in a year I was the lump of lard I am today.'

'Your way of taking control of your life?'

She raised her right thumb. 'Tell that to WeightWatchers. I shaved my head as well in case anyone missed the point. I continued to play, of course. The joy has never gone away. I've played as a soloist with some of the great orchestras. Vivaldi wrote twenty-seven concertos and I've learned almost all of them. What I absolutely refused to do was put myself in the clutches of the popular classical music merchants. If you follow music at all you'll know the process. They take second-rate artists with pretty faces, groom them, call them the voice or the player of the century and turn them into stars, whether they're singers, violinists, pianists. The quality of the sound is crap, they're off-key, and the great gullible public doesn't seem to notice. I could find you literally hundreds of finer voices and better players completely overlooked.' She stopped and shook her head. 'I've lost my thread, haven't I? This is one of my pet beefs.'

'You saw off the vultures.'

A broad smile. 'That sums it up. I might have made millions, but as a musician I'd have been dead meat. When all is said and done, you keep your musical integrity. These second-rate performers know they cashed theirs in. So I scraped away in an orchestra making real music and no money. Gave lessons, did some work on film scores and TV commercials. That's allowed in my scheme of things. I wasn't cheating anyone. This went on for a few years until I met Ivan and he told me he was thinking of forming a string quartet. Ask any string player and they'll tell you that's their dream, to play in a high quality quartet.'

'How did you meet him?'

'Ivan? In the Liverpool Philharmonic. I was temping for a month, but he was the leader. Very solemn, very earnest. I didn't think we'd get along at all, and I was gobsmacked to be asked, but desperate enough to give it a try. Ivan is all

191

right, a bit pompous, only it's not self-conceit. That would be death to any ensemble. He respects the music and his tone quality harmonised with mine from the beginning. That's as vital as technical ability.'

'I expect if he gets too serious you know how to bring him down to earth?'

'I do my best. He doesn't lack emotion. You hear that in his playing. He just finds it difficult to express his feelings in everyday life. We were talking about Japan just now. Ivan used to visit the geisha houses and I always thought that was a perfect arrangement for him, very proper, with clear rules, just like the chess he plays. He'd be waited on and entertained by these gorgeous young women. No hanky-panky at all. Hints of it all around, but the rituals forbid it. He felt secure. He doesn't like surprises.'

'How does he deal with all the success?'

'Of the quartet? He doesn't let it go to his head.'

'The groupies?'

'You're on about them again? Listen, Ivan's not a young man. If he was in danger of making a fool of himself, which isn't likely, I'd tell him. I keep my boys in order.'

Diamond believed her. He was getting a useful insight into how the group functioned. 'Getting back to the time when the quartet was formed, how did you find the others?'

'We needed a second violin and a violist. Ivan knew of a Ukrainian called Yuriy and I remembered Harry from a summer school I did at Dartington. Two totally different personalities. Yuriy was a bear of a man. You'd expect him to have been a percussionist, but he was a red-hot fiddle player. I think there was gipsy blood in him. He'd launch into gipsy music in the middle of a rehearsal discussion just for a laugh, or to take the heat out of an argument, and it always worked. He was great company and a good influence on Ivan, but he did over-indulge with the vodka. I think he got lonely. He had a wife back in the Ukraine and they'd separated on some understanding that they'd stay in touch. Eventually he went back to her. Happy ending for her – I think – and not so happy for us.'

'And Harry?'

She sighed and shook her head slowly. 'Poor, benighted Harry. He was my recommendation, so I still feel responsible. A gifted violist, no question. He adored the instrument and talked it up at every opportunity, which made him an easy target for viola jokes, of which there are many. He was with us a long time, but I never felt I got to know him as well as I wished. On tour, he'd clear off and not say a word about where he was going. We all did our own thing. I hit the shops, Yuriy the bars and Ivan the local chess club.'

'Or the geisha house.'

'When possible. You don't find many of those on the average tour.'

'So where do you think Harry went?' he prompted her.

'None of us knew and he didn't encourage us to ask. He'd be back for rehearsals and play divinely, so we had no reason to complain until the day he didn't show up.'

'Don't you have any theories?'

'Got into bad company, I suppose, but whether it was of his making or theirs, I don't know. We were in Budapest at the time. He must have had his viola with him, because it wasn't found at the hotel. It was a Maggini worth probably two hundred thousand pounds, and it didn't belong to him. He had it on extended loan from some rich patron. This happens. We poor beggars can't afford instruments of that quality and the owners buy them as investments and want them played. Harry vanished and we found some dreadful stand-in from a local orchestra. We sounded like four cats stranded in the Battersea Dogs' Home. For months after that we were a lost cause. Couldn't fulfil our bookings. We didn't know if Harry would suddenly reappear. It would have been easier if he'd just put a gun to his head. At least we could have looked for a replacement.'

'In the end, that's what you did.'

She pulled a face. 'With mixed results. A series of violists who weren't up to it musically. There's a treacly, sentimental tone – a lingering in the action of the slide – that is death to any quartet. We heard it from the first guy and told him in the nicest way to look for another job. The next stand-in was a woman whose fingering was sloppy. She couldn't sustain the vibrato and it ruined our tone quality. I think she didn't have the expressive feeling within herself. When we asked her to make the sound continuous it was worse, forced and insincere. God knows, we tried and she did, too, but it was obvious it would never work. She knew it. She walked.'

'Was that when you found Mr Farran?'

'Mel? After a much longer gap. We'd just about broken up. Anthony – he's our second violin and a whole different story – became so impossible that Doug found him a job with the Hallé. The Staccati was a forgotten group. Quartets are breaking up all the time and everyone in the music world assumed we were finished, but dear old Ivan wouldn't accept it. He's a brilliant player and he could find work anywhere and yet he loves quartet playing and he wouldn't accept that we were through. He used all his contacts to look for a truly gifted player and Mel's name kept coming up. Luckily for us he wasn't committed to any orchestra so we pounced. Good result, too. He's fitted in well.'

'Better than Harry?'

She hesitated. 'It's early days. Harry knew the rest of us and our quirky ways so well. He was a lovely guy and I miss him. The day he disappeared I toured the streets of Budapest looking for him. I still would if there was any realistic hope. But Mel is shaping up nicely.'

'This has been helpful,' Diamond said. 'A real insight into the quartet. The one you haven't said much about is Anthony.'

'Special case,' she said.

'In what way?'

She shook with laughter. 'You name it. I'll say this. Anthony is a terrific violinist. Technically he has the edge on Ivan, but I wouldn't want either of them to know I said that. He could make it as a virtuoso if his head was right.'

Diamond leaned forward and almost fell off the stool. 'What's wrong with it?'

'Not exactly wrong, just out of balance. He sees the world in a different way from the rest of us. Very focused. His power of concentration is amazing. But he has no sense of humour and he makes no allowance for the feelings and opinions of anyone else. Music is all-important to him. His work-rate is phenomenal. He'll master a new score sooner than any of us. It used to worry me that he had no life outside the quartet. Over the years I've come to accept that he found his goal in music and he wants nothing else. Any change of arrangements can throw him. That's why Harry going was a major crisis. I seriously feared Anthony would kill himself if we didn't get playing again. It's that essential to him.'

'A personality disorder?'

'I would say so. Have you heard of Asperger's?'

'I don't know a lot about it.'

'It's a form of autism, but the people who get it can still function at a high level.'

'Is that what he's got?'

'It's in that area. They call it the autism spectrum, apparently.'

'How did you recruit him?'

'We needed a second violin to replace Yuriy.'

'Who returned to his wife in the Ukraine?'

'Yes. And almost at once Anthony appeared and asked for an audition. News travels fast in our little world and he'd got word that Yuriy had quit. I'm not even sure Yuriy had actually left. It was obvious at once that this earnest young man was twice the player Yuriy had been. He told us frankly that he'd pulled out of three string quartets and a trio in two years because they weren't up to standard and we looked at each other and wondered if we would make the grade. He was so damn good that we decided to give it a whirl. In the first weeks he was with us it felt as if we were on trial, not Anthony.'

'Did you go on tour with him?'

She laughed. 'It was a hoot. In many ways he's like a baby. The basic things in life pass him by. He forgets to shower, to eat breakfast, to carry money. He can't be relied on to pack. You tell him and he'll do it. Next time you have to tell him all over again. Between us, we cope with him and get a few laughs along the way. Anything you say, he takes as gospel truth so we have to be careful not to speak ironically. Once at rehearsal I had a noisy chair – a regular hazard for cellists – and I said in jest that I'd had baked beans for lunch. "No you didn't," Anthony says. "You had an egg and mayo sandwich. I saw you." Fortunately he's right up with the music, and that's what counts.'

'How is he with the audiences?' Diamond asked.

'I don't think he's aware of them. He's immersed in the music.'

'You meet some of them afterwards, no doubt?'

She pointed at Diamond. 'Hey, this is the groupie question in another guise. You're a sly one.'

'Better answer it, then, in case I turn nasty.'

'The leeches get nowhere with our Anthony.'

'They're going to try. He's good-looking.'

'We know that, but he doesn't. He has no self-image. If they just want an autograph he'll sometimes oblige even if he can't fathom why it's required. If they ask a musical question such as the most common one – "Is your violin a Strad?" – he'll answer. But if they were to ask what he's doing after the concert he'll tell them he's going back to the hotel for a room-service meal and a sleep, which is true. End of conversation. He's got a way of dismissing them with a look.'

'So you don't think it's possible he could end up spending the evening with a woman through some misunderstanding of the sort you mentioned?'

'She'd need to be very devious. And she'd need to understand how his strange logic works.'

'And if he felt he'd been tricked?'

Cat shook her head. 'I don't know. I don't even like to think about it.'

'Doesn't he like women?'

'He isn't capable of liking anyone, male or female. If you're asking me about his love life, there isn't any. He goes to sex workers when he gets randy. Paying for it suits his mentality. No relationship, no affection. And he feels no shame. He'll tell us straight he was with a whore next time we meet. I expect he'd say exactly what happened if we asked. He can be very candid.'

'Yet you say he's a brilliant violinist. Isn't it all about expressing emotion through the way you play?'

'Right on. And communicating emotion to your audience. He succeeds and that's the biggest mystery to me. It's almost as if he comes alive through the instrument. Pathos, tenderness, humour, even love. Where it comes from I can't tell you. His soul, I suppose, finding an outlet that doesn't exist in the locked-up person he is.'

This was getting into areas outside Diamond's competence.

'The only person I haven't asked you about is your manager.'

'Doug? He's normal enough and that's a good thing. He looks after the business side, makes sure we earn enough to survive. All the gigs and recording sessions are down to him. He tells us when and where and we decide what. The musical decisions are ours.'

'So was it his decision to bring you to Bath?'

'We wanted a residency, a chance for the new combination to gel. Being in one place is so much better than touring when you're adjusting to a new member. From what I recall, Doug got on the phone and found out quickly that Bath Spa University were looking for some kind of professional ensemble to teach and play. We agreed the same afternoon.'

'How is it working out?'

'Wonderfully, apart from you lot giving us the third degree.'

'I wouldn't call it that,' Diamond said.

'You're not on the receiving end.'

'These concerts you give. They're small by your standards, aren't they?

'Intimate. They're lovely. That's how quartets were played originally, for small, invited audiences in gracious surroundings.'

'I'm hoping to attend your next one.'

'Really? You don't strike me as a string quartet aficionado.'

He smiled. 'I don't claim to be that.'

'I hope you don't suffer, then.' She glanced at her watch. 'Is the grilling over now?'

'Not yet,' Diamond said. 'You said there are lots of viola jokes. I can't think of one.'

She tilted her head back. 'If I tell you one, am I released without charge?'

'Only if it's a good one.'

'All right. This man walked into a bank carrying a viola case. Why did everyone get nervous?'

'They thought it was a machine gun?'

'No. They thought it was a viola and he might take it out and play it.'

16

'Mine wasn't much help.'

'Mine was an obstacle race, and I don't think I won.'

'Mine was a waste of time.'

'Snap out of it, guys,' Diamond said. 'You're supposed to be professionals.'

Leaman shrugged. 'He refused to talk about anything except the music they're rehearsing.'

'This was Anthony Metcalf, the second violin?'

'I'd get more sense from a talking clock.'

The debrief was taking place in a quiet corner of the senior common room at the Michael Tippett Centre. The team had helped themselves to instant coffee from a jar marked *staff only*. In one of the practice rooms nearby, the quartet had begun their delayed rehearsal.

'Anthony thinks of little else except music,' Diamond said. 'I heard that from Cat Kinsella, who was good company once she got warmed up. Even told me a joke.' He put up his hand. 'Later. Did any of you get a reaction when you showed the picture of Mari?'

Leaman and Halliwell shook their heads.

Ingeborg said, 'Mel Farran reacted. He actually calmed down quite a lot when he saw it. Before that he was a different bunny from the one I met here before.'

'Different in what way?'

'Tense. He sat clutching his instrument case across his

200

knees like a barrier. I've seen women hold their handbags like that. It's unusual in a man.'

'Not many blokes have handbags,' Leaman said.

She looked at him as if he was something she'd trodden in. 'I don't know what Mel thought I was going to ask, but I got the impression it wasn't about Mari.'

'Does he have form?'

'No, I ran a check. He's clean.'

'So what did he say when you gave him a sight of the picture?'

Ingeborg's eyes rolled upwards. 'Said he never forgets a pretty face. Then he smirked a bit. He sees himself as God's gift to women.'

'You've changed your tune,' Leaman said. 'He was nice-looking and friendly when we last spoke.'

'He's still nice-looking and friendly – and he still thinks he's God's gift.'

'So not one of them appears to have met the victim,' Diamond said.

'Mel did admit Mari could easily have been in the audience at one of the concerts and he wouldn't have known.'

Diamond aired the small piece of expertise he'd learned from Cat. 'Because they have a light on the music stand and they can't see anything over it?'

'No. Because they concentrate on the music.'

He tore open three strips of sugar for his coffee. 'Disappointing, then. No apparent link to our victim. It's only our assumption that she came here to listen to her favourite string quartet.'

'I can't be entirely sure how much Anthony knows, or how little,' Leaman said, and for once he wasn't trying to score points. 'I showed him the picture and he hardly gave it a glance. Wasn't interested.'

'Did you ask him the question?'

'Had he met her? He said he was a musician – as if that said it all.'

'In his case, it probably does,' Diamond said. 'He has some form of autism. People don't interest him.'

Ingeborg took a sharp breath. 'So it's entirely possible Mari spoke to Anthony and he paid no attention.'

Halliwell was some way ahead of her. 'And he killed her and dumped her in the river and blanked it from his mind.'

'I find that impossible to believe,' Ingeborg said. 'Anyway, why would he do such a thing if he's only interested in music?'

Halliwell turned up his palms to show it was mainly guesswork. 'Mari became a nuisance, got in his way.'

'How?'

'She was a groupie, like we said.'

'I get you now.' She nodded. 'He's the poster-boy, the one most likely to have attracted women.'

'Okay,' Diamond said. 'I'd better have a try with Anthony.'

'You won't get anywhere,' Leaman said, blunt, if not actually insubordinate.

Diamond carried on as if no one had spoken. 'I'm not sure if he really can't recall things, or if he just doesn't want to talk about it.'

'Using the autism as a get-out?' Halliwell said.

'That's got to be considered.'

'I said you're on a loser,' Leaman said.

'I expect you're right, John, but I'm having a go.' He turned to Halliwell. 'You said Ivan Bogdanov was an obstacle course. What did you mean by that?'

'Treated me as if I was the KGB. Kept talking about his rights and what a waste of his precious time it was and how we ought to be hunting the real killer instead of persecuting innocent musicians.'

Leaman smirked. 'You mean he didn't melt under the Halliwell charm?'

'You slay me.'

Diamond asked, 'Did he respond at all when you showed Mari's picture?'

'Claimed he hadn't seen her. I asked him if the fans ever became a problem and he took the line that people who appreciate good music keep their distance. If he's hiding anything, he's well defended.'

'Ivan is a chess player. I got that from Cat. She respects him. In fact, she spoke well of all of them. Sees herself as the mother hen. She wants the quartet to succeed.'

'They all want that,' Ingeborg said. 'They've got a name, a reputation, a cosy little number here in Bath. It's in their interest to stay together now they've got a good viola player. They'll cover up for each other, I'm sure of that.'

'The question is,' Diamond said, plucking at the lobe of his ear, 'do they have anything to cover up?'

The practice went on for almost two hours before the quartet took a break. When the door of the rehearsal room opened, Diamond was waiting outside. The rest of the CID team had already left for the police station.

Cat emerged at speed and made a beeline for the ladies' room. Her reaction to Diamond was to raise both hands. 'Not now.' Over her shoulder, she added, 'Talk about groupies. You're one of them.'

Diamond stepped into the rehearsal room.

Ivan looked up, but not to welcome the visitor. 'You people have a damn nerve. What is it now? We're in the middle of a practice.'

'A few words with Anthony during your break won't hold you up.'

'Anthony's already answered questions.'

'Not from me.'

'He's within his rights to refuse.'

'If you want to talk about rights, we can take up all of the break before I even start to question him.'

'Intolerable.' Ivan looked across the room to where Anthony was studying the score, apparently oblivious of what was being discussed. 'This policeman wants more time with you. Can you spare him a couple of minutes?'

Diamond said, 'He'll spare me as long as it takes.' He curled his finger at Anthony, turned and left the room, confident that he would follow.

And he did, entering the percussion room and seating himself on the stool behind the drum set.

Diamond looked the young man up and down and understood Ingeborg's remark about the dark good looks. The high, narrow cheekbones and finely shaped mouth were likely to appeal to any woman, however stone-faced Anthony appeared. The unattainable has a strong sexual attraction. A confident woman would expect him to respond to the right signals.

A burly male detective had no such optimism. Getting any kind of response would be a challenge. But there was one thing that might work in Diamond's favour. People with autism generally speak the truth if they say anything at all. They are honest to the point of rudeness.

Start on safe ground, he decided. Get the man talking about what he knows best. 'How's the practice going?'

'Okay.'

Better than no answer at all. 'Preparing for tomorrow's concert, are you?'

This time Anthony settled for a nod.

'Beethoven, wasn't it?' Diamond ventured.

Anthony was supposed to get the idea that Diamond was a fellow lover of music. He didn't show a glimmer of appreciation.

'I couldn't place the piece,' Diamond added, which was

true. He was about as capable of placing a piece of Beethoven as he was of riding a Derby winner. 'Do you mind telling me what it was?'

'Opus 59, Number 3,' Anthony said.

'Silly me. I'm a duffer with numbers.'

'In C major.'

'C major.' Diamond raised his thumb as if all had been made clear. 'Any particular part?'

'The fugue.'

'And to me it sounded just as a fugue should.'

'It was too fast.'

'A shade quick, I'll give you.'

Hearing this, Anthony with his care for the truth must have assumed he was in the company of a connoisseur. 'You're right about that. Beethoven's tempo instruction is just about impossible.' Now he wanted to discuss the playing of the fugue, which would be a minefield for Diamond.

'I didn't appreciate that,' Diamond said, 'about the tempo instruction.'

'It's a metronome mark.'

'Does that make a difference?'

'The metronome wasn't invented when the piece was written.'

This was information any self-respecting detective could work on. 'Beethoven added his note at some later date?'

Anthony nodded. 'Much later, when he was stone deaf.'

'So you think he got it wrong?'

'It's meant to be quick and energetic, but . . .'

'Not so quick as you played it?'

Anthony made a fist and held it up in solidarity with Diamond. 'You're right. Something is lost at the tempo he gives. I keep telling Ivan to slow up a touch. The music is without fault. It can take it. He won't listen. He's implacable. He treats the score as gospel.'

'Don't the others have something to say about it?'

Anthony shook his head.

'Maybe they don't want to make an issue of it,' Diamond suggested. 'Cat is all for peace and harmony and Mel is too new to the quartet to take a stand.'

From Anthony's wide-eyed look this was an insight he had missed. 'Do you play?'

Diamond shook his head. 'Too busy with other things, unfortunately.'

'But you know Beethoven.'

'I wouldn't go that far.'

'You can speak to Ivan, tell him you were listening to us and it was too quick.'

'Me? He wouldn't take advice from me.'

'For all he knows, you could be one of our audience.'

'With luck, I will be tomorrow night, but I'm in no position to tell a man of his experience how to play.' He was fast running out of musical conversation, but he knew it was the only way to make progress with Anthony. 'Is there an interval?'

Anthony frowned. 'It's full of intervals.'

'Not the music. I mean a break during the concert for people to walk about.'

'That will be too late.'

'I'm not planning to speak to Ivan. I was wondering what comes after.'

'After the interval? Some solo pieces.'

'From you?'

Anthony shook his head. 'The others.'

'All three?'

'All three instruments. Violin, viola and cello.'

'Nice. I can't wait. But what about you? I heard you're a brilliant violinist. Don't you give solos?'

The lips tightened.

'Sorry I asked,' Diamond said. 'You're more of a team player?'

No response. After going so well, this had hit the buffers.

'Do you happen to remember what music you played in the first few concerts the quartet gave?'

'Yes.'

Anthony's precise responses came with the mental condition. They could be a barrier to progress when you expected more. 'I'd like to be told,' Diamond said.

'Beethoven Opus 131, Quartet Number 14 in C sharp minor. Schubert Number 14 in D minor. Haydn Opus 74, Number 3 in G minor. Shall I continue?'

'Wonderful, but no need. And do you also recall where you played?'

Anthony frowned. 'No.'

'I heard you go to some splendid houses, perfect for chamber music.'

'I've forgotten.' The gracious drawing rooms of Somerset and Avon, their Baroque splendour enhanced by candlelight, had already been deleted from this young man's discriminating memory. Only the music counted for anything.

'They don't make an impression?'

'I'm not there for the architecture. You can ask one of the others.'

'But you remember every note of the music? Am I right?'

'Not every note. We have the score in front of us.'

'And how was your playing received?'

'All right.'

'Would you happen to remember if one of the audience spoke to you afterwards about your playing?'

'Depends.'

'On what?'

'What they had to say. If it was only praise I wouldn't bother. We get a lot of that.'

'I'm sure it's all well meant,' Diamond said. 'Is there anything you *would* remember?'

'Intelligent remarks.'

'Intelligent remarks about what?'

'The music.'

One relentless track.

Diamond took a deep breath and tried again. 'Such as?'

'Such as the stress we give to the fourth note in the opening of the Beethoven Opus 131, Number 14. Ivan is the player, not me, and it's a signature moment that sets the tone for all that follows. It can sound disruptive, the transition from G sharp to A. They're separated by a full bar. He draws it upwards a fraction on the G and then slips back to the same pitch after leaving the A.'

It was about as clear to Diamond as the second law of thermodynamics. 'Thank you for explaining. Did one of the audience raise this with you?'

'Yes.'

'A woman?'

'A man.'

Another hope dashed.

'Can you think of a comment a woman made after one of those early concerts?'

Anthony frowned, as if deciding whether the question came within his span of attention. 'One told me our performance of the Schubert was superior to the recording she has of the original Staccati. Since then I've listened to the piece myself, and she was right.'

'Do you remember who she was, this woman who spoke to you?'

'The wife of the man who owned the house.'

In his long career, Diamond couldn't remember an interview as tough as this. Each door slammed shut before he could get inside. 'Wasn't there another woman who approached you, a younger woman, Japanese?'

'I don't remember.'

'You would if she had something of interest to say about the music.'

Anthony shrugged as if to say, 'You tell me.'

Now it was Diamond's turn to be logical. 'I can't tell you because I wasn't there. Have you played with the quartet in Japan?'

'Yes.'

'The Japanese like classical music, don't they? I expect some of them are very knowledgeable.'

'Yes.'

'You see, I'm wondering if a certain young woman who heard you play in Tokyo, or wherever it was, loved your playing, came to England this summer and got herself into one of the soirées the quartet gave. She could have introduced herself after the concert and told you she was a fan.'

'Plenty do,' Anthony said.

'Plenty of Japanese women?'

'All sorts. I don't pay attention to fans.'

'But you would pay attention if she made an intelligent comment about the music?'

'I told you that already.'

Diamond decided the only way forward was an appeal to Anthony's better nature. 'Help me, Anthony. Try and remember. Whatever she said may not have seemed worth listening to at the time, but it could be important. She was Japanese and her name was Mari Hitomi and you've seen her picture before.' He took the photo from his pocket.

There wasn't a glimmer of recognition.

'If she didn't have anything to say about the concert, she may have asked a question about your violin, how old it is, how valuable, who made it, whether you have other violins.'

A shrug and a shake of the head.

'She could have asked you to autograph her programme.'

'I wouldn't remember that.' Anthony looked at his watch. 'I must get back. The others will be ready to start again.'

'She had a musical note tattooed on one of her upper teeth.'

'A quaver,' Anthony said at once, 'on the lateral incisor, right-hand side. Right to me, left for her.' He didn't add, 'Why didn't you ask?' but Diamond felt as if he had. Even so, it was the breakthrough he'd been working for.

'Did she say anything to you?'

'She must have, for me to notice the tooth.'

'Do you remember what was said?'

'It couldn't have been important.'

'Take another look at the photo. Is this the woman?'

'I don't know. I can't see her teeth.'

'But is the face familiar?'

'I told you I don't remember faces.'

He got no further with Anthony.

Before allowing the quartet to resume their rehearsal, he addressed them as a group. 'You've all been shown a photo of a Japanese woman called Mari Hitomi who was found dead in the river Avon a few days ago. We happen to know she was a fan of the Staccati Quartet visiting Bath about the time you began your residency here. Earlier, each of you claimed you hadn't seen her before, but I have since learned from Anthony that he was approached by a woman of her description after one of the concerts you gave. He spotted the tattoo of a music note on one of her front teeth and this leads me to believe this was Miss Hitomi. Obviously this is significant. We'll need to ask more questions of each of you and I'm advising you as individuals to contact me if you have any more information about her.'

Nobody spoke for several seconds. Then Ivan said, 'Are you telling us we're under suspicion?'

'I was careful with my words,' Diamond said. 'I'm seeking information.'

Cat said, 'You want to be careful about what Anthony tells you. He's a sweetie, but his memory isn't the sharpest when it comes to anything other than music.'

'Thanks, but we'll treat everything we learn from any of you with the same respect.'

'I didn't say he isn't honest. He's the most honest guy you could hope to meet.'

'I'll second that,' Ivan said. 'We trust him totally.'

17

After Diamond had said his piece and left, Ivan stated in a few trenchant words that he wanted to get straight back to work on the Beethoven without any more being said about the Japanese woman. Nobody objected. A surge of energy in the second part of the rehearsal reflected the tension among the quartet. They played Opus 59, No. 3 from the beginning. This time when they reached the fugue they attacked it with a pulsating tempo that almost did justice to Beethoven's impossible metronome mark. The intensity of the task galvanised them all, yet the bowing was crisp and always under control. It was as if they were resolving their own anger through the playing – anger at Diamond, the police and the suspicion hanging over them.

'I think we're in shape,' Cat said after they lifted bows from strings and sat back.

'It was a better rendition, without question,' Ivan said in a rare expression of satisfaction. 'And this new viola of Mel's has a richness in tone that I, for one, welcome.'

'You should,' Cat said. 'We all should. That's a Cremona fiddle if ever I heard one. 'Fess up, Mel. Where did you nick it from?'

Mel had a powerful urge to put the precious instrument out of sight in its case. He had a lingering disquiet about the way it had come into his possession. 'It's an Amati, from 1625.'

'Then it must be the work of the last and greatest of the family, Nicolò Amati,' Ivan said. 'About that time there was a famine and plague that killed every other violin maker in the city. May I?' He held out both hands.

The request to handle the antique viola was understandable. For Mel, the act of passing it across was a wrench. A mother with her newborn child couldn't have felt more protective. Of course it would be safe in the hands of another musician, he told himself. If you can't trust the members of your own quartet, you shouldn't be one of them.

He steeled himself and placed the Amati in Ivan's hands.

Ivan turned it over and stroked the maple surface, tracing the grain with his fingertips. 'Exquisite. A thing of wood, hair and gut that can touch the soul and lift the spirit.' One-handed, he raised it by the neck. 'Nice weight.' He tucked it under his chin. 'Good length.'

'Watch out, boys,' Cat said. 'Our first violin is about to change into a violist.'

Mel decided he had better explain how he came to possess such a treasure. 'I was approached by a collector who wants it played.'

'Nothing unusual in that,' Ivan said. 'It would be difficult to name a soloist who didn't at some stage play with an instrument loaned to him.'

'Or her,' Cat said.

'He made me promise not to reveal his name.'

'The super-rich have their reasons, which is why they stay super-rich. Don't be so anxious, Mel,' Cat added. 'You look like the stick insect who found himself in the middle of a rave-up.'

'I can't help it,' Mel said. 'Some years back, when I was starting out as a professional musician, taking any work that came my way, I was mugged outside the Royal Festival Hall and had my viola snatched. They were clever. A girl looking

213

like a student, pretty, Asian, asked me for my autograph. I had my fiddle in its case under my arm and while I was distracted by this girl some guy on a bike pulled the thing from me and rode off with it. I gave chase all the way down to the river and I thought at first he'd slung it in, but there was a speedboat nearby and they may have collected it and got clean away. I never saw my viola again and I've never forgotten the feeling of loss.'

'You're afraid of someone stealing this?'

He nodded. 'My old fiddle had sentimental value and I was deeply affected, but as a responsibility it doesn't compare with this.'

'A salutary tale,' Cat said, 'but you're safe with us, kiddo.'

Ivan was still holding the Amati. 'I can't resist.' He picked up his bow and played the C string from heel to point, pianissimo, long and slow.

'You've kissed goodbye to it now,' Cat told Mel. 'Is anyone else going to get a try? Anthony is practically wetting himself.'

In the end, they all took a turn at handling the Amati, although no one else played on it. Mel was deeply relieved when Cat handed back the object of so much admiration, if not envy. He stowed it in its case. This should have been the cue to leave, but there was unfinished business.

'So what are we to make of that policeman?' Cat said before they left their seats.

'Nothing,' Ivan said at once. 'We make nothing of him. He's a distraction. He has his job to do and we have ours. The fact that the unfortunate young woman was an admirer of ours is a trivial coincidence. Life is full of chance events.'

'I doubt if Detective Diamond sees it that way, O Wise One,' Cat said. 'He struck me as a man without much faith in chance events. We had enough hassle from the *Polizei* when Harry disappeared. I think we'd better brace ourselves for more. Did he rough you up, sweetie?' she said to Anthony.

'No.'

'Offered you plastic surgery and a safe house in Outer Mongolia?'

'No.'

'Then how did he wear you down?'

'Kept asking questions.'

'Well, he's a smart guy if he got an answer. I've known you six or seven years and most times I can't get two words out of you.'

'Will you listen to me?' Ivan said. 'We're musicians and we have a performance tomorrow night. The last thing we need is to get involved in speculation about a death in suspicious circumstances.'

'Too late,' Cat said. 'The big detective means to rub our noses in it.'

'He'll go away if we ignore him.'

Then Anthony announced, 'He said he'll be at the concert tomorrow.'

There was a shocked silence. Ivan chewed at his thumbnail.

'See what I mean?' Cat said. 'Don't kid yourself he's coming to listen to Beethoven. He'll have a pair of handcuffs in his pocket.'

'We've done nothing wrong,' Mel said.

No one spoke.

'Have we?' Mel broke the silence, looking at each of the others.

'You wish,' Cat said finally with a peal of laughter. 'Don't all speak at once. Now let's organise our taxis.'

Mel was to share with Ivan and both taxis were slow in coming. Cat climbed into the first with her cello, assisted by Anthony. Before it drove off, she called out of the window,

'We're hearing over the intercom that your cab went to the tip instead of the Tippett. He's stuck in the garden waste queue. Could be another hour.' Their taxi zoomed away.

'That woman doesn't amuse me,' Ivan said. 'Never has.'

'Was she making it up?'

'Of course she was. Three-quarters of what she tells you is made up. Ours won't be far behind.'

Mel had spotted a stationary black saloon car parked at the edge of the approach road. Someone was in the driver's seat. 'Could that be it?'

'Where?'

He pointed.

Ivan sniffed. 'It looks to me like a private car. Probably waiting for some student.'

'I might go and ask. Stupid if he's waiting there and we're standing here only thirty yards away.'

'As you wish,' Ivan said. 'I've never known them to park there.'

With his cased viola gripped to his chest, Mel strode towards the parked vehicle. True, he couldn't see any writing on the side or any sign that it was licensed. Sometimes it was difficult to tell.

He hadn't gone ten yards when the driver started up, made a screaming U-turn that must have left rubber on the tarmac, and drove off at speed, just missing a student on a bike.

Shaking his head, Mel returned to Ivan's side. 'What was that about?'

For once, Ivan had no answer.

'Bloody dangerous,' Mel said. 'Someone could have got killed.'

'Yes,' Ivan said. He'd turned pale.

Their transport arrived soon after, a recognisable cab with a Bath Spa Taxis emblem on the roof.

Most of the journey was in silence. The reckless driving of the car seemed to have affected Ivan. Mel tried saying something about the venue for the soirée and got one-word answers. It was like being with Anthony. 'See you at Corsham tomorrow, then,' he said when the taxi stopped outside his lodgings. 'Early as usual to get ready?'

'Yes,' Ivan said.

Inside the house, Mel closed the front door as quietly as he could, crept upstairs, let himself into his room and slid the precious Amati viola under the bed. Later, he would practise scales, still getting the measure of this marvellous new outlet for his talent. For now, playtime of a different sort was overdue. He stripped to the waist, washed at the hand-basin in the corner, refreshed the deodorant and the aftershave, put on a fresh shirt and checked his hair in the mirror. Then he reached to the back of his sock drawer for two miniatures of gin and a small can of tonic and left his room to cross the passage to Tippi's bedroom. She liked her G&T and Mel liked the result. It took the edge off her sarcasm and made her even more randy.

He didn't knock. They had an understanding. He opened the door and said, 'Better late than never, huh?'

'Late for what?' said a voice he didn't expect.

Tippi's mother, with a crocodile smile, was sitting on the bed.

A better man might have thought of some clever excuse. Mel sighed and said, 'Fair cop.'

This was no bad response, as it turned out, because it avoided an elaborate lie and had a sense of contrition. Mrs Carlyle must have been expecting some tall story she could lay into. Instead she was thrown off course. Rather than attacking Mel, she started to account for her own behaviour, explaining what she was doing in her daughter's room. 'I came up here to put away some of her washing. She leaves it for days on the clothes-rack in the kitchen if I don't, and she may not mind you seeing her frillies, but I'm old-fashioned enough to think it isn't quite the thing.'

Mel nodded as if he approved every word.

Mrs Carlyle said, 'Is that gin and tonic you're holding, Mel?'

'Would you like some?' he said, pleased to find anything to say that wouldn't land him deeper in trouble.

'I wouldn't mind, but not here. We don't want Tippi walking in and finding us.'

'True.'

'Heaven knows what she'd think Mummy was up to. Bring it across to my room.'

Mel had alarming doubts of his own about what Mummy was up to, but he'd offered the drink and he couldn't easily refuse. 'Is she about?'

'Carry the booze across and I'll tell you.'

He felt he had no option.

'Last door on the left,' Mrs Carlyle said. 'Don't be surprised how bijou it is. When I took a lodger I switched rooms.'

He pushed open her bedroom door. Certainly it was small, and dominated by a double bed that was a nest of pink, with ruched satin along the headboard and sides. The walls, too, were pink, with a design of ribbon and roses.

'Don't stand on ceremony,' Mrs Carlyle said. 'Make yourself comfortable on the bed. I don't have room for a chair, as you see. I have to perch on the edge of the mattress when I'm using my dressing table.'

Uneasily he lowered himself into the softness of goose down and foam rubber. He was facing the window, which was mostly covered by pink velvet draped in two deep curves held by tiebacks. He couldn't help thinking it was the shape of a pair of enormous buttocks.

'There isn't much choice over seating arrangements, is there?' Mrs Carlyle said. She took her place beside him and they both sank a few inches deeper. 'Yours is the master bedroom, which is right and proper for a masterful man.'

'I wouldn't say I'm masterful.'

'We'll find out presently. I'm ready for that snifter now.'

He felt the warmth of her hip against his. In this new predicament he'd almost forgotten he was still holding the miniatures. 'Do you have a glass?'

'Not here. Let's be depraved and drink the gin straight from the bottle and chase it with the tonic.'

'All right.' He handed her one of the gins.

She unscrewed it and tipped the contents straight down her throat.

He handed her the tonic and she took a gulp of that.

'Nice,' she said. 'Next time, we can do it properly with my Waterford glasses and ice and lemon, but you made an offer I couldn't refuse. Seize the moment, I say. Do you believe in seizing the moment?'

'I like a drink, if that's what you mean.'

'How old are you, Mel, if you don't mind me asking? And don't say old enough to sit on a lady's bed and sink gin. That's self-evident.'

'Twenty-nine.'

'Are you sure? Not an itsy-witsy bit over thirty?'

'It's the truth.'

'You just appear more mature than that. Far be it from me to complain. The reason I asked is that I was lying here on the bed a couple of nights ago thinking about you – in a totally innocent way, I must add – and it struck me that you must be quite a bit older than Tippi.'

'Tippi?' Mel said as if he hadn't heard of her. 'I've no idea. How old is she?'

'Eighteen last August twentieth. Not quite a Virgo.'

Mel couldn't follow that, so he looked steadily ahead.

'And I had her when I was twenty-one, so I'm thirty-nine, only ten years older than you. Do you realise what that means?'

'Not really.'

'You're closer in age to me than you are to Tippi.'

'Is that a fact?' he said with all the enthusiasm of a man told that a pit-bull terrier wanted stroking.

'And I was reading in the *Daily Mail* that it's become very fashionable for men to be attracted to women older than they are. It's all about sophistication and experience, on the part of the women, I must add. I'm not saying men aren't sophisticated and experienced about certain things we won't go into – not after only one G&T – but when a knowledgeable woman takes the initiative it enriches the man's enjoyment, and I can understand why.'

Was this a try for more gin? It could be a way of escape if he could leave the room and find some reason not to return. A sudden emergency? A blackout? A coronary?

'The shame of it is that there's this wealth of experience in my generation that men aren't aware of,' Mrs Carlyle continued while Mel was weighing the options. 'They get distracted by young things who know nothing at all. Surface impressions are so misleading, Mel. A pretty face with a figure to match and they think that's all there is in life. What fools they are. And the biggest fools are the old fools, middle-aged men who chase after girls scarcely out of school.'

Mel wouldn't mind betting Tippi had left school two years ago, at sixteen, the earliest possible opportunity. She wasn't the brightest. But he'd got an opening here. He could take a strong line and get out of this unscathed. 'Are you talking about me, Mrs Carlyle?'

'Cyn,' she said.

'I don't follow you,' he said, already undermined.

'My first name is Cynthia, but I prefer Cyn if we're getting on closer terms, and you don't need to state the obvious. If I've heard it once, I've heard it a hundred times.'

'Well . . . Cyn . . . I didn't like the drift of what you were saying. I'm not a middle-aged predator.'

'Lord love us, Mel, it wasn't you I was talking about. It was the man who parks his car across the street and sits there waiting for her.'

Another surprise. She was full of them. 'Who's that?'

'Don't ask me. I don't know anything about him except he's no spring chicken. Anyone can see that.'

'What's he like?'

'Quite good-looking, dark-haired going grey at the sides. I've been watching him through the binoculars I use when I'm watching the birds on my feeders. He's forty if he's a day.'

'When did he first appear?'

'A couple of days ago.'

'Is he there now?' Mel started to get up.

Mrs Carlyle grabbed his arm and pulled him down again. 'He'll see you. It's better to look through the lace curtains downstairs.'

'Shall we go down, then?'

'He won't be there now. Tippi went out for a manicure and he'll know that. He's probably parked outside the shop.'

'Are you sure it's Tippi he's interested in?'

She giggled a little. 'What are you suggesting, Mel – that I'm the star attraction?'

This wasn't what Mel was thinking. It was far more likely some crook had got a sniff of the Amati. 'As the man of the house, I'd better go downstairs and check. Where do you keep your binoculars?'

'They'll be where I left them, on the sill in the front room. I'll come with you.'

'No need.'

'I insist.'

Any excuse to be out of here, he thought – and the man in the street interested him as well. He took the stairs fast, with Cyn Carlyle not far behind. He grabbed the binoculars. 'Which direction?'

'A little to your right if he's still there. Oh, I say. That's him, our stalker.'

Mel adjusted the focus and felt his blood run cold. He was looking at a black car, a Megane, and he was pretty sure it was the same car that had raced out of the forecourt of the Michael Tippett Centre.

There was definitely someone in the driver's seat, but in shadow.

'I think it's me he's tailing,' he said, handing the binoculars to Mrs Carlyle. 'I've seen him before. I'm going out to have a word with him. Shut the door after me.'

'Is that wise?' she said.

Mel was already through the door and crossing the street. He headed straight for the car at a fast step, but the driver was faster. Two massive roars from the engine and the vehicle was in motion.

Mel was about to cross in front of it, to the driver's side. When the car powered away from the kerb, he jerked to a stop and took a step back. Even so, it caught his right leg below the knee, tipped him off balance and threw him on to the road. It was a good thing he wasn't any closer or he would have ended up dead. As it was, his left hand and arm took most of his weight. His shoulder crunched against the tarmac and his head followed.

The driver must have known he'd caused an accident, but he didn't stop. Mel watched the car race to the far end of the street and over the crossroads without a flicker of the brake lights.

Crazy. It had to be the same fool who'd been at the Tippett Centre. The pity of it was that Mel still hadn't got a sighting of him.

Shaken and angry, he heaved himself into a sitting position. His hand was smarting. There was grazing from the smallest finger to the heel of his palm. Blood was starting to ooze from the flesh. And this was the hand he used for fingering. He didn't think anything was broken, but it could so easily have been. He got to his feet, checked that nothing else was coming up the street, and returned to the house.

The door was opened by Mrs Carlyle. 'Are you all right?'

'Just about.'

'You're not. You're bleeding.'

He looked at the hand again. 'It's not serious. I'd better run some water over it.'

'That was masterful,' she said.

'Idiotic, in my opinion.'

'You, not him,' she said. 'He could have killed you. He wasn't going to stop. It's a disgrace. I'll call the police right away.'

'Don't do that. I don't want all the hassle.'

'I think I should.'

'It's more trouble than it's worth. I didn't get the number. Didn't even get a proper look at the driver.'

'He shouldn't get away with it, whoever he is.'

'Can I use the tap in the kitchen?'

She followed him along the passage and ran the water for him. 'Look at your hand, you poor dear. Is it painful?'

'It's numb. It just needs cleaning.'

'I'll get some paper tissue. I was so impressed by you, Mel, dashing out there to deal with the stalker. He panicked at the sight of you bearing down on him.'

'Did you get a look at him?'

'No,' she said. 'My eyes were on you alone. You're shaking.'

'I'm not surprised.'

'I'm all of a quiver myself. What we both need is a socking great G&T. Shall we go to the master bedroom and see if the master has any more supplies?'

'My legs wouldn't carry me up there,' Mel said. 'Right now all I want is a strong black coffee.'

18

The only member of CID claiming to know anything about classical music was John Leaman, so next morning he got the job of listing all the Staccati tours and concerts he could trace from the internet. The quartet's website was unhelpful. It had obviously been relaunched recently with all the emphasis on the current players. Whoever had designed it was under instructions to gloss over the problems of the past four years, so there was no detailed log of past performances. A summary of the cities they had visited and concert halls they had played in was provided, but without dates. He had to look for the information elsewhere. By degrees he got there. In their prime they had toured widely and earned rave reviews, but it became obvious that they had done little as an ensemble since 2008.

'When exactly was it formed?' Diamond asked.

'Sixteen years ago,' Leaman said. 'Ivan Bogdanov and Cat Kinsella were founder members. The others are replacements for people who left.'

'And who was Staccati?'

There was some sniggering behind the computer screens.

Leaman studied his boss's face, uncertain if he was being led into a trap. 'It's a musical term for short notes sharply separated from each other, from the Italian, *staccato*, meaning "detached".'

'Strange choice,' Diamond said with an effort to cover up

his ignorance. 'It's the opposite of what you want for a team of people. They ought to be called Unison. That's what they should be projecting.'

'It hasn't held them back. They were very successful, up there with the best, doing concerts across the world and making recordings – until the viola player dropped out.'

'Dropped out or dropped dead?'

'He went missing on one of the foreign tours and wasn't heard of again.'

'Ah, yes. Harry . . .?'

'Cornell.'

'Cat told me about him.'

'It threw them right off course. Big efforts were made to find him. Interpol were notified. The theory seems to be that he gambled heavily.'

'On what?'

'Casino stuff. They think he got on the wrong side of some bad people and was taken out.'

'Gambling doesn't fit my idea of a classical musician.'

'It comes with the territory. Quartets, in particular. Four is the right number for card games. The Budapest were well known for playing bridge, and for high stakes. I think the Amadeus preferred poker.'

'But that's in-house. You're telling me Harry Cornell played with professionals.'

'And rather badly. It's the best guess, that's all.'

'I still can't see it, a serious musician wasting his time gambling.'

'Plenty have, from Mozart to Elgar. It could be to do with calculating the odds. There's a well-known link between music and maths.'

'I'll take your word for it,' Diamond said. 'So when Harry went missing, why didn't they get a quick replacement? They were famous. They could take their pick.'

'It's not so simple. For a long time they expected he would turn up again so they couldn't offer anyone regular work. They performed with stand-ins who didn't cut it for one reason or another. The mix has to be right. Everyone has to blend in. You may find a brilliant soloist who can't work with others. It's as much about temperament and team-building as musical ability. They were unlucky or unwise in their choices and for a time they went their own ways.'

'Broke up?'

'In all but name. Some time last spring they found this new man Mel Farran and he seems to be doing okay. It clinched the residency at Bath for them and soon they'll be touring again.'

'If they aren't involved in a murder trial.' Diamond picked up the printout of Leaman's list. 'Is this their itinerary? They certainly travelled. I heard about the Japan trip from Cat.'

'They've been there a few times.'

'Was this with Anthony on board?'

'The last couple of visits.'

'When Mari was probably in the audience. I'm assuming Anthony was the main attraction.'

'Why him in particular?' Leaman asked.

'Obvious, isn't it? Good-looking, intense and a brilliant violinist. I expect she wasn't the only young girl who lay awake thinking about him.' Diamond continued to study the list. 'Budapest was where Harry went missing. Before that they were touring other European cities. Paris, Rome, Vienna.' He stopped. 'They performed in Vienna in October 2008?'

'A city noted for its music,' Leaman said.

'I know. I was there this summer.' A tingling sensation crept over his face. He called across the room to Ingeborg. 'Remember the Japanese woman you researched for me who drowned in the Danube canal?'

'Miss Kojima.'

'I don't recall the name. I doubt if I even asked you. This was something I didn't want to get involved in for personal reasons.'

'She took her own life.'

'So they reckoned. They found the little ivory thingummy representing suicide.'

'The netsuke.'

'Didn't you tell me this happened as much as four years before I was there?'

'That's right, guv. She wasn't a student, like Mari. She was in her mid-twenties, from Tokyo, and she'd come to Europe as a tourist, apparently alone. Do you think there's a link?'

'I don't know, but I intend to compare dates. If this happened while the Staccati were performing in Vienna, we could be on to something.'

'I'll check right away.'

Images that pained him coursed through his brain. The embankment beside the Danube canal. Paloma spotting the bunch of lilies on the ground and then seeing the other flowers, dead and brittle, forced between the lattice struts of the stone wall. He'd insisted on moving on and she'd refused to treat it as an unknown tragedy that didn't concern them. She'd seemed to think discovering the lilies in their path and replacing them in the pathetic little shrine was significant, a symbolic call to find out the true facts about whoever had died.

Against all his instincts he'd pandered to her superstition, getting Ingeborg to check the story on the internet. The way he'd dealt with it, trying to steer Paloma away from the depressing story once he had related it to her, had led directly to another unhappy waterside encounter, this time beside the Avon, their argument and break-up. In her eyes he was a lost cause, a stony-hearted professional unwilling to open up to sympathy for others or even for himself.

The whole episode still pained him deeply. In an effort to move on, he'd been trying to put it out of his mind, but without much success.

And now it might touch on the case he was investigating,

Ingeborg looked up from her computer screen, 'Found it, guv. The body in Vienna was discovered on the tenth of November, 2008.'

'Yes, but when was she reported missing?'

'I'm not sure if she was.'

'Nobody noticed she'd gone?'

'She wasn't travelling with friends or family. When they found the body, they estimated she'd been in the water three to four weeks, which would make it October.'

Trying to sound calm, he checked the list in his hand. 'When the Staccati were giving a series of concerts in Vienna. A Japanese girl. A canal. The quartet in town. I should have been on to this before now. Was there any evidence that the dead girl, Miss . . .'

'Kojima.'

'. . . was into classical music?'

Ingeborg shrugged. 'I don't recall anything like that. I can access the report again.'

'Where did you find it?'

'In one of the Vienna papers. It wasn't a huge story. I had to read it in translation.'

'Get it on screen again, everything you can. I'm going to call the Viennese police. And the Japanese embassy. They were helpful over Mari, but it always takes longer than you expect to get anything out of these government agencies.' He'd written the name of the Vienna victim and the estimated date of her disappearance on a notepad he'd picked up from one of the desks and he now saw that the

229

top sheet was smeared with black ink. It was all over his hand as well. In his fury with himself he'd squeezed the pen so hard that it had splintered and leaked. 'Okay,' he said, addressing the entire room. 'I want the full life histories of each of the Staccati people – everything we know about them – on my desk before the end of the afternoon. And when I say Staccati I'm including previous members and the manager. What's his name? Christmas.'

'Douglas Christmas,' Halliwell said.

'Yes, he's part of it. He may have an office in London, but he makes the key decisions and I wouldn't mind betting he turns up for the foreign gigs.'

From across the room someone had started humming a tune.

'Who's that?' Diamond said.

Silence shut everything down like a power cut.

'Come on,' Diamond said. 'Share it with us.'

Everyone in the team knew it was best to come clean when the boss was in this sort of mood. The junior member, Paul Gilbert, cleared his throat and started up again with a half-hearted rendering of the old Band Aid number, "Do They Know It's Christmas?".

'That's more than enough,' Diamond said, flapping his hand. 'You must be older than you look. I was a mere youth when that came out. If that's your take on my comments, DC Gilbert, you'd better investigate Mr Christmas. Make him your specialist study. Get his background, how he took on the quartet and where he was at the time of these two murders. With your investigative skills we can look forward to finding out if it really is Christmas.'

Gilbert had got off lightly. Humour can be the saving grace of something as grim as a murder investigation, but it has to be well timed. He'd picked the wrong moment.

*　　*　　*

The evening soirée at Corsham Court had taken on an added importance, a chance to see the four main suspects in performance. Ingeborg collected Diamond from his home in Weston and watched him wedge himself into her Ka.

'You're looking different, Sergeant Smith,' he said when he'd got the belt across his middle.

'Is that meant as a compliment?' She'd fastened the blonde hair high on her head with two glittery combs and was in a burgundy-coloured suit.

'Statement of fact.'

'Now come on,' she said, laughing. 'If we're supposed to appear like a couple enjoying an evening of culture, you'd better start acting the full gent. It's a posh do, this one.'

'Okay, you look like the Queen of Sheba. How's that?'

'Better.'

'Better? It's spot on. It's a musical reference, in case you didn't know. What do you think of my get-up?' he asked.

'Not very different.'

'It's the best I've got. Will it pass?'

'It passed a good ten years ago. If you want a musical equivalent, it's the "Dead March" from *Saul*. Are we quits?'

'But this is my best tie.'

'I'd call that the *Pathétique*.'

'You win,' he said. 'Don't know enough to compete. Seriously, am I dressed right for a soirée?'

'You'll get by, guv – just about.'

'Good enough.'

'If we sit at the back.'

'I didn't get a lot of time for thinking about my wardrobe. I was still at the office at six, on the line to Vienna.'

'Any joy?'

'They promised full cooperation. This was the police I'm speaking of. They regarded the case as closed, but they're

231

willing to send over everything they have on file. And the Austrian embassy are going to look at their records.'

'It's worth pursuing,' Ingeborg said. 'Too close to our case to be a coincidence.'

'I just wish I'd cottoned on before this.' He checked for the crease in his trousers and found two. Should have been more careful before hanging the suit last time he put it away. 'Is there much socialising at these things?'

'I couldn't tell you. I haven't been to one.'

'There's got to be some. You do the chat and I'll drink the bubbly and watch the action.'

Corsham Court, off the A4 to Chippenham, is a grandiose hotchpotch of English architecture, originally Elizabethan and home over the centuries to the elite of Wiltshire families, the Hungerfords, the Thynnes and the Methuens. They all brought in builders, with mixed results. Even the illustrious Capability Brown had a go. As well as landscaping the grounds and extending the building he converted the East Wing into a magnificent picture gallery, and this was the setting for the Staccati concert.

The guests were assembling in the anteroom, where it soon became obvious that most of them knew each other. Diamond spotted several who could be numbered among the great and the good of Bath society.

'Forgot to wear my chain of office,' he muttered to Ingeborg as they faced each other on the fringe of the gathering.

'What's that, linked handcuffs?'

'Where are the musicians?'

'They'll be tuning up. Can't expect them to circulate.' She froze.

'What's up?'

'Don't look round. Someone you know just came in. Keep talking to me.'

'Who is it?'

'Your friend Paloma.'

His voice went up an octave. 'Paloma? Here?'

'She's with someone. I don't think she's seen you. They're on the opposite side, near the fireplace.'

'Who? Who's she with?'

'A guy in an expensive suit. Can't say I recognise him.'

Diamond's above-average blood pressure soared to well above average. Who was this dog's dinner Paloma was partnering? The prospect of her taking up with someone else hadn't entered his head. He glanced over his shoulder. 'Which side of the fireplace?'

'This side. They're being served drinks. You could look now.'

Paloma was in an outfit he hadn't seen before, black, with a wispy blue scarf or pashmina. She looked taller. New shoes. Extra high heels. She was laughing at something, clearly enjoying herself.

The dog's dinner was taller than Diamond – allowing Paloma to wear the high heels without towering over him. He was also slimmer and younger. Certainly had more hair and it was only slightly silver at the sides. In a dove grey three-piece suit, he exuded privilege and class. Even had a pink tie.

Diamond had no idea who he was.

'Take it easy, guv,' Ingeborg said.

'I'm okay,' he said through clenched teeth.

'You're staring.'

He took a deep breath and looked away. 'When everyone goes in, we'll hold back and let them find seats. Then we can make sure we're not too close. I need another drink.'

The champagne was coming round on silver trays. He reached for a glass, downed it fast and took another.

'You might need to get to a seat earlier than you think,' Ingeborg told him.

'She's had her hair done differently.'

'I wouldn't let that bother you, guv.'

Someone in a pinstripe and purple shirt who seemed to be acting as host approached them with another man in tow. 'Here am I, doing my best to introduce people and I don't even know your names.'

'Ingeborg Smith.'

It took a nudge from Ingeborg to get Diamond to speak his name. Mentally he was over by the fireplace.

'Bathonians both?' the host man said.

'Locals, yes,' Ingeborg said.

'This is Mr, em . . .' The host turned to the other man.

'Christmas. Doug Christmas, the manager of the quartet, down from London.' Dark, with longish hair brushed back, he flashed a smile, but more at Ingeborg than Diamond. 'I do my best to smooth the way for them.'

'Did you arrange all this, then?' Ingeborg asked Christmas after the host had moved on to make more introductions. Diamond, still in a state of shock, plainly wasn't up for polite conversation.

'Not tonight's concert. That's down to the university. They have the use of some offices here, so they have a foot in the door, so to speak. Have you heard the Staccati before, Ingeborg?'

'Not like this, not live,' she said. 'We're looking forward to it, aren't we?' She turned to Diamond. 'Looking forward to it,' she repeated as if to a deaf man.

'Can't wait,' he said after a pause.

Ingeborg turned back to Douglas Christmas. 'Do you go on tour with them when they perform abroad?'

'Not for the entire tour. Can't spare the time, more's the pity,' he said. 'I make a point of visiting them at various concerts. Bring them a few treats from home, new shirts, the latest paperbacks, music magazines, a large box of chocs for Cat the cellist. It keeps up their spirits. You can get depressed living in foreign hotels for long periods.'

'I expect you're in regular touch with them.'

'Daily. Hourly, if there's a crisis.'

'What can go wrong?'

'You name it. No one to meet them at the airport. Sub-standard hotel. Cock-ups over the concert programme. There was even one horrible tour when our violist went missing. A very gifted musician, too. I had to drop everything and take the first flight to Budapest to sort things out.'

'What happened?'

'They cancelled the concert. I arrived in a murderous mood, after Harry's blood, and I still feel bad about that, because the poor fellow stayed missing. No one has seen him or heard anything to this day. It was a massive setback. We muddled through for a time with substitute players, but it wasn't the same. We've only recently got back to some kind of normality.'

Part of Diamond's brain had been taking in what was said. He dragged his attention back to this side of the room and turned to Christmas. 'Was he scared of you?'

This brought a frown and raised eyebrows. 'Who?'

'The violist who disappeared.'

'Harry? Good Lord, no.'

'You said you were in a murderous mood.'

'A turn of phrase, no more.' He laughed. 'I may be known in the trade as Jaws, but I treat the quartet like my own kids. I'm still broken up about Harry.'

'What could have happened?'

'I wish I knew. He was a loner. I suppose they all are in their different ways, only he was always more secretive than the others and always strapped for cash, asking me for something ahead of payday. I discovered he was a compulsive gambler, off to the casino each time they arrived in a new city. He didn't tell the others, as far as I know. He was always back in good time for each rehearsal and performance and always played divinely.'

'Did he get on all right with the others?'

'No problem I ever heard of. There are always tensions between talented people and we have strong characters in the Staccati, but Harry dealt with personal relationships in an adult way.'

'Was he depressed?'

'He didn't appear so. We went through all this at the time with the Budapest police.'

'I'm sure,' Diamond said. 'Have any of the quartet told you about their current problem?'

'Problem?' His face turned a shade paler. 'What's that?'

'Here in Bath.' Diamond pitched his voice lower. 'I'll be straight with you, Mr Christmas. Ingeborg is a detective sergeant and I'm the head of CID. We're investigating the suspicious death of a young Japanese woman who seems to have come to Bath because she was a keen fan of the quartet. She was found in the river some days ago.'

'You don't think my clients have anything to do with it?' Christmas said in an appalled tone. 'They're not going to kill fans. They need them.'

'There may be a connection with a case in Vienna four years ago. Another Japanese woman. She went missing at the same time the Staccati were performing there. She was found in the Danube canal.'

'I know nothing of this.'

'But you know they were in Vienna in 2008?'

'True. They played several nights at the Konzerthaus. I was there for one of them and it was a perfectly normal gig. This is the first I've heard about a missing woman and it's outrageous to suggest such a thing has any connection with the quartet.'

'The body wasn't found until after you'd all left. So you were in Vienna yourself?'

'It's one of my favourite cities.'

'Mine, too,' Diamond said as if he was a world traveller. 'Was this visit prior to the Budapest engagement when your violist went missing?'

The manager's face creased in alarm. 'By God, it was. All part of our 2008 European tour. How extraordinary. It's got to be a ghastly coincidence.'

Diamond didn't need to comment on that. A voice from across the room announced, 'The concert will begin shortly. Kindly proceed into the picture galley and take your seats.'

'Are you going in?' Christmas said.

Diamond nodded. 'Wouldn't miss it for the world.'

'Better not delay.' He was off.

Diamond's gaze returned to the opposite side of the room, where Paloma and her partner were in conversation with some other people. 'They're in no hurry,' he said to Ingeborg. 'Why don't they bloody move?'

'Cool it, guv.'

The anteroom was emptying fast. His plan to hold back would misfire if he and Ingeborg were left there, conspicuous.

'We'd better go in,' Ingeborg said.

Still he hesitated.

And then Paloma turned her head and saw them. Her brown eyes held Diamond's briefly and widened in shock. Of all the people she might have expected to see at a chamber music recital, he would not have been high on the list. Clearly embarrassed, she swung away, grasped her partner's forearm and almost tugged him towards the door.

'Did you see that?' Diamond said to Ingeborg. 'She was holding his arm. Do you think they're an item?'

'Guv, I've no idea.'

He was hurting. 'The body language says everything, doesn't it? They're more than just friends.'

'Don't let it get to you. It may be quite innocent.'

'What's she doing here anyway?'

'I expect she's saying exactly the same about you. We'd better go in.'

They took the end seats in the last row but one. Paloma and her escort were closer to the front, in the middle of the second row. Capability Brown's gallery was seventy-two feet by twenty-four and the seating had been arranged lengthwise, but in a shallow arc facing a white marble fireplace. Chairs and music stands for the performers were positioned in front.

Diamond's police career had put him in some unlikely places. This, by his standards, was among the most alien. Classical art was not his thing any more than music was. The pictures were hung in the style of the early nineteenth century, when the objective was to use as much wall space as possible. Large gilt-framed paintings from the Methuen family's collection were suspended one above the other in twos and threes. To his eye the pictures looked sombre and repellent. He had no confidence that the music would be any more congenial.

A ripple of applause started and grew in volume. The quartet made their entrance. Ivan Bogdanov led them in, violin and bow in hand, a squat, bald figure in a white jacket and white bow tie that was their uniform. Even Cat Kinsella had a jacket over a white top and wore dark trousers like the others. Her waist size was probably more than twice Ivan's. But she walked well and had no difficulty carrying her cello. Anthony Metcalf was the tallest, handsome, expressionless, indifferent to the audience. Finally came Mel Farran and he was definitely interested in the sea of faces, taking nervous glances as he moved towards the music stands.

A strip of white plaster covered the outer edge of his left hand.

'Pick your killer,' Diamond said to Ingeborg and the woman in front of them stopped clapping and turned to see who had spoken.

The musicians took their places and spent a moment adjusting the lights on their music stands.

'What are they going to play?'

'It's on the sheet,' Ingeborg said out of the side of her mouth.

'What sheet?'

'On the chair when we came in.'

'Ah.' He'd been too interested in Paloma to notice. He shifted his weight to the left, delved under his thigh and retrieved it.

Beethoven, Opus 59, No. 3 in C major.

The quartet must have tuned their instruments off stage. Ivan gave a nod, put bow to string and they were straight into it.

19

'Is that it?' Diamond asked. The clapping had finished and everyone was moving.

'Only the interval,' Ingeborg said.

'God help us.'

'Be thankful for small mercies.'

He stood up to get the feeling back into his legs. The seats weren't the most comfortable. At the same time he looked across to where Paloma had been.

She'd gone.

He'd spent much of the concert debating with himself whether to go over and speak to her. She had definitely spotted him. It seemed churlish to go through the evening without saying anything. Yet weeks had passed with no contact and the last words she'd spoken had been about as final as you can get between people in a relationship. He wasn't good at peacemaking.

And yet . . .

If she'd come here alone, he told himself, he would have seized his chance. She might well have given him the frost, but at least the pain would be private to the two of them. The new companion – or whatever he was to her – made any approach a minefield. Diamond knew for sure that if the dog's dinner pitched in with backchat or sarcasm he'd give him more than a mouthful, and what use was that? Paloma would side with her new man and a bad situation would get massively worse.

'I'll be back presently,' Ingeborg said.

'Oh, sure.'

Needing to get his head straight as well as pumping some blood into his legs, he stepped over to the nearest wall and stood in front of the pictures. They held as much interest for him as outdated copies of *Country Life* in a dentist's waiting room. Reynolds, Romney and Rubens weren't his choice of painters. The Diamond theory of art required scenes and figures that looked real, as these did, but not so laboured over that they lost all vitality. He preferred the style of Hockney, fresh, bold and cheerful.

'Didn't expect to find you here.'

He swung round and there she was. Give Paloma her due: she wasn't letting their recent history stop her from speaking to him.

No problem now with circulation. Heart thumping, he managed to say, 'Likewise. How's it going?'

'Fine. And you?'

'Soldiering on.'

Something was different about her, apart from the hair colour. He realised her eyes were level with his. Those crazy heels made her taller.

But the eyes weren't angry, as he'd seen them last. Her mouth curved upwards. 'In all the time I've known you, string quartets were never mentioned.'

'That's for sure. I'm no expert.'

'But it's nice you're giving it a try. The Staccati are about as good as it gets. Did Ingeborg persuade you to come?'

She'd spotted Ingeborg, then. What did she think – that he was dating one of his team? 'No. I invited her in case I made a fool of myself clapping in the wrong places.'

'Is she into classical music?'

'Not really. As an ex-journo, she's done most things.' He'd skirted around the real reason for his presence here. Paloma seemed so encouraged that he was doing the cultural bit that he didn't want to disillusion her and admit he was on police business.

'Invitations to these soirées are hard to come by,' she said.

'I got ours through Georgina. She's well connected.'

'Through her choral singing? Of course. So did you enjoy the Beethoven?'

'I'd have enjoyed it more if I hadn't got pins and needles in my legs. The seats aren't the most comfortable.'

'I know what you mean. I wanted to stand up halfway through. I expect they hired them specially for the concert.'

'Those look better.' He was eyeing the long row of padded chairs ranged along the wall below the pictures.

'They're Chippendale,' Paloma said, 'and not for sitting on. Not these days, anyway. I'll tell you something that will amuse you. See the fabric they're covered with? What do you notice about it?'

'Matches the walls?'

'Right. It's exactly the same stuff, crimson silk damask. At some point the original chair coverings got worn to shreds and needed replacing. Unfortunately the same fabric couldn't be got for love nor money, so some bright spark came up with the idea of cutting out patches of the wall-covering from behind the pictures and using them on the chairs. If you took the pictures down, you'd see a lot of large square holes. It means they can't change the arrangement, so they're stuck with this crowded display that was okay two hundred years ago, but looks all wrong now.'

'How did you find out?'

'I know the house well. It's sometimes used for period dramas. *Northanger Abbey. The Remains of the Day.* They usually get my help.'

'Should have realised. Seeing you here, I didn't think of that. Is the business thriving?'

'Doing okay. And yours? Still keeping the crime rate down?'

He smiled. 'Mostly.'

'How's Raffles?'

'The same, running the house the way he likes.'

The small talk would run out soon. Diamond hadn't found out for certain if she was in a new relationship.

'People seem to be returning to their seats,' Paloma said.

'Where exactly are you?' he asked as if he hadn't been watching her all evening.

'Over there. Third row back. You haven't met Mike, have you? The tall guy in the light grey suit. He'll be wondering where I am. Better get back to him. Enjoy the rest of the music.'

She was away. A civilized exchange had been ruined for him by the way she spoke about the dog's dinner: Mike – not Michael, but the shorter, more familiar name, suggesting a closeness that hit Diamond like a low punch. The very fact that she'd left the guy alone for the whole of the interval indicated that they'd passed the stage of dating. *He'll be wondering where I am.* She could have been talking about her husband.

Diamond slunk back to his seat.

Ingeborg was already looking at the programme. 'The cellist is doing a solo next.'

'Ah.'

'"Salut d'Amour".'

Cat Kinsella's arrival was warmly applauded. The confident way this woman with the girth of a sumo wrestler carried in her cello and positioned it between her knees spoke volumes for her temperament. She began playing with a clear, strong note.

Elgar's bittersweet music was never going to lift Diamond out of his low mood, but he was here for a reason and by

243

degrees he forced himself to give all his attention to Cat. What was it that made her prefer playing in the quartet to giving solo performances like this? By all accounts she was in the first rank as a cellist, capable of any of the great concertos in the repertoire. She could be a virtuoso, a top name in her own right.

There are people who think of themselves as team players. Mostly they relish the support of those around them. He wasn't sure if this was true of the Staccati. They were more like talented individuals who tolerated each other. Of the four he'd met, Cat had the most regard for the others. She spoke well of them all, even the nitpicking Ivan. With her sharp wit, she was good at defusing tensions between the men. As the solitary female, did she see her role as a peacekeeper or something more? Were they a foster family for a woman without children of her own? Or was she living the dream that she had three lovers? Who could say what her sexual fantasies might be – or what actually happened.

Out here alone, the focal point of the entire room, interpreting Elgar with skill and sensitivity that even Diamond could appreciate, she still left him puzzling how it could be that she was happier when performing with the men around her.

The piece came to a plaintive end. She stood and dipped her head as the audience responded. Seated again, and as if to demonstrate that there was another side to Cat Kinsella, she launched into the 'Ritual Fire Dance'. The audience had its passions well stirred and quite forgot that it was middle class in middle England in midwinter.

'How about that?' Ingeborg said over the cheering at the end.

'Best I've heard tonight.'

'Me too.'

Difficult to follow a turn as gripping as that. Next on was Mel Farran, the new member. He looked even more ill at ease than when he'd made his original entrance with the others. He knocked one of the music stands with his foot and almost tipped it over. Some of the sticking-plaster on his hand had come unstuck and he had to press it back into place. Mel clearly wasn't comfortable in this situation. Before he played the first note he seemed to be scanning the rows as if he expected a gunman out there. Diamond watched, intrigued. *All right, chum. The worst you'll see is a couple of detectives you've already met, and they ought to give you confidence. If you've done nothing wrong, that is.*

Mel played two pieces by Fritz Kreisler. Once under way, he became calmer and so did the audience. Difficult for Diamond to tell whether he was playing well. More out of relief than anything else the audience gave him a generous reception, after which he was joined by Ivan Bogdanov for an arrangement for viola and violin of Handel's Harpsichord Suite No. 7 in G minor. The two blended well.

While the piece was being played, Diamond's concentration wasn't total, or even partial. He'd heard almost as much of this stuff as a man could take in one evening – a man whose musical education hadn't up to now stretched beyond Freddie Mercury and Montserrat Caballé singing 'Barcelona'. His attention wandered to the huge painting over the mantelpiece, a particularly gruesome hunting scene. People mostly on horseback were slaughtering wolves and foxes with clubs and spears. Dead and dying animals testified to the success of the day's sport. A strange backdrop for a musical soirée. How ironic if one of the quartet turned out to be a killer.

All four returned to play the last piece on the programme, *Andante Festivo*, by Sibelius. At this stage of the evening the term 'strung out' summed up Diamond's condition in more senses than one. But the piece was mercifully over in about five minutes. Then to his despair the audience demanded an encore. They wouldn't stop clapping.

Ivan led the musicians off.

'Thank God,' Diamond said to Ingeborg.

She said, 'Hang about, guv. They're coming back.'

Diamond's buttocks flexed. Amazing any life was left in them.

Ivan stepped forward to speak. 'We would like to offer you a piece neglected by many ensembles: the Sibelius String Quartet in D minor, Opus 56.'

Huge applause.

The buttocks went into spasm. Another entire quartet.

As if he was a mind-reader, Ivan continued, 'But it's late and unfortunately we don't have time for the entire composition, so with apologies to Sibelius we'll pick it up at the start of the fifth and final movement. Thank you for being such a splendid audience.'

The quartet knew what they were doing. Whatever it was that made the Sibelius a neglected quartet, its climax was a sure-fire audience-pleaser, the Allegro, dynamic, demanding and impassioned. When the bows were lifted from the instruments a standing ovation followed. Diamond was among the first to rise. He needed no prompting.

'I've become a fan,' Ingeborg told him. 'Wasn't that awesome?'

'Yes, but don't overdo the clapping.'

'Such talent. It's almost impossible to believe one of them could be . . .'

'I can believe it, no problem,' he said.

20

'What's the matter with you?' Ivan asked.

'My hand, you mean?' Mel said. 'It's not serious.'

'Your whole performance. You were pathetic. Timing, intonation. And don't blame the new instrument. You were perfectly good in rehearsal.'

The quartet were using the gothic library in the West Wing at Corsham Court as a base. Their manager Douglas had joined them. Tired and drained from the performance, they were supposed to be unwinding before travelling home. This wasn't unwinding; it was winding up.

Cat came to Mel's defence as if she was shaping a passage with her cello, a stabilising counterpoint. 'Ivan, that's way over the top. He wasn't that bad. He was a damn sight better than most of the so-called violists we've played with, and I never heard you slag one of them off.'

'Because we know he can do better.' Ivan turned on Mel again. 'Are you a drinker? If you are, we have a right to be told.'

With the musicians almost squaring up to each other, Douglas tried his old-school best to calm the situation. 'Steady on, old man.'

Mel decided the others deserved an explanation. More than anyone, he knew his playing hadn't been up to standard. 'Ivan is right. I was rubbish. I had a fall today. Well, to be honest, I was knocked down by a car.'

Douglas said, 'Stone the crows!'

'And it wasn't due to drink, not on my part, anyway.'

'Where did this happen?' Cat asked.

'In the street outside my lodgings. My landlady spotted this stationary car with someone seated inside staring at the house. He'd been there a long time and she thought we had a stalker. She has a rather attractive daughter. I went over to speak to the guy. When he saw me coming he drove off fast. I don't think he meant to hit me. He just wanted to be away, but the side of the car brushed against me and sent me flying.'

'So he *was* a stalker?' Cat said.

'He wasn't staying to talk about it, whoever he was.'

'That's how you did your hand?'

'It was grazed and bled a bit. My arm is the problem. It's stiff today and I bashed my head on the road as well.'

'And still turned up tonight and gave a performance?' Cat said. 'Played your solo pieces and the duet as well as the Beethoven and the Sibelius? That's heroic.' To Ivan, she said, 'I hope you're about to apologise for the snide remarks you made.'

'I do.'

'In all humility?' Cat said with a stare worthy of a headmistress.

Humility was an alien concept to Ivan, but he mumbled something that wasn't a denial.

'Your left hand is the one you use for fingering, isn't it?' Douglas said to Mel. 'I don't know how you got through the evening.'

'All those vibratos,' Cat said, her face creasing in sympathy.

'The fingers weren't damaged, I'm glad to say. I'd have let you know if I thought I was going to mess up. More than anything, my state of mind was the problem.'

'Listen, darling, you weren't pathetic, as Joe Stalin over

there so unkindly put it. I don't suppose any of the audience noticed.'

Douglas said, 'I certainly didn't. And from the reception you were given there's no doubt Cat is right. Nobody was any the wiser.'

'I wouldn't count on it,' Mel said.

'Get a grip, people,' Cat said. 'This was one evening in front of twenty or thirty rich punters who think the only good note is a banknote. The bigger picture is that Mel's playing has raised our game. We're better now than at any time since we formed. Isn't that a fact, Anthony?'

The laconic second violin gave a nod.

'He says bang on, back of the net, hole in one,' Cat said.

Douglas shifted the focus back to the accident. 'Didn't the driver stop?'

Mel shook his head.

'Hit and run, the bastard,' Cat said.

'Did you get a look at him?' Douglas asked.

'My landlady did. She said he was in his forties, going grey and quite good-looking. Not much of a description, I know, but she'd probably know him if she saw him again.'

'Did you call the police?'

Mel shook his head. 'Didn't get the number. And I don't think he meant to knock me over.'

'It was dangerous driving, whatever you may think.'

'Aside from the fact that the man's a menace to women,' Cat said.

'We can't be certain he was a stalker,' Douglas went on. 'Has it occurred to you, Mel, that this may have nothing to do with your landlady's daughter – that he was spying on you?'

'What for?' Ivan said.

'It crossed my mind, I have to say,' Mel said. 'I've been over it a few times. I wondered if it he was interested in the Amati, waiting for a chance to break in and steal it.'

Cat was frowning. 'How would he know about the Amati? You've only had it a couple of days.'

'I've no idea.'

'It's not as if it was written up in lights. Only a handful of people know and most of them are in this room.'

'Well, it's news to me,' Douglas said. 'An Amati viola? That's a rare beast, isn't it? Where did you get it?'

'He's not at liberty to say,' Cat said. 'A secret millionaire. They never come my way.'

Ivan was still brooding over the mystery. 'There's some other explanation. Must be.'

'Wait a mo,' Douglas said, raising a finger. 'Have any of you thought this may be connected to Harry's disappearance?'

'Someone targeting violists?' Cat said. 'Come off it, Doug. Lightning doesn't strike twice.'

'We never discovered the reason.'

'That was four years ago in Budapest. It's history now and we're in England in case you haven't noticed. We've moved on. Don't put scary ideas into Mel's head. The poor lad has suffered enough.'

'Even so, we must take care of him. How are you getting back to Bath?'

'Taxis as usual,' Ivan said.

'I'll give Mel a lift in the Aston Martin. I'm still thinking we should report this incident to the police. Did you know they were here tonight? I met two of them before the concert.'

'A big guy called Diamond?' Cat said.

'Yes, and a blonde with a foreign-sounding name.'

'We knew they were coming,' Cat said. 'It's all about this unfortunate Japanese girl.'

'The police said something about this,' Douglas said. 'There's so much to catch up on.'

'She was found dead in the river, murdered apparently. They're saying she was a fan of ours.'

'Doesn't mean you're responsible.'

Ivan said, 'A point we all made clear. Once the police get a sniff of something they think is suspicious, watch out. They're well capable of planting evidence. What's the term?'

'Stitching us up?' Cat said.

'That might be true in your country,' Douglas said. 'I can't believe the British bobby would stoop to anything so low.'

Ivan rolled his eyes. 'It's quite possible that the man who knocked Mel down was a plain-clothes policeman keeping him under observation. Maybe we're all being spied on. There was a suspicious-looking car outside the Tippett Centre yesterday and he drove off fast when we spotted him. Mel saw it, too.'

'I'm totally confused now,' Douglas said.

'So am I,' Mel said. 'Some of these theories must be wrong. A sex pest, an instrument thief, a kidnapper of violists and a police spy? Let's try and keep a grip on reality.'

Douglas turned to Mel and smiled. 'Well said. This seems as good a moment as any to announce some good news.'

'We could certainly use some,' Cat said. 'What is it?'

He rubbed his hands. 'News travels fast these days, as we all know. There's a real buzz among concert managers around the world that the Staccati have re-formed. The enquiries are coming in thick and fast and I'm now in a position to offer you a five-week South American tour as soon as you've completed your stint here in Bath. You'll be going to some wonderful places – Rio de Janeiro, São Paulo, Montevideo, Buenos Aires, Santiago, Lima and Bogotá. Some of these cities have facilities you wouldn't believe, amazing concert halls that will sell out within hours. Five-star hotels all the way.'

'And fees?' Ivan said.

'The best I've ever negotiated for you. South Americans adore their music and they're passionate about the chance of hearing you. I know it's a lot of travelling, but, believe me, you get well rewarded.'

'I'm tempted,' Cat said. 'As you know, I prefer longer stays, but this will be new territory, new shopping opportunities.'

'And a new market for your backlist,' Douglas added. 'A huge boost to your CD and video sales. Already several of them are talking about press calls and TV appearances.'

'What do you say, boys? Are we up for it?' Cat said.

After the build-up, the decision was low-key, a matter of looks, shrugs and nods, but no one disagreed.

'Super,' Douglas said. 'I'll confirm it all when I get back to London tomorrow.' At a stroke he'd removed all the negative feelings after the concert. 'And on that high note, I recommend a well-earned sleep. I'll bring the car round to the front entrance. I can find room for one more.'

It was agreed Ivan would travel with Douglas and Mel, leaving Cat to share a taxi with Anthony.

Mel and Ivan walked together to the main entrance, an opportunity for Mel to raise a point that had caused him some concern. 'I didn't say anything back there because everyone seemed to be getting paranoid, but there's something I should tell you about the car you and I saw out at the Tippett Centre.'

'What's that?' Ivan's tone was as friendly as a January night in Riga.

'I'm almost certain it followed my taxi home. It was the same car that knocked me down.'

'Unlikely,' he said. 'Talk about paranoid. You're sounding paranoid yourself.'

'You saw it. What make do you think it was?'

'A Megane.'

'That's the car that hit me.'

Ivan was silent a moment. Then he said, 'They're a common make. They're everywhere.'

'I'm telling you this because it seemed to me at the time you were visibly shaken just by the sight of that car. You went silent. You scarcely said a word all the way back to Bath.'

'I was tired from the rehearsal.'

Mel said no more. In this sour mood, Ivan was giving nothing away.

Shortly after midnight he let himself into the house. In darkness he removed his shoes and left them by the door. Clutching the Amati to his chest he crept up the stairs fearing each creak of the boards might waken the household. The last thing he wanted was a late-night meeting with Mrs Carlyle in her night-clothes. On tiptoe he moved along the landing to his room and let himself in, closing the door with stealth. He didn't risk turning on the light. In this small house the click of a switch was audible everywhere.

He slid the Amati safely under the bed next to his other viola. Then he stripped to his Calvin Kleins, leaving the clothes heaped on the floor. No bathroom visit tonight. He'd give his teeth an extra go in the morning.

Relieved to have made it and more than ready for sleep, he eased himself under the quilt, turned on his side and found he wasn't alone. His chest was in contact with a warm, bare back. His pelvic area had come to rest against the divide of a chunky pair of buttocks, also bare.

She made a not unwelcoming murmuring sound. She was nine-tenths out to the world.

For the next few seconds Mel stayed still and silent, considering his options. From the shape and smell of her, this was unmistakably Tippi. She'd sneaked into his bed naked and ready for his return. Warmed by the quilt, she'd fallen asleep. Normally he'd not think twice what to do next. Tonight he had a sore left arm and his head was aching.

He'd psyched himself up for the concert and now fatigue had caught up with him.

The bed was pleasantly warm. Would it be any use easing back from her and hoping she would drift off again?

He made the attempt.

Without success.

'Mel?'

He tried breathing evenly.

She turned right over and reached unerringly for his Calvin Kleins. 'You're late, but not too late.'

'It over-ran,' he said.

'Never mind,' Tippi said, giving the elastic a tug. 'Get 'em off.'

'Can I have a raincheck?'

'What?'

'It's an American expression. Means: could we make it another time?'

'You're joking.' She explored the front of his pants and then said with less certainty, 'Aren't you?'

'I've had a rough day, Tippi. Got knocked down by a car.'

'Mummy told me.'

'Yes. She saw it all.'

'She says you were like Superman charging across the street. She's got it into her head that the driver was a stalker, stalking me. To be honest I haven't noticed him myself.'

'It was the first I'd seen of him.'

'But as you did it for me I decided to give you this nice surprise.'

'I'm touched,' Mel said.

'I wouldn't know it yet,' Tippi said, checking again.

'The thing is, I hurt my arm and it's still quite sore.'

'Your arm?'

'Yes.'

'Nothing further down?'

'Oh, no. I'm fine in that department.'

'Prove it, then.'

'I can't, because of the arm.'

'Come again.'

'The arm. That's why I suggested a raincheck.' Just in case that hadn't settled the matter, he tried giving her something else to think about. 'The man in the car may not be stalking you. He may be interested in a new viola I've been given to play. It's a valuable item, extremely valuable actually.'

'He shouldn't have driven the car at you, whoever he is.'

'I agree, but I reckon he was trying to drive past me.'

'Mummy doesn't think so. She told the cops he meant to hit you.'

'What did you say?' he said in alarm. 'The cops?'

'Keep your voice down,' Tippi said. 'You'll wake her up. She called in at the police station in Manvers Street tonight and told them what happened. She said it's her public duty to report him.'

'For Christ's sake why?'

'Well, he was stalking me and he almost killed you.'

'I wish she hadn't,' Mel said.

'Too late now. I expect they'll want to hear from you.'

'I was never in any danger.'

'Your arm's hurt. You just said.'

'Aches a bit. I wouldn't want to put any weight on it. That's the problem.'

'No problem at all.' Tippi grabbed his pants and yanked them down his thighs. 'Move into the middle. This'll be fun. Me on top.'

Tired as he was, he felt himself responding.

At breakfast, he waited for Mrs Carlyle to raise the matter of the police. He was keen to hear what they'd said, but he couldn't turn back the clock. What was done was done. And this morning *he* was done. It had taken a superhuman effort to get downstairs.

'You were late coming in last night,' she said while she was cracking the eggs.

'I hope I didn't disturb you,' he said, meaning every word.

'Not really. I may have heard something. If you disturbed anyone, it was my Tippi. I heard her moving around in the small hours. I'm not expecting her down for breakfast.'

'I took my shoes off.'

'Very considerate.'

'I mean when I first came in.'

'I believe you. I saw them when I came down this morning. So was it a good concert?'

'Not really. I was a bit off.'

'Played some wrong notes, did you?'

'It was more a matter of rhythm and tempo. You need to be on top of your form to respond to the other players, and I wasn't and it showed – not all the time, but enough to shake my confidence and theirs.'

'Maybe you should have cancelled after all you went through. You're still looking pale.'

'It has to be something drastic to call off a concert. People were going to turn up. It was too late to let them know.'

'If they were told what happened to you and why, they'd be sympathetic. How's your arm today?'

'Improving.'

'They say exercise is the best remedy. Are you up for it?'

For a moment, he was unsure what she meant. Then the plate of bacon and eggs arrived in front of him.

'Get your knife and fork working on that,' Mrs Carlyle said. 'I told the police you're a superhero. It's all on tape. They took me into a special interview room. This was yesterday evening. I decided it was my duty as a mother to report what happened, so I went down to Manvers Street and saw this nice young man in plain clothes called Paul. Far too young to be a copper, in my opinion, but he knew how to treat a lady. Tea and a biscuit, I got. He told me to take as long as I wanted and I had a wicked thought that I can't repeat to a gentleman like yourself. Anyway, I said what happened, how brave you were and everything, having a go like that.'

'I wouldn't call it having a go,' Mel said. 'I only went over to speak to the guy.'

'You got knocked over and injured for your trouble. He's a danger to the public and I told them so. I don't want him across the street ogling my Tippi. I know she dresses to attract the men but that's no reason to have them sitting outside the house like tom cats. You don't know what they're thinking. Well, you do, and you don't want it. He wasn't her age. He was out of the ark compared to her. I gave them a description, as much as I could.'

'Are they going to do anything about it?'

'I don't expect so, but they'd like a statement from you and I think you ought to go along and volunteer like I did.'

'They'll have got as much as they need from you. I didn't get a proper look at the guy.'

'But you saw his Renault Megane, rather too much of it, in fact.'

'It's a common make. They'll never trace it.'

'That's not the point. He could be back today. Show them your injuries and they'll get him for dangerous driving and attempted murder.'

'I don't think so. They're minor injuries.'

'He needs to be locked up, Mel. If he doesn't come after my Tippi you can be sure he'll pick on some other young girl and it could be far worse next time. You don't want that on your conscience. Besides, they know your name

and where you live and what you do for a living. I told
them.'

'Oh, thanks.'

She missed the sarcasm. 'A mother's instinct, caring for
her young. Under all that make-up is an innocent child.'

21

'I won't be making a habit of it,' Diamond said of the soirée. Ingeborg was more positive. 'It was really good in parts.'

'The part that matters is that we met the manager,' Diamond said. 'We weren't there for the music.'

'What did you make of him?' Keith Halliwell asked.

'Douglas Christmas?' Ingeborg said. 'A smooth operator. I guess you need someone like that fronting a cultural group. He'd make a good impression abroad with his old-world charm.'

'Rather less with you?' Halliwell said.

'Charming people always have a hidden agenda.'

He grinned. 'If you're a blonde.'

The CID team were all present and there was a sense of anticipation. Diamond's case conferences tended to be informal, for whoever happened to be around. This one had been scheduled in advance as not to be missed.

'Listen up, people,' he said. 'Yesterday as you know an international dimension was added to the case. It emerged that another Japanese woman went missing in a city where the Staccati were performing – in this case, Vienna, in 2008 – and was found dead some time after in the Danube canal. We can't be certain of a link, but it has to be investigated.'

While Diamond was speaking, Ingeborg pinned a new photo to the display board. Posed against a whitewashed wall, a woman's face making no effort to please stared forward from the centre of the frame. This was no family snap. Everyone in the room knew a mugshot when they saw one.

Diamond continued, 'Points of similarity. One, her nationality, of course. Two, the body was recovered from a city waterway. Three, she was submerged too long for a cause of death to be determined. Four, no obvious injuries. Five, she was clothed. Six, there was no great alarm when she went missing. And seven, she died at about the time the Staccati were in town.'

He waited for that to take root.

'And these are the differences. One, this woman, Miss Emi Kojima, was about five years older than Mari Hitomi. Two, she'd been out of touch with her family for rather longer. Three, she was found with a netsuke under her T-shirt. That's a small antique ornament of a particular design that led the Viennese police to deduce she took her own life.'

'But it could have been planted by her killer,' John Leaman said, keen as always to chip in.

'Goes without saying.' Diamond folded his arms and lulled everyone into thinking there was little else to report. 'Nothing we don't know already, you're telling yourselves. But I asked Ingeborg to run a search on the Vienna victim and she's discovered some background that I'm sure you'll agree is new and significant.' He turned to Ingeborg. 'Over to you.'

'Getting straight to it,' she said, 'from an early age Emi Kojima attended one of the famous Tokyo violin schools.'

Murmurs of interest rippled through the room.

'Music again?' John Leaman said.

'She was said to have been an exceptionally gifted player. They take them young and get them up to an amazing standard. But at seventeen she was caught in possession of

260

cocaine and asked to leave the school. After that she seems to have left home and drifted into petty crime and prostitution. She lived in one room in a notorious Tokyo slum. The picture you see was taken after an arrest, one of many. Her family despaired of getting her back to some kind of normality. A sad story, but far from uncommon.'

Most eyes had returned to the photo on the display board. Emi Kojima's jaded look seemed to confirm that she had been pulled in and charged so often that it had no meaning for her.

'So,' Diamond said, 'we can add one more point of similarity: an interest in classical music. And one difference: this woman had a police record.'

'How did she make it to Vienna if she was in poverty?' Halliwell asked.

'Three guesses. She wasn't there on a city break.'

'Are we talking organised crime?'

'We could be.'

'Trafficking?'

'That's well possible.'

'To work as a hooker in Europe?'

'What do you think?'

'Excuse me,' Paul Gilbert said, 'but how would this link up with the string quartet? None of them are Japanese.'

'Doesn't stop one of them paying for sex with her,' Ingeborg said. 'Guys on tour for weeks on end.'

'Classical musicians?' Gilbert said in disbelief.

'They need to get their rocks off, same as you, ducky,' Ingeborg said.

Young Gilbert turned puce and everyone else enjoyed the moment.

'He's right to ask the question,' Diamond said. 'It comes down to this: did one of the Staccati pick up Miss Kojima in Vienna and kill her, and also Miss Hitomi in Bath?'

261

'Someone who fancies Japanese girls?' Halliwell said.

'Or hates them.'

Paul Gilbert was still grappling with the concept. 'Something doesn't add up. If she was working as a prostitute in Vienna and got picked up and killed by one of the Staccati, the fact that she went to violin school is neither here nor there. That was all in the past.'

Ingeborg looked as if she was in free fall. In her eagerness to join up the dots she'd missed this basic flaw in the logic. 'Now you put it like that, the music link may be a red herring. It must be what she was doing in Vienna that got her killed.'

'That makes sense to me,' Diamond said, moving smoothly on. 'Let's stay with it.'

'If we're talking about the Staccati in Vienna,' Halliwell said, 'this was before Mel Farran joined. There are only two males in the frame, the old guy and the silent one.'

'"Old" is a relative term,' Diamond said. 'He could be my age.'

No one else spoke a word.

'Losing some of his hair doesn't make him decrepit. But as you say, either of these might have gone looking for paid sex. And we shouldn't ignore the third man.' Diamond stopped and looked around the room. 'Do I hear someone whistling?'

A few heads turned towards the source of the Harry Lime Theme.

Caught again.

Paul Gilbert seemed to shrink within himself.

Diamond could have hung the young man out to dry. Instead he gave a disarming comment. 'It sounds better on a zither.'

Relief all round.

Diamond wasn't departing from his script. 'The third man – Harry Cornell – known to go off on missions he discussed

262

with nobody. He's in the frame with the others. It's possible he was with this woman and killed her. The next city they visited was Budapest and he went missing there.'

Leaman was encouraged to develop the scenario. 'He dumped her in the canal in Vienna and he expected the body would be discovered any time soon, so he went into hiding.'

'Yeah, down the sewers,' Halliwell said.

'Don't try me,' Diamond said. 'The joke's been done.'

Halliwell clearly wasn't impressed by the third man theory. 'For this to make any sense, Harry would have stayed in hiding for four years and turned up again in Bath and killed another Japanese woman. For Christ's sake, why?'

Ingeborg said, 'We haven't discussed the motive.'

Leaman agreed. 'All we have is the vague idea that some nutter has a kink about Japanese women.'

'Two very different women,' Ingeborg added.

Gilbert said, 'Should we be checking all the cities the Staccati have visited for unsolved murders of Japanese women?'

'Speak for yourself,' someone murmured.

'A serial killer?' Diamond said.

Gilbert hesitated. 'That's possible, isn't it?'

'Fair point. Do that, would you, Paul? We have a list of all their gigs for sixteen years, thanks to John Leaman.'

Gilbert looked as if he'd just grown older by all of those years. 'Me? How would I do that?'

'Interpol. That's why they exist, for something like this.'

The young man's face relaxed. 'Thanks, guv.'

'Then if they're unable to confirm anything it's a matter of trawling through the international press.'

The appeal of teasing Gilbert was that every emotion was as vivid on his face as if he was a silent film actor.

'Don't despair. A lot of it's digitised.'

'The Japanese papers should be helpful,' Halliwell said.

Ingeborg said, 'This is getting mean. You'd better come clean, guv. Are we seriously looking at a serial killer?'

'Personally, I think it's unlikely,' Diamond said. 'A series of killings would have shown up on the radar before now. The Japanese police are no slouches. So it won't be necessary to go back all those years, Paul. But it's not impossible some maniac has just started on a psychopathic career, and I'm serious about checking for a similar case in the past five years. Meanwhile for the rest of us it's back to the nitty-gritty of probing the secret lives of our musicians. And I'm not ruling out their manager. He flew out to Vienna while they were performing there.'

'Is Mel still in the frame?' Ingeborg said. Her tone suggested he ought not to be. Mel had made a favourable impression on her when she interviewed him. 'He wasn't around when the first girl was killed in Vienna.'

'You saw him at the concert,' Diamond said. 'Of the four, who looked the most nervous?'

'He *is* the new boy, guv.'

'He's had several months to settle in. This wasn't the first concert they've played.'

She nodded. 'Okay. I'll keep digging.'

Paul Gilbert still hadn't been silenced by the drubbing he'd received. 'There could be a reason why Mel was nervous.'

'Better tell us, then,' Ingeborg said before any of the others could inflict more punishment.

'It's in the copy of the message log I put on the guv'nor's desk.'

A show-stopping moment followed. Everyone in the room except young Gilbert knew Diamond was a word-of-mouth man who rarely went near his desk.

'Message about what?' Diamond asked.

'The statement I took yesterday evening from a Mrs Carlyle.'

Diamond drew a sharp, impatient breath. 'Never heard of her. Is it relevant?'

'It could be.'

'Go on, then.'

'She came in and made this voluntary statement. Only the thing is she happens to be Mel Farran's landlady and it was all about a hit-and-run incident outside the house yesterday afternoon. Mel was knocked down.'

The old blood pressure rocketed. 'And you wait until now to tell us?'

'It was in the message. I thought you must have seen it by now, guv. If you want to listen to the statement it's all on tape.'

Diamond managed to contain himself. Strictly speaking, the lad had acted correctly. Not sensibly, with the way things were done in CID, but correctly. 'We'll do that. Fetch it in and play it to us.' While Gilbert went off to retrieve the cassette, Diamond told the rest of the team, 'This may have nothing to do with our investigation, but we can't take that chance.' He frowned. 'How come Gilbert interviewed this woman? A voluntary statement about a traffic incident ought to be dealt with downstairs.'

No one knew why, so he asked the young DC when he reappeared with the cassette-player.

'When she first came in she wasn't talking about the car accident, guv. She was on about a sex maniac stalking her daughter. Uniform said it was a CID matter and I happened to be the only one here.'

'We'd better hear this.'

He switched on.

They listened enthralled to Mrs Carlyle's melodramatic account of the stalker and his all-too-obvious lust for the innocent Tippi. They heard how her gallant lodger Mel went to investigate and was almost killed by the escaping car.

Diamond was gracious enough to say at the end of it, 'Difficult interview. You handled her well, finally got to the real facts.' He pressed his forefinger against his chin. 'Why didn't Mel report this himself, I wonder?'

'Too busy with the concert, I expect,' Ingeborg said.

'Maybe.'

'Perhaps what actually happened wasn't as dangerous as the woman described it,' Leaman said. 'She sounds hyper on the tape.'

'Mel did have a plaster on his left hand,' Ingeborg said. 'And at the soirée he was looking every which way as if he expected someone to attack him.'

'But he didn't report the driver,' Diamond said, refusing to excuse the omission. 'I want to know why. And if the mountain won't come to Mohammed . . .'

Mel's lodgings were in Forester Road, north-east of the city centre. Diamond asked Ingeborg to drive him there since she was the member of CID who knew the violist best and had a good rapport with him. In his twitchy state Mel would probably appreciate some female reassurance. Which wouldn't stop Diamond putting the boot in when required.

It was best to call unannounced, so they'd made no appointment. This was still before midday. The quartet rehearsed mainly in the afternoons. Mel shouldn't have left the house.

'What was the make of the stalker's car?' Diamond asked as they cruised up the road looking at house numbers.

'A Renault Megane. Black.'

'Haven't noticed one along here, have you?'

'In view of what happened he'd be an idiot to come back the next day,' Ingeborg said.

They stopped outside a house with a crimson door and gleaming metal fittings.

'You must be Tippi,' Diamond said when their knock was answered by a young woman in a bathrobe with her hair colour matching the door.

She gave him a suspicious look. 'How do you know? And what's it to you anyway?'

'Police,' he said, showing his ID. 'Your mother reported an incident yesterday and we're following up on it.'

'Mum's out.'

'Good. We'd like to speak to Mel if he's in.'

'He's out, too.'

'Any idea where?'

'He walks in the park sometimes.' She pointed along the road in the direction of Sydney Gardens.

'Your mother seems to believe you have a stalker,' Diamond said. 'Has he troubled you before?'

'Who – me?'

'That's what I'm asking, Tippi.'

'A stalker? Give me a break.'

'What's that meant to mean? Don't you believe your own mother?'

'I wasn't here, didn't see him.'

'And nothing like it has happened before?

'Dunno, do I? If he's any good at it, I wouldn't notice him.'

They drove down to Sydney Gardens, originally an eighteenth-century pleasure garden that suffered a major assault soon after its opening when the Kennet and Avon canal was driven through. And forty years later it was sliced through a second time by the track of the Great Western Railway. But thanks to deep cutting and the building of ornamental bridges and a parapet, the worst horrors were averted. Jane Austen walked there often in its heyday and remarked that one of the advantages was that it was wide enough to get away from the music. These days the gardens are a haven of quiet in a busy city. Helpfully for Diamond, it wasn't the sort of park where you had no chance of finding anyone. There is a central path almost from end to end with views to either side.

They spotted Mel Farran near the Temple of Minerva, the faux Greek structure of Corinthian columns at the centre of the gardens. Clearly he saw them coming and seemed undecided whether to make an about turn, but thought better of it.

'How are you doing?' Diamond said when they got close enough. 'You had a run-in with a Renault Megane yesterday, I was told.'

Mel was quick to dismiss. 'It was nothing. My landlady got excited, but I'm fine.'

'Any idea who was driving?'

'It all happened too fast. As much my fault as his, I reckon. I don't want to make a complaint.'

'How was it your fault?'

'I was dead set on speaking to him and I kept going when he started the car. Walked right into it.'

'When you say "dead set"—'

'I thought I recognised the car. Saw one just like it the same day outside the Tippett Centre, some idiot who drove off fast and almost knocked down a student. But I could be mistaken.'

Diamond didn't let that pass. 'You think you saw him twice the same day?'

'I didn't get the number or anything. I'm not a hundred per cent sure.'

'Can you think of any reason why anyone is tailing you?'

Mel hesitated, 'No.'

'Just that you seemed nervous at the concert last night, as if you were looking out for him.'

He pulled a disbelieving face, as if somebody else was being discussed, and then seemed to remember and gave a shrill laugh. 'That's nothing to do with the driver of the Megane. I was playing a new instrument in public for the first time and I thought the owner might be in the audience.'

'Don't you own your viola?'

'I couldn't possibly afford an Amati. They're worth a fortune. This sometimes happens with professional players – if you get lucky. We get offered top quality instruments by the people who own them. In a few cases they're gifts, but mostly they're on extended loan.'

'I guess that would make anyone nervous.'

'Especially as I once had my own instrument stolen.'

'When was this?'

'Years ago, when I was doing orchestral work.' Mel related the story of the mugging outside the Royal Festival Hall and it was obvious that the experience had deeply affected him. Even at this distance in time his voice broke up a little in telling it.

'That's so cruel,' Ingeborg cried out suddenly.

'Mean,' Diamond said. 'What would they want with a viola that had very little value?'

'Maybe they thought it was worth more,' Mel said. 'For me, it was valuable.'

'A young musician, trying to earn a living?' Ingeborg stressed in sympathy. 'I should think it was irreplaceable.'

'So who does your Amati belong to?' Diamond asked.

Mel vibrated his lips and became cagey again. 'I'm not allowed to say. The owner likes to remain anonymous. That's a condition of the loan.'

'From what you were saying, you only acquired it recently. Can I infer that he lives in Bath?'

'No, you can't.'

'Meaning he doesn't live here – or I shouldn't be asking?'

'No comment.' Followed by a twitchy grin.

'We've heard those words a few times before, haven't we?' Diamond said with a glance at Ingeborg. 'Let's walk a bit, Mel.'

They crossed the bridge over the railway and headed through a wooded area towards Sydney House, a large private building at the eastern end of the gardens, but screened by another pseudo-classical folly known as the Loggia, a semicircle of Ionic columns and pilasters fronting a cement wall.

'Tell us about your background, how you came to join this quartet – or is that another secret?'

'Not at all.' Mel seemed to welcome the change of emphasis. 'It was a phone call from Ivan. They needed a violist and they'd got to know about me and came to some recital to hear me play. I met them by stages, Ivan first, then Cat, and they called me in to do an audition, playing with them. I was in a blue funk but it seemed to go well and I was welcomed in.'

'Did you have any qualms about joining?'

'I jumped at the chance.'

'And now you're fully signed up.'

'Yep.'

'For how long?'

'Indefinitely.'

'Foreign tours?'

'They're planning one for South America as soon as we finish our stint in Bath.'

'Up the Amazon?'

He smiled. 'I hope not.'

'Have you played abroad before, Mel?'

'Heaps of times, filling in with orchestras and ensembles.'

'Europe?'

'Paris, Warsaw, Berlin, Vienna, Amsterdam.'

Trying not to reveal that every neuron in his brain was transmitting at peak capacity, Diamond threw in a question that could have passed for small talk. 'So you've been to Vienna? Who was that with?'

'You name it. I must have played there a dozen times. The first was with the London Symphony Orchestra. Last winter guesting with the Vienna State Ballet.'

'When you say "guesting" . . .?'

Mel grinned. 'I wasn't dancing. They needed a violist at short notice and one of the orchestra remembered me from a previous visit. In the music business it's who you know.'

While the two were in conversation, Ingeborg had left them to it. They appeared to have hit it off without any input from her. But she'd noticed something Diamond had not. Her difficulty was finding how to tip him off without Mel knowing. She touched Diamond's arm. 'Guv.'

He ignored her, still high on the discovery that Mel had worked in Vienna. 'So when were you first there?'

Mel was still talking in a relaxed way. 'With the LSO? That was a shorter trip. Two or three concerts as far as I remember. Mahler, I think. As you approach the stage there's a bust of the composer staring at you. Slightly unnerving.'

'Yes, but when?'

'2008, if my memory is right.'

'Weren't the Staccati performing in Vienna in 2008?'

'Don't know. I wasn't following their progress at the time.'

'I believe they were.'

'Coincidence, then. But Vienna is a stop-off on most of the European tours, so it's no big deal if we overlapped.'

Diamond was like a sniffer dog in a cannabis plantation. His list of strong suspects had increased. 'Which part of Vienna were you?'

'Now you're asking,' Mel said. 'Must have been Karlsplatz. We played at the Musikverein.'

'The Staccati were at the Konzerthaus. That's a different location, is it?'

'I didn't run into them, if that's what you're asking. There are several concert halls.'

Ingeborg caught up with them and gave Diamond a nudge. 'Guv, can I have a word?'

'Presently.' He continued to question Mel. 'Can you recall what time of year you were there with the LSO?'

'At this distance in time?'

'I can check with their management, I expect.'

'Why do you need to know?'

'It's all part of our investigation into the death of the Japanese girl,' he said, not wanting to give more away at this stage.

They were crossing the white-painted cast-iron bridge over the canal, more than a mile from where Mari's body had been recovered, but still a reminder of why they were there. Ahead, the path would end at the Loggia in front of Sydney House.

Ingeborg refused to be sidelined any longer. 'Guv, we're being watched.'

'What?'

'I noticed this hooded guy standing among the trees by the temple where we first met Mel and he's been trailing us ever since, using the trees as a cover.'

'Where is he now?'

'Not sure. I just caught glimpses through the bushes.'

'Why didn't you say?'

She didn't answer.

'He'll have to cross the bridge if he's coming after us.' Diamond said. 'He'll be out in the open then. Wearing a hoodie, you said. What colour?'

'Dark blue.'

'I'll walk on with Mel. Why don't you double back and see if you can catch him and find out what his game is.' For Mel's benefit he added, 'Parks are favourite places for weirdos.'

Ingeborg did as she was asked. On the other side of the bridge she left the path and headed into the undergrowth to the right.

'Will she be all right?' Mel asked.

'He's the one who should be worried,' Diamond said, glancing back. 'She's a black belt.'

They stopped to look. A minute or two went by. They'd lost sight of Ingeborg. The scene was peaceful. People were playing tennis on the courts to the left. A light breeze rustled the leaves.

'There he is.'

A dark figure broke from cover and sprinted through the trees with Ingeborg in pursuit. At first the hoodie appeared to be heading across the open ground towards Beckford Road. Then Ingeborg cut the angle to intercept him and he veered in their direction again.

'She'll trap him,' Mel said. 'He won't get over the canal.'

'Dead right,' Diamond said. 'He's had it.'

22

The hooded man was less fit than his pursuer. And unfortunately for him, he'd picked the wrong direction.

'He doesn't know he's heading straight for the canal,' Mel said. 'You can't tell from where he is.'

Diamond just folded his arms and watched.

At the end of the eighteenth century when the canal had been dug through Sydney Gardens the main demand of the committee was that it should be invisible to the promenaders, so it was sited at a depth of twelve feet. From where Diamond and Mel stood, its sinuous route was obvious, but you had to be really close.

'Does *she* know it's there?' Mel asked.

'Ingeborg? She was on the bridge with us.'

Gasping and flailing like a marathon runner in sight of the finish, the hoodie was no more than thirty yards ahead of Ingeborg. He covered the last uneven stretch and reached the stone parapet that was there for safety purposes. Now he would see the sheer drop.

Instead of giving up, or turning to fight, he didn't hesitate. He bent low, gripped the top of the wall, heaved himself over, swung his body down and held on with his fingertips. For a moment he hung there. Then he dropped the remaining six feet or so to the towpath. He could have broken both ankles, but he didn't. He bent his knees as he hit the ground, staggered a few steps and straightened up.

Then he was up and running again, jogging along the towpath towards the north end.

Diamond put his hands to his mouth and yelled to Ingeborg. 'Don't try it. Let him go.'

She would have followed, but had the sense to obey instructions. Hands on the wall, she leaned over to see where her quarry had gone.

He was about to disappear into the long tunnel beneath Beckford Road.

'It's not worth it,' Diamond called out. He'd walked that tunnel more than once with Paloma and he knew it wasn't far short of a hundred yards.

He grabbed the mobile from his pocket and called Bath Central. He couldn't really expect a patrol team to be close enough to arrest the stalker as he emerged at the other end, but it had to be tried. And even as Diamond was doing his limited best to describe the suspect, part of his brain was asking what crime the guy had committed. Threatening behaviour? Resisting arrest?

Not too convincing.

'Who was he?' Mel asked when Diamond finished the call.

'If you don't know, I'm sure I don't. It's you he was following.'

'How do you know?'

'It can't be us. We only came into the gardens because Tippi told us you were here.'

'D'you think he's the Megane driver?'

'I can't think of anyone else.'

Ingeborg crossed the bridge and joined them, in a foul mood. 'He was slowing up, for God's sake. I could have caught him.'

'You did okay,' Diamond told her.

'I'm not feeble.'

'Whatever gave you that idea?'

'Yes, but—'

He knew better than to get into an argument about her physical ability. 'It's taken care of. I told control, asked for assistance.'

And she had the good sense not to persist. 'What can we do him for?'

'I want to know what he's up to, that's all.'

'Me, too,' Mel added. He appeared genuinely mystified by all the attention he had been getting.

They made their way back through the gardens to Forester Road, where Ingeborg's car was parked. Diamond questioned Mel closely about the company he kept and whether he'd made any enemies recently.

'I don't have time to go out,' he said. 'It's all rehearsals and tutoring.'

'Who do you tutor?'

'Music students. It's part of our deal.'

'Female?'

'Some are.'

'Could anyone be jealous?'

'I can't think why.'

'Come on, Mel,' Diamond said. 'Even I know students get crushes on lecturers. It wouldn't be unheard of for a man of the world like you to get his leg over.'

Mel shook his head. 'No chance.'

'Oh, yeah?'

'Look, if I want sex it's on tap at my lodgings.'

There was a pause for thought.

'It crossed my mind, I have to say,' Diamond said, 'but her mother seems to think she's Snow White.'

'Have you met her mother?'

'No, I got that second-hand, but I've met Tippi.'

A nod from Mel was enough. No elaboration was needed.

'Just a thought here,' Diamond added. 'Does Tippi have

a boyfriend who might suspect you have home advantage, so to speak?'

'She's never mentioned one.'

'She wouldn't, would she?'

'A jealous lover?' Mel said, as if surprised by the idea.

'It's you he's following now, not Tippi.'

Mel scraped the hair back from his forehead. 'I hadn't really thought about that.'

'Better be on your guard. Up to now he seems content to watch you, but that could change.'

They were approaching the house and Diamond hadn't finished with Mel. 'What time are you leaving for the rehearsal?'

He looked at his watch. 'In just under an hour.'

'Because I'd love to see this valuable instrument of yours.'

'All right.'

Mel had his own key. There was no need to bring Tippi to the door again. She wasn't about when they went in. Probably getting dressed, Diamond decided. But he was mistaken. After they'd gone upstairs and Mel opened the door of his room, they found Tippi sitting on the bed with her feet up.

'Wrong room,' Mel said.

'You don't mind?' she said coolly. 'I was checking my nails. The light's so much better in here.'

'I've got visitors,' Mel told her.

'See you later.' In the act of wriggling off the bed to leave the room, she treated them to a view that was more page three than Snow White. Diamond thought she winked at him as well.

Mel wasn't embarrassed. He'd explained the situation already. He reached under the bed and withdrew the instrument case.

'I still can hardly believe this,' he said as he unzipped it and opened up. 'Four hundred years old, near enough.'

The Amati was a beautiful object regardless of its antiquity, the glazed wood almost orange in colour, the finger board and pegs darker.

Mel lifted it one-handed from the case. 'Isn't the graining superb? Would you like to hold it? Mozart himself could have played this. He was a viola player, you know.'

Diamond, congenitally clumsy and fearful of doing damage, put both arms underneath and cradled the precious thing Mozart may have handled.

'Compare it with my own, and see the difference.' Mel fished under the bed and came out with another case and opened it. This second viola was in a darker wood, but to an inexpert eye looked similar. 'Mine is a William Hill, and pretty well regarded.'

Diamond occasionally placed a bet with William Hill, but doubted if there could be any connection.

'It can't live with this, can it?' Mel said.

'Well it has to, under the bed. Is that the best place?'

'As good as any if it isn't locked in a bank vault, and that's not what the owner wants.'

Diamond handed the Amati back to Mel with the same sense of relief as the vicar at a christening. 'What about the bow? Is that special?'

'Oh, yes. It came with the instrument. The very best bows sell for about a hundred grand. I can't tell you the maker of this one. I was so staggered to be presented with the viola that I forgot to ask. To be honest I'm not using it. Tough enough getting used to a new viola, so I still play with my old Tourte. If it's comfortable and gives the sound you want, why switch?'

'And the case?'

'That isn't special.'

'I'll take a look, if you don't mind.'

Diamond picked the case up and turned it over. He was checking for clues to the true owner's identity. He found

278

none. Maybe ultraviolet would have picked up some security marking you couldn't see with the naked eye.

'I thought Stradivari was the great violin man,' Ingeborg said.

'He made only about ten violas that survive, compared to five hundred violins and fifty cellos,' Mel said. 'He was said to be a pupil of the guy who made this. Nicolò Amati was the third generation of instrument makers in their family, and the greatest. Sadly most early violas have been mutilated.'

'In what way?'

'Cut down in size to something not worthy of the name viola. This one escaped, fortunately. I was told it dates from 1625 and that's of interest because for some reason almost every other Amati you hear about is said to have been made in 1620 and some are fakes, so the date itself has to be regarded with some suspicion. To find one from 1625 gives it a touch more credibility.'

'But there's no question that this is the real thing, is there?' Ingeborg asked.

'Not to my mind. Listen.' He picked up his bow and played a snatch of something neither of them recognised, but with a golden tone, warm and soul-stirring. 'Can that be a fake sound? I don't think so.'

'Beautiful,' Ingeborg said. 'Will you ever go back to your other one?'

'Not while I have the use of this. I don't really feel it's mine. But in a sense you never truly own a fiddle. It's passed down over the centuries from one musician to the next, so you're a caretaker.' He replaced the Amati in its case.

'Forgive me,' Diamond said. 'I know nothing about musical instruments. It's hollow, of course?'

'For the sound,' Mel said with a tentative smile, uncertain if he was being sent up.

'But it has these S-shaped holes.'

'Known as f-holes,' Mel corrected him. 'The old-fashioned f looked like an S. The Amati family perfected the shape. It's remained the same ever since.'

'What if some small object was dropped inside – a cigarette, say, or a coin, or a ring. Would it affect the sound?'

Mel looked surprised by the question. 'A hard object like a ring would rattle. I'd know as soon as I picked the instrument up. In fact I think I'd know if something as light as a cigarette was in there.'

'My distorted way of thinking,' Diamond said, continuing to play even more clueless than he was. 'If someone wanted to ship drugs through customs, the inside of a violin or viola might be a good place to stow it. Mind you, a cello would be better still.'

Mel gave a prim response. '*Drugs*? That's too far out for me.'

'The holes are too small,' Ingeborg said.

'Just a thought, that's all,' Diamond said.

Like Mel, she didn't think much of Diamond's theory. 'It wouldn't fool a sniffer dog.'

'Probably not.'

'I can tell you something for sure,' Mel said. 'I wouldn't let anyone interfere with this instrument.'

'Good for you,' Diamond said.

'I'm not in the business of drug-running, anyway.'

'And I don't suppose you've ever indulged.'

'No chance.'

'Not while you're stuck in Bath,' Diamond said. 'But the South American tour might be a different story. Put that in your fiddle and smoke it. Are any of your fellow musicians drug users, would you say?

Mel grinned. 'Can you picture it?'

'They get their highs from Beethoven and Brahms, do they?'

'And why not?'

'Well said,' Ingeborg murmured, confirming her high regard for Mel.

'Is Colombia on the itinerary?' Diamond asked. He wasn't leaving this.

'Not that I've heard.'

'If a fellow in a sombrero called Speedy Gonzales offers to carry your case, don't let him.'

'I get the message,' Mel said with a forced smile.

'But in the meantime – and this is serious – if you get another sight of the stalker, let us know at once. No heroics.'

In the car on the way back to Manvers Street, Ingeborg said, 'What was all that about drugs, guv? You don't seriously think they're a factor, do you?'

'Testing the ground,' he said. 'There's an extra element in this case that I doubt is music.' He fished in his pocket. 'I'm going to call control, see if they picked up our hooded man.' He wasn't yet managing one-handed, but he used the mobile more often these days.

After exchanging a few words with the CAD room he told Ingeborg, 'No joy. Not even a sighting.'

'What description did you give them?' she asked.

'Average height and build, wearing a hoodie, dark blue or black. Dark trousers and shoes.'

'It's not a lot, especially if he has the sense to take off the hood or tuck it out of sight.'

'I suppose. What do you think his game is? Have we covered all the angles?'

'All the obvious ones. Anything else would be stretching it.'

'And you still think Mel is on the level?'

'Don't you?' She gripped the wheel so hard that the steering shuddered.

* * *

281

In the CID room a surprise awaited them in the shape of a young blonde woman with plaited hair coiled on top of her head. In a houndstooth suit and white blouse, she was sitting on the edge of Keith Halliwell's desk drinking coffee from the machine.

'Guv, this is Dagmar,' Halliwell said, as if Diamond should know all about Dagmar.

'Right,' Diamond said, with an enquiring glance towards Ingeborg, who amazed him by saying, 'Dagmar? How did you manage this?' She turned to Diamond and said, 'Dagmar is my contact in the Vienna police. I never expected to meet her in person.'

Dagmar eased herself off the desk, which involved a small jump. She was not much taller than the three-drawer filing cabinet. She formally extended a hand and addressed Diamond in a voice so deep that it more than compensated. 'Pleased to meet you, Detective Superintendent. I am Detective Inspector Aschenberger of the Bundespolizei, Vienna District.'

'We didn't know they were sending anyone,' Diamond said, impressed by the strength of her grip.

'I flew in this morning.'

'That was quick.'

'But you are not my reason for coming.'

'No?' He scratched his chin, uncertain where this was leading.

'I am here for a course in forensics at Bristol University, but I volunteered to make a special visit to Bath after we heard from you yesterday.'

Ingeborg said, 'You're a star.'

Diamond said, 'So why are you here – apart from meeting Ingeborg?'

Dagmar stooped and picked her backpack off the floor and made a startling noise ripping open the Velcro flap. 'As you know, most of the material you requested was sent electronically, but there is a piece of evidence that by law we must keep in the possession of our police service.'

'The netsuke?' He felt like picking Dagmar up and kissing her on both cheeks. He had become increasingly curious about the strange little ornament found with Emi Kojima's body. 'You brought it with you?'

'I can allow you to examine it as long as I am present. This way, we observe the letter of the law.'

'Understood.'

Dagmar produced from the backpack a transparent evidence bag and handed it across. It contained an object not much bigger than a table tennis ball, but less white. It was intricately carved.

'May I take it out?' Diamond asked.

'No problem. Many people have handled it since it was found.'

'Not many as clumsy as me, I bet.' With care, he tipped the netsuke into his palm. It weighed very little. 'Nice carving!' He held it up with his left hand. Two figures, male and female in traditional costume, formed the upper portion, with hands joined around the rim, exquisitely detailed. The doomed lovers were finely worked by the sculptor, but only to waist level. The lower half of the piece had been left as a mainly flat surface representing fallen snow, giving the impression they were half submerged in a drift.

'Do you know the story?' Dagmar said.

'The lovers who commit suicide by going into deep snow?'

'Chubei and Umegawa. We learned about this when we consulted Japanese experts to find out whether the netsuke had some significance.'

'As an emblem of suicide?'

'Exactly.' She brought her small hands together in a gesture of finality. 'With their advice we reached the conclusion that the victim meant it to symbolise her choice of death.'

'So we heard. And did the evidence back this up?'

She shrugged. 'There were no obvious signs of . . . what do you say?'

'Foul play?'

'Yes. No foul play.'

Diamond didn't relish challenging the Bundespolizei, Vienna District, interpretation, but it had to be done. 'The body had been in the water for some time, right?'

'Correct.' Dagmar looked at him with all the respect she would show to a man who had arrived at her door to sell double-glazing.

'So it was difficult to be certain?'

'We don't claim it is certain. These questions had to be decided by a jury and they could have been mistaken.'

'They wouldn't be the first. And who carried out the autopsy?'

'A hospital doctor.'

'Not a forensic pathologist?'

'She was a qualified pathologist.'

'Not a forensics expert. We had two autopsies done on our victim. The second revealed that she was strangled. A small bone in her throat fractured. Unless your pathologist was looking for it . . .'

Dagmar said, 'Nothing like this was in the report of our autopsy. But even if there was damage to the throat and it wasn't discovered, it is too late now. The body was returned to Japan for disposal.'

He didn't press the point any more. He wanted to stay on speaking terms. 'Did you discover where this netsuke came from? They're collectors' pieces, aren't they?'

'Usually they are, particularly if they are antique. They can be extremely valuable. We had this one valued by an expert and he said the workmanship was of high quality.'

'Even I can see that,' Diamond said holding the ivory piece up to the light. 'It's obviously handmade, not cast.'

'That is true,' Dagmar said, 'but the value is not especially high. It's not antique. There are craftsmen working with modern precision tools who make these as copies of ancient designs.'

'Forgeries?'

'If they are traded as antiques, yes. But if they are sold as what they are, modern artefacts, you can't call them forgeries. They have some intrinsic value for the workmanship.'

Ingeborg came in on the conversation. 'But if they're ivory, they're illegal. Ivory products have been banned since 1989, and rightly so, in my opinion.'

'That is true and no right-minded person would argue with you,' Dagmar said in a tone suggesting she was about to do exactly that. 'True of elephant ivory. But this netsuke is not elephant ivory.'

'What is it, then?'

'Mammoth.'

'Get away,' Diamond said.

Dagmar continued in her solemn voice, 'Don't you know about this? The melting of the ice-cap has revealed large quantities of mammoth remains in the Russian tundra. The tusks are workable as ivory and can be traded within the law. They are not particularly valuable.'

'Yet this thing I have in my hand is actually thousands of years more ancient than the netsuke that are so prized. That's weird.'

'Weird, but true. Mammoth ivory netsuke are increasingly being worked and traded, and not just by Japanese.'

An awed silence had descended. Visions of mammoths roaming the Siberian wastes half a million years ago were pretty remote from the CID room in Bath.

It took Paul Gilbert to bring everyone back to the twenty-first century. 'So how does this affect the case?'

'It doesn't,' Dagmar said. 'The symbolism would still be just as valid if it was made from plastic.'

'Where would she have got it from?' Diamond asked for the second time.

'In Vienna? From some private source. You don't find these in good antique shops.'

Diamond said, 'We may sound ungrateful, Dagmar, but we're not. We're looking at it from the perspective of another case.'

'I know about this. Your Japanese woman.' Even so, her lip curled slightly as she added, 'But if I understand correctly there was no netsuke found with her.'

'Yet there are other things in common.'

'But your woman was strangled, you said.'

'And we must decide if we agree with that jury of yours that Emi Kojima committed suicide.' Back to confrontation, but it had to be said.

Dagmar shot him a withering look.

He refused to blink. 'Just now you said there were no obvious signs of foul play. I noted your words. Might there have been something you wouldn't classify as obvious?'

'Have you read the autopsy report?' Dagmar asked.

'It only landed on my desk this morning.'

'We provided a translation.'

'Thank you. I haven't got to it yet. Is there anything we should know about?'

Keith Halliwell said, 'I've been through it. Some of the fingernails on both hands were broken. She had quite long nails.'

Dagmar said, 'It all depends on your interpretation. This may have happened when the body was underwater, or being recovered.'

'Or when she was fighting an attacker,' Halliwell said.

Dagmar shrugged in a dismissive way.

'You went to some trouble finding out about her background in Tokyo,' Diamond said. 'The drugs and the prostitution.'

'That was all provided by the Japanese authorities.'

'Before, or after, the autopsy?'

'After. But we had it in time for the inquest.'

'Did you discover why she came to Vienna? Was she selling herself there?'

'We had no reports that she was.'

'It's hard to understand how a woman who used drugs and traded in sex managed to get herself to Europe.'

'Maybe,' Dagmar said, 'but it happened.'

'Perhaps there was trafficking going on.'

'Quite possibly, giving her a reason to kill herself.'

'Or be killed. Is there much of a Far East influence on organised crime in your city?'

'There is some for sure, just like the mafia, into all kinds of illegal money-making. They are the yakuza, a network of Japanese gangs with international connections, increasingly in Europe.'

'I know a little about them,' Ingeborg said. 'They're rooted in tradition and go back a long way, but it comes down to the usual rackets like drugs, loan-sharking, gambling, protection and prostitution. They had a stake in a large swathe of Japanese industry, but the authorities have cracked down hard in recent years and they're starting to make inroads elsewhere. This poor young woman could have been part of the process.'

Diamond sensed the discussion slipping away from the investigation. 'There's a point you may not be aware of,' he said to Dagmar. 'Both of these victims had a grounding in classical music. Emi was trained to a high level in a Tokyo

287

violin school. And Mari's mother was also a product of one of those schools and Mari inherited the passion for it. I don't think she performed, but she spent all her pocket money on concerts. We believe she came to Bath specially to hear a string quartet called the Staccati. She had them as a screen-saver on her phone.'

'Three of them,' Ingeborg was quick to correct him. 'The fourth is a late addition.'

'True,' he said, 'but all four were in Vienna in 2008 when Emi ended up in the canal.'

'Not Mel,' Ingeborg insisted, her face flushing.

'He happened to be there with the London Symphony Orchestra,' Diamond informed her. 'I don't think you heard him telling me in Sydney Gardens. You were keeping tabs on the stalker at the time.'

Now Ingeborg went white. 'I didn't know this. You didn't tell me.'

'Probably just coincidence,' he said to pacify her. There was a bigger issue here than Ingeborg's cosying up to Mel.

Dagmar asked, 'Have you interrogated these people?'

'"Interrogated" is putting it too strongly. We're talking to them. We have it confirmed by one of them that Mari Hitomi attended the first concert they gave. She wasn't seen alive after that.' He let that sink in before saying, 'Now do you understand our interest in what happened in Vienna?'

She said tersely, 'We are not aware of any link between this quartet and the death of Emi Kojima.'

Diamond lifted the netsuke high. 'I'm thinking this could be it.'

23

If Diamond had thought of catching up on some paperwork (unlikely) or making peace with Ingeborg (more likely) or going for a pie and chips (the best bet), none of it happened. As soon as Dagmar hoisted her backpack and left, there was a call from downstairs to say a gentleman had arrived and wanted to see him urgently.

A gentleman? That endangered species was not often sighted in Manvers Street nick.

Douglas Christmas was waiting in the front hall. The pinstripe suit, MCC tie and dolphin smile would without question have impressed any desk sergeant, as would the voice like a BBC newsreader from seventy years ago. 'Remarkably decent of you to see me at short notice,' Douglas told Diamond. 'The car's outside, being guarded by one of your obliging chaps.'

'I wasn't planning a drive.'

'But you'll change your mind if I treat you to a strawberry tart and a proper cup of tea, served in a pot. There's a charming place up the street.'

Now that food was mentioned, Diamond's stomach groaned. He hadn't had a bite since breakfast.

Douglas knew he was on to a winner. 'If you prefer, there are gateaux to die for. Don't you agree with me that tea in the afternoon is the highest expression of life, liberty and the pursuit of happiness? And I do have that small matter to raise with you.'

The red Aston Martin convertible was illegally parked in the street at the front of the police station. A uniformed constable was in the act of directing a bus around it. How Douglas had negotiated this was a mystery. Diamond made a mental note never to underestimate the man.

'Hop in,' Douglas said.

'If the place you have in mind is Patisserie Valerie, it isn't worth taking the car,' Diamond said. 'It's a five-minute walk.'

'I'm not much of a walker, old boy.'

'There's nowhere to park in the High Street.'

'What do I do with the jalopy, then?'

'I can tell you one thing. I'm not being party to a parking offence.'

'Look the other way, then.' Douglas solved the problem by slipping a banknote into the top pocket of the officer doing duty for him.

In the teashop, Diamond studied the menu. He was a newcomer here, but he'd heard Paloma sing its praises more than once. He asked the waitress if the breakfast was still available. She said in the nicest way that it was too late in the day, whereupon his go-getting companion switched on the heat of his charm. First Douglas asked the waitress her name. He then introduced himself and said he was a regular at the Soho branch in Old Compton Street, which had been opened by Madame Valerie herself as a replacement for her Frith Street shop bombed during the war. He said his guest, Mr Diamond, was a food expert who had come specially to sample the quality of the service. Sadly – he continued without pause – the lovely Madame Valerie had long since baked her last croissant but he was confident she was with them in spirit, delighted that all these years later this splendid shop bearing her name existed in Bath and that a waitress called Jeannie was willing to speak to the chef about a special request from a VIP customer.

After all that, what else could Jeannie say except that she would see what could be done?

'Food expert?' Diamond said.

'Everyone is, my dear fellow. You know what you like, don't you?'

'God knows who she thinks I am.'

'The food critic of the *Sunday Times*, I expect,' Douglas said. 'You'll get your breakfast.'

First he got the chef in person saying he would be delighted to cook a breakfast and would the gentleman care to sample his eggs benedict with salmon?

'A simple fry-up, thanks,' Diamond said.

It had been a telling demonstration of Douglas's persuasive talent.

'So what's the small matter?' Diamond asked him.

Douglas poured the tea. 'I'll be heading back to London shortly and I promised my clients I'd speak to you about all the interest you and your people have been showing in them. They're artists, you see, sensitive plants, not men of the world like you and me. I can see a real danger that their music-making will suffer.'

'They've been on to you, have they?'

'I noticed it myself. The new man, Mel, is very jumpy. You put him under the cosh, this morning, I gather.'

'That's overstating it,' Diamond said. 'A few civil questions.'

'But deeply alarming to a chap who lives a sheltered life.'

'I needed to get at the facts about an incident his landlady reported to us. A man in a car was stalking him yesterday and actually knocked him over.'

'I heard about this. Very bizarre.'

'Did Mel use those words, about being put under the cosh?'

'Not directly. Ivan acts as their spokesman.'

'Ivan? I can hear him saying it.'

'Yes, a wonderful artist and a difficult personality. Ivan is waspish in his better moods and positively rebarbative when he feels there is an issue to pursue. He lived in a police state for much of his youth, so anything that smacks of authority gets him going. He feels the quartet are being persecuted.' Douglas then softened the statement with all the polish of a professional negotiator. 'You and I know this isn't true. You're just doing your job. I did my best to explain. I can't remember a time when Ivan was so agitated.'

'Maybe something else is agitating him.'

'Is there anything else?'

'The stalker, I suggest,' Diamond said. 'Ivan was present at the Michael Tippett Centre when they first noticed the car and saw it drive away at speed. He's heard from Mel what happened later. Something is going on there, and Ivan knows it.'

'Did you see this stalker yourself?'

'A bloke in a hoodie running away.'

'Pity you didn't catch him.'

'He took a risk, jumping from a dangerous height. He was able to leg it through a canal tunnel and away.'

The breakfast arrived soon after.

'That looks a treat,' Douglas said. 'I almost wish I hadn't asked for the raspberry tart.'

'What about the other two, Cat and Anthony?' Diamond asked. 'Are they agitated as well?'

'To a degree. Anthony doesn't say a lot, but he picks up the vibes when the others are in a flap.'

'Does he ever get violent?'

Douglas hesitated. 'He's a single-minded chappie, is our Anthony. It's not a good idea to cross him, but I don't think it's ever come to blows, if that's what you're asking.'

'And Cat? How is she behaving?'

'On the surface, no different. She makes light of everything in the interest of harmony. She's a good balance for Ivan, a positive force. However, I do detect some real concern underneath all the levity. There's a look in her eye I haven't seen since Harry went missing.'

'No one is threatening her. I haven't spoken to her for days.'

'Yes, but any threat to her boys, as she calls them, makes her anxious. The quartet is her lifeline.'

'Would she fight to defend it?'

'Like a tigress.'

'I'll watch out, then,' Diamond said as he took another mouthful. 'This is good. The chef gets five stars from this critic.' He looked straight into Douglas's brown eyes. 'And what's in it for you, apart from your twenty per cent?'

For a moment, Douglas was lost for words. He wasn't used to such bluntness. 'The quartet are my friends, for one thing, and immensely talented for another. They need a manager, and I do my humble best for them.'

'Isn't there ever a time when you wish you were one of them?'

'Not in a million years. I don't have a musical bone in my body. Between you, me and the blessed Valerie, it's an ordeal sitting through their concerts, but I have to show the flag.'

'Yet you know the music business.'

'From top to bottom. That's my job.'

'Your talent.'

Douglas smiled. 'Kind of you to say so, but I don't think one should confuse the gift of the gab with the gift of the gods. What they have is genius.'

More than a hint of envy lay behind those words, in spite of what had been said, Diamond decided. 'Are they your biggest earners?'

'I shouldn't really say, in fairness to my other clients, but it's blindingly obvious. Yes, they keep the wolf from my door, bless them.'

'If they stopped performing for any reason, you'd feel the draught?'

'And I'd know the door was open and the wolf was coming in. It happened, of course, when Harry went AWOL. Quite a crisis, that was.'

'What's your theory about what happened?'

Douglas leaned so far across the table that he had to stop his tie from straying on to his raspberry tart. 'This is strictly between you and me. Not even the sainted Valerie should be a party to it. Harry played a heck of a lot of poker, rather badly. You know what they say? If you're invited to join a game, look around the table and if you don't see a sucker, get up and go, because it's you.'

'He lost badly?'

'Catastrophically badly and the sort of people he played with let the debts run up to a ridiculous level and then called them in. Several times he asked me for payment in advance for concerts that weren't even in rehearsal yet. I did my best to help him out, poor fellow, because I could tell he was terrified.'

'Under threat?'

'No question.'

'Do you think his creditors killed him?'

'Sadly, I do.'

'How would that have helped them?'

'*Pour encourager les autres.* You don't mess with the mafia.'

'Is that who they were?'

'He called them the mob. "The mob have called time on me," were almost the last words he used to me. When I told the Budapest police, they seemed to take it as a reason to drop the case.'

'When exactly did he speak these words?'

'On the phone shortly after they arrived in Budapest.'

'Did the others know he was in hock to the mafia?'

'It's hard to tell. The group dynamic is complex. They appear to respect each other's privacy, but they spend so much time together on tour that they must have an idea of everyone's comings and goings. I'm in a privileged position because I hold the purse-strings. Occasionally they need bailing out. I'll get a call asking if I can transfer some funds urgently.'

'Which of them have called you?'

'All, from time to time.'

'What does Cat spend her money on?'

'You name it. She's a shopaholic. You should see the luggage she brings back.'

'And Anthony?'

Douglas gave the benign smile of a father figure. 'The poor boy is hopeless with money. He'll give it away. He visits call-girls and the smart ones get the measure of him and demand gifts of jewellery and exorbitant fees. It's happened in several cities. Cat tries to keep tabs on him, but it's not possible all the time and she can't follow him into all the sordid addresses he visits. I wouldn't ask her to.'

'Which brings us back to Ivan,' Diamond said. 'He strikes me as the sort of guy who looks after number one. I can't imagine him going to you for help.'

'You're right in a way,' Douglas said. 'There's never an emergency. When he requires an advance it's as an investment.'

'In what?'

'Hasn't he told you? He's a chess player.'

'That much I know. Does he play for high stakes?'

'I doubt it. No, he deals in chessmen. When the quartet are on their travels, Ivan always has a few beautiful handcrafted chess sets with him. He sells them to the people he plays with – at a handsome profit. If you're fanatical about the game, these gorgeous carved figures are irresistible, I'm told.'

'I see. So the investment you mentioned is to stock up with chess sets?'

'Exactly.'

'Who is his supplier?'

'Someone from Russia or the Ukraine he knows from years back. Must be Russia, come to think of it, because he wants his cash in roubles. It's the black economy, I'm sure. None of this nonsense over VAT, or whatever tax they operate there. I turn a blind eye.'

'And it's big money, is it?'

'Pretty impressive. And of course he's paid in the local currency.'

'There's a chess club here in Bath, but I doubt if the members are in that league financially.'

'He has contacts all over the world and some of them are very rich men. They tend not to be the sort who join the local chess club. But you'd have to ask Ivan if he's done any business locally.'

'I don't want him to get the idea I'm in league with the taxman.'

'Do you play chess yourself?' Douglas asked.

'A bit. I know the moves.'

'Offer him a game. Give him a chance to show you how good he is. He never ducks a challenge. He's a chess junkie.'

'And do you think he'll talk as we play? I'd like to ask him about the Russian connection.'

'Be sure to get your question in early, then. He doesn't take long over a game.'

The afternoon session at the Michael Tippett Centre should have felt flat, coming, as it did, the day after the concert at

Corsham Court. But Ivan suggested they were ready to play the *Grosse Fuge* in its entirety and, strange to relate, the challenge energised them all. The Everest of quartet music was written originally as the finale of String Quartet Opus 130 in B flat major, but Beethoven's publisher persuaded him later to substitute a less demanding movement, and the *Fuge* was republished as a stand-alone work. Unlike anything else Beethoven created for strings, incomprehensible to many of his contemporaries, this overwhelming piece leaps forward musically into dissonance. Stravinsky famously called it 'an absolutely contemporary piece of music that will be contemporary for ever'. Strident, tempestuous, uneven, it makes huge demands on each player. Only in the fifth and final part does the composer relent a little and show harmony emerging from the skewed rhythms and variations.

They finished exhilarated, their spirits lifted.

'I've got the shakes,' Mel said.

'Tell me about it,' Cat said. 'This must be an electric chair I'm sitting on. Hey, no one ever got a better sound out of the Amati than you did just then. Listen. I swear it's purring.'

'Thanks.'

'And you guys on the end weren't rubbish, either. What do you say, Anthony? Was that the best yet?'

'I was playing, not listening,' Anthony said.

'Not waving, but drowning.'

'What?'

'Ignore me, sweetheart. Just something that popped into my head as you spoke. I know exactly what you mean. I wish we'd recorded that. Personally, I think the composer himself would have clapped. D'you think God has fitted Beethoven with a hearing aid? I hope so. Ivan, have you taken a vow of silence? We're all waiting for your verdict.'

'You're right. We should record it,' Ivan said.

'Do you mean that?'

'It's a step on from the recording we made with Harry. A significant step.'

'Count me in.'

'If only for ourselves we should do it,' Ivan said. 'I can book the studio and the technical people. Let's go for it tomorrow.'

'All agreed?' Cat said.

The others nodded.

'Better call those taxis, then. I'm getting an early night. I suddenly feel bushed.'

The unexpected sound of a cough came from above them. They all looked up. The rehearsal studio had a gallery. Nobody was in sight, but they heard a door closing.

'Someone was up there,' Cat said. 'Damn cheek, listening in.'

'Students, I expect,' Mel said. 'You can't blame them. After all, it is a music department.'

Ivan was out of his chair and across the floor to the door.

'Where are you going?' Cat said.

He didn't answer. They heard him running along the corridor towards the stairs.

'He's getting more paranoid by the day,' Cat said.

Mel stowed the Amati in its case and said with what he hoped was a voice devoid of urgency, 'I'll just take a look out the front.'

'You're no better than he is,' Cat said. 'All right. Leave it to Big Momma to fix the transport.'

The entrance hall was crowded with students when Mel got there. After threading his way through to the plate-glass front he checked the open area where cars drew up. Nothing was parked there. But a black hatchback was speeding away along the drive and might just have been the Renault Megane. Difficult to be certain from that distance.

He returned to the others. Ivan was back with them,

fussing with his music sheets, clearly frustrated. 'Where have you been?' he asked Mel.

'Out front.'

'Did you see anything?'

'Only a load of students. How about you?'

'Negative.'

Cat folded her arms and emitted a sharp, displeased breath. 'What's happening here? You guys are as jumpy as toads in a thunderstorm. Isn't it time you let me in on the secret?'

Ivan busied himself returning his violin to its case.

The focus shifted to Mel. As the new man, he'd received nothing but friendship from Cat. He felt he couldn't ignore her. 'I told you about my little accident,' he said. 'What I didn't say is that I'm pretty certain the car that knocked me down outside my lodgings was here the same afternoon, waiting out front. When Ivan and I took some interest, he drove off fast. I just went to check in case he was back today.'

'And he wasn't?'

'I saw a car disappearing into the distance. It could have been the same one.'

Ivan looked up. 'You didn't say that when I asked.'

'Because I don't know for certain.'

Any of the others could have seen that a struggle was going on in Ivan's mind. His cavernous Slavic eyes held Mel's for a moment and then moved to Anthony and finally fixed on Cat. 'I've been keeping something to myself because I didn't think it was helpful for any of you to know. I can't explain it. I don't like to think what it means. I recognised the man in the car the other day, the man who is stalking us. I'm absolutely certain it's Harry.'

24

Just when he'd scaled the heights, Mel was in free fall. His place in the Staccati had seemed secure, the *Grosse Fuge* mastered, the South American tour confirmed. His magnificent new instrument was producing sound of such purity that his soul rejoiced each time he put bow to strings.

And now this.

For all the amazement everyone had voiced, Ivan had insisted he was not mistaken. He wasn't given to exaggeration. Precision was innate to his character, a Slavonic insistence on stating the facts with accuracy. No question: he had seen Harry Cornell sitting in that car.

So if Harry was alive and secretly watching the quartet, what was his game? It seemed obvious to Mel. The man had decided he wouldn't muscle in right away and demand his place back. He'd chosen to play it cautiously and get a sense of what was going on. His musicianship wasn't at issue. He was a brilliant violist who had served the Staccati well, toured with them, played concerts, made recordings. They'd always spoken of him warmly. They'd surely welcome him back.

After Ivan's shock announcement, they had all made a point of saying it was the best news possible that Harry was alive. What else could anyone say? As to taking him back, they had the tact to stay silent while Mel was there. But there's only one violist in a string quartet.

Shocked and depressed, Mel sat in his room brooding on

what would happen next. Without difficulty he could see himself back to the grind of playing for weddings and anniversaries, filling in when orchestras needed a stand-in for one of their regulars.

Worse still, he'd be stuck with his old William Hill. Mr Hamada would want the Amati back as soon as word reached him. What a wrench that would be. Mel had fallen in love with his new viola. It was a deeply emotional attachment. With that superbly crafted fiddle he experienced fulfilment, a richness of experience he hadn't dreamed was within his capacity. He'd felt ready to join the company of the masters.

Depression simmered for a while and turned to anger. Where had Harry bloody Cornell been for the past four years? He'd let his fellow musicians down, allowed them to think he was dead. They'd gone through a grim period when the quartet was in decline and virtually defunct. Now they were on the brink of success again, he expected his place back, all forgiven.

Selfish git.

Mel turned his left hand and looked at the graze-mark, still obvious. A great way to get back into favour, driving your car straight at your replacement on the team. And now he began to see the hit-and-run in a different light. Harry had followed him home, checking where he lived and waited for him to appear again. When the opportunity came he'd revved the car and sent him flying. Immediately after, Mel had been of a mind to dismiss the knockdown as partly his own fault. Now he was telling himself it was more sinister.

Harry had deliberately tried to injure him.

Or kill him.

His first assumptions had been mistaken. Harry wasn't playing the waiting game. He'd had long enough to get to know the quartet and their moods. They were a contrary bunch of people. Considering how shabbily he'd treated them, they may have decided he didn't deserve a second chance. And if so, his remedy was to make certain they needed him by removing his replacement.

It was a grotesque idea, but Mel had a sore arm to prove it.

What was to stop Harry from trying again?

Mel got up and stared out of the window. The street lights were on, but it was difficult to tell one parked car from another. Fear crept over him.

Behind him he heard the door handle being turned.

He swung round.

'Only me,' Mrs Carlyle said. 'You've got a visitor downstairs and he looks awfully like the stalker, but he's an absolute charmer and he seems to know you, so I said I'd see if you're in.'

Typical, Diamond thought.

Ivan's lodgings were at one of the best addresses in Bath, Great Pulteney Street, palatial, quiet and only five minutes from the city centre. If anyone in the quartet was going to get the best digs, it would be their wily spokesman.

Diamond wanted this to seem like a social call. He'd even thought about letting Ivan know in advance, but decided against that. Control freaks always change arrangements to suit themselves. He decided a surprise visit at about eight in the evening was best.

The man wearing eye-shadow who answered said he was sorry but Mr Bogdanov had made it crystal clear that he wasn't at home to visitors tonight.

'It's all right,' Diamond said. 'I'm family.'

Well, he was – to his sister Jean in Liverpool.

Quite a few flights of stairs to the top flat. What a good thing it was, Diamond thought, that Ivan had only a violin to lug up there. A double-bass would have put him at risk of a coronary.

It was dark on the top landing. Diamond couldn't find a

bell. He knocked with his knuckles, heard a movement from inside, and was ignored.

'Ivan?'

No response.

'This is only Peter Diamond.' He knocked harder. 'From the Bath police . . . Are you all right in there?'

He gave it a few seconds before upping the ante. 'I know you're in there.'

He was getting impatient.

'I don't want to kick it in unless I have to.'

He heard a safety-chain being slotted in. The door opened a couple of inches. 'Didn't they tell you downstairs? I'm not to be disturbed.'

'Well, it's happened, so you might as well see me.'

'What do you want?'

'Just a few minutes of your time. I'm not here officially. May I come in?'

'About what?'

Some flattery was wanted here. 'I'm looking for some expert advice.'

'From me?'

'Who else? No one is better placed to help me.'

After some hesitation: 'Are you alone?'

'Absolutely.'

Ivan released the chain and admitted him. In a silk dressing gown, pyjamas and leather slippers, he could have been a character out of a Noël Coward play. It seemed right for a flat in Great Pulteney Street.

'Were you practising?' Diamond asked.

'No, but I'm busy.'

They were in a large sitting room with an Afghan carpet, three-piece suite, music-stand and TV set. A violin in its case lay on one of the armchairs. Some foreign newspapers were scattered over another.

'Is this what you're busy at?' Diamond had spotted a chessboard on a nest of tables, the pieces spread, as if in mid-game.

'It's a match that was played many years ago between two grand masters you won't have heard of,' Ivan said.

'Try me.'

After a beat a different note entered his voice. 'Do you play?'

'To a modest level. Care for a game?'

'I thought you were here for advice.'

'We could talk as we play.'

'All right.' Ivan didn't need any more persuading. He crossed to a sideboard, picked up a box and another board. Then he reached under the unfinished game and drew out a second table. He opened the board. 'You can be white.'

'I'd rather draw for it.'

'Very well.' Ivan picked out two pawns, enclosed them in his hands behind his back and allowed Diamond to make the choice.

White.

Red and white rather than the more usual black and white, the pieces were housed in a velvet-lined box.

'These look special,' Diamond said as they started setting up.

'Ivory.'

'The red as well?'

'Stained.'

'It's a magnificent set.'

'This is the Staunton design everyone has. I could show you better.'

'You trade in them, don't you?'

Ivan shrugged. 'Only as a sideline.'

'But they're not antique.'

'No,' Ivan said. 'Are you going to start?'

Diamond pushed his king's bishop's pawn forward two squares.

'Bold.' In the offhand manner born of long experience Ivan advanced his king's pawn two squares.

Diamond made an early pause in the play. 'You're safe with me as someone who enjoys the game, but isn't ivory banned these days?'

'It's not elephant. It's the ethical alternative, mammoth ivory, from northern Siberia.'

Hey ho, Diamond thought, this sounds familiar. 'Perfectly legal, then.'

'It's down to global warming. More and more skeletons are being uncovered each year as the tundra melts.'

'So you still have contact with the old country?' Diamond nudged his king's bishop's pawn one square forward.

'You must be bluffing,' Ivan said.

'Not at all.'

'Then I've got you checkmate in two.' He slid his queen on the diagonal as far as it would go. There was no escape. Diamond's king was trapped. Ivan gave him a glare worthy of the customs hall at Heathrow. 'Fool's mate, supposedly, but I believe you're making a fool of me.'

'It's not in my interest to do that,' Diamond said. 'Well done. I'd offer you another game, but it wouldn't last much longer. How much do you charge for these?'

'The going rate for a Staunton set is ten thousand dollars, something over six thousand pounds sterling.'

'And you said you have other designs?'

'Knights on horseback and so on. They cost rather more. But I don't think you came here to buy.'

'How does it work? Are the sets carved in Russia?'

'Why are you so interested?'

'This is where I need your advice. There may be a connection with the case I'm investigating. An ivory netsuke

305

was found on the victim in Vienna and proved to be mammoth ivory.'

Ivan showed no reaction.

Diamond asked, 'Do you know anything about the trade in Japanese ornaments?'

'I don't deal in them, if that's what you're thinking,' Ivan said.

'I know you don't,' Diamond said, 'and even if you did, I wouldn't expect you to tell me. I'm still keen to know where these beautiful chess sets are made.'

'In Archangel, by a master carver. It's a business arrangement. I buy from him. I travel with the quartet to some of the great cities of the world and I play a lot of chess. From time to time I am asked about the sets and I will sell at a reasonable profit.'

'Guilt-free ivory.'

Ivan nodded.

Diamond took a photo from his pocket. 'This is the netsuke that was found. It's definitely carved from mammoth ivory. As a connoisseur of these things—'

'Not of netsuke. I don't trade in netsuke,' Ivan interrupted him.

'That isn't what I meant. You appreciate Japanese culture.'

He flushed deeply. 'No more than the next man.'

'I was told you like to visit the geisha houses when in Japan.'

'Who told you that?' Ivan said in a clipped, angry tone.

'I forget,' Diamond said. 'Must have been one of the quartet. It's the truth, isn't it?'

'What if I do?'

'Nothing to be ashamed of,' Diamond went on. 'Traditional Japanese dancing and music and the famous tea ceremony. All highly respectable, isn't it? Highly expensive, too.'

'The way I choose to spend my time and money is no

concern of yours,' Ivan said. 'I have a long-standing interest in the geisha. As a musician, I have studied the shamisen, the three-stringed instrument they play with the plectrum.'

'So the music is the pull, and not the young ladies?'

If looks could kill, Diamond would have been ashes ready for scattering. 'Geisha is an aesthetic experience. This isn't some catchpenny tourist attraction. I go to the genuine okiya in the geisha district in Kyoto.'

'Don't get me wrong, Ivan. I'm not accusing you of anything. It's your advice I came for. The geishas wear traditional dress, I'm told, and this would surely include at least one netsuke on the sash.'

'I'm not an expert on the costume.'

'But it's part of that aesthetic experience you mentioned.'

'Correct.'

'I was going to ask what you think of this particular example.'

'I wouldn't have a view. Anyway, it's only a photograph. You can't tell.'

'I've held it in my hands,' Diamond said, 'and it's a marvellous piece of carving. Would you happen to know where objects like this are created?'

'In Japan, I should think.'

'Of Siberian mammoth ivory?'

'I expect it gets shipped there.'

'Might there be craftsmen working in Eastern Europe?'

He gave a shrug. 'Conceivably.'

'But you wouldn't know any? The man in Archangel who makes the chess sets doesn't have a second line in Oriental objects?'

'Not to my knowledge.'

'Has anyone ever discussed this with you before?'

Ivan swayed back as if Diamond had thrown a punch. He didn't answer, but he didn't need to.

'One of the quartet?' Diamond pressed him.

The conversation had hit the buffers.

'I'm sure this is difficult for you,' Diamond said. 'They're friends and fellow artists, but I'm investigating two suspicious deaths and I can't allow your loyalty to obstruct me. They all know about your sideline selling the chess sets and one of them may have taken a particular interest in where they came from.'

'Douglas Christmas knows more about my business than any of them,' he said finally. 'He assists with the finance.'

'Providing you with the roubles. He told me.'

Ivan tensed. 'That's confidential. He had no right.'

'Don't worry,' Diamond said. 'Tax evasion isn't my department. Leaving Douglas aside, which of the others has talked to you about the trade?'

'I really think you should leave now.'

'One of them saw an opportunity of branching out on his own. It was Harry, wasn't it?'

Although Ivan didn't speak a word, his face had turned deathly white.

'I need to know, Ivan. You're a frightened man. Anyone can see that. You could be in need of my protection. This isn't chess, this is life and death.'

Frightened he certainly was. His lips gave an involuntary twitch before he got control. 'I only learned about this through a mistake. Seven or eight years ago we were performing in Paris and I was stupid enough to invite a potential client to the hotel. There was some kind of mix-up at the desk and they sent him to Harry's room instead of mine. Of course Harry wanted to know everything. He questioned me repeatedly until I told him the truth about the dealing I did. He was deeply in debt from his gambling.'

'And saw this as a way out of his troubles?' Diamond said.

'Exactly.'

'Except that he chose to deal in netsuke?'

'It's more profitable than chess sets.'

'The Japanese woman who was found dead in Vienna had a netsuke in her T-shirt. They took it to be a suicide emblem. Convenient.'

Ivan shrugged and didn't comment. He seemed to feel he'd said enough already.

'One more thing,' Diamond said. He took out the photo of Emi Kojima. 'On the evening of your last concert in Vienna, did you see this woman?'

It was obvious from Ivan's eyes that he recognised Emi at once. He made a performance of studying the photo to take time to prepare an answer. 'She was in the audience.'

'Did she speak to you afterwards?'

Another silence followed. This was being played like the serious chess match they could have had.

'She spoke to us all,' Ivan said. 'You might as well know.'

'And did she end the evening in Harry's company?'

A nod. 'We saw them in the hotel bar together.'

'When you say "we" . . .'

'Anthony, Cat, Douglas and me. After a time they walked to the elevator. The bar was on the ground floor. They could only have been going up to Harry's room.'

Diamond gave voice to the conclusion he'd been heading towards for days. 'And now Harry is alive and here in Bath secretly watching you all.'

25

The man in Mrs Carlyle's front room was instantly familiar to Mel from posters of the Staccati, the sort of well-proportioned, rugged face that attracted women and put men at ease, yet now looking creased with fatigue or strain. He couldn't have shaved for days. He was in some kind of padded jacket with the hood turned down. Far from threatening, he was obviously ill at ease.

'Hope you don't mind me calling. I really do need to meet you. I'm Harry Cornell.'

His unkempt appearance belied the educated voice. It was all so disarming that Mel reached for the hand that was offered. 'Mel Farran.'

'Can we talk here without being overheard?'

Mel thought about the Carlyle women and their interest in everything he did. 'Probably not. We can go out if you want.'

'I'd rather not. How about your room?'

They went upstairs. Mel sat on the bed and allowed Harry to use the chair.

'I hate this cloak-and-dagger stuff,' Harry said, 'but I can't take chances. What I have to say is for you alone.'

'Okay. Want to take your coat off?'

He shook his head. He kept his hands buried in the pockets. 'First, I want to say how sorry I am for knocking you down the other day.'

'That was you in the Megane?' Mel said, more as a statement than a question, confirming what he had already worked out for himself.

'You weren't seriously injured?'

'More shocked than hurt.'

'I know you played in a concert that evening. It was unforgivable of me. I'm truly sorry. I panicked when it was obvious you were coming towards the car to speak. I wasn't ready to meet you then. All I could think was I had to get the hell out of there.'

'Why were you there at all?'

'Making sure.'

'Of what?'

'Where you lived. I'd already followed a taxi as far as the street, but I didn't see where you went in. If nothing else, I got that confirmed.'

'What exactly do you want?'

'You're a fine musician,' Harry said. 'I heard you playing today. You bring out the best in the others.'

'Thanks, but—'

'What's your instrument?'

'I thought you knew.'

'The maker, I mean.'

'Nicolò Amati.'

Harry's eyes widened. 'I thought it sounded out of this world. May I see it?'

A firm line was needed here. The man's behaviour had done nothing to engender confidence. 'Sorry, but no.'

'You don't think I'd damage it?'

'It doesn't belong to me.'

'Ah.' A short silence from Harry. 'This is something I wanted to ask you about.'

No, no, no, a voice screamed in Mel's head. 'I can't say any more.'

'A very rich man owns your viola and wants it played to a high standard. Am I right?'

'Shall we talk about something else?'

'Soon after I joined the Staccati, I was given a Maggini to play,' Harry said, smoothly overriding Mel's request. 'From 1610. Any of us would go through fire to own a fiddle like that. Extraordinary workmanship and a wonderful tone. You must have heard it on one of our recordings.'

'I have,' Mel said, 'and I know exactly what you mean.'

'None of us in the quartet owned our instruments,' Harry said. 'We were all indebted to the super-rich, but that's the way things have been for as long as music has been played. Fat cats buying antique instruments as investments.'

'I know.'

'And then they're horrified to discover the damn things need to be played to preserve their sound quality. Paganini presented his own Guarnerius to his native city of Genoa and they kept it in a glass case in the municipal palace and buggered the tone. To be fair, my patron may have been a fat cat, but he actually knew a lot about fiddles. He had an amazing collection from what I could gather. I don't know if he owned an Amati.'

Mel didn't rise to the bait.

'A Japanese guy who didn't speak much English,' Harry went on. 'I never discovered how he made his millions. You don't like to ask, do you? Anyway, I was offered the little beauty on indefinite loan and I played it all the years I was in the quartet. I didn't even get a chance to kiss goodbye to it.'

'You had to return it?'

'It was collected.' His look was so bleak that he could have been saying a knife had been thrust into his gut.

Mel didn't like the way this was heading. 'So what do you play now?'

'I don't play at all.'

Difficult to believe. 'Why? Did you take against it, or something?'

'Long story,' Harry said. 'I don't know how much the others told you.'

'They don't know anything. They thought you were dead.'

'I might as well be.'

Mel didn't comment. How can you follow a remark like that?

'I'm constantly on the run,' Harry said. 'I sleep in the back of my car, never in the same place twice. That's okay. I've lived on the streets and survived, but I can't feel safe anywhere.'

This was all so alien to Mel's idea of the life of a top musician that the best he could do was try to appear sympathetic.

'Do they ever talk about me?' Harry asked.

'The quartet? Occasionally.'

'What do they say?'

'They have good memories of you.'

'All of them?'

'In their different ways, yes. They still have huge respect for your playing – and your company.'

'That's nice.'

'After you went missing, they were devastated. Cat roamed the streets of Budapest looking for you. Anthony went all to pieces. They had to find work for him with the Hallé.'

'And Ivan?'

'He's more philosophical, as you'd expect. He seems to think women were your problem. He saw me eyeing up some students in short skirts the other day and gave me quite a lecture about it.'

'Using me as an example?'

'Actually, yes.'

It was difficult to tell whether the twitch of Harry's lips was a smile or a grimace. 'But they think I'm dead?'

Mel shrugged. 'As time went on . . .'

'The other day,' Harry said, fixing Mel with a steady, questing look, 'out at the Michael Tippett Centre, I wasn't sure, but I thought Ivan looked at the car and recognised me.'

This was a minefield. 'I wouldn't know. We're all a bit jumpy now. Was that you in Sydney Gardens running away along the canal?'

A nod.

The conversation seemed to have ground to a halt. Mel felt more comfortable when Harry was talking. 'What is the story?'

'All right, I'll tell you,' Harry said after a pause. 'Some of this you'll have heard already. I used to play poker. Fancied I was a red-hot player. Whichever city we fetched up in, I'd seek out the casino, or, better still, a private game without the house edge. But most serious players these days use casinos. We earned good money on tour so I could play big games. It turned out I wasn't the whizz I thought I was. I was too much of a bloody optimist. Wouldn't fold when I should have. I won a few times and then lost big. Started stacking up debts. In the end, it got silly. You must have heard some of this from Cat or Ivan.'

'Hardly anything.'

'I never borrowed from the others. Sometimes I'd ask Doug for a bit on spec.'

'They weren't sure if it was poker or women taking up your time.'

He smiled. 'There were a few one-night stands, I admit. You know how they come on to you after a concert? Sometimes you're in the right mood. But no, I wouldn't say women are my weakness. Anthony is the one for that. Even before we'd check in at the hotel he'd ask the bellman where the red-light district was. How's the old goat doing these days?'

'All right, I think.'

'I like Anthony. Terrific fiddler. Better than Ivan, which is saying a lot. I was telling you about my poker debts. They got worse than serious. I was blacklisted in several of the major casinos. They're syndicated, you see. They wouldn't let me play, but they still chased me for what I owed, and some of the debts are collected by gentlemen who call themselves family.'

'The mafia?'

'You don't mess with those guys. I needed another source of income – and fast. You may not know this, but Ivan, the crafty old bugger, has a nice little earner in hand-carved chess sets.'

'That's news to me.'

'He wouldn't tell you unless you asked. It's all cash in hand, no tax. I only found out accidentally when the hotel in Paris sent one of his customers to my room by mistake. This French guy didn't have much English, but he had a stack of Euros with him. He was waving them at me and talking about *les échecs*. I thought he was telling me cash is better than a cheque. Finally he produced a card with Ivan's name on it and I sent him to the right room. In my cash-strapped situation, I was more than a little curious what all this was about, I can tell you. I asked the concierge the meaning of *échecs*. When I put it to Ivan he was tight-lipped, as you'd expect, but I wormed out the truth. He has an arrangement with some craftsman in Archangel, that Russian port right up near the Arctic Circle.'

'Making chess sets?'

'Ivory chess sets.'

'Isn't that illegal?'

315

'Mammoth ivory isn't. They're digging it out of the permafrost in Northern Russia when the snow melts. It's a huge resource. They believe millions – literally millions – of woolly mammoth skeleton remains are waiting to be uncovered. It's cheap and legal and every bit as good as elephant ivory.'

'Is Ivan selling it as elephant ivory?'

Harry shook his head. 'He wouldn't take the risk. He's straight with his customers. He still has a sizeable mark-up on the chess sets, hawking them everywhere the quartet goes on tour.'

'And did you ask for a stake in it?'

'Ask Ivan? No chance. You couldn't blackmail him. What he's doing is legal. Well, he's paying no tax, but I wouldn't shop him to the revenue. No, I thought a lot about it, how I might turn a few honest pennies. There are all sorts of ivory products in short supply because of the ban on killing elephants. The trading still goes on, obviously, and thousands of elephants are shot each year. The main market is the Far East. Decorative combs, chopsticks, fans, all that stuff. And netsuke. You know what they are?'

Mel nodded.

'I decided to branch out on my own as a mammoth-ivory netsuke dealer. The idea wasn't totally new. Netsuke were already being created and supplied. I just had to find my own carver and eventually I did. We gave a concert in Vladivostok and had two days to ourselves. I don't know how good your geography is. Vladivostok is the last station on the Orient Express run, only a boat trip from Japan. It has a thriving Japanese quarter. I found a whole street of shops selling ornaments, mostly antique. There were a few new netsuke for sale there, quite highly priced. By this time I'd read up about ivory and how you identify it, which is quite a study in itself. Basically, in a cross-section you look at the graining, called Schreger lines, and how narrow they are. I wasn't an expert by any means, but I managed to convince the shopkeeper I was. With the help of a magnifying glass and some bluffing I let him think I was some kind of inspector from the Environmental Enforcement Agency. He was bricking it. He assured me his netsuke were legitimate mammoth ivory and produced the paperwork with the name and address of his carver. Just what I needed.'

'Was the carver local?'

'Three or four blocks away. I looked up my guy the same afternoon and did a deal. He was Japanese born, a sensational carver, and of course apart from the quality of the workmanship the beauty for me was that the product was small, light in weight and just about unbreakable – ideal for travel. Much more cost-effective than Ivan's chess sets, which take up a lot of space in his luggage.'

'Did you tell Ivan what you were up to?'

'No. He's a prickly character, as you must know by now.'

'Then why are you telling me?'

'I'll come to that. My netsuke business really took off in Europe. I'd seek out the upmarket shops and sell at profit of more than a hundred per cent. Even better, it was becoming a hobby, weaning me off the poker. I got a real kick out of having a product everyone admired and coveted. I was paying off my casino debts. I thought nothing could go wrong – which, as anyone knows, is exactly when you're due for a kick where it hurts most.'

'What happened?' Mel asked.

'I was green as owl-shit. Should have realised if there was money to be made this way, then someone else would already be doing it.'

'Who was it?'

'A Japanese syndicate. I didn't know they were already trading in ivory objects in just about every capital city in

Europe and Asia. But their trade was the illegal kind, ivory from slaughtered elephants. Ten tonnes a year. That represents around a thousand elephant deaths.'

'That's horrible,' Mel said.

'There's still a huge demand for the stuff. People don't seem to make the connection with a noble, giant creature that has a time-honoured right to exist. But you don't need a lecture from me. You obviously feel the same disgust I do. Okay, I was profiteering, too, but from fossilised material. As it turned out, this was my undoing. Some alert member of the syndicate got to know about me and decided to act. But they believed I was in direct competition, trading in elephant ivory. They decided to take a close look at my carver's work, so they set a honey trap.'

'A woman?'

'In 2008, the Staccati gave a concert in Vienna, at the Konzerthaus. We were at the top of our form that night, playing the Debussy in G minor – all those restless harmonies – followed by Mendelssohn's charming A minor with its quotations from Beethoven. I was elated when we finished, fair game, I suppose, for the young Japanese woman from the audience who came up afterwards and spoke to us, thanking us in turn for enchanting her with our playing. You'll know yourself that some fans just gush and you wish they'd go away. It became obvious that this woman was a scholar of music. She talked about the closing bars echoing the ending of the Cavatina from Beethoven's Opus 130 and how our interpretation of those final four quavers had brought the homage to a perfect conclusion. Do you know the piece?'

'I do. We've played it and Ivan likes to give a special emphasis to each note.'

'It works a treat, doesn't it? Anyway, this lady was spot on with her comments. She charmed us all. While I was packing up she said – just to me – that she was staying at our hotel and would like to talk music if I wasn't too exhausted. I knew from the look in her eyes that there was more on offer than conversation.'

As a self-confessed soft touch for the ladies, Mel sympathised.

'I suggested we had a drink back in the hotel, but warned her I was tired and couldn't stay long. As hotel bars go, this one was okay, with a fountain and some nice lighting. The others were in there with our manager Doug having a nightcap a few seats away. When you're on tour it's just about impossible to make a move without everyone knowing.'

'You have to be thick-skinned.'

Harry grinned. 'Speaking from experience? Anyway, believe it or not, when she came to my room we continued to talk music intelligently for a bit, about the Debussy, that fantastic passage near the end of the first movement when second violin and viola play together. She'd noticed how Anthony was leading because he had the upper voice and she appreciated how I was reacting to him. A musician's observation. It brought us closer together and the sex, when it came, was all the more satisfying because of it. This wasn't "wham-bam, thank you, ma'am" as I'd rather expected. Afterwards I offered her a drink from the mini-bar and we talked about my touring. And since she was Japanese, it seemed natural to mention the netsuke and show her some samples from my suitcase.'

'She appreciated them?'

'God, yes. She almost had another orgasm. She said the carving was the best she'd ever seen, and she may have been telling the truth, because my little guy in Vladivostok was a genius in his way. I could tell she would have loved to own one. I don't know if it was the champagne or the nice things she'd said about my playing, but in a rush of generosity I

319

offered her one as a memento of the evening. She was thrilled. Yes, it was a valuable gift, but I told myself I could have lost three times as much in one session at the poker table. So it was a happy evening. She left my room some time after midnight and I slept well.'

Mel had listened to all this with mounting concern. He knew the police were investigating the murder of a young Japanese woman in Vienna at the time the Staccati had been performing there four years ago. She'd been dumped in the canal. If Harry had slept with her, he had to be the prime suspect. Why was he admitting so much unless it was to shift the blame elsewhere?

There was more. 'Our next concert was in Budapest and we moved on the next day. I gave no more thought to Emi, my Japanese fan. We were flat out rehearsing a new programme. I barely found time to do my rounds of the shops that sold ivory objects. A pity I did, because when I got to one of the last I was invited into the back room. This was normal for doing business. But the way I was treated certainly was not. I was grabbed from behind, thrown to the ground and held there. I thought I was being mugged by at least two strong men. I had quite an amount of cash in my wallet and there were still a few unsold netsuke in the case I carried. You're outnumbered, I thought. Best not to fight. So I lay still. Next I felt my jacket being grabbed off my shoulder and my shirt ripped open to expose my arm. Out of the corner of my eye I caught sight of a syringe poised to inject me with something – and that's all I remember until I regained consciousness in total darkness, doubled in a foetal position with my hands cuffed behind me. From the bumping I was getting and the engine noise I guessed I was imprisoned in a car boot.'

'Incredible,' Mel said.

'Well, it happened to me, I promise you. I had no idea

how long I'd been unconscious or what this was about. I thought of the concert we were supposed to be giving and my precious Maggini back in the hotel. It was a nightmare. Hours went by, or so it seemed, before we stopped. The boot opened and two young Japanese guys were looking down at me. One had a bottle of water and a straw and I was allowed to sit up and take some liquid. I tried asking questions, but there was no communication. He shoved me down again, slammed the lid and I was left for a while, I suppose while they were eating. More hours of driving followed. I had no way of telling where we were headed.'

If this is an invented alibi, it's an elaborate one, Mel was thinking. 'So where did you end up?'

'No idea,' Harry said. 'When I was finally allowed out of that bloody car boot, I was blindfolded, taken into a building and thrown into a cellar. It could have been anywhere. I was given the basics, bucket, water and some kind of bread.'

'What did they want from you?'

'I didn't find out for days. Finally a little guy in a suit arrived to interrogate me.'

'Japanese?'

'Definitely. He knew all about Emi coming to my room in the hotel and he knew I traded in netsuke. But he didn't seem to know they were mammoth ivory or where they were made. Gradually it got home to me that my selling around Europe had got up their nose. They had a good thing going trading in ivory objects, illegal elephant ivory, and they viewed me as unfair competition. My netsuke were getting a reputation as superior work and they weren't happy. They wanted a closer look at some of my merchandise and Emi had been instructed to sleep with me and beg, borrow or steal a piece.'

'Which she'd done successfully.'

'Right. But she hadn't reported back. She'd disappeared.

And he wanted to know what I'd done with her. I couldn't tell him where she was. I had no idea she was dead. In this situation I had no reason to hold back, so I told him what happened that night. He didn't believe me. He talked about codes of behaviour and certain penalties prescribed by the organisation he belonged to.'

'Which organisation?'

'Have you heard of the yakuza?'

'No.'

'You'd better know. They're the Japanese mob. A network of huge syndicates making money out of crime. They still command some respect, even though they're the biggest managers of organised crime. Like the mafia, they have their tentacles into just about every institution, banking, the stock exchange, the media. You name it. Like you, I knew nothing about them. I picked this up gradually.'

'You were down in the cellar some time, then?'

'Weeks. They were in no hurry. I lost weight and went into a deep depression. Then one morning the guards came in and made it clear I was being moved again. I allowed myself to hope they might be returning me to Budapest. Some hope. I won't bore you with all the discomforts of the journey. We ended up in Vladivostok.'

'That's a huge distance.'

'Tell me about it. I was taken there to be questioned by someone else from the organisation. And this guy didn't mess about. He told me I was a murderer, that Emi's body had been found in the Danube canal in Vienna and she had one of my netsuke tucked inside her clothes. I denied knowing anything about it, of course, but I wasn't believed. He talked about honour and punishments. He was definitely out to scare me. It was only at the end of this grilling that I realised what they really wanted was the name and address of my carver.'

'Hadn't you told them?'

'It hadn't come up before, but now I was in Vladivostok I sensed that the guy interrogating me was the local yakuza don. He was miffed because he'd lost face from not knowing who had been carrying out this beautiful work in his own backyard. He expected me to volunteer the name and address of my carver, but he was too proud to ask in front of his henchmen. You have to understand that dignity is paramount to these people. The thing was, it gave me something to bargain with, or so I told myself. So I kept shtum. There were two more sessions and I let him know my terms. If I supplied the name, I expected to get my freedom. They would have no reason to keep me.'

'What was his reaction?'

'Inscrutable, to say the least. He wasn't going to grovel for sure. No promises were made. But one afternoon I was blindfolded and taken out of my cell by two of his thugs and driven a short distance. They removed the blindfold and I knew exactly where they'd brought me. It was the Japanese quarter in Vladivostok. At first I thought they were about to release me. Ever the optimist.'

'They wanted you to take them to your carver.'

'You've got it. And of course there was a slight ethical dilemma. Did I want to lead the mob to my obliging little helpmate? You wouldn't wish that lot on your worst enemy. But I'd gone past the point of behaving honourably. I figured they wouldn't kill him. The worst they would do was pressure him to work for them, using elephant ivory instead of mammoth. He was my ticket to freedom. So, driven by desperation, I led them to his address.'

'And was he there?'

'Gone. No sign. Another family had moved in. It was a different business altogether, run by women selling silk fabrics. I was shocked. I definitely had the right building. I

323

knew the houses on either side. Yet the women there claimed to know nothing about my guy or where he'd gone. Of course the heavies who were with me took a poor view of this. They talked to the women in Japanese and still got no help. Then they turned on me, accusing me of taking them on a wild goose chase.'

'Did you make a run for it?'

'No chance. It may have crossed my mind, but they each had a hold of one of my arms. I was marched back to the car and blindfolded again and taken back to my prison. That was a low point, believe me. I'd played my ace and lost. I'd had my first glimpse of freedom in weeks and now I was back in captivity having angered my captors.'

'Do you think your carver had got wind that he was about to be visited?'

'He must have. He would surely have let me know if he was changing his address. I was his best customer. Maybe the women with the silks were his own family, covering for him. Whatever it was, I was shafted.'

'What happened then?'

'It gets worse. The guy I called the don came back next day with his helpers. He said I was a murderer and a liar and his organisation had a time-honoured way of dealing with such people, to warn others what to expect. It was known as *yubitsume*. Do you know about it?'

'No.'

'It's a form of penance or apology and generally the offender is expected to carry out the punishment himself. In my case, the don said, I couldn't be trusted, so they would do it for me. They placed a square of white cloth on a table and grabbed me by the wrist and held my hand over it. Then the don himself took a knife from his pocket and cut off the end of my left little finger, just below the top joint.'

Mel felt a crawling sensation along the length of his spine. 'God – that's cruel.'

'Painful, anyway,' Harry said. 'The original idea of *yubitsume* was that it weakened your ability to use a sword. In Japanese martial arts the bottom three fingers are used to grip the hilt. So you become more dependent on your yakuza brothers defending you. And of course everyone who saw your maimed hand knew you had disgraced the family in some way. If you transgressed a second time they cut it to the next joint, leaving you with a stump . . . like this.'

He removed his left hand from his pocket and held it up. He had a thumb and three fingers. The mangled end testified to the truth of his story.

'They took the second joint?' Mel said in horror.

'A few days later. I was considered a serious offender.'

'But it means . . .' Mel's voice trailed away.

'I can't do the fingering on the viola. I won't be asking for my job back.'

The cruelty of the punishment would have been savage enough for anyone. On a professional musician it was the loss of his life's work. Mel understood why Harry had said earlier that he might as well be dead. There was no way he could ever play again. A few times during Harry's account Mel had wondered if he was being strung along. This ugly stump was proof of Harry's integrity.

'When did they let you go?'

'I escaped. I think they were planning to take the finger on my right hand. Certainly they showed no sign of letting me go. I pretended the wound had gone septic and asked to see a doctor. They drove me out to see one of their own doctors in the city. I was acting as if I was weak and delirious from blood poisoning. This put them off their guard and between the car and the surgery I made a run for it. They chased, but I managed to escape through the side streets.

So there I was, a free man again, but with no money, no form of identity, and on the run from the yakuza, who were not going to hand me the keys of the city if they found me. Not much use throwing myself on the mercy of the Russian police either.'

'What did you do?'

'Lived rough, begged for food, joined the homeless community. Vladivostok is already full of beggars and not the best place to be a vagrant. I spent a few nights in jail, got ill drinking bootleg vodka, survived two Russian winters. I'm not proud of some of the things I did to survive.'

'You were there as long as that?'

'A broken man. Psychologically, it took a long while to get over the shock of not being able to play the fiddle any longer. If I got back to the West I couldn't foresee any future. From all I'd been told by my captors, I was the number one suspect for Emi's murder in Vienna. The Brits would hand me over to the Viennese police. I didn't have the strength to face all that. In the end I got some money – don't ask how – and smartened up enough to travel again. Worked my way slowly across Europe. Actually passed through Vienna and visited the place where Emi's body was found. Bit of a risk, but I wanted to do it. I know she wasn't totally truthful with me, but she was under duress as well and she was sweet.' He shrugged. 'And here I am.'

'Why? Why seek us out again?'

'I saw in the papers about the Japanese girl murdered here in Bath and thrown in the canal. The tooth tattoo. The interest in music. It seemed to link up with Emi's murder and I want to find out the truth.'

Mel was trying to think how he could get rid of Harry. 'I wish I could help, but . . .'

Harry shook his head. 'I'm not looking for help from you. I'm here to warn you of what you could be getting into.'

Mel did his best to make light of it. 'Good thing I don't trade in ivory.'

'I'm talking about that,' Harry pointed under the bed. He'd spotted the viola case.

'My instrument? Thanks, but I'm being ultra-careful with it, as you appreciate.'

'I'm thinking about who owns it. I don't know for certain that the guy who presented me with the Maggini is the same who owns your Amati. I don't know for certain that he's a high-up in the yakuza. All I can tell you is that I've looked online at the press accounts of when I was first reported missing in Budapest. They all say that when my hotel room was searched, my two Tertis Model violas were found. Not one of them mentions the Maggini. It must have been collected. For this to have happened so quickly, before even the police got there, someone must have known about my abduction – someone with inside knowledge of the yakuza, someone acting on behalf of the owner, Mr Hamada.'

Mel felt a definite tingling sensation at the tip of his left little finger.

'So, my friend, you've heard my story,' Harry said, 'and now it's time for some straight talking from you.'

Mel shook his head. 'I don't have anything to say.'

'I'm serious,' Harry said. 'This is how serious I am.'

The right hand had come out of his coat pocket holding a handgun, an automatic.

26

'It's bloody frustrating,' Keith Halliwell said to those of the team who were listening, 'but there's no point in us buzzing around Bath like blue-arsed flies. The boss has put out an all-units call. Wait for the shout. It'll come. Then we can reel him in.'

'Is he dangerous?' Paul Gilbert asked.

'Lethal when DCs ask daft questions.'

'I mean Harry Cornell.'

'Anyone on the run has to be considered dangerous. After four years he's probably got himself a shooter.'

'He must know he's taking a risk coming here. What's he doing it for?'

'How would I know? He's the one you want to ask. Old scores, maybe. If he's stalking the people he used to know, he must have something to settle with them.'

'Could it be sour grapes that they replaced him in the band and he's a forgotten man now?'

'The *band*?'

'Quartet.'

'You could be right. These performers have inflated egos.'

'The guy who replaced him had better watch out, then. I wouldn't want to be in his shoes.'

Diamond treated himself to a later start. He'd worked overtime the evening before, not only visiting Ivan, but making a late trip to Manvers Street to set up the dragnet for Harry. He phoned in early. No news. It was too much to hope for a quick arrest.

He caught himself talking to the cat again as he put down food, a sure sign of stress. Raffles ignored him, and after a sniff ignored the pieces of salmon squeezed from the pouch and sat by the plate waiting, a way of informing a dim-witted owner that rabbit, lamb or beef were preferable every time. Cat food in packets of twelve always included some flavour Raffles rejected.

'You're too picky for your own good, Mr Cat,' Diamond said. 'A contented mind is a continual feast. It's a lesson in life.'

A short lesson. Ten minutes later he softened and put out a plate of lamb. Raffles had been Steph's cat and he could almost hear her urging him to open another packet. So the cat got the continual feast and the contented mind.

The big man pottered around, making tea and toast until he noticed the message light winking on the kitchen phone. A call must have come in while he was shaving. He pressed *play* in case it was Manvers Street to say they'd found Harry Cornell.

The voice was Paloma's.

He stopped everything, stood still and listened.

'Peter, this is me. I expect you're still hard at work on the case of those poor Japanese women. Well, I was thinking back to our Vienna trip and that little shrine of flowers we found by the canal. It may mean nothing at all, but on the other hand . . . Listen, I've been doing some research of my own and I ought to speak to you about it. Is there any chance we could meet? Let me know if you think I could be helpful.'

If you think I could be helpful.

No need to think. This was Paloma wanting to meet again. He called her mobile.

329

She had switched it off. Nothing is ever simple. So he left a voicemail message saying he'd be grateful for any help she could give and would call her again to fix a time and place.

He'd not slept well. His brain had kept returning to Harry Cornell, asking why the missing violist had resurfaced after so long. Was the man dangerous, as Ivan believed? Almost certainly.

Emi Kojima had last been seen alive in Harry's company late at night in October, 2008, in the bar of their hotel in Vienna. She was a Tokyo prostitute who had mysteriously arrived in Vienna and turned up at one of the Staccati concerts. Working girls don't make expensive trips to Europe. Someone must have funded her, and for a reason. She had some knowledge of classical music so she'd been chosen for this job. What was the job? Surely to learn more about Harry's trading in netsuke – a lucrative private enterprise that was upsetting the big boys. Some criminal syndicate had arranged for Emi to sleep with Harry and get the truth about his dealings. She was later found dead with one of Harry's netsuke hidden in her clothing. This suggested she'd stolen it as a sample of his wares, but was killed before she could report back and deliver the goods – which made Harry the prime suspect.

Any of the quartet, or Douglas Christmas, could testify in court that they'd witnessed the pair drinking together and stepping into the lift. It wasn't too much to surmise that the action moved from the hotel bar to Harry's room.

Harry, already deeply in debt to the mafia, needed his second income. He would have been alarmed when Emi got interested in his business activities.

Alarm, panic, violence. A deadly sequence.

The hotel where all this had happened backed on to the Wienfluss, which fed into the Danube canal, where the body was found.

Then Harry went missing in Budapest, the next stop on the quartet's tour. With the mafia calling in his gambling debts and the yakuza closing in on his netsuke dealings, and the Vienna police likely to discover the body, his only sensible option had been to disappear.

As it turned out, Emi's death was assumed to have been suicide and no one made the connection with the quartet. They had never been questioned about their enthusiastic fan and who she slept with.

Four years on, the quartet had re-formed and were based in Bath. If Harry took the slightest interest in his fellow musicians, he'd have looked at the website. Curiosity may have brought him here, or envy, or the pull of the quartet-playing he loved and missed. Whatever the reason, he was in the city and a second Japanese woman had been strangled. By now, Harry would be desperate to know if there were fresh suspicions about the Vienna death and if his old companions had been questioned and how much they remembered.

This would explain the stalking.

Diamond tried putting himself in Harry's situation. There was a limit to what he could learn by stalking. He needed to speak to one of them. Who would he approach? Not the prickly old Soviet defector, Ivan. Not Cat, who would blab to everyone and think it a huge joke. And certainly not Anthony whose tunnel vision recognised little else but music.

Which left Mel, the new man, an unknown quantity for Harry, but without direct knowledge of what had happened in Vienna. As a fellow violist Mel ought to be a twin soul. And well placed to report on what the others were saying these days. This explained why Harry's car had been seen outside Mel's lodgings. And why Mel had been followed into Sydney Gardens. It was even possible Harry had been on the point of approaching Mel that morning in the gardens

– neutral ground – when Diamond and Ingeborg had appeared.

At the cost of a decent night's sleep, Diamond had a better grasp of events. A meeting with Mel was next on his agenda.

But not quite.

As he was about to leave the house, his phone rang. He snatched it up and heard Paloma's voice: 'Peter? I was in the shower when you called. Any chance we could meet?'

'Every chance,' he said. 'Can I come now?'

Her Georgian house in Lyncombe Vale doubled as home and business premises. Maybe it was understandable after their recent history that she chose to see him upstairs in her office with her mahogany desk between them and her personal assistant Judy in the same room working on the computer. Once in Vogue was a thriving international company that supplied period illustrations for television and stage designers. Two large bedrooms had been knocked into one to store the prints, books, bound magazines and newspapers. It was a huge archive, yet you had the sense that everything had its place and Paloma knew exactly where each item was to be found.

'Coffee?'

'Too early, thanks,' he said. 'It's not my caffeine rush hour yet. But don't let me stop you.'

'How's work?' Her unease was obvious. They were both as stiff-backed as guests at a state dinner. And Judy's presence didn't help.

'Hectic, as usual. Yours?'

'Much the same. You look tired.'

'Do I? It must be all the clubbing.'

He wasn't going to ask how her personal life was going. All too painfully he was minded of the tall guy he'd seen her with at the concert, the one he had dubbed the dog's dinner.

'I got your message about Vienna,' he prompted her.

'Oh, yes. Vienna,' she said with obvious relief. 'The little shrine of flowers by the canal. I've been thinking about them. The woman who died was Japanese, you discovered?'

'Yes, and we thought she committed suicide, but we now believe she was murdered.'

'Like the woman found in Bath?'

'Strangled, yes. That's the theory.'

'Don't you know for certain?'

'The body was returned to Japan and cremated. Our suspicions are based on circumstantial evidence, a growing amount of it.'

'You sound confident.'

'I am. She'd been working as a prostitute in Tokyo. Then she turned up in Vienna at one of the Staccati concerts. We reckon she was employed by the Japanese mafia.'

'Doing what – apart from the obvious?'

'Basically, spying. One of the quartet – the one who later went missing – was dealing in netsuke made from mammoth ivory. It got up the noses of the mob because they wanted the monopoly on the netsuke trade. So they ordered Emi to find out more.'

'Who was the dealer?'

'The violist. Not the one we heard at Corsham. He's new. This was a man called Harry Cornell.'

'And he was in Vienna?'

'In 2008, when all this happened.'

'Did he murder her?'

'It looks a strong bet.'

'Was he a Brit?'

Diamond nodded. 'Why do you ask?'

'Let me tell you about the flowers. Do you remember the

bunch I found lying on the pavement and pushed back into the wall?'

'The lilies.'

'We called them lilies and it's true they are a variety of lily. There was no message with them that I could see. Most of the dead flowers were bunches of carnations, some of them with cards attached in Japanese writing. I assume they were put there by Japanese people who knew the woman.'

'I expect so.'

'The Japanese like carnations. But I was more interested in the living flowers, the long-stemmed ones we called lilies. Do you remember them, with the pinkish-white star shapes and long yellow-tipped stamens?'

'Just about,' he said.

She opened a book that she'd marked with a Post-it note and handed it across the desk. 'They were asphodels.'

He remembered them now. 'I wouldn't have known. Is it important?'

'I don't know. You must decide. They have a strong association with death. In Greek mythology, the underworld, where dead souls went, had asphodel meadows. The best place to find yourself in was the Elysian fields, where the blessed went. The asphodel meadows were a stage lower, for indifferent and ordinary souls. You'd probably sinned a bit if you ended up there.'

'Just a bit?'

'Let's say you weren't considered a total write-off.'

'I think I know where the write-offs went.'

'Happily it doesn't concern us.'

'Yet.'

She conjured up a smile. 'Speak for yourself. Do you know about the language of the flowers?'

'I've heard there is one,' he said. 'All Greek to me.'

'No, this isn't Greek. This is English. The asphodel has a

meaning all its own, a precise message that hasn't changed in two hundred years. You'll find it in pre-Victorian books and even today on the internet. It's this. "My regret follows you to the grave."'

He needed a moment to take it in. 'Strange. Like a message to a dead person?'

'All the main flowers have some kind of significance according to this system and most of the sentiments are pretty bland, like snowdrops meaning hope, campanulas gratitude.'

'Roses for love?'

'Red roses. But this one is specific. It may be pure chance that someone settled on asphodels, but if they were using the language of the flowers intentionally, they were making a statement that was very suitable for a shrine.'

'"My regret follows you to the grave." Are you thinking this could have been left by the murderer?'

'That's why I phoned you. It sounds like someone with a guilty conscience.'

'I suppose,' he said. 'But let's not forget all the carnations already left there by Japanese friends or family. They knew Emi back in Japan and wanted to pay respect while they were in Vienna.'

'So you're thinking friends or family must have left the asphodels?'

'Don't you?'

'I would,' Paloma said, 'except that the Japanese have their own language of the flowers and it doesn't include the asphodel. This is a peculiarly British thing.'

'I get it now,' he said. 'You're thinking some Brit must have left them because of what they're supposed to mean. Harry?'

'They were not more than a day old when we found them. They could only have been placed there while we

335

were in Vienna ourselves. If it was Harry, he'd have needed to be in Vienna in July.'

'That's not impossible,' Diamond said. 'We don't know where he disappeared to after Budapest. I suppose he could have come through Vienna. He'd need to know the symbolism.'

'He's a musician,' she said. 'An intelligent, sensitive person, one assumes.'

And not a yob like me, he thought, who couldn't tell an asphodel from an asparagus. 'Maybe I underestimate these musicians.'

'It may be a long shot, Peter, but once I started checking it seemed to make sense. Isn't there something about murderers returning to the scene of the crime?'

'That's a myth. Only if they're taken there in handcuffs to show where they buried the body.'

'Have you checked whether any flowers have been left by the Avon in memory of the other girl?'

He shook his head. Checking bunches of flowers wasn't part of the investigation process.

'Might be worth your while,' she said.

'Possibly.' He didn't say it with much conviction.

'Anyway,' Paloma said with a trace of annoyance, 'I decided it was my duty to bring it to your attention.'

Her *duty*? With that short, uncompromising word the gulf between them had grown into Death Valley. He'd kidded himself this was about something more than obligation. 'Thanks. You've obviously done some homework.'

The disappointment must have been written all over his face. He felt himself reddening.

'I didn't phrase that very well,' she added.

'That's okay.'

'It's strange,' she said. 'When I saw you at the concert the other evening I was flabbergasted. I wouldn't have expected to meet you there in a million years.'

'There you go.'

'But now I understand. The link with the Staccati. Peter, I do hope one of them hasn't killed these women. I can't believe they're capable of such dreadful crimes. They're fabulous musicians. Even you must . . .' She clapped her hand to her mouth. 'Sorry. That's so patronising.'

'True, even so,' he said. The earlier remark had wounded him more. 'A lot of what we heard was way above my head. I recognised the "Ritual Fire Dance".'

'Enjoyed it?'

'Always have.'

'Perhaps we should do another concert some time. Quartet music is an acquired taste.'

It sounded like a peace offering, but he couldn't tamely accept it. Too much had come between them. The real issue hadn't been faced. Impulsively, he blurted it out. 'I'd spoil your enjoyment. You're better off with someone who knows this stuff, like your latest man.'

At her computer in the background Judy the PA continued to gaze at the screen, but her ears must have been flapping.

Paloma frowned. 'My what?'

'Your tall friend in the grey suit.'

'That was Mike.'

'Yes, you told me.'

'My brother Miguel. I must have mentioned him before now. He likes to be known as Mike.' Now it was her turn to blush. 'Oh my God, you didn't really think I was seeing someone else. Peter, I know we had our difference of opinion, but I'm not so angry with you that I'm going out with other men.'

The relief surged through him. He was speechless, far more emotional than he expected.

She filled the silence with more explanation. 'Mike lives in London. He's a Beethoven fanatic, and I was offered

337

tickets through my connection with Corsham Court, so I thought of him.'

He blinked and his eyes moistened.

Paloma said, 'Why don't I walk downstairs with you? Judy can look after the office.'

They left the PA in charge.

'This hasn't been a total waste of your time if it's cleared up that misunderstanding,' Paloma said as they went down her grand, crimson-carpeted staircase.

'Far from it,' he said. 'Far from it.'

She linked her hand under his arm. 'I'm glad you came.'

'You could be on to something with the asphodels.'

'Stuff the asphodels. I've missed you, Peter.'

'If I'm honest, it hasn't been much fun for me.'

'Truce?' she said when they reached the front door. She offered her lips and they kissed lightly.

'Truce,' he said. 'Sorry – and not just for jumping to the wrong conclusion. Sorry for being an oaf on the towpath that evening.'

'And I'm sorry for being such a grouch. Can we start over?'

'That would be good.'

They kissed again and held each other before he got into the car and drove away.

Mrs Carlyle came to the door of the house in Forester Road. 'You're the policeman.'

Diamond didn't deny it.

'You want to speak to Mel?'

'That's the general idea. Is he out in Sydney Gardens again?'

'Definitely not. He had a phone call from one of his musical friends and ordered a taxi straight away. He was in a bit of a state if you ask me.'

'Which friend?'

'How would I know? But it seemed to be an emergency. Something about a cat.'

'Cat? She's the cellist. Has something happened to her?'

'I couldn't tell you. Funny name for a cellist.'

27

Cat was living south of the river in a two-up, two-down terraced house, a relic of Bath's industrial past. Compared with Ivan's grand address in Great Pulteney Street, Sydenham Buildings was a slum, bordered by the railway, the main road and the cemetery, but there was an advantage in that Cat had sole use of the furnished house. There are definite compensations in living apart from one's landlord.

All the curtains were across when Diamond arrived. He was getting wise to the lifestyle of musicians. Used to working late, they were in the habit of lying in. He rang twice and stepped back to see if the bedroom curtains moved.

He rang again.

Nothing.

He put his ear against the door and couldn't hear anything from inside.

If Cat wasn't at home, who was Mel visiting?

Another of the quartet – Anthony, the second violin – was in lodgings a short walk away. As the member most in need of day-to-day assistance he'd doubtless been housed close to Cat so that she could keep a sisterly eye on him. His digs were at the bottom of Westmoreland Street, parallel with Sydenham Buildings.

Still seized with the urgency he'd got from Mrs Carlyle, Diamond drove the car round there instead of walking.

His ring was answered and it was Cat who opened the

door. She was looking distressed. Faint lines of mascara marked the paths of tears down her cheeks. 'Man, do we need you!' she said, opening her arms. 'Come in. They're all inside.'

He sidestepped her embrace.

The other three members of the quartet were standing in the living room facing the window as if something of surpassing interest was happening in the street.

'Relax, guys. The Old Bill are on the case,' Cat told them with an effort to be cheerful.

When the three musicians turned, it was obvious they were anything but relaxed. Anthony had the shakes. Mel looked ten years older. Ivan could have passed for Hamlet's father.

'What's up?' Diamond asked.

'What's up?' Cat said. 'Harry's out there in a car with a bullet through his head, that's what's up.'

She was a natural jester, and you couldn't take much she said at face value.

'Oh, yes?' Diamond said, preparing to grin.

'Fact,' she said and took a big tearful sniff. The men weren't smiling either.

He was forced to accept that she probably meant what she'd said. 'Where exactly?'

'The other side of the street, opposite your car.'

He went to the window. Some detective I am, he thought. Drove up and never noticed.

Harry's black Megane was out there with a man slumped over the wheel.

'Anthony found him, poor lad,' Cat said. 'Imagine the shock.'

'Have you called the police?'

'Of course.' She gave Diamond as disbelieving a look as he'd just given her. 'That's you, isn't it?'

'I didn't get the shout. They must be on their way. Stay here, all of you. Don't leave this room.'

Harry dead, when everyone had barely adjusted to the surprise that he was alive.

When Diamond opened the front door, the two-tone wail of the first response car soared above the growl of morning traffic. His grasp of events could be faulted, but his timing couldn't. He'd beaten the emergency service.

He ran across the road.

The man with his head flat to the steering wheel was unmistakably dead, with a neat, star-shaped red hole below his right ear. Hardly any blood had been shed. Never having got a full sight of Harry Cornell, Diamond couldn't identify him except from a general likeness to photos he'd seen. But the jacket was similar to the one the runaway had been wearing in Sydney Gardens except that the hood was now drawn back from the head.

From the nearside he saw that a handgun, a black automatic, was wedged in the space between the seats. Both of the dead man's hands hung limply over his left thigh above the weapon. The fourth finger of the left was missing.

He knew better than to touch any of the car doors, all of which were unlocked. Quite an array of food packets and cans littered the back seat. A blanket was on the floor. Harry must have been using the car as his home. Forensics would have a field day.

The police siren had been getting louder and was joined by others, and now two blues and twos in quick succession swung off the Lower Bristol Road and powered towards him. He raised a hand in greeting in case some idiot failed to recognise him and used a taser.

Fortunately he was well enough known. 'You got here fast. How did you manage it, sir?' the driver of the first asked.

'I'm Superman. Tell control we have a man here shot through the head who answers to the description of Harry Cornell, the guy we've all been looking for. We need forensics, a police surgeon to certify that death has occurred and enough tape to secure the scene. Then it's a matter of doorstepping for witnesses. You know the drill.'

'Has he topped himself?'

'Unlikely, but that's not a question for you or me. For the present we try to keep an open mind. Get on with it, would you? I'll be in the house opposite when I'm needed.'

The response teams were trained to deal with incidents like this. No two scenes were ever the same and there was much to be done, yet Diamond's priority had to be with the living, the people with a link to the dead man.

He called Manvers Street and told Keith Halliwell and Ingeborg Smith to get to Westmoreland Street fast to assist with the questioning.

Back in the house he asked the shocked members of the quartet to be seated. In the small front room this was only possible with Mel and Anthony perched on the arms of a two-seat sofa shared by Cat and Ivan. They could have been posing for a group photo, and a strange one it would have made, fit to be a Charles Addams cartoon. 'Right you are, people. I need to know the sequence of events. Anthony, when did you raise the alarm?'

Cat said, 'His landlady called me—'

Diamond stopped her. 'Thanks. He's got a voice of his own. We'll come to you shortly.' He wanted particularly to hear from the one steadfast truth-teller of the group.

Anthony said, 'Seven forty-five.'

'Good. How did you come to discover the body?'

'Looked out the window.'

'And saw?'

'Harry's car.'

'So you knew what he was driving?'

'We all knew.'

There were murmurs of confirmation.

'Could you see from the window that he was dead?'

'No.'

The previous interview with Anthony at the Michael Tippett Centre had taught Diamond to take one-word answers as encouragement, better than silence.

'Tell me what you saw.'

'Harry's car.'

'Sorry,' Diamond said, mindful of the logical process of Anthony's thinking. 'I already asked you that. Could you see anyone inside?'

'Harry.'

'And what was he doing?'

'Leaning forward, against the wheel.'

'What did you do about it?'

'Went out for a better look.'

This was the only way with Anthony, patiently prising out information. The brain that was so expressive with music had to be helped to make a connected narrative in words. 'What did you see?'

'The bullet-hole in his head.'

'What did you do next?'

'Went back to the house.'

'And?'

'Told Mrs Oliphant to phone Cat.'

'Mrs Oliphant being your landlady, I suppose. Is she around?'

'No.'

'Where is she?'

'The corner shop.'

'Shopping already?'

'She works there.'

'But she found time to call Cat before she left? You did the right thing, Anthony.'

Anthony didn't register any emotion.

Diamond put one more key question to his truth-teller. 'Do you know how Harry was shot?'

A shake of the head.

'That's no, is it? I want to hear you say it.'

Anthony, expressionless, said, 'No.'

Ivan said, 'Isn't that obvious? He wasn't there when it happened. None of us were. We know Harry was carrying a gun and he put it to his head and took his own life.'

'Did I hear right?' Diamond said. 'You knew he was in possession of a gun?'

'He showed it to Mel and Mel warned us all last night on the phone.'

Mel cleared his throat. 'I decided everyone had a right to be told.'

'I'm obviously missing something here,' Diamond said, turning to Mel. 'Did you have a meeting with Harry?'

'Last night. He came to see me at my lodgings.' Mel launched into an account of almost everything Harry had told him, about the poker debts; the mammoth ivory; the netsuke carver he had found in Vladivostok; the sex with Emi Kojima in Vienna; the gift to her of the netsuke piece; his capture by the yakuza in Budapest; the long, uncomfortable journey by car to Vladivostok; the mysterious disappearance of the carver; the refusal of the yakuza to believe Harry knew nothing about Emi's killing; the amputation of his finger joints; his escape; and his eventual return to Britain.

A short silence followed, time required to absorb the extraordinary sequence of events.

Diamond couldn't see any way Mel had invented such an elaborate story. Nothing in it conflicted with his own

345

discoveries. Moreover it was evident from Ivan's twitchy reactions that each mention of his personal influence on events touched raw nerves.

'The one thing you haven't spoken about is the gun,' Diamond said.

'He only produced it after he'd said all this,' Mel said. 'I was shocked.'

'Who wouldn't be?' Cat said. 'None of us slept last night wondering if Harry would come knocking – or without knocking.'

'Did he threaten you with it?' Diamond asked Mel.

'Not at any point. He made enough of an impact by simply producing it. He held it out in the palm of his hand. It scared me.'

'What did he want from you?'

'An update on what the others were saying about him.'

'Did he say why?'

'No, but it was clear he was feeling insecure.'

'How did you answer?'

'With the truth as I understood it. I told him straight there had been the full range of feelings from annoyance that he failed to turn up for the Budapest concert to concern when he went missing, to resignation after years went by that he could well be dead. He asked if the quartet really believed he'd killed Emi and I said nobody had ever suggested to me he was a murderer.'

'It didn't cross our minds,' Ivan said, 'but in view of what's happened this morning . . .'

Cat said, 'What are you trying to tell us, Comrade Bogdanov? Do you think he shot himself because of a guilty conscience?'

Ivan spread his hands. 'We'll find out, presumably.'

'There's more, isn't there?' Diamond pressed Mel. 'What else did he want to know?'

'The name of the person who supplied my new viola. I didn't tell him. I'm strictly bound to keep that a secret.'

'Even at gunpoint you held out?' Ivan said.

Mel clicked his tongue in impatience. 'I told you he didn't once point the gun. He had no intention of shooting me. He told me the gun was for his own protection and I believed him. He'd escaped from the yakuza, as I told you, and he thought they were still after him.'

'Not to mention the mafia wanting their poker debts settled,' Cat said. 'If that wasn't a rock and a hard place I don't know what is. Poor old rascal didn't know where to turn.'

'And then the second girl was strangled and the two cases were linked,' Ivan said. 'He became a suspect for the first, if not the second. We don't know how long he's been in England, do we?'

'He didn't say,' Mel said.

'Could Harry have murdered Mari Hitomi?' Cat asked, big-eyed. 'I can't think why.'

'Maybe she also was working for the yakuza,' Ivan said.

She took a sharp breath. 'I hadn't thought of that.'

The speculation wasn't helping Diamond. He'd run through similar possibilities in his own mind already. He picked up the last point Mel had made. 'Why was he interested in your viola?'

'It's a beautiful instrument, an Amati,' Mel said, nodding. 'As a fellow violist, he wanted to handle it, but I didn't let him. He didn't insist. The owners of these fabulous instruments set strict conditions about their use.'

Cat said, 'Harry knew that. He had a Maggini on loan to him. None of us can afford the beautiful toys we play with.'

Diamond asked Mel, 'Was anything else said that might help me to understand Harry's mind-set?'

'I've covered it,' Mel said. 'He acted more like someone

on the run than a threat to me or anyone else. I know he had the gun, but in the end he put it away and left quite tamely.'

'Would you say he was suicidal?'

'Under stress, for sure. He did make one remark.' Mel put his hand to his head and scraped it through his hair. 'I'm trying to think back to how it came up. Yes, I was telling him that while he was missing for so long we gave him up for dead and he said, "I might as well be."'

'Poor lamb!' Cat said.

'Did he say where he was going next?' Diamond asked.

'No. It was getting late by then. After ten, anyway.'

'But you phoned each of the others to let them know?'

'Because they had a right to be told Harry was around, and armed. And if I'm honest, I was shaken up by the visit. I felt I wanted to speak to someone who would understand.'

Diamond glanced out of the window. A forensic tent was being erected around Harry's car. The police surgeon had arrived and was struggling into a blue protective overall.

'And this morning,' Diamond said, turning back to the group, 'what happened after Anthony's landlady got on the phone?'

'I phoned the others and we met here and decided the right thing to do was call 999,' Cat said.

'Who was first here?'

'I was,' Ivan said. 'I took a taxi. Cat wasn't long after me. She came on foot, living nearby, as she does. We were outside looking at the car when Mel's taxi arrived.'

'Did you touch anything?'

'Naturally we did,' he said as if the question shouldn't have been asked. 'We looked inside to see if he was still breathing. When it was obvious he wasn't, we shut the door and came in here and made the emergency call.'

Cat had a better idea what Diamond was thinking. 'You

don't even need to say it. Our prints are all over the car. If there's anything dodgy about the suicide theory, Ivan and I are going to be the prime suspects, but what else could we have done? We had to check whether life was extinct. Don't they always say the first few minutes are critical?'

'Do we know when he died?' Mel asked.

'We may get an estimate from the doctor,' Diamond said, 'but times of death are difficult to pin down. If someone heard the shot we'll have a better idea. We'll ask at all the houses.'

'Could have been last night, I was thinking.'

'What would he have been doing here last night?' Cat asked.

'What was he doing here at all? Visiting Anthony, obviously.'

'Except he stayed in the car and shot himself.'

Diamond glanced outside again and saw that Ingeborg's car had arrived on the other side of the taped-off section. 'I'll be needing statements from each of you.'

Ivan folded his arms in a defiant way. 'It had better not take long. We're booked for a digital recording session this afternoon.'

'Where?'

'At the Michael Tippett Centre. The technicians are expecting us.'

Mel said, 'In view of what's happened, maybe we should cancel out of respect.'

'Not at all,' Ivan said. 'We'll dedicate the recording to Harry. He would have wished us to go ahead. And I asked Douglas to come back for it.'

'You're right for once,' Cat said. 'We've got to do this for Harry, we really must. He loved the *Grosse Fuge*, for all its challenges.'

This was getting a momentum that Diamond would find

difficult to stop. For the moment he said, 'We'll see how long it takes to get those statements.'

'You can't hold us indefinitely,' Ivan said. 'Besides, we have very little to make statements about.'

'Apart from Mel,' Cat said. 'His will take the rest of today and tomorrow, I should think. All that stuff Harry told him last night. Can he record it?'

Diamond shrugged. 'It still has to be written down and signed. A statement is a document.'

'Best get started, then.'

Ivan was at his most crotchety. 'I really don't see the urgency of this. The man is dead. He shot himself. It's not as if anyone else was involved. We could take all week and it wouldn't make a jot of difference.'

'You're wrong,' Diamond said. 'It's clear to me that Harry was murdered.'

28

Out in the street, Ingeborg Smith and Keith Halliwell were awaiting instructions.

Diamond was chirpier than he had been for weeks. 'Top of the morning to you. Raring to go, are you?'

All he got was puzzled looks.

'I need statements from all four, an account of their movements from nine last night until I arrived this morning. They'll probably tell lies and I want it as evidence.'

'All of them will lie?' Ingeborg said.

'Maybe not. Anthony may not say anything at all.'

'Really?'

'The little he does say is going to be true. He'll need drawing out, though. I'm not sure how much he knows.'

'Is it a conspiracy then?' Halliwell asked.

'It could become one. This is like nothing else I've come across, four strikingly different individuals who don't mind sniping at each other, but in reality are as close as atoms in a nucleus. They must stick together to survive as performers and their music-making matters more to them than morality or law-breaking. They're not comfortable going it alone, any of them. They have no family commitments. The Staccati is their family and quartet-playing is what they do. One goes, and it's curtains for all of them.'

'A few mixed metaphors there, but we get the point,' Ingeborg said.

Diamond gave her a pained look. 'Do you want to go through it with a red pen?'

She bit her lip. 'Sorry, guv.'

'Are they as good as they think they are?' Halliwell said to defuse the tension.

'Musically as good as it gets. Morally, the jury are out,' Ingeborg said, diplomatically picking up Diamond's theme.

'Better dive in, then,' he told them. 'Who's going to be first to split the atom?'

With that, he lifted the Do Not Cross tape and entered the secure area.

He was handed a package wrapped in polythene.

'XL for you,' the crime scene woman said.

'I'm taking that as a compliment.' He stepped to one side and started the undignified process of stepping into the protective suit. These things weren't designed for people with more flesh than figure. A well-cut suit hides a lot.

Inside the forensic tent three similarly clad crime scene officers were at work. He had to squeeze around the open doors of the car and step over legs and equipment to make his presence known to the police surgeon, who was standing over Harry Cornell's corpse.

'Anything I should be told, doc?' Diamond asked.

'I can tell you one thing.'

'What's that?'

'You need a forensic pathologist for this, not a family doctor. They've sent for Bertram Sealy.'

'Him.'

'I've done my bit. Life is extinct. I'm off to see someone who really needs me.'

'Before you go, did you look at the bullet hole?'

'I did, and the bullet passed right through the head,' the doctor said. 'But don't expect any *CSI* stuff from me.'

The body was still in the position Diamond had first seen, head against the steering wheel with only the right side of the face visible. 'Would this be the exit wound?'

'We can agree on that, going by the stellate shape,' the doctor said, ignoring his own injunction. 'I believe that's due to bone fragments being forced out by the action of the bullet. If you lift the head to look at the other side, you'll find a neat round hole where it went in. Is that what you wanted to know?'

'Thanks. It confirms what I thought.' He paused. 'No chance you could estimate the time of death?'

'Yes.'

Diamond's eyes opened wide. 'You can?'

'I mean yes, there's no chance.'

Still wearing his forensic jumpsuit, Diamond returned to the house. Ivan and Cat remained in the sitting room, sombre and silent. They each gave his mode of dress a long look, but passed no comment.

'Are we under way with the statement-taking?' he asked.

Cat nodded. 'They're limited by the poky accommodation. The young woman is in the kitchen with Anthony, and Mel is upstairs with the man. We were just saying it could take a while.'

Ivan made a point of looking at his watch. 'We'd better be through before lunch, all of us. We're due in the recording studio at two.'

'What are you hoping to record?' Diamond asked.

'There's no hoping about it. The session is fixed. The *Grosse Fuge.*'

'Can't say I know it,' Diamond said. 'Can you whistle a few bars?'

Ivan scowled.

'Beethoven,' Cat said. 'It's in our contract. The first recording we've attempted since Mel joined us.'

'If you get there I may listen in.'

Ivan stared through him. Obviously anyone who hadn't heard of the *Grosse Fuge* was a waste of space.

Dr Bertram Sealy arrived within the hour holding his trademark flask of coffee and the case he called his guts-bag. Diamond watched from a distance, allowing him to make some progress before going out to join him, wondering what insult Bath's least congenial pathologist would have for him.

Clad in his own rather superior pale blue overall, Sealy was on his knees by the car studying the victim's hands. Without looking up, he said, 'Right up your alley, this, Peter Diamond. Grotty little backstreet tucked away between the railway and the cemetery. Home from home for you with your charity-shop suits. Are you enjoying yourself?'

'I always enjoy seeing a genius at work,' Diamond said. 'Where did you buy your Andy Pandy outfit? The pound shop?'

Sealy stood up. Ever prepared with all the comforts, he'd been kneeling on a rubber cushion. 'The deceased isn't much of a fashion plate either. Do we know who he is?'

'A viola player who was once in a famous quartet.'

'He wouldn't have played too famously with a digit missing from his left hand,' Sealy said.

'It hadn't passed me by.'

'I presume he was like Charlie Chaplin.'

Diamond frowned. 'How does Chaplin come into it?'

'Played the fiddle left-handed, didn't he? You want to sharpen up your observational skills. What I'm saying is that this fellow must have done the same, used his left hand to hold the bow, so as to do the fingering with his right.'

'That isn't so,' Diamond said. 'He played the orthodox way. Couldn't play at all after losing the finger.'

'Should have been more careful, then.'

'It wasn't an accident. Have you looked at the head wound yet?'

Sealy was not ready to move on. 'Are you one hundred per cent certain he was right-handed?'

'I've seen pictures of him playing.'

Sealy tapped his chin with his surgical-gloved finger. 'That's odd.'

'The exit wound being on the right side of the head?' Diamond said.

'Well, yes.'

'I thought so, too.' Diamond aired his new bit of expertise. 'It *is* the exit wound because it's stellate, agreed?'

'Swallowed a forensic manual, have we?' Sealy said. 'This is the problem. The bullet entered the head from the left side. Did a right-handed man put the gun to his left temple? Or use his left hand to fire with? Difficult and unlikely. Ergo if he really was right-handed he didn't fire the gun himself. It was murder.'

'From close range?'

'Look at this.' Sealy grasped the hair on the dead man's head and pulled it back far enough to display the circular hole on the left side. 'It's too neat for a contact discharge and there's no muzzle stamp, but there is what we call an abrasion collar caused by friction, heating and dirt. That's close range.'

'Right.'

'The burning and powder tattooing wouldn't be present if the gun was fired from a distance of more than, let's say, a metre. Do you have any suspects?'

'Several.'

'Better look for GSR, then.'

'You've got me there.' Diamond had a blind spot for acronyms and abbreviations.

'Gunshot residue. The thing was fired in a confined space. And don't just check the hands and clothes. It can get into nostrils, ear canals, places you wouldn't think of.'

Diamond wasn't ignorant of forensic procedures, but he didn't look forward to literally getting up the noses of the quartet without arresting them. He'd only just confirmed that murder had been committed and any evidence he had against the four was circumstantial. They wouldn't think it a privilege to be asked for swab samples.

Sealy was still talking about the gun. 'I wonder where the bullet ended up if it didn't smash the window.'

'He may have ducked,' Diamond said, 'in which case the angle could have been downwards and we'd find it lodged in the bodywork.'

One of the CSI team spoke up. 'We already found it in the offside door, sir.'

'Where is it, then?'

'In an evidence bag with my boss. It's a nine millimetre. Fits the Glock 17 that you see between the seats.'

'Thanks.' Diamond turned back to Sealy. 'Is it too much to ask for an estimate?'

'Of what? My fee?'

'Time of death.'

'Has any pathologist *ever* given you an accurate time of death? If so, he was either a bloody good guesser or the killer.'

'Thanks for nothing, then.'

'If I could give you an answer, believe me I would triple my fee.'

Diamond exited from the tent and squirmed out of the protective suit. He'd formed a pretty clear picture of the killing. At some point last evening or early this morning Harry had parked the car opposite Anthony's lodging with the intention of visiting him. His proven method was to sit in the car and observe before doing anything else. He may have spent the night there. The gun, his protection, would be kept somewhere handy, in a pocket, or the glove compartment, or lying on the passenger seat.

The killer had approached the car and seen Harry sitting behind the wheel. They knew each other, so it was not immediately a conflict situation. Harry hadn't apparently wound down his window to speak. He must have reached across and opened the door on the passenger side, allowing the killer to lean inside or sit beside him and talk. At some point Harry must have mentioned the gun, as he had when speaking to Mel. The moment it was produced was the opportunity for the killer to grab it and fire at point blank range.

An impulsive killing.

The short period following the shot was critical. Had anyone in the nearby houses overheard? Quite likely. But if they went to their windows and looked out, what was there to see? Just the usual line of parked cars. The killer would wait five or ten minutes before quitting the scene. And there was time for a decision. Take the murder weapon away, or leave it close to Harry's hand to suggest suicide? Maybe attempt to wipe it clean of prints and DNA first. Press it against Harry's hand before placing it between the seats, and then slip quietly away.

But in the pressure of the moment basic errors had been made. The most obvious had already been made clear: a right-handed man doesn't put a gun to the left side of his head. Suicide was never an option.

Firing the shot inside the car was another mistake. Sealy was right about gun shot residue, but in addition there would be DNA from the killer deposited on and around the passenger seat. It was a maxim of forensic science that every contact leaves a trace. Wiping the gun wouldn't work either. These weren't sterile conditions. Traces would remain.

All very encouraging for the investigation.

But there's always a snag. The snag here was the familiar one that bedevilled modern detectives. Forensic science won't be hurried. This was a complex scene. The car had been lived in for days, if not weeks. Talk about traces: it teemed with traces, of skin particles, hair, food, blanket fibres and all the other droplets and driblets that are deposited in a car every time it is used.

The evidence would be agonisingly slow in emerging. Weeks, probably.

Diamond needed a swifter result. He returned to the house.

Ivan and Cat were still waiting to have their statements taken. Ivan was like a corked volcano.

'Can't you speed this up? You're supposed to be in charge.'

This was a helpful opening. 'All right,' Diamond said. 'We can make a start right away.'

'On what?' Ivan said. 'My statement as to where I was last night? It comes down to one sentence. You visited me yourself and I didn't leave my lodgings until this morning when I got the call from Cat.'

Cat said, 'Mine is a one-sentence statement, too. A seven forty-five call from Anthony's landlady.'

'Before we go into that,' Diamond said, 'I need some help from you both about what happened four years ago in Budapest.'

'Budapest?' Ivan said as if Diamond had named Timbuktu.

Cat was faster on to it. 'Where Harry went AWOL? Not much we can help with there, your honour. It was a mystery at the time and I'm not much clearer now.'

'You told me you searched the streets for him.'

'It was panic stations. Ivan can tell you. We had a concert to give. Brilliant and talented as we are, we haven't yet discovered how to play a string quartet without a violist.'

'Was it unusual for Harry to let you down?'

'Unheard of,' Cat said. 'Ivan will bear that out.' She almost had to nudge him to speak up.

'That is true,' Ivan said after a pause for thought. 'He would go off alone for hours on end – you now know where – and always be in time for concerts and rehearsals. He had a playboy streak, but there was a responsibility there as well.'

'And a sensitive side,' Cat said.

'Sensitive in what way?'

'Whenever we performed in Vienna, he would visit Beethoven's grave in the Central Cemetery and place a single sprig of rosemary there, for remembrance.'

'The language of flowers?' Diamond said with an upsurge of interest.

'It is, isn't it? I don't know all the meanings, but Harry must have.'

He tucked that away in his memory. 'What interests me in particular is what happened to his viola after he disappeared.'

'The Maggini?'

'Going by what he told Mel, it must have gone missing from his hotel room before the police made their search. A valuable antique instrument.'

'A thing of beauty,' Ivan said.

Cat asked Diamond, 'What are you getting at? Do you think he took it with him?'

'Highly unlikely,' Diamond said. 'He was doing the rounds of the shops trying to offload the ivory netsuke when the yakuza kidnapped him.'

'Well now. That is a point,' Cat said. 'Of course he

wouldn't take the Maggini with him. He had it on trust and he looked after it. We're all using priceless pieces of wood and gut to make music, including Mel. My cello is a Strad. Are you thinking our instruments are behind these crimes?'

'People are behind them,' Ivan said.

'Of course, O Wise One,' she said, 'but people can be motivated by greed.'

Ivan snorted in impatience.

Diamond turned to him. 'Don't you agree?'

'The instruments have nothing to do with any of this,' Ivan said emphatically.

'You sound confident.'

'Because I am.'

'So was it you who removed the Maggini from Harry's room?'

Ivan flushed scarlet as if the suggestion was monstrous. He took in a deep breath. Then he sighed, his shoulders sagged and he admitted, 'I took it into safe-keeping as a precaution. It was eventually returned to the true owner.'

'I wish you'd told me earlier.'

'There was an issue of confidence. The same owner presented me with the Guarnerius I play. He pledges us to secrecy.'

'Who is the owner?'

'I'm not at liberty to say.'

'You won't be at liberty much longer if you don't say.'

Another sigh. For all his tough talk, Ivan's resistance was habitually paper-thin. 'His name is Hamada and he is a Japanese collector of rare and beautiful instruments. He heard of Harry's disappearance and asked me to make sure that the viola was safe. I gave a generous tip to one of the chambermaids and she let me into the room knowing I was a colleague of Harry's.'

'When you say "heard of Harry's disappearance" it begs a question.'

'Was Mr Hamada a party to the kidnapping? Definitely not,' Ivan said. 'He's a powerful man who guards his privacy, but his intentions towards us are wholly supportive.'

Diamond wasn't convinced. 'He knew about the kidnapping before the police were on the case. He must have links to the yakuza.'

'That's not impossible,' Ivan admitted. 'But yakuza isn't a unified group. It's a generic name given to more than twenty Japanese gangs who compete for the best pickings from organised crime. Their codes and traditions, including the amputation of fingers, may be similar, but they rival each other. Mr Hamada's interest in the quartet has been positive from the start. I've known him for years and he wants his instruments played by the best musicians and in the world's top concert halls. Not long ago he came to Bath and presented our new member Mel with a priceless Amati viola. That isn't a man who would be party to the kidnapping of one of us.'

This was a new insight for Diamond, and believable. A super-rich man might well keep tabs on the yakuza to know what crimes were committed by some of its many factions.

'You say you've known him years.'

'I've only met him a few times, but we keep in touch. I delivered the Maggini to him personally in London some months after recovering it. He entrusted me with it until I could place it into his hands.'

'You didn't tell the rest of us,' Cat said.

Ivan shrugged. 'You know what he's like.'

Cat turned to Diamond. 'If it's any help, I can also vouch for Mr Hamada. He's on our side. I'm sure if he'd had the power to stop them kidnapping Harry, he would have done so.'

'It was a disaster for us all,' Ivan said. 'Harry should never have got into so much financial trouble.'

'If we'd known the full facts, we would have rallied round,' Cat said. 'We suspected he was into something flaky at the time, but none of us guessed it was so serious.'

Ivan said with a shake of the head, 'The idiot.'

'Too late in the day to chuck insults after him,' Cat said. 'The poor boy's had a hellish time ever since and now he's dead.'

'We all had a huge stake in the quartet's existence,' Ivan said, addressing Diamond. 'Our professional lives were bound up in it. We tried to look out for each other. I was usually the spokesman and leader. Cat was like a mother to us all and kept us in good spirits. Anthony with his focused brain is like a child in some ways and needs practical help. And Harry with his laid-back manner kept us from getting too intense about our music or anything else. It was a nice balance.'

This touching tribute to the Staccati came to an end just as Ingeborg emerged from the kitchen with Anthony.

'All done?' Diamond asked.

Ingeborg nodded and ran a hand through her blonde hair. The session had obviously been stressful.

'Anything I should be told?'

She shook her head.

Then Keith Halliwell came down the stairs followed by Mel.

'We could murder a coffee,' he said.

'They did it!' Cat said at once. 'Take them down to the nick and throw the book at them.'

'Do you want one?' Halliwell asked Ingeborg.

She shook her head. 'Why do you think I picked the kitchen for my interviewing?'

Diamond said, 'The last two statements shouldn't take long.'

Ivan said, 'After that, are we free to go?'

'I'll need you all to read them through and sign them, but that can be done at the end of this afternoon's recording.'

There were smiles of relief from three of the musicians. Even Anthony managed a nod.

29

'What's the boss up to now, letting them record their party piece?' Ingeborg asked on the drive to Newton Park.

'Don't ask me,' Halliwell said. 'We had all four in that house this morning. We could have pulled them in and got to the truth.'

'There's a change in him today. He's more like he used to be.'

'Cocksure and pushy?'

'I was going to say frisky, but I guess it's much the same.'

'As if he knows something we don't.'

'By the way he's behaving, anything is possible. Only it could be down to something else,' Ingeborg said. 'His love life is looking up. He came in wearing aftershave this morning.'

'Doesn't he usually?'

'Only when he's seeing Paloma.'

They parked behind the Michael Tippett Centre and zigzagged around clusters of gossiping students on their lunch-break towards the two digital recording studios. Diamond was waiting outside, still unmistakably frisky. 'Don't look so hard done by,' he said. 'I've asked and this lasts only sixteen minutes.'

'For one take,' Halliwell said. 'They're never satisfied with one.'

Diamond hadn't thought of that. 'Today, they have to be.'

'Have they all turned up?' Ingeborg asked.

He nodded. 'And so has Douglas Christmas.'

'I'd almost forgotten him.'

'He's in there already. Shall we join him?'

Extra seats had been placed at the rear of the narrow control room. The technical team were already manning the digital audio workstation, headphones on, testing the controls. Through the glass the Staccati were seated in the usual formation, violinists to the left and Mel and Cat right. Deep in concentration, they were fine-tuning, obtaining the A from Ivan and making their own small adjustments. In addition Cat and Mel would compare C strings, a wise check for accuracy allowing that the pitch of the instruments was an octave apart. There was an air of anticipation, that mix of excitement and nerves that is the dynamic of any performance.

Diamond took the chair beside Douglas. 'Glad you made it here.'

The manager nodded. 'I support them whenever I can. After all, they're my breadwinners.'

'Enjoy your last meal, then.'

Douglas clearly missed the point but registered with a grin that it must be humorous. In fact, he followed with a quip of his own. 'And what are you chaps doing here – making an arrest?'

Diamond said straight-faced, 'All in good time.'

'Are you familiar with the piece?'

'That would be an overstatement.'

'I'd better warn you, then. It can be difficult to the untrained ear, even brutal.'

'Up my street, then.'

Everyone smiled.

'Ghastly news about Harry,' Douglas said. 'A sad end to a fine musician. I'm going to suggest they dedicate this to his memory.'

'Difficult and brutal?'

Douglas was lost for words. He clearly wasn't on Diamond's wavelength.

The producer touched a switch on the console and spoke through his mike to the artists. 'How are we doing, folks? Almost ready to go?'

In the studio Ivan turned to the others and got their agreement. He raised his bow towards the window.

'In your own time, then. We're running now.'

The players took their cue from Ivan and began.

The overture, as the composer termed it, of the *Grosse Fuge* made no concessions. It demanded attention to what amounted to snatches of unrelated music separated by long pauses that would only have relevance as the piece developed. Eventually they would be identified as a kind of running order for what was to come, but perversely Beethoven had turned the whole thing on its head and started with the finale.

Fair warning.

The sound was relayed to the control room for the benefit of the little audience. The technicians in their headphones concentrated on getting the ideal mix, oblivious of any conversation from behind them. There *was* a voice speaking. At the back, Diamond had begun a performance of his own.

'While this goes on I'm going to explore the evidence and see if we can agree what actually happened. We have three unexplained deaths, three murders as it turns out, with the Staccati featuring in some way in each one.'

'The common factor,' Halliwell said, rather like the second violin developing the theme.

'Let's start in reverse order,' Diamond went on. 'Why was Harry killed? On impulse, apparently. The opportunity presented itself and the killer snatched the gun and shot him. If you're planning a murder you can't expect your victim to supply the loaded weapon. So it was unplanned. A crude attempt was made afterwards to suggest it was suicide. Crude and poorly executed.'

'There must have been a reason for the killing,' Ingeborg said.

'There was. Harry had to be silenced.'

'Why?'

'It goes back a long way. He had unfinished business with the quartet. He naively supposed he could return and learn the truth about the murder of Emi Kojima in Vienna in 2008. The police had been led to believe she drowned herself, but the yakuza knew better. They knew the netsuke she was carrying in her clothes – a suicide emblem – wasn't a statement of intent, but a sample obtained on their instructions and for their inspection. She had been working for them, brought to Vienna to get the inside story of the trade in ivory objects, and they were angry. They decided, rightly, that she had been murdered. Harry was the obvious suspect and they removed two of his finger joints to try and extract a confession. But Emi's death was a mystery to Harry. He couldn't say who killed her, or why.'

'What a nightmare,' Ingeborg said. 'It's bad enough being tortured for information, but when you don't have the information to give, that's too horrible to imagine.'

Diamond was trying to keep imagination out of it. 'Harry remained in terror of the yakuza. He'd escaped and gone into hiding, but he lived in constant fear of being caught again and put through more agony, or executed. When he learned that the Staccati were fully functioning again and were in Bath with a new violist he decided to visit his former colleagues and ask if they knew the truth of what happened in Vienna in 2008. He returned to Britain, rented a car, drove to Bath with the idea of observing them first, armed with a gun for his own protection. After so much had gone wrong in his life he was cautious.'

'Can't blame the guy, after all he'd gone through,' Ingeborg said.

Diamond continued the story. 'But first came the shock of Mari's body being discovered in the canal, another Japanese woman murdered and disposed of in the same way. What was he to make of it? Could one of his old colleagues be the killer? He wasn't sure which of them he could trust.'

'Mel,' Halliwell said. 'Mel was the new man. And he thought Mel hadn't been in Vienna.'

'As we later discovered, he had, playing with the London Symphony Orchestra, but Harry didn't know that. To Harry, Mel was clean, the new man, his replacement as viola player. So Harry found out where he was living and after spying on him for a time and nearly getting caught at it, he called at the house and found out from Mel how things currently stood. A calculated risk. Fortunately they got on well, particularly because there was no threat of Harry claiming back his place in the quartet. After the loss of his finger he would never play again. The meeting passed off peaceably and Harry planned his next move. He would make an approach to Anthony.'

'Why Anthony?' Ingeborg asked.

'Because he could rely on him to tell the truth. There's no sophistry with Anthony. He gives it to you straight if he gives you anything at all. That's a symptom of his condition. So if Anthony knew what really happened in Vienna – even if he had killed the woman himself – Harry had a chance of extracting a truthful account. He drove to Westmoreland Street last night and waited for the right moment.'

The quartet were already into the second section and it was complex. The essence of any fugue is that a melody or theme, known as the subject, is introduced and then taken up by each of the other players until all four are weaving an elaborate mesh. Connective passages lead on to other variations of the theme. That can be demanding enough. Here, Beethoven had a double fugue in play from the start, a remorseless deluge of counterpoint, savage in its intensity. The term 'brutal' that Douglas had used was not unwarranted. Fingering too quick for the eye to follow, frenetic bowing and faces taut with concentration testified to the severity of the journey through this jungle. The players were at the limit of what was musically possible.

Diamond, too, was developing a difficult new subject. The music wasn't entirely lost on him; he expected to evoke moods of disquiet and dissonance that matched. 'For the moment let's leave Harry sitting in his car outside Anthony's place. I want to return to the night Emi Kojima was murdered in Vienna. Remember she was a talented musician herself. She'd been chosen by the yakuza as the honey trap for Harry, to get the lowdown on his ivory trading. She attended the recital at the Konzerthaus and made a point of approaching the artists afterwards and talking intelligently about the music. She was there to pull Harry, and she did. Later in the evening the other players were drinking in the hotel bar and saw Harry get into the lift with Emi, the last time she was seen alive.' Diamond turned to Douglas. 'You were there that night.'

Douglas jerked as if he'd been punched. Up to now he'd been staring through the glass, obviously trying to give the impression he wasn't listening to Diamond. 'Aren't you interested in the music?'

'It's over my head,' Diamond said. 'You'll be able to hear it on disc later. I'm asking about Vienna, what was said in the hotel bar.'

'I hope you're not suggesting I had something to do with these tragic events.'

Diamond smiled. 'I don't mind telling you I've had my

suspicions. You seemed to be around at the critical times.'

'It's my job. I'm their manager.'

'Yes, and just to be certain, I made a call before coming here to check if you were in London this morning, and you were. You couldn't have shot Harry.'

'I'm glad that's clear, then. I don't kill my own clients, even ex-clients. What did you just ask?'

'What was the talk about Harry in the Vienna hotel bar?'

'It was a long time ago,' Douglas said. 'I think we passed a few remarks. He was up to his old ways with the ladies, that sort of thing. He had a spicy reputation.'

'Anything else?'

A shrug and a sigh. 'We were all quite relaxed about it, as I recall. We recognised the young woman as the music buff who came up after the concert. Someone – it may have been me – laughingly suggested she might have been trying to lure Harry away to the Tokyo Quartet. Good violists, you see, are much in demand. And Vienna is the place where musical wheeling and dealing is done.'

'It wasn't a serious remark?'

'Not from me, of all people. I didn't want anyone to defect.'

'Would the others have taken it lightly?'

Douglas tilted his head one way and the other like a parrot under scrutiny. 'Cat will have laughed it off, or topped it with something more outrageous. You never know how Ivan or Anthony will react. They can get far too uptight and obsessive about the quartet, but I don't think they rose to the bait. I honestly can't remember how it was left. Soon after, we all went to bed ourselves.'

As if on cue, the quartet had started the third part, a more accessible sequence at a slower tempo, tender by contrast with what had just gone before. The players' faces reflected the lyrical nature of the theme. The lines of anxiety had gone from Ivan's brow. Beside him, Anthony's lips had formed into something near a smile. Mel was leaning back as he played. And Cat had time to brush away a wayward strand of hair.

Diamond resumed. 'Emi didn't remain all night with Harry. She left after they'd had sex and she'd persuaded him to part with the netsuke. Earlier, she'd given the impression she was a guest at the hotel, but this wasn't true. She was under instructions to report back to the yakuza with the netsuke. She took the route beside the river Wien that links to the canal and she must have been followed. Someone was deeply alarmed about her.'

'Harry?' Halliwell said. 'He'd worked out what this was all about?'

'Unlikely. He wouldn't have dropped her into the canal without recovering the netsuke. After all, it linked her to him. But someone attacked her and almost certainly strangled her and dumped the body in the canal. The reason, the motive, is the key to this whole mystery.'

In the studio, a dramatic change in the music sent the players careering into the fourth part. The jarring fugal themes returned at full pitch, outrageous in complexity, skewed into ever-changing variations, playing havoc, twisting, reversing, rollercoasting into dissonance and darkness. Eyes wide, the musicians strove to stay with it, the strain as extreme as it gets.

'We can't consider the killing of Emi without leaping forward to Mari Hitomi,' Diamond said. 'The deaths are related. We know for certain that Mari was strangled and thrown into the Kennet and Avon canal. The same method of disposal. And why? Because up to this time the killer appeared to have got away with the first murder this way. A rotting corpse recovered after weeks in water doesn't yield many clues. If she hadn't been identified from the tooth tattoo we might never have made the connection. Once we had the facts, the parallels were striking. Two Japanese women with knowledge of classical music who attended Staccati concerts and approached the players afterwards as fans. Two women who ended up murdered in canals. What can we get from that?'

'The killer had a thing about Japanese women?' Halliwell said.

Ingeborg rounded on him. 'What do you mean – a "thing"?'

'I don't know what psychologists would call it. A love–hate complex? All his sexual fantasies revolve around Japanese women.'

'Ivan,' Ingeborg said at once.

'I've been thinking hard about Ivan,' Diamond said. 'He's a regular visitor to the geisha houses. He told me himself that he visits Kyoto and plays the three-stringed instrument with the geishas. These aren't knocking shops. They're highly respectable places controlled with long-established rules. It's genuinely about traditional culture. But with my suspicious mind I wondered what really motivates Ivan. Is he secretly wishing he could have sex with these unattainable women? And when a Japanese woman says she's a fan and wants to hang out with the quartet, does it start an adrenalin rush in Ivan? Is he transferring all those pent-up desires to these hapless women? It's not difficult to see how it could get nasty if, for example, they reject the advance.'

'How would it have happened?' Ingeborg said.

'He'd see Emi going up to the hotel room with Harry and he'd wait for her to come out. Something similar with Mari. He thinks because the geishas dance attendance he's got a special way with all Japanese women. With these two it doesn't work out and he turns violent.'

'Is that it?' Ingeborg said. 'Ivan is the killer?'

Behind the glass they could see Ivan's piston movement with the bow, ferociously rising to the demands of the score while the fingers of his left hand kept a continuous vibrato in play.

'He seemed more shaken than anyone else when Harry reappeared this week,' Diamond went on. 'He recognized him in the car and kept the knowledge to himself. When I called on him at his lodgings he was fearful that I was Harry. I had to threaten to knock the door down.'

'Did Harry know Ivan was the killer?' Halliwell asked.

'Harry knew nothing. Ivan was in a state of near-panic because he thought Harry wanted reinstating as the Staccati violist. He didn't know about the missing finger. Ivan can't take disruption. He wants the quartet to stay as it is. After four years in the wilderness they had only just got back to peak performance again. He had no strategy for dealing with Harry. As a chess player that alarmed him.'

'So the panic wasn't because Harry could turn him in?'

In the studio, the ferocious drive of the violins reached a pitch of intensity that caused Diamond to break off.

There was a difference of tone when he resumed. 'When all is said and done, these crimes aren't down to Ivan,' he said with certainty. 'Remember he's the controlling one, the chess expert. There was too much left to chance, too many mistakes, too many unknowns. Do I have to go over them again? He wouldn't dream of attempting a murder without a master plan. Ivan would make sure he committed the perfect crime.'

'I can agree with that,' Douglas said. 'He covers every angle.'

'Is it Anthony, then?' Ingeborg said.

'What's the case for Anthony?' Diamond said. 'The ball's in your court.'

'Pretty straightforward,' she said. 'He's obsessive, autistic,

373

liable to tantrums. Yet he's no child. He has a sex drive and visits prostitutes. He's been around when each of the killings took place. Harry was murdered right outside the house where he lives.'

'Why would he have killed these women?'

'Because he has no ability to relate to us,' she said, as if speaking for all women. 'He can't form relationships. We're sex objects, and that's it. The tragic irony is that he's a young, attractive-looking guy who is going to appeal to women. But when they show interest he assumes it's sex they want and if they don't immediately respond he kills them.'

'Simple as that?' Diamond said.

'Issues are simple for Anthony.'

'So you're saying he murdered Harry as well?'

'Harry made the mistake of parking outside Anthony's lodging and sitting there. Anthony went out to him and asked what he wanted. Harry started asking awkward questions about what happened in Vienna and Anthony grabbed the gun and pulled the trigger.'

'Do you know this for sure? You interviewed him.'

Assertive as Ingeborg liked to appear, she was sometimes betrayed by a blush and it happened now, spreading with the speed of a flash fire. 'I didn't in fact get much from him. I've told you my theory.'

'You think he shot Harry because questions were asked about the killing of Emi?'

'Awkward questions.'

Diamond was shaking his head. 'Awkward questions aren't awkward for Anthony. What's done is done. He gives it to you straight. He told us what happened this morning, how he went out and saw the bullet-hole in Harry's head and how he told his landlady and she phoned Cat.'

'Yes,' she said, still pressing her theory, 'but what he didn't say is what matters. He didn't say he'd gone out to the car and shot Harry last night, which I believe is what happened. You didn't ask him, so he didn't tell you.'

'In fact I put the question to him when I first got to the scene before you came,' Diamond said. 'These were my actual words to Anthony: "Do you know how Harry was shot?" He shook his head and I insisted on a verbal answer and got one. He gave me a clear "No". Are we all agreed that he speaks the truth?'

Douglas said, 'Every time. Even when it's uncomfortable for other people.'

Halliwell said to Ingeborg, 'You took his statement. Did he say anything about speaking to Harry last night?'

Her gaze slipped away to the musicians pounding out a fortissimo passage in great sobs of sound, and then came back to Diamond. 'All right, guv. I agree with you. Anthony is in the clear.'

There would have been a pause for thought if thought was possible in a maelstrom.

When the volume decreased a little, Halliwell said, 'That leaves the least likely.'

'Mel?' Ingeborg said, mystified. 'He's only just joined them. Anyway, he's not violent. He's a normal, well-adjusted guy.'

'We all know how you feel about Mel,' Halliwell said.

'That's below the belt. If you remember, I commented after first meeting him that he thinks he's God's gift to women.'

'So we've got that clear,' Diamond said to get some order in the ranks. 'Shall we examine the case for Mel being the killer? You say he only just joined them, Inge, and that's true. However, we discovered he was in Vienna performing with the London Symphony Orchestra in 2008, in the month Emi was killed. Coincidence, or evidence of guilt?'

'Pure chance. There's nothing to connect him with Emi or the Staccati at that time,' Ingeborg said.

'But he does act like God's gift.' Halliwell couldn't resist quoting her. 'From all we hear, he shags anything that moves – his landlady's daughter and probably his landlady as well. We know what Emi's profession was and we know she was a musician herself. He could have coupled with her. We can't rule it out.'

'What – strangled her and dumped her in the canal? Mel?' Ingeborg said with scorn.

Diamond said, 'There's a story about Mel that may have some bearing on this.' He turned to Ingeborg. 'About his viola being stolen outside the Festival Hall. You were there with me. You heard him tell it.'

'I know. A really mean trick on somebody's part,' she said, 'but I don't see the relevance, guv.'

'Can you recall the details? You and I heard it, but Keith hasn't and it may be new to Douglas.'

In a slightly mystified voice Ingeborg started repeating the tale. 'He was on his way home from a concert at the Festival Hall one night and this student stopped him and asked for his autograph.'

'Stop there,' Diamond said. 'You've missed the point. She was from the Far East.'

'Why does that matter?' She put her hand to her mouth. 'Oh. He's got a thing about Asian women. He was tricked by this one and never forgot it.'

'Finish the story.'

For the benefit of the others, she told it to the end. 'It didn't strike me as important at the time,' she added. 'I suppose it could have turned his mind.'

'Let's move on,' Diamond said. 'Mel joins the quartet. They recruit him. He doesn't go looking for the job. But here in Bath he's as likely as anyone else to have met Mari at the concert she attended.'

'He claimed to have no memory of her,' Halliwell said.

'He would, wouldn't he?' Diamond said. 'I don't see that as significant. He could have fixed to meet her later, on some pretext like a walk along the towpath.'

'And strangled her because she reminded him of the girl who set him up for the mugging?' Ingeborg said. 'It still seems far-fetched.'

'Unless you can think of a better motive.'

Halliwell returned to the point he'd made already. 'He's a letch. These women came on to him and he responded.'

'You mean a murdering letch,' Diamond said. 'In other words, a psychopath.'

'We don't know if either victim was killed as part of a sex act, but they could have been. The bodies were too far gone to show any signs.'

'They were dressed,' Ingeborg said, contemptuous of Halliwell's theory.

'Doesn't mean nothing happened,' Halliwell said.

Diamond wanted to move on. The sixteen-minute fugue was at least two-thirds through. 'I'm willing to look at that. But what would have caused Mel to shoot Harry, a totally different kind of killing?'

'We agree Harry knew too much for the murderer to allow him to live,' Halliwell said.

'Or was too curious and likely to find out the truth,' Ingeborg chimed in. 'Harry had visited Mel earlier the same night. Something he said caused Mel to panic. He knew where to find him. It was obvious Harry would try and see Anthony next.'

'What's all this? Are you warming up to the idea of Mel as the killer?' Diamond said to her, faintly amused at the U-turn.

'He knew Harry was carrying the gun. He may have thought he could fake a suicide.'

'Hang on a minute,' Diamond said. 'Let's inject some

reality into this. The reason Harry called on Mel last night is that he felt safe with him. He'd get the updated story from him. If he'd thought for a moment that Mel was the killer he wouldn't have gone near him. They had their conversation and he left in peace. And even supposing Mel *is* the murderer, how would Harry know? At the time Emi was murdered, Harry wasn't around. He was in bed in his hotel room. We all agree Emi had sex with him and left the hotel alone after midnight. And as for Mari, if Mel had some kind of date with her in Green Park, we don't even know if Harry was in the country by then. The first time he was spotted was less than a week ago. Mel had no reason to kill Harry. Mel is innocent.'

A crescendo from the Staccati appeared to salute this conclusion.

There was another short period when nothing was spoken and the control room was filled only with the dissonant wail of the strings.

'We've eliminated them all,' Ingeborg said.

'Except one.'

The fifth and final part of the *Grosse Fuge* restores sanity. It picks up and develops the transparent, tuneful theme that was briefly employed in the second part. It is recognizable Beethoven, a coda in pianissimo that pacifies and pleases.

'To quote a smarter sleuth than any of us,' Diamond said, '"When you have eliminated the impossible, whatever remains, however improbable, must be the truth."'

30

'If you mean who I think you do,' Ingeborg said in a voice that was calm, but challenging, 'women are not stranglers. It's not a woman's crime.'

'Have you seen her hands?' Diamond said.

Everyone looked to where Cat was still pressing the strings with strength and mobility, extracting trills from the cello that matched anything the three men were producing. Fleshy they may have been, but they were long-fingered, workmanlike hands. Given a slender neck to grip, they could have ended a life, no question.

'Both female victims were petite,' Diamond reminded them.

Ingeborg tried reasoning with him. 'You don't want to go down this route, guv. She's a caring person. She keeps the men from getting quarrelsome. She's quick, witty, takes the heat out of any argument.'

'Why on earth would she want to kill anyone?' Halliwell said, finally finding a common cause with Ingeborg.

'All will be revealed,' Diamond said. 'I'm pulling her in for questioning.'

The *Grosse Fuge* came to its serene conclusion, a sense that a mountainous journey had been completed and the travellers were safe. The quartet lifted their bows and lowered them. Relieved smiles all round.

'Terrific,' the voice of the producer penetrated the studio. 'I don't think you'll better that.'

Ivan gave a nod. 'Shall we settle for it?' he asked the others.

'Even Anthony is satisfied,' Cat said. 'Somebody please collect me from cloud nine.'

In the control room, Diamond said, 'We'll give them ten minutes.'

It was fully two hours later when a solicitor had been found and Cat was seated beside her in Interview Room One at Manvers Street.

'What's all this about, then?' she said, arms folded defiantly, after the formalities had been gone through and the tape was running. This wasn't going to be one of those 'no comment' sessions.

Diamond had asked Halliwell to sit in with him. Most of the others would be on the other side of the one-way observation window. 'It's about what you've been up to, and why,' Diamond said.

'Recording the *Grosse Fuge*,' she said with gusto, 'and you were there to be blown away by it, lucky man.'

'It would have blown anyone away. But I want to ask you about Vienna in 2008. Your quartet was equally brilliant then, but with a slightly different combination.'

'Harry on viola.'

'Before he went missing.'

'Before he was kidnapped, poor lamb.'

'You know about the kidnapping, then? That's a good start.'

'Mel filled us in this morning. Harry called at his house yesterday evening. What a horror story it was, too.'

'You were the originals, you, Harry and Ivan.'

Cat remarked to her solicitor, 'He wants us to know he's done his homework.'

'You've always been the mainstay of the Staccati,' Diamond

said. 'Be they alcoholic, autistic or exiles, you mother them all.'

'Is that what they told you?'

'It's what you repeatedly tell everyone. The first time we spoke at any length, you told me you keep your boys in order.'

She said to the solicitor, 'He doesn't miss a trick.'

'I'm sure they appreciate it,' Diamond said. 'In their different ways, they all need mothering, don't they? They're your family. You told me how, after Harry went missing, you wandered the streets of Budapest searching for him.'

'Where are you going with this?' Cat's long fingers beat an impatient rhythm on the table.

'I'm thinking a single woman like yourself found an ideal outlet for her strong maternal instincts.'

'I thought you were a policeman, not a shrink.' Her tone was less playful now.

'We have to understand people's motives,' he said. 'Let's talk about the music, then. You're one of the best cellists in the world, I'm told. You could have a solo career, but you prefer playing in the quartet.'

'There's nothing criminal in that. I'm a team player, an ensemble person through and through.'

'You've said it for me,' Diamond said. 'You keep the Staccati going. It's your personal mission, creative and fulfilling.'

'I won't argue with that.'

'But if anyone threatens its existence, you see red. I was told you're like a tigress then.'

'Who said that?'

'If it's true, does it matter? There was that evening in Vienna when you were having a drink after the concert in your hotel bar with the others.'

'Most concerts end like that.'

'This one was different because Harry wasn't drinking with you. He was in another part of the bar with a Japanese woman you'd all met.'

'Harry was like that. Never known to refuse an offer.'

'You were all discussing the two of them and Douglas remarked that this woman – who knew a lot about music – could be out to persuade Harry to join another quartet.'

'Douglas said that?'

'He tells me he did.'

She arched her eyebrows in a show of surprise. 'I have no recollection at all.'

'Harry took the woman, whose name was Emi Kojima, to his hotel room.'

'Tell us something new, sunshine. Stuff like this has been going on since Adam and Eve.'

'But you were deeply suspicious of her motives. You considered Emi a serious threat to your beloved quartet and, let's face it, your personal and professional life. You waited on the same hotel floor for her to leave. She was alone and you followed her along the river bank towards the Danube canal. I'm guessing now, but I reckon at some point you caught up with her and challenged her to say what her intentions were. She was terrified of you. She tried to get away, but she was small, no match for you. You may have simply pushed her, or you may have put your hands around her throat. Either way, she ended up dead in the canal. She wouldn't be found for some weeks. You returned to the hotel shaken by what you'd done, but thinking you'd stopped her from poaching Harry. The tour continued, but unfortunately in the very next city, Budapest, Harry went missing.'

'The last part is correct,' Cat said to her solicitor.

The solicitor said, 'I'm advising you not to comment.'

'I'm only agreeing that we lost Harry. Of course we did.

382

The rest, about me attacking the woman, is up there with UFOs and little green men.'

Diamond wasn't put off. Cat had clearly decided to bluff her way through this and he hadn't expected her to tell all after the first salvo. 'So in spite of all the risk you took,' he continued in the same steady manner, 'the quartet was in trouble. All credit to you and Ivan for trying to keep it going.'

'Desperate times.' She took up the narrative as smoothly as if nothing had passed between them. 'I had Anthony throwing tantrums because he wanted work. You've no idea how childish he can be. And Ivan had to be stopped from jumping ship. I kept reminding them both that we had a brand name and a fan base and a backlist of recordings.'

The solicitor touched her arm to silence her, but Cat wasn't of a mind to underplay her achievement. 'You've no idea how much competition there is among quartets. All these pushy kids coming out of Eastern Europe and the Far East were only too keen to fill the vacuum.'

'And you didn't know at the time that Harry had been kidnapped by the Japanese mafia?'

'We thought he was dead. What else could we think after so long? That's why we hired Mel to replace him – eventually. Years had gone by. We weren't even history. We were forgotten. We needed to build our reputation all over again.'

'So you got the residency here.'

'Thanks to Doug. He kept the faith. Top man.'

'And everything was coming up roses until you gave your first concert and a small Japanese woman said she was a fan and started cosying up to the men. To you it must have seemed like a rerun of Vienna in 2008, except that this time Anthony was getting the attention. She talked intelligently to him about the music. She'd played the violin to a high level herself. Do you remember the shock this gave you, Cat?'

White-faced, she was about to say she didn't, but Diamond added, 'Anthony does, and he's selective in his memories. He particularly noted her tooth tattoo.'

Again, the solicitor put a restraining hand over Cat's forearm.

She wouldn't be silenced. 'Anthony wouldn't stitch me up. He needs me. He can't function without me.'

'His mind doesn't work like that,' Diamond said. 'He takes each day as it comes. He didn't stitch you up, as you put it. You stitched yourself up. You were incensed. You weren't going to allow Mari Hitomi to threaten the Staccati after the tough times you'd been through. I don't know what went through your mind, whether you believed she was trying to recruit Anthony for another quartet, or if it was pure jealousy that she was young and pretty and might sleep with him. You weren't having it. You spoke to her yourself and offered some kind of lure – perhaps a private meeting with the quartet. She was to meet you after dark at Green Park, that remote patch of ground just across the river from where you live.'

'This is the biggest load of horse hooey I've ever heard,' Cat said.

The solicitor said, 'Miss Kinsella, in your own best interest—'

'I'm not giving anything away, darling,' Cat said with an effort to sound unconcerned. She looked Diamond squarely in the eye. 'On with the fairy story, matey. We're dying to hear what the wicked witch did next.'

'I prefer the image of the tigress,' Diamond said. 'You had your cubs to protect.'

'Oh, give me strength.'

'Your boys, then. This unfortunate young woman – who simply came to that concert as a fan wanting to meet the musicians she adored – was grabbed and strangled and dragged to the river and dropped in. You'd got away with it in Vienna, you figured, so why not a second time?'

She gave no sign of caving in. 'You can do better than this,' she said, trying to bait him. 'What about the hundreds of other fans I killed because they came on strong with the boys? It's farcical when you think about it.'

'There was another victim, and that was Harry.'

'I knew we'd get around to him,' she said, rolling her eyes upwards. 'And how are you going to slot dear old Harry into this catalogue of slaughter? He was one of my boys, a Staccati player and a lovely guy in spite of all his demons.'

'No longer a Staccati player.'

'Because of his missing finger? True, but that doesn't mean he wasn't family.'

'Yes, I believe you really liked Harry,' Diamond said, 'but he made the fatal mistake of trying to find out the truth of what happened in Vienna, and how Emi Kojima's murder linked up with Mari Hitomi's. If he could discover who killed Emi he'd have an answer for the yakuza if they caught up with him again. Harry wasn't behaving as family should. He was poking the tigress with a pointed stick.'

'God help us,' Cat said. 'I'm getting weary of this *Jungle Book* stuff.'

'Yesterday evening you and Anthony shared a taxi home and when it stopped outside Anthony's lodging you saw Harry's car there with Harry waiting inside. It was obvious what he intended. He reckoned if he spoke to Anthony about what was going on, he'd get honest answers. Anthony might not be capable of putting two and two together and identifying you as the killer, but Harry was. You had to act quickly.'

'Oh, yes?'

'You live only two or three minutes away. After the taxi dropped you at your house, you returned to Westmoreland

Street to speak to Harry yourself. He was still in his car, waiting. You sat beside him in the passenger seat and listened to his story. To show how desperate he was, he showed you the gun. You seized your chance, grabbed it and shot him dead.'

Cat sighed and shook her head. 'Are you for real?'

'It was an impulse killing and a big, big mistake. Suddenly you had a corpse sitting beside you and this time there was no easy way of disposing of it. Panic. The best you could think to do on the spur of the moment was rig it up to look like suicide. You wiped the gun, pressed it into Harry's hand to get his prints on it and let it drop between the seats. Then you walked home and showered and washed all your clothes. Next morning when the call came through from Anthony's landlady, you made sure you weren't the first on the scene. Ivan got there first. By the time I arrived, you were inside the house with the others weeping crocodile tears.'

'Pardon me,' she said. 'The tears were genuine. I was heartbroken Harry was dead.'

'Heartbroken because you couldn't put the clock back. What a mess you made of it – a so-called suicide on the left side of the head from a right-handed man.'

'You keep going on about this as if it was me, but you're wrong,' she said, but on a shrill, petulant note. 'You're way off the mark and I can sue you for false arrest.'

'No chance,' Diamond said. 'Don't you know about gunshot residue? When a gun is fired the explosive gases and particles escape and cling to the hands, clothing and hair of the person who fired the gun as well as settling on anything else in the vicinity. While you were cutting your disc this afternoon, a forensic team was going through your flat collecting evidence. Yes, you showered and washed everything, but you can't prevent these tiny particles being scattered over the floor of your bedroom and bathroom. We have enough to prove you fired the fatal shot.'

386

'You're bluffing,' she said in a fierce, combative voice.

'Why do you think I let you go ahead with the recording? We needed time to get a warrant and search your house.' He reached under the table and held up an evidence bag containing the murder weapon. 'And if you think you wiped this clean, think again. We'll be taking your prints and DNA presently after I've formally charged you with Harry's murder.'

'You can't do that,' she said. 'I've admitted nothing, nothing at all.'

'Doesn't matter when we've got the evidence,' he said with all the authority he could muster, allowing that forensics would take weeks to produce enough for a prosecution. He was banking on this effusive woman talking her way into proof of guilt. 'You could say nothing at all and still go down with a recommendation that life means life.'

The solicitor was on her feet. 'That's enough. You're trying to elicit a statement by the use of oppression. You're in flagrant abuse of the Police and Criminal Evidence Act.'

'Oh, shut up,' Cat said. 'I need to know the worst that can happen, don't I?'

It was a seismic moment.

To Diamond, she said, 'What are the chances of a lighter sentence if I plead guilty to all three?'

'It wouldn't be up to me,' he said evenly, 'but an admission of guilt is always taken into account.'

'I'm up for it, then,' she said with some of her former bounce. 'Where shall we start? Vienna, 2008?'

The following weekend, Diamond took Paloma for a candlelit dinner at the Hole in the Wall in George Street. No awkwardness lingered between them. He felt relaxed after bringing the Staccati case to a successful conclusion. And Paloma had landed a contract to be the costume consultant on a new TV series set in the 1940s.

'So you obtained a confession?' she said.

'We did.'

'Without violence, I hope.'

'She sang like a blackbird on the first day of spring.'

'Is that usual?'

'No. Their brief generally makes sure they don't, but in this case Cat insisted, and when that woman insists, no one had better stand in her way.'

'She'll get a long sentence, I expect.'

'Life. For three murders, that will be seriously long.'

'So the Staccati is no more?'

'Not necessarily. Ivan is looking for another cellist.'

She looked wistful. 'Pity if they have to break up. What will that poor autistic man do?'

'Anthony? He'll join another ensemble. I don't have any worries over him.'

'He'll miss all the mothering from Cat.'

'I doubt if he will,' Diamond said. 'A lot of it was more about Cat's need to feel wanted. Anthony is such a good musician that people will put up with his strange ways.'

'I hope you're right.' She smiled. 'Cat will keep the prison entertained. She'll probably form an all-girl quartet.'

'I'm sure of it. We're doing the prison service a favour, sending them someone as chirpy as her.' He poured more wine into her glass. 'But let's talk about your new project. It's a bit more modern than the shows you've been dressing lately, isn't it?'

'Yes, I may even ask to see some of your old black and white movies.'

'You know you're always welcome.'

'And I was thinking before you get wrapped up in another case that it might be good to fit in another city break.'

'I'm all for that,' Diamond said at once.

'You are?' She couldn't hide her surprise.

'I enjoyed Vienna – probably more than you did.'

She laughed. 'I had some fun out of it, too. A lovely city. Where shall we go next?'

'That could be difficult.'

'Why?'

'I don't know if I've seen it in the brochures.'

'Which city do you have in mind?'

'Fits in with your new project.'

'Don't keep me in suspense.'

'I was thinking Casablanca.'